The Christmas Secret

Karen Swan is a *Sunday Times* Top Five bestselling writer. She is the author of eleven other novels, although she's been a writer all her life. She previously worked as an editor in the fashion industry but soon realized she was better suited as a novelist with a serious shopping habit. She is married with three children and lives in East Sussex.

Come to find her at www.karenswan.com or on Instagram @swannywrites, Twitter @KarenSwan1 and Facebook @KarenSwanAuthor.

Also by Karen Swan

The CHRISTMAS SECRET

KAREN SWAN

MACMILLAN

First published 2017 by Macmillan
an imprint of Pan Macmillan
20 New Wharf Road, London N1 9RR
Associated companies throughout the world
www.panmacmillan.com

ISBN 978-1-5098-3804-2

1 3 5 7 9 8 6 4 2

A CIP catalogue record for this book is available from the British Library.

Typeset by Ellipsis, Glasgow
Printed and bound by CPI Group (UK) Ltd, Croydon, CR0 4YY

Visit **www.panmacmillan.com** to read more about all our books
and to buy them. You will also find features, author interviews and
news of any author events, and you can sign up for e-newsletters
so that you're always first to hear about our new releases.

For Sally, Mhairi and Muirne.
My three graces.

Prologue

Out there.

The first time he had escaped death was out there, in those treacherous waters that stretched from here to the coast of Ireland. But from these cliffs, on this day, when the sea was stretched pale and smooth like a bolt of cerulean silk, there was no sign of the horrors of that long-ago night – when force ten winds raged above the surface and missiles were fired beneath it.

She stared out to the horizon, the wind in her face as though blowing breath into her, bringing her back to life. He felt closer here and she thought, if she prayed hard enough, she might see his footprints in the sand, detect his scent on the breeze. Oh, but for this tiny isle to have held something of him in its embrace; the landlady of her lodgings had told her the seeds of the bright yellow gorse bushes that dotted these moors could remain dormant in the soil for forty years, and still germinate. Could she not hope for just such a trace?

But hope was lost and had been for many years. Death had been chasing him, snapping its jaws at his ankles for a second time, refusing to let him get away. He had fought so hard, they said, these kind strangers with their rich, rolling vowels and still eyes.

1

Several times they thought he was lost, only for him to break through the fevers like a ghoul from the mist, hollow-cheeked and panting from the chase.

He had strong fibre, they said, a tender smile; eyes that whispered, hands that danced. Even so many years later, he was remembered here, he had been admired.

And to think he had been hers . . .

She closed her eyes, letting the breeze buffet her. There was indescribable comfort in that simple truth: he had been hers and Death – though triumphant on its third attempt – could not cleave it from her.

A sound – a voice? – carried over to her ear and she looked around to find a woman hurrying towards her. Though the wind played with her hair like a kitten after string, she moved with ease and grace. Her frame was slight and quick, with intelligence in her eyes, breeding in her bones. But if her beauty was delicately spun, there was nothing fragile about her. She looked strong and resolute. Formidable.

'Are you the American?' the woman asked with a clear-eyed directness.

'Yes.'

The woman gave a single exhale and a nod. 'They told me I could find you here. I thought I had missed you.'

'What is it?'

'Before you leave . . . there's something you should know.'

But she already did. Instinct told her.

He had been hers too.

Chapter One

Mayfair, London, Friday 1 December 2017

'Alex Hyde's office.'

Louise Kennedy's clipped voice pierced the silence of a thickly carpeted room whose still air was only otherwise punctuated by perfumed wafts from the snowball peonies.

'No, I'm sorry, she's not available. Who's calling, please?'

Her French-manicured fingertips hovered, poised, above the keyboard, the cursor on the screen flashing as she awaited the name. On the right side of the keypad, a red light was flashing. Another client, incoming; she was like an air-traffic controller managing the perpetual flow of aircraft coming in to land: rack 'em, pack 'em, stack 'em.

'I will need a name if she's to—' She was careful to avoid exhaling into the mic of her headset as the caller prevaricated, not believing her, not used to being told no. Her fingers twitched in the air as though twiddling a pen, restless to get on. The red light was still blinking. She had to pick up within the minute. One never knew when it could be urgent and at this level, urgent meant exactly that: jobs, fortunes, very lives could be on the line.

'No, that isn't possible.' One threaded eyebrow arched as the caller's voice became more strident. 'Because she's in

New York.' Her eyes fell to the red light again. 'That's confidential,' she said more briskly, more than used to dealing with self-importance. It was probably the single most common defining trait of Alex's clients; it was probably what enabled them to become one of Alex's clients in the first place. 'But I can ask her to call you. Does she know what it's in regard to?' Her fingers twitched again.

Outside, the blue lights of an ambulance whirled past the mink-grey slatted windows, the woolly white sky tumbled thick with rain clouds. People in heavy coats walked past in profile, heads bent to their phones, the pavements still slick from the last cloudburst a few minutes earlier.

Her lips pursed as the man talked. She had thought as much. 'I see. So this is a *new* client enquiry.' His presumptive tone had suggested deep personal acquaintance but in all likelihood they had perhaps shaken hands at a cocktail party, or Alex's name had come up at a celebratory dinner, murmured in hushed tones and passed over with the same furtive secrecy as a Mason's handshake.

'I'm afraid we operate a waiting list and Ms Hyde doesn't have any openings before May.' Her eyes glanced across to the red light. Still there. Just. Ten seconds . . . 'Would you like me to book you in and we'll be in touch nearer the time?'

Her eyebrows buckled as presumptive became didactic; he perhaps didn't realize that no one got to Alex without first going past her, and she was paid to vet the clients, as much as to diarize them. 'Well, as I said before, Ms Hyde is not in the country at the moment and I'm not at liberty to tell you when she'll be back. Now if you'll excuse me, I have other clients trying to get through. You are very welcome to call back at your convenience if you change your—'

Her finger hovered over the disconnect button, her eyes on the flashing red light.

Three, two, o . . .

Her hand dropped to the desk as though shot down, the words still ringing in her ears as though every single one had exploded down the line with a bang. She leaned forward on her elbows, concentrating harder as she stared at the flashing cursor on the still-blank screen, the red light now gone. Completely forgotten, in fact. There was a long pause.

'I'm sorry, could you repeat that?' she said finally, an uncharacteristic waver in her cut-glass voice. 'I don't think I heard you correctly.'

New York, same day

Alex Hyde stared down at Wall Street. It was teeming with ego, pulsing like a muscle as people ran into the traffic – late for meetings and seemingly armour-plated against the flood of yellow cabs that hooted furiously, red tail lights blinking – and wove a bravura dance from one side of the road to the other. At street level, their signifiers of status would be both discreet (the colour-threaded buttonhole of a hand-stitched suit, perhaps) and overt (a Rolex Oyster, a Caribbean tan) but from this height, these people looked like nothing more than metal shavings on a magnetic board, darting this way and that as though propelled by an outer force, all desperately trying to get somewhere. Get here, in fact. Up here on the 98th floor was where they wanted to be, and the man she was talking to was who they wanted to be. A master of the universe; a power hub – the source of all energy, all money.

But none of them would ever make it this far. They didn't see themselves from her perspective. They couldn't see themselves from two paces away, much less two hundred metres high. Even their own reflections in the mirror wouldn't reveal to them what she saw because they didn't know they had to understand that ambition wasn't enough, talent wasn't enough, hunger wasn't enough. And if they didn't even know that they had to know this, how could they possibly expect to climb the stairs that led to this vaunted position in the sky?

The man behind her knew it, but then he had been lucky enough to meet her when he was a newly appointed president of Bank of America and the best career move he had ever made had been not just to realize, but also to admit, that he was out of his depth. She turned her back on the hard December sun throwing a white slant down the street and faced him again. Apprehensive blue eyes stared back at her from a lined face as she walked slowly back into the room.

'Howard, do you remember in our last session we talked about edge?'

He watched her as closely as an antelope tracking a lion in the long grass. 'Yes.'

She returned to sitting in the chair opposite him, her lean figure discreetly flattered by the ivory crêpe Phillip Lim dress, her mid-length chestnut-brown hair tumbling artfully at her shoulders thanks to this morning's blowout – God, she *loved* this city's blowout bars – and wearing only the lightest slick of make-up, her olive skin still glowing from last month's mindfulness retreat in Costa Rica. 'What did we say, can you tell me?' She tilted her head empathetically, her expression soft although her deep brown eyes retained a quizzical expression.

'You said that in order to have edge, there needs to be a coming together of the whole person?'

She nodded. 'That's right. We need to have the *blend*, to get the *edge*.' She smiled. 'It sounds contradictory, doesn't it? Blend, edge – surely they're opposite terms? But only when the four areas of our lives – the physical, the mental, the social and the spiritual elements – are in balance, can we expect to perform concordantly. And when they are, *because* it's such a rarity, that's when you have the edge to see things more sharply, to make smarter decisions, to act with clarity and confidence. But –' her expression changed – 'we neglect any one of these aspects of our psyches at our peril. How can we possibly expect to be flexible in our thoughts if we're not reading or learning anything beyond the confidential memos circulating in the bank? How can you absorb the stress of making your targets if you cancel on your trainer? You cannot let the body become weak, the mind mechanical, your emotions numb or your spirit insensitive. You cannot operate in a vacuum. Not at this level. The air is too thin up here, Howard.'

He sighed, knowing what she was getting at. 'You're telling me to give her up.'

'You know I never tell, I simply advise,' she demurred, feeling the single silent vibration of her phone on the arm of her chair. 'But if there's no longer anything there, if what's between you is just –' she shrugged – 'dead energy, then you need to ask yourself whether you're getting the correct blend.'

Howard's knuckles blanched slightly as he gripped the

armrest, a look of incredulousness dawning. 'You mean, *Yvonne*?'

'Well, let's examine the idea,' she said, spreading her hands, invoking awakening. 'Is it simply obligation that's making you stay?'

'Ob-obligation?' he stammered. 'We've been married thirty-four years! That's a lot of life to share with someone.'

'Yes, it is. Has it been too long, would you say? Do you think with hindsight you should have moved on sooner?'

Howard looked scandalized. 'It's not that easy. We've got four kids.'

'Four grown-up kids, who are all married with families of their own,' she nodded calmly. 'You know, guilt can't change the past, Howard. And anxiety won't change the future. This is a big decision, but perhaps it's the one we've been avoiding confronting.'

Howard looked down and then back at her, apprehension and insecurity creasing a patrician face that featured in the *Wall Street Journal* at least twice a week, that had been papered all over the city as the lead financial advisor to the mayor during the previous election campaign. 'But last time we met, you said it was Kayleigh I should leave.'

'No, I never told you to leave anyone, Howard,' Alex said firmly, resting her chin on her thumb and index finger. 'I told you to look at the *blend*, remember? And back then, you said Kayleigh was "acting crazy" – making unreasonable demands that you leave Yvonne for her, threatening to turn up at your house, to go to the press. You said you couldn't sleep, you couldn't concentrate on your work. Now, that clearly wasn't an equilibrium you were going to be able to maintain going forward and you recognized you couldn't deliver an edge for as long as all that was going on.

8

So, we discussed the idea of you giving *her* up.' Alex twirled her hand out. 'On the other hand, you've just spent the past forty-five minutes telling me you can't stay away from her; in spite of all the crazy behaviour, she makes you feel alive.' She shrugged. 'So if that's really the truth, then don't – don't give her up. If she makes you feel that good, then maybe it's time to rethink the equation. Maybe this change is what you need to achieve the perfect balance for now. People change, Howard, our needs mutate. What worked for you thirty-four years ago isn't necessarily what works for you now. We need to be brave and face up to that. Too many people let themselves get stuck in the rut. They allow themselves to be straitjacketed by bourgeois conventions. But you're not one of them, Howard, you're not one of the little people. Those rules don't apply to you. You can do what you want and if Kayleigh makes you feel alive, feel awake, then go and be with her.'

'But . . . what about all that stuff she did? The threats?'

'She only did those things because she wanted you to be with her; if you leave Yvonne, she's got no reason to act crazy.'

She sat back in the chair, her chin dipped, one leg swinging lightly. There was a long silence.

'I don't know,' he hesitated.

Alex leaned forward in the chair, her elbows resting on her knees, hands clasped together out front. 'She makes you feel young again, doesn't she?' she asked intently.

He nodded.

'Invincible. Powerful. Virile. The man you used to be.'

He nodded again.

'She's your key to getting back to being that man again, Howard.'

Howard blinked. 'But what about . . . I mean, she broke into my house for Chrissakes. I think she might be unstable.'

'Listen, forget all the reasons why something may not work. You only need one why it will. And you two are crazy about each other; you told me yourself, she's a hunger you can't satisfy. That's all the motivation you need.'

The phone vibrated again but Alex kept her gaze on Howard. She could see the doubt in his eyes, the outright fear that came with bringing fantasy into the real world. 'This is exactly what we've been exploring in our previous sessions – if you want to keep the blade sharp, you have to promote growth and change in your life. Now, initially we were working to achieve that through the charitable initiative in Angola and the attempt on K2 –' she sat back up again – 'but if Kayleigh is the answer, then let's embrace it. Let's not be rigid or fixed in our views, Howard. Keep in mind that whatever makes *you* feel whole, benefits the bank. Perfect the blend and you sharpen the edge.'

'But Yvonne—'

'Is a big girl. And I'm sure you'd honour your thirty-four years together by looking after her financially. You're a gentleman, after all.'

Howard blinked. 'I'm not sure this is—'

'This is about you, Howard. It's about what makes you feel whole.' She smiled. 'Do you know what's the most common lie? The one that millions of people tell every single day?'

He shook his head.

'"I'm fine." That's what they say, all the time, when they're not – *especially* when they're not. Are you fine, Howard? Is your life how you want it to be when you're with Yvonne? Or is it how you want it to be when you're with Kayleigh? Who are you with when you say, "I'm fine"? Where are you living the lie? Because it's with one of them. I think we can say we've fairly established that you can't have both; your attention is too divided – and besides, you're too good a man for that sort of compromise, Howard. You've got principles, honour, pride.' She inhaled deeply. 'All of which means you're standing at a crossroads. It's decision time. Get this right and you'll get your edge back.'

Her phone vibrated for the third time – the signal that it was urgent. She smiled and rose. 'Look, I can see it's a lot for you to absorb. Change can be daunting. Why don't you take a few days to let it all settle and we can work on strategy for implementing this next time we meet?'

Howard rose too and nodded. 'Settle, yes. Okay.' He looked stunned, as though caught in the electric grip of a taser.

Alex walked him to the door. 'I'll get Louise to follow up with Sara and book something in your schedule. Lunch, perhaps? Maybe we should actively go out and celebrate this exciting new change.'

Howard fiddled with the buttons on his jacket as she opened the door. 'Lunch? I'm not sure. I think I'm pretty booked—'

'Of course, everything gets crazy in the run-up to Christmas, doesn't it? No problem, we can leave them to sort out the logistics between themselves.' She held out a hand, shaking it firmly. 'It's been a great session, Howard. I think we're on the cusp of the change we've been reaching for. Mull everything over and let's regroup when you're ready.'

Alex shut the door as he walked slowly towards the elevator, reaching for her phone and calling the only number that ever rang her on it.

'Louise?' she asked, walking back to the windows and looking down again at the metal shavings still shifting and twitching their ways to magnetic north. 'No, it's fine, we were winding up anyway.'

She stepped out of her shoes, feeling a wince of pleasure-pain as her feet spread and she dropped down three inches.

'Oh, you could say that,' she sighed. 'I just gave him what he thought he wanted and saved his marriage. Ring his PA and get in a follow-up for within the fortnight.'

A sudden flash past the window made her startle and step back. It was another moment before her eyes tracked what she had seen and she realized it was a peregrine falcon, one of the huge number that were making their home in the city, roosting on the multitudinous ledges of the city buildings, soaring on the thermals provided by the concrete rooftops and hunting the pigeons that flapped merrily up and down the avenues. She watched as it glided effortlessly on an updraught. 'Anyway, what's up?'

She pressed a hand to the glass and looked down as it suddenly swooped into a dive, making for a hapless, oblivious pigeon several storeys below. Its speed was dizzying – someone had told her they could reach up to 200 mph in a stoop – and helped by the skyscrapers acting like mountains, funnelling the air. These falcons now lived in greater numbers in Manhattan than anywhere else in the world, and they were thriving far better than their counterparts in the wild. She gasped, thrilled, as the falcon made the kill; the pigeon didn't even know what had hit it. It had been outclassed by a predator that had every advantage: not just height, or speed, but adaptability. These peregrines were the living embodiment of everything she preached to her clients.

Wait . . . It was another moment before the words in her

ear caught up with the vision before her eyes. She turned away from the window and stared, unseeing, back into the empty room. 'Say that again . . . he wants me to do *what*?'

Edinburgh, two days later

Sleet patted at the windowpanes like a kitten trying to get in from the cold and the room was draughty, sending the fire into leaping kicks as occasional gusts worried the flames. But Alex, sitting in the orange velvet wing chair, felt warm. She had been warm for two days now, ever since she had put the phone down to Louise in New York, the promise of this deal sitting like a hot coal in the very heart of her.

Sholto Farquhar looked back at her with a slow, unhurried blink. He wasn't a man who ever needed to rush. 'So there you have it, Ms Hyde. Our cards are on the table.' He brought his fingers to a steeple before his lips, his cheeks ruddy-flushed. 'What do you think?'

'Well, I agree you need my help,' she replied, mirroring him at an equally relaxed pace. 'From everything you've just told me, I think it's remarkable you've managed to get to this point without further damage to the company. You should congratulate yourself on containing the problem thus far.'

Sholto rose from his chair and walked across the tartan-carpeted room to a round rosewood table, upon which sat a decanter and a pair of cut-crystal tumblers. She watched as he poured them each a finger of whisky.

'Ice?'

She shook her head.

Nodding approvingly, he walked back with the drinks.

'Our thirty-year reserve,' he said, handing her one with appraising eyes.

'My favourite.'

He settled himself in the plum velvet chair opposite hers. 'You know, you are very young to have such a formidable reputation.'

'I'll take that as a compliment, thank you.'

'I had a devil of a time getting your number. I had heard of you long before I could get hold of you.'

'Well, I prefer not to make myself available to cold-callers. I only take on a handful of clients each year. I prefer to work closely with just a select few. I find that those who need me have the means to find me.'

He raised an eyebrow. 'Getting past your PA was no mean feat either. I've had warmer phone calls with the Russian embassy.'

Alex chuckled. 'I couldn't do without her.'

'Well, I'm grateful to you for agreeing to meet with me, particularly on a Sunday. I'm sure your weekends are precious.'

'I'm available to my clients at any time.'

Sholto raised an eyebrow – seemingly pleased by this – and his glass. '*Sláinte.* Your good health.'

'*Sláinte.*'

He watched as she sipped the amber liquid, but she didn't betray the heat in her throat as she swallowed it down. After a moment, to her mild surprise, she found she rather liked it.

'No one's sorrier than I that it should have come to this, but he's a loose cannon,' Sholto said, getting back to business.

'It certainly seems so. The affairs are ill advised, at the

very best – he's laying the company open to God only knows what in terms of sexual harassment charges. But to punch a board member in the face at the family assembly?' she said, looking – and feeling – disgusted. 'Throwing a computer terminal through a window . . . ?' she tutted, shaking her head. 'I've never heard of anything like it. He sounds temperamentally and physiologically unsuited to the role; he physically can't handle it. In CEOs, what you want to find – if you could peer into their brains – would be high levels of testosterone, the "can do" hormone, but low levels of cortisol, the stress hormone. He is a classic high testosterone, high cortisol mix which is a disaster. When the pressure's too much, he's going to blow and that makes him a liability.'

Sholto sighed, looking regretful. 'It's not necessarily all his fault; I'm afraid his father was overly indulgent and you know what they say about sparing the rod.'

She tilted her head, expressing empathy. 'Do you have children?'

'Two boys. Torquil and Callum.' He chuckled lightly. 'I say "boys". They're both in their thirties and have stood six inches taller than me for the past fifteen years.'

'And do they work for the company or are they just shareholders?'

'They're both company directors – Tor's our CFO, and Callum heads up our wealth management division in Edinburgh.'

'How do they find him?'

'They were close as boys – Callum and Lochie particularly – but they tend to keep their distance from one another now. They've all changed and become very different people.'

Alex thought for a moment. 'So how many family members are sitting on the board of directors? You, Lochlan . . .'

'Torquil and Callum.'

'Any non-family members?' she asked.

'Yes, four. Two external directors, one former employee and one current employee – our master blender. Why?'

'I'm just interested in the make-up of your board. Family businesses with high proportionate representation are less likely to fail but this effect is cancelled out if family members have fifty per cent or more of the directorships. That's because whilst family businesses *can* benefit from the closer emotional ties, sibling rivalry, identity and succession rivalries also mean conflicts blow up more easily – as seen at your family assembly.

'Well, no one could argue it's a close relationship, genetically speaking I mean. Lochie is my second cousin once removed, and he and my boys are third cousins so I don't know whether that plays into your hypothesis or not.'

Alex considered for a moment. 'It probably does. They're sufficiently linked to be unable to escape each other, but not so closely that they truly care. Are there any women on the board?'

'One. Mhairi MacLeod. She's a senior partner at Brodies.'

Alex nodded. 'Depending upon your Articles of Association, it might be worth looking at bringing in at least one more female director. There is strong evidence that boards with gender diversity are more stable with lower resignation rates and less conflict.'

'Ms Hyde, I'm quite sure you're right but the only conflict at Kentallen emanates from one person: Lochlan Farquhar. Always operating *just* within the limits of corporate by-laws, he persistently and repeatedly obstructs both the will of the board and the family assembly.' His expression darkened. 'My company is responsible for employing three hundred and forty-one people from the town. Our distillery brings in over one million visitors to the area annually and we donate one per cent of our operating profits – which were sixty-five million pounds last year – to local charities. The board is not the only group who cannot afford for Kentallen to fail.'

'Understood.'

'He simply cannot be allowed to continue as he is – God knows, he's gone downhill since his father's death. It's clear he's in pain and we've all tried intervening in our various ways – talking to him, offering support, a shoulder. But he's a renegade, hell bent on self-destruction, and I now fear he's going to bring us all down with him, whether he intends it or not.' He frowned. 'His actions over the past few months have been tantamount to gross misconduct and he knows it.'

'Indeed, you've been incredibly tolerant. If you were anything other than a family-owned and managed business, he'd have been out on his ear by now.'

He leaned forward in his chair, the whisky in his tumbler sloshing against the cut crystal. 'I realize that what we're asking is unorthodox, but I think, also, you can see the predicament we're in. The usual routes of solving such a problem aren't open to us and besides, we wouldn't want family relations to break down further.' He cleared his throat. 'Can you do what we're asking?'

'Yes.'

'In the timescale we discussed?'

'That depends on how resistant he is going to be to working with me.'

'Almost entirely opposed to it, would be my guess.'

'Well, given that mindset and the scale of the task, weekly sessions and remote conferencing are out; I'll have to go out there and work with him intensively.' She met his gaze. 'But yes, I believe I can get it done by Christmas.'

He smiled and held out his hand, one bushy grey eyebrow hitched up. 'So then we have a deal?'

Alex looked at him, blinking slowly; she was never one to be hurried either. 'Yes,' she smiled, taking his hand and shaking it firmly. 'We have a deal.'

Chapter Two

Thompson Falls, Montana, 23 January 1918

The snow lay in deep drifts in the early-morning light, puffed up like a marshmallow and as yet undotted by animal tracks. The land stretched out before her, perfectly still and silent as though to make a point of his absence – it had been twenty-one days now since he had left for Washington, and eighteen hours since they had night-trekked from there, the five and a half miles through the snow to the train. By now, he would be in New York.

New York; so far from here. Until last month, it had felt like a world away, foreign even, but within the fortnight his boots would tread in the blood-riven battlefields of Europe. Then he would know the difference.

She stood on the porch step, her woollen shawl offering scant protection around her shoulders as she watched a fox emerge from the bare, bony trees and trot belly deep in the powder, its russet coat like a stray flame in the snow.

She watched as he stopped – nose pointed, one paw poised in the air, like one of their old hunting dogs – detecting a noise or smell. A deer mouse? A kangaroo rat? A least chipmunk? If he was lucky, a white-tailed jack rabbit? He looked thin and in need of that meal. She held her own breath as he froze, waiting with him. Then he pounced suddenly, all four legs in the air, his body tucked under and his muzzle pointed downwards as he landed with a small 'pouf', face first and part buried.

A moment later he emerged, triumphant, the limp body of a meadow vole dangling from his jaws, and she watched as he trotted back into the trees again and disappeared out of sight.

He might be the only other living thing she would glimpse today, or this week, and she knew her gesture was futile – what point was there in hanging a blue star in a window that no one else would see? But it was all she had to symbolize her sacrifice: a star to honour him – her love – fighting someone else's war.

She stared out at the walls of her world, sending prayers into the ether. She had to remain strong. She had to be brave and do that hardest of things: just wait.

Port Ellen, Islay, Wednesday 6 December 2017

The ferry docked with surprising grace, the rust-freckled hull of the 1950s vessel knocking politely against the giant tyre fenders of the jetty wall. Alex watched from behind the thick glass windows as ropes were thrown, men in calf-length yellow boots and waterproof boiler suits hauling and winding the unwieldy ropes around mighty bollards, tethering them in place and seemingly quietening the swell that had pestered them on the route over from the mainland.

She disembarked quickly, eager to feel still again. She had never been an able sailor and she knew without needing to check that her complexion would be green-tinted, even with her Chanel Les Beiges foundation on.

'Miss Hyde?'

A stocky man with a bushy grey moustache stepped forward and took her overnight bag from her grasp. 'Hamish

Macpherson, from the distillery,' he said, shaking her hand briskly. 'Welcome to Islay. You've picked a fine day for it.'

Not sure whether he was serious, Alex resisted the urge to look up either at the torrid sky that was tussling only metres above her head, or back at the frothing heaving sea. 'Hello. Thank you for coming to collect me.'

'Aye. Well, it can be a wee bit tricky finding the turn-off unless you know where to look. Apparently, "Turn right past the rowan tree" has been too obscure for some guests in the past.'

She glanced across at him, still not sure whether he was being wry or grumpy. 'Oh dear. I take it they found you eventually, though.'

'Nope,' Hamish shrugged. 'They were never heard of again,' he said ominously, but a very faint glint twinkled in his hazel eyes.

Alex laughed lightly, following after as he turned and led her back up the jetty; she kept pace with him easily, in spite of the difficulties of wearing heels on wet cobbles – Louise always joked she could run a marathon in Choos – but the wind blew hard at their backs, blowing her dark hair in front of her face, and she tugged the collar of her coat tighter to her neck. Orange fishing nets lay in heaps along the stone wall, lobster creels upended and empty beside them. Two fishing boats were docked alongside and a couple of men were slopping water from a bucket over the decks. Ahead, Port Ellen – the second-largest town on the island – stood on guard as though awaiting her inspection, a rack of large white terraced houses stretched out along a curved beach before her, each one handsome but spare with not a door wreath or window pot to be seen. Beyond, the land rose in gentle increments like a lumpen mattress.

They stopped at an ancient pale olive Land Rover that looked as though it had served in the Great War and had not so much been parked as just stopped in the road, blocking the path of a blue tractor that – although stationary – was still chugging breathlessly and bouncing on its springs. Alex saw the driver leaning against the wall of the local Co-op, dragging on a cigarette and reading the community noticeboard.

'Hi, Euan!' Hamish hailed, waving a hand in greeting as he tossed Alex's bag in the back of the Landy and hoisted himself into the driving seat. Louise had already sent up her bigger suitcases on the earlier train from London.

'Aye!' The tractor driver waved back in return, taking another deep drag of the cigarette before dropping it on the ground, grinding it out beneath his boot and heading back to his own cab.

Alex smiled to herself as she fastened her seat belt – the same scenario in Mayfair would have played out entirely differently. The cap of a thermos flask peeped from beneath the lid of a cubby between the two front seats and the radio appeared to be held in place with duct tape. Alex was sure it was colder inside the car than out.

They pulled away, past a couple more rows of stern white houses, and then almost immediately they were in the open countryside, thick hedgerows bordering lush pastures, the distinctive smell of peat heavy in the air. 'Which distillery is that?' she asked, pointing to the smoking chimney across the bay.

'Lagavulin,' Hamish replied without having to look.

'Ah. The enemy.'

Hamish made a strange sound that suggested they might well be, pulling a hard right up a lane that travelled past the ruins of an old church and headed towards the gently swelling hills.

'And what do you do at Kentallen?'

'I work in the copper shop.'

Alex narrowed her eyes, trying to work out where this figured in the life of a distillery. Thanks to Louise's excellent research skills, she had spent the past few days and the entire journey reading up not just on the company but on the wider industry as a whole and now felt sufficiently well versed in the technicalities of distilling to be able to set up whisky shop herself should she choose (which she didn't).

'Copper shop? That's where the stills are worked, isn't it?'

'Aye.'

'They all have to be beaten by hand. The shape determines the amount of condensation and the liquid run-off determines the character of the whisky?'

'You've been doing your homework.'

She smiled. Preparation was her middle name. 'If I remember correctly, the shape of the still is the most critical part of the distilling process,' she added, showing off a little now.

'Aye, but don't tell the blenders that or they'll have your guts for garters.'

'Guts for garters,' Alex murmured to herself with a smile. 'Right.'

Hamish didn't seem to feel the need to fill the silence with chat (well, what silence there was over the guttural racket of the Landy's engine) and she was grateful for the opportunity to take in her new home – for the next three weeks, anyway – in peace. The landscape was modest and muted; she had been expecting craggy mountains and windswept moors, but the hillocky fields were parcelled with crumbling stone walls and the palette of gunmetal grey, heather and pine had been softened with a white gauze as Atlantic clouds smudged the sun from the sky. In the distance, she saw a small herd of red deer grazing by a thicket, the stag nosing the air imperiously, protectively.

'Have you had any snow?' she asked as they rounded a deep bend, the left-side wheels dropping into a pothole and sending them both bouncing on their seats.

'A dusting a fortnight back. Not enough to get excited about.'

'It was just starting to dump as I was leaving New York. Apparently over a metre fell the night I left. I think I got out in the nick of time.'

'Isn't that always the case?'

'I'm sorry?'

'Getting out of the city. Escape is always in the nick of time.' A wry expression hovered over his features like that low-lying Atlantic cloud.

'I take it you're not from the big smoke?' she asked, looking for an overhead handhold with which to steady herself; but finding none, having to make do instead with pressing one palm to the window and the other to the seat.

'I was born four miles from here and the longest I've been off the island was nine days in 1982.'

'What necessitated that?'

'My mother dying in a hospital in Glasgow.'

'I'm sorry.'

Hamish glanced at her, a kernel of scorn in his gaze though whether it was because the tragedy was so long past or so clearly unconnected to her, she couldn't tell.

'Is there a hospital on the island?'

'At Bowmore, across the way, but there's a doctor's practice in town. You're not sickly, I hope?'

She shook her head. It had been more of a command than
a question. 'No.'

'Good. The weather would make short work of you otherwise. December can be an unforgiving month. It's no time
to be peely-wally.'

'Peely-wally,' Alex repeated quietly, slowly. She was
fluent in French, German, Spanish, Italian and Mandarin,
but Scots was new to her.

'Aye,' Hamish nodded, staring dead ahead. A sheep
stuck its head over a low stone wall as they passed and she
winked at it. 'You'd best not be expecting postcard weather.'

'Don't worry, it's not the weather that's brought me
here.'

'No,' Hamish said, glancing at her again, a note of disap-
proval in his gaze as he took in her red Proenza Schouler
coat, dress and heels. 'I heard you're coming here to boost
morale.'

If he had said 'coming here to plant rainbows', he
couldn't have sounded more sceptical. 'That's right,' she
smiled, looking straight across at him this time to gauge his
reaction. 'The board feels some fresh thinking is required.
You know, getting everyone out of their funk,' she said
with a wrinkle of her nose.

'Funk?' Hamish looked genuinely perplexed and Alex
could imagine he'd be as perplexed by corporate-speak as
she was by Scottish.

'Don't worry, I'm not going to have everyone paint-
balling around the oak casks in the name of team bonding.
I've only been tasked to work with specific management
personnel.'

At this, to her astonishment, Hamish threw his head back and openly laughed.

'What?' she grinned. 'What's so funny about that?'

'I hope for your sake you're not going to be including Lochie in those fun and games?'

'Lochie?'

'Aye, the boss. I can't see him standing for much of that nonsense.'

'No?' she asked, not at all insulted. 'And why's that?'

'Because Lochie's not exactly . . .' Hamish glanced across at her, biting his tongue suddenly. 'Och, you'll see for yourself soon enough.'

Disappointed by his discretion, Alex faced forward in her seat again and straightened up. 'Well, do you at least have any tips for me, for dealing with the boss?'

Hamish chuckled. 'Aye. Hold on to your wits, don't bother trying to lie to him and never make him want to punch the wall.'

Alex frowned. 'Why not?'

'Because he'll punch the wall.'

'Oh. I see,' she said as they continued bouncing along the road, cresting a hill to another vista of open fields, sheep and not much else. 'Good tip. Noted.'

Chapter Three

The home of Kentallen whisky was set back from a small, deeply curved bay just outside the port. In front of it, the grey North Channel still swelled with suppressed menace but within the encircling embrace of the bay's arms, the water was millpond calm and so clear that, even from this distance, Alex could see stray fronds of seaweed lilting in the pale water. The land around the bay on the far side rose steadily, forming the bedrock of the impressive purple-hued mountains in the near distance, and a couple of fields away sat a humble stone chapel and a crofter's cottage. The distillery buildings were all painted white and, apart from a run of three-storey buildings across the back and a chimney pointing like a finger to the heavens, they were low and squat, with thatched roofs and bumpy walls. 'Kentallen' was written in bold black lettering along the entire length of one long building and hundreds of barrels were stacked in rows in the courtyard. And in the middle of it all sat a decommissioned copper still, as smooth and bulbous as a giant metal-cast onion.

'Here we are.' Hamish cut the engine and, leaving the keys in the ignition, he hopped out.

Alex followed suit, her eyes already noting the details: the couple of bicycles propped against a wall, a ginger cat sleeping on one of the barrels, the clatter of copper being beaten, barrels being staved, casks being charred, steam escaping the stills. A lorry was parked alongside one of the bigger buildings and being loaded, a team of thickset men rolling the enormous barrels up ramps the way she'd only ever seen in strong-man competitions. The ends of some of them had been painted red and all were stamped with '*Kentallen, since 1915*'.

'If it's the boss you'll be wanting, his office is this way,' Hamish said, heading for the low, small run of outbuildings in the middle of the courtyard, which had the bikes beside the door.

'Should I bring my overnight bag?' she asked, thumbing towards the back of the Landy.

'Not unless you're intending to sleep under the desk,' Hamish replied.

Alex dodged the puddles, keeping up in her dainty heels as he strode across the courtyard oblivious to the muddy splashes on the backs of his trousers, one hand automatically patting the head of a handsome blue-black-and-white smudged English springer spaniel that came out to greet him as he knocked hard on the door. He entered without stopping.

'That's Rona,' Hamish said to her whilst casting a quizzical eye around what appeared to be an empty office. 'Huh. Where the devil's he gone this time?' he muttered. 'Don't worry, she won't bite. She's gentle to the point of daftness,' Hamish said, glancing back at Alex and seeing her apprehension. 'It's Diabolo you need to watch out for.'

'Diabolo?'

'The cat.'

'Oh.'

Hamish shrugged. 'Well, I don't know where the boss is at. I told him I was going to fetch you.'

'It's fine. I'm sure he won't be long,' Alex said, taking her gaze off the dog and looking around. The room was dark with low ceilings, the floor laid with huge blackened stone slabs that were so old as to have been polished to a shine, and a small open fire – set into the right-hand wall to the side of the desk – was smouldering and crackling quietly. Alex had to resist the urge to switch on the table lamp; the dank, grey light outside the Crittall windows suddenly seemed blinding by comparison to this dark space.

How could anyone work in here? she wondered, remembering her own light-flooded office with underfloor heating and inviting kid-leather chairs, and the coral garden in the whole wall-set aquarium that emitted a gentle blue light perfect for soothing her frazzled CEOs.

'I'll go see if he's in the maltings. Uh . . . make yourself at home,' Hamish said, disappearing through the doorway.

Alex and Rona stared at each other again, before the dog gave a weary sigh and padded across the room to settle herself in front of the fire once more. Alex stayed rooted to the spot, trying to make a first reading of the person who inhabited this space.

The mess on the desk suggested he was . . . messy. She curled her lip at the sight of papers strewn, shuffled and towered across the work surface, two . . . no, three half-empty coffee mugs buried beneath like structural pillars; the half-moon of a plate emerging on the far side – she hardly dared look – revealed yesterday's leftovers (spaghetti bolognese?); a pair of muddy trainers, the laces still tied and the backs pushed down, had been kicked off beneath the desk; a jacket and tie, still in the dry-cleaning bag, were hanging from a set of antlers on the wall behind the desk chair; the antlers were also decorated with a string of gold tinsel, and what was that red thing . . . ? She walked over and peered at the something she'd glimpsed behind the dry-cleaning bag. A bra.

A green-and-white vase that had to be of 1986 vintage was perched on one deep windowsill, with several desiccated sticks inside that Alex guessed had once been fresh flowers. Probably in 1986. A boxer's punchbag dangled from one of the roof struts, some red gloves slung across the top by the laces.

She took a closer look at the papers on the desk – there appeared to be no discernible filing system, with one sheet bearing no relation to the one above or below it. There was a report from the Scotch Whisky Association about overseas growth in India and South America; an inventory of whisky stocks; a spreadsheet showing lots of big numbers; a copy of the *Field*; a printout of a blog for whisky connoisseurs; a catalogue from Sotheby's for a Fine Wines and Spirits auction in 2012; a birthday card featuring a fart joke and signed *'All the lads at KW'*; a yellowing copy of the *Sun* open on the third page; a 2016 desk diary (although it was opened to 6 December, today's date – she couldn't decide whether that made it more or less alarming) . . .

Having seen enough, Alex stepped back and did a quick summary in her head. From a cursory glance, she could say this man was messy, yes, but also chaotic, adrenaline-fuelled, too close to the staff, disorganized, distracted. In short, she could already see he was unprofessional and she didn't imagine it was going to take much to persuade her to Sholto's conviction that he was incompetent too. The guy was heading up the single largest independent malt whisky distillery in Scotland (ergo, the world) and yet his office could have been that of a bookie or an NCP attendant.

Alex wandered over to the window and stared out into the yard. She always preferred to observe unseen; people revealed their true selves when they didn't know they were being watched and from this vantage point, she could see into the open doors of the L-shaped buildings opposite. A few people in gumboots, black work trousers and red polo shirts were walking back and forth, sweeping the floor in one of the units to the left. One man in his early twenties was talking on his phone by the door. Hamish, just across the way, was standing past a set of sliding double doors and talking to someone out of sight. He didn't use much body language when he talked but she saw enough of his eye roll and a head bob in her direction to know he was talking about her.

She waited. His hands went onto his hips. Impatience. Frustration.

Was it the boss he was talking to? Was he refusing to come over and talk to her? Sholto had warned her his CEO would be a truculent client.

With a quick glance at the sleeping dog, she walked out of the office and across the courtyard to where Hamish was talking. The clamour enveloped her and Hamish looked surprised to see her as she strode in, one arm already out-stretched to a man who, she saw now, was in his early-to-mid-thirties with a thick thatch of golden hair, high-coloured complexion, freckles and the most raffish smile she had ever seen. He was incredibly attractive but even at first glance it was apparent he also knew it.

She inwardly congratulated herself on her assessment of him as their palms met. If she had had to choose from a line-up the man allied to the state of that office, she would have chosen him: arrogant, entitled, conceited. Why tidy up when someone else could do it for him? She could see he had been spoon-fed privilege his entire life. Everything had come too easy to him. He and his desk were made for each other.

'Mr Farquhar, I'm Alex Hyde,' she smiled, shaking his hand with a firm grip and having to talk more loudly over the din.

'Miss Hyde? Mrs?' he asked with a voluptuous accent.

'Miss.'

His smile widened.

'But please, call me Alex.'

'Alex,' he repeated, his smile still growing.

She paused, expecting him to reciprocate and ask her to call him Lochlan, at least, but when he made no move to do so, she added, 'I'm very much looking forward to working with you, Mr Farquhar. I trust the chairman gave you the heads-up I was coming?'

'Oh yes, absolutely, we all got the memo,' he said with great warmth, before suddenly noticing Hamish was still standing there. 'Oh, thanks, mate, I'll take it from here.'

'But—'

'I said I've got it.'

'Thanks for the ride, Mr Macpherson,' Alex said as Hamish walked away with a dark expression and muttering to himself under his breath.

'Och, don't mind him. He's as dour as we get round these parts. You had a good journey, I trust?'

'It was fine. Well, until the ferry ride. I'm not great on the water.'

'There's a mighty swell all right; they're predicting

storms for the next couple of days. You were lucky to get here when you did. The ferries are going to be suspended from six o'clock tonight until the storms pass.'

She smiled. 'How super.'

His eyebrows knitted together in bafflement. 'Really?'

'Yes, of course. It's my first full-blown, authentic experience of island life – being cut off from the mainland!' she said, loading her voice with intrigue.

'Oh, I see. Well, I think we'll have just about enough provisions to see us through,' he grinned. 'We certainly won't go thirsty, that's for sure!'

'Quite,' she said, looking around her properly now. The space was vast, far bigger than it seemed from the outside, with a vaulted ceiling, open to the rafters. Teams of men were moving about busily, some knocking out the staves of huge wooden barrels, others stacking them on pallets; some of the barrels were being reassembled within tight iron hoops and uploaded onto a conveyor-belt system, ready to be charred. She had read about the processes in such depth, she almost felt she'd experienced them already. 'It's an impressive set-up you've got here. How many people do you have working at the site?'

'Oh, uh, it's about . . . five hundred? Five fifty? Something like that,' he said, looking around at the teams, all engaged in their hard labours.

'Really? That many?' Alex asked, watching his body language whilst knowing perfectly well they employed three hundred and forty-one people here and another twenty-four in positions around the globe, and that for every direct-line operative on site, they employed three times that number in the supply-chain industries of glass, closures, tubes, labelling, packaging, inspection, warehousing and distribution. That he didn't know the numbers on his own payroll was alarming, to say the least. He might be an attractive, highly personable figurehead but charisma alone couldn't yield profits.

'Would you like to have the grand tour? I don't usually do them myself, but I'd be happy to make an exception for you,' he volunteered.

She nodded, keeping her opinions hidden. 'Thank you. That would be very interesting.'

She let him lead her out of the building they were standing in and head across the cobbles towards the building next door. The wind had become gustier even since her arrival on the island and she could just about see the crests of white horses topping the waves out to sea. There were only a few more hours till the ferries stopped but she had to wonder whether they might call them off even sooner.

'So how long are you staying with us for?' Lochlan asked, pushing open a sliding door and stepping back to allow her in. 'Long enough to allow us to take you for dinner, I hope?'

Alex didn't startle as she stepped past him; she was more than used to being fed this line (although not normally so quickly); she was also perfectly aware that it was usually done in an attempt to deflect attention away from performance to personality. 'I'll be here for as long as you need me,' she said neutrally, making direct eye contact with him. It was the best method of dissipating a half-baked seduction and firmly batting away any illusion of romantic subtext.

Well, it usually did.

'Great,' Lochlan replied, his grin growing. 'It's a date then.'

Alex frowned and went to correct him, but at the same moment he turned and gestured expansively to a couple of tall red geometric machines that looked agricultural in form. 'So, these are the grinding mills. It's where the dried malt is—'

Reduced to grist. Yes, Alex knew this, but she kept nodding interestedly as he talked, noticing how he stretched his neck slightly in a sort of tic when he talked business, how he kept rubbing his ankle with his left foot, his arms crossed over his torso. He was sending out conflicting messages, though she didn't think he'd be aware of that.

She followed him into the adjoining unit where two enormous steel tubs sat squatly, dominating the space. A man in overalls looked up as they walked in. 'Hi,' he said, clocking the boss and making to come over.

'Hi! Hi!' Lochlan said quickly. 'Don't mind us. We're just doing a quick tour. We'll be out of your hair in a jiffy.'

'Who's that?' she asked quietly, watching as the man hesitated and then nodded, moving back to his workstation.

'That's, uh . . . that's Jock.'

'Jock . . . ?'

Lochlan's eyebrows shot up in surprise that she was pressing for more detail. 'Jock, uh, gah, what's his surname . . . ?' There was a long pause. 'No, it escapes me. It'll come back.'

'And what does Jock do?'

'He's the guy who works these beauties,' Lochlan said, gesturing to the giant vats.

'Oh, he works the mashing tuns?' Alex asked, watching him closely.

'You know about . . . ?' Lochlan's eyes widened again. He was easy to surprise. Almost too easy. 'So you're not a complete novice to the trade then?'

'On the contrary, I'm afraid I'd never drunk a glass of Scotch before this week—'

Lochlan looked scandalized. 'Never had a dram?'

'Not my poison, I'm afraid, but I've no doubt I'll be a connoisseur by the time I leave.'

He tutted. 'It would be a dereliction of our duty if we let you leave as anything less. So what's your usual tipple then? Don't tell me, a champagne spritzer.'

Alex looked at him disapprovingly. 'Vodka. Preferably Kauffman Luxury Vintage edition. Distilled fourteen times and filtered twice.'

'It sounds powerful.'

'It's pure. No hangovers.'

'You don't like hangovers?'

'Does anyone? Besides, I don't have the time. I can't afford to lose days lying on the sofa.'

'Och, but those are the very best days.'

Alex hitched up an eyebrow as she smiled. He seemed oblivious to the hole he was digging around himself. Unprofessional, unproductive, inefficient . . . Sholto had been right – he was spoilt, just playing at his role. He was only in the job because his father's death put him there. This was going to be easier than she'd expected. At this rate, she was going to be off the island within the week.

'Well, I'm afraid we can't promise a hangover-free experience with Kentallen,' he went on. 'It comes from the very earth we're treading, so it's peaty and rich and complex. I promise, if you finish a bottle of this, you'll need sunglasses to open the fridge the next morning.'

Alex couldn't help but laugh. 'I'll be sure to stick to a single glass then.'

They went back out to the courtyard; it was not so much

a guided tour as a chatty preamble but it gave her an opportunity to assess him in a neutral setting and so far, he was
going to great pains to manifest his authority via flirtatious
chatter (men often used flattery as a form of containment)
and an easy-going manner that bordered on loucheness
(implying supreme confidence in his abilities). But she wondered how he was going to feel sitting across from her in a
one-to-one session when he wouldn't be able to call on
either of those tools and he wasn't the one in control.

'So? Where to next?' she asked, noticing a small group of
women emerge from a long, low building on the opposite
side of the square; they were the first women she'd seen so
far. 'What's over there?'

'That's the canteen. Would you like to take a look? Or
. . .' He looked around him. 'Or shall we go to the malting
house?' He pointed to a tall building behind her right
shoulder.

Alex saw the women throw them curious looks as they
passed, two of them openly appraising her all-red outfit,
one of them smirking and trying to catch Lochlan's eye.
Alex remembered the bra; Sholto had already told her he'd
had several affairs. With one of them, she wondered?

'Hmm? No, see one malting house, you've seen them all,
right?' She pulled her gaze away, turning slowly. 'What's
that over there?'

She pointed to a glossy, glassy single-storey building at
the furthest point of the courtyard. It was set behind the
converted outbuildings where his office was situated, overlooking a field and the sea beyond a low stone wall.

'That's the blending labs and visitors' centre.'

'Ah, where the magic happens? Let's go there then.'

'Right you are,' he said, leading the way. 'So . . . what

exactly is your job title?' he asked, curiosity colouring his voice.

'I'm a leadership consultant. Or executive coach. Business coach, whatever you prefer.'

'A leadership consultant,' Lochlan echoed, looking at her with fresh scrutiny. 'You're awful young to be in such a . . . *bossy* position, aren't you?'

'There's nothing bossy about it,' she laughed lightly. 'My role is to support you, not direct you. You already have the answers – that's why you're in the position you're in. My job is simply to keep the ship steady when the waters get choppy.'

'And how do you do that?'

'Listening, empathizing, deploying a few strategic tips to improve confidence, boost productivity. It's a science, and once you know the formulas, you can apply them to most business models.'

'You still look far too young to be directing crusty old dinosaurs.'

'Do you include yourself in that covey?'

'Huh?'

'Age is irrelevant. I'll never know what you know about the whisky trade, but I don't need to. I just need to apply my techniques to help you become a stronger, better, more enterprising, dynamic, flexible leader – delete as appropriate.'

'You don't think I'm strong and dynamic?' he asked, that flirtatious note back in his voice again, his eyes twinkling with mischief.

'I couldn't possibly comment whilst I'm still assessing you, Mr Farquhar.'

'You're assessing me?'

'Of course.'

His eyes gleamed brighter. 'And what have you decided so far?'

'It'll all be in my report. We can talk more closely about it in our first meeting.'

'At dinner?'

'In whichever room you have designated as my office.'

'I think dinner would be more conducive to establishing a rapport. Tonight? Say eight o'clock?'

'Tonight I shall be making initial notes and recovering from the long journey.'

They were at the threshold of the visitors' centre now, the lights from inside glowing golden through glass Crittall doors. He had a grip on the handle and she took a step towards it, forcing him to open the door, in no mood to stay out in this weather; the growing wind was blowing straight through the fibres of her unlined coat, and her core felt chilled. She shivered appreciatively as she stepped into the warmth, rubbing her hands together and blowing into them.

Her eyes instinctively roved around the room. It was a good size, perhaps seven metres by five, with backlit glass shelves on every wall showcasing seemingly hundreds of bottles, and the light that they cast inside was an even warmer amber than had appeared from the courtyard. A wood-burning stove crackled with life in one corner and various oak barrels were scattered around the space, set on their ends to be used as tables. There was a small group gathered around one, their anoraks in a heap on the floor by their feet, enjoying a tasting session that was being led by a spectacled young woman with hazel-brown hair pulled up into a ponytail. Several of the people in the group turned to stare as they came in, their eyes resting upon Alex curiously. It was because she was in red, she knew. A misjudgement; she'd wanted to convey energy – maybe a little festive friendliness – but the colour was too forthright in this environment where everything was watercolour pale.

She noticed two men standing by the till, heads bent as they read something, talking in low voices.

'Tomorrow – tomorrow then,' Lochlan said, lowering his voice as he came in after her and clocked the tasting in progress. She was wandering around slowly, looking at the labels and differently shaped bottles of the vintage editions.

'Tomorrow? Yes, at eight a.m. I shall look forward to it. I'm glad to see you too like to be productive in the mornings. That's a positive sign.'

'No, I meant—'

'I know exactly what you meant, Mr Farquhar.' She stopped walking and turned to face him directly. 'Or may I call you Lochlan?' she asked outright, seeing as he clearly wasn't going to offer it himself. But he was right about one thing – they did need to start building a rapport and that meant getting onto a first-names basis and initiating a little physical contact. She placed a hand lightly on his arm. 'We are, after all, going to be working together very closely for the foreseeable future.'

Lochlan hesitated, his gaze flicking over to the two men by the till, and she looked over to find them watching them.

'Well?' she pressed, looking back at him when he didn't answer. 'Are you comfortable with that?'

'O-of course.' Lochlan nodded, his gaze flitting to the two men again as she saw from the corner of her eye that they were heading for the door. Who were they?

'Oh, would you introduce us, please?' she asked,

intrigued by his evident discomfort at their presence. 'I'd like to start meeting the teams. I'll need to interview people in the coming days anyway.' Would he know these work-ers' names this time? she wondered. She was determined to witness some direct interaction between him and his man-agers; their body language would tell her a lot about how they regarded him: their respect for him and how comfort-able they felt with him.

'Uh . . . guys,' Lochlan said, calling them over.

Both men looked displeased at being hailed, and Alex's smile grew as theirs diminished.

'I'd like to introduce you to Alex, uh . . .' His voice faded away. He had forgotten her name; another fail.

'Hyde. Alex Hyde,' she said, offering her hand.

The closer man shook it. He was five foot ten and in his late fifties she guessed, his small eyes deeply set, his cheeks full and weathered. 'Jimmy MacLennan.'

'Pleased to meet you, Jimmy. I'm going to be working here in a consultancy capacity for the next few weeks. May I ask what it is that you do here?'

Jimmy looked at both the other men before he answered. 'I'm the warehouse manager.'

'Great,' she nodded. 'Well, I hope we'll get a chance to talk at some point. I'd be interested to hear your views on things.'

Jimmy nodded, looking less thrilled at the prospect than she was.

Alex looked across at the other man who was openly scowling. 'Hi. Alex Hyde,' she said again, offering her hand with a benign smile even as she felt a sudden, surprising jolt as their eyes met.

The man looked at her for a moment, his body language

hostile and closed, before reluctantly taking her hand and shaking it. He looked to be in his mid-thirties, with light brown hair and hazel eyes with golden flecks. His hair was tousled, his clothes – jeans and a shirt – smartly casual but still somehow rumpled, as though he'd been tussling with bears or chopping wood or tossing cabers for fun. He was ruggedly handsome, wearing a deep frown and regarding her with an overt suspicion, and she wished again she'd worn navy; she was spooking the natives in her cityscape colours. 'And you must be . . . ?'

He flicked his eyes towards Lochlan. 'I'm his cousin,' he said, as if that was an answer.

But it was, of sorts. Now that he'd pointed it out, she could see he looked just like a darker version of Lochlan, only with none of her host's easy, friendly manner.

'Ah, another of the Farquhar clan,' she said, glossing over his rudeness with even greater politeness. It was a failsafe trick; people found it hard to maintain hostility in the face of a smile. 'Torquil, I assume?' And when he didn't imme- diately reply, 'No? So then you must—'

'Be late, yes,' he nodded curtly. 'If you'll excuse me.' And with just a cursory glance towards his cousin and not another word, he turned and left.

Alex watched him go in astonishment, a cold gust billow- ing into her as the door opened and closed behind him. Both Lochlan and Jimmy were looking aghast too, but when she met their gazes, the best response they could manage was an apologetic shrug.

'Don't mind him,' Lochlan said. 'He warms up.'

Jimmy gave a snort. 'Usually.'

Chapter Four

Islay, Scotland, 2 February 1918

'Come away from the window.'

Her father's voice was wearied, his face still turned to the newspaper, reading spectacles perched at the very end of his bulbous nose as he frowned in the dim light.

'But, Father, he said he'd write.'

'And he will. When he can. You must show more patience, Clarissa. This blasted war isn't conducting itself to your convenience.'

She sighed and moved away from the window, the glass still fogged from her breath, the first sea mist beginning to roll in over the lawns. Her father was right. She could afford to wait; it was the very least she could do. Her brother would put pen to paper when he could.

She came back to her reading chair by the fire and picked up her book again, wondering what he was doing right now and where he was. Somewhere in France was all she knew. Had he seen Paris? It had been a childhood dream of theirs to visit – to make their own Grand Tour – back in the days before war had thrown a black cloak over Europe, blotting out the sun, the future, all hope.

'No news is good news,' that was what her mother kept saying as she paced the hall, wringing her hands fretfully. Clarissa knew *she had to believe that too, even as her mind ran through all the different horrors he might have seen or lived through just last week or yesterday or today. Her parents had always accused her of an excitable imagination but this was more terrifying than anything she might make up; the newspapers were running headlines of flamethrowers and machine guns; of noxious yellow and green gases, men stumbling blind over bodies, fleeing the guns, suffocating in the trenches, their lungs and skin blistered raw. If Percy did make it back, how could he possibly be the same person he had been before? Archie she didn't worry about; he had always had a fine-tuned sense of self-preservation, but Percy – he was too good, too kind.*

They were all changed by this war. Her own days in the barley fields were long and back-breaking, the cold numbing her hands and feet with dangerous chill, leaving them calloused and red and blistered. She stared at them in the firelight. It was almost impossible to remember their pale softness of years past, how Phillip had smiled as he pressed them to his lips, promising her a life of rose gardens and music that would now never come, torched to ashes somewhere in a field in Ypres.

Mrs Dunoon, the housekeeper, came in with their evening tray: a wedge of cheese, barley wafers, a sliced apple and a pot of tea. The china cups trembled in their saucers as she set it down. She was worn down by her duties too, trying to single-handedly cook for the three of them, manage all the laundry, and keep clean and warm the five rooms they had been reduced to using, the other twenty-eight now shrouded in dust sheets and shut off. The previous staff of nine had been whittled down to just two: Mrs Dunoon and her husband who had had to maintain the estate's boundaries, tend the kitchen garden and drive for her lame father. But now he too had been called up, along with everyone else either conscripted to the front, labouring in the fields, or those forced to leave the isle altogether for the city, to work in the shipbuilding docks and munitions factories. 'Mrs Farquhar will be down presently and asked that you start without her.'

'Thank you,' Clarissa's father said as the housekeeper retreated with a nod.

Clarissa poured the tea for him as he folded his newspaper and looked into the flames. 'Would you like to listen to the wireless?' she asked as she handed the cup to him.

'No, but one must,' he sighed, bracing himself for the news of another day's slaughter in foreign fields. 'We cannot turn away from the truth, irrespective of how hard it is to bear.'

Clarissa walked over and tuned the dials, the static an undulating whine and crackle until a well-dressed voice fell into the room. She took her seat again, straight-backed and stiff as she lifted her cup and saucer with quivering hands.

No news was good news. He would come back.

She just had to wait.

Islay, Wednesday 6 December 2017

The B&B where she was staying was only two miles from the distillery, further up the 'main' road and set just back from the coast on a fledgling cliff that was forming as the land rose towards the uplands and the nearby mountains. It was a bare and rather austere-looking farmhouse but it had a pleasing symmetry with eight windows and a centrally set front door. Unlike the rest of the local housing stock, it was unpainted and its granite stone walls looked weather-beaten; a tendril of smoke puffed and twisted from one of the chimney-tops, but it was gathered and spirited away by a sudden gust in the next moment. The farmyard and outbuildings were located just beyond the gated approach to the house and in the small, stone-walled garden, a washing line was pegged with a white sheet that billowed and flapped furiously in the wind.

The lights were on in the bottom left windows and as Alex thanked Hamish for the lift again and climbed out, she could see shadows flickering on the walls inside, someone moving about. It was dusk and apart from a red thread bleeding into the grey at the world's edge, the sky was a volatile mess of tall, overstacked clouds that looked like water buckets on the verge of overflowing and tipping their load.

The storm was about to break, fat raindrops already beginning to fall intermittently and thudding to the ground. Alex ran up the stony path, her overnight bag bouncing awkwardly behind her, one hand above her head feebly trying to protect her hair as she knocked at the door and waited.

'Yes?' The woman who answered had eyes like currants, dark and small and set in a doughy, pliable face. She was tall for a woman of her generation – five foot nine or so – and her white hair was fastened in a bun that was just beginning to come undone at the sides. She was wearing a half-apron over a tweed skirt and what appeared to be a hand-knitted Aran cardigan, a black-and-white border collie standing by her ankles, its eyes never leaving Alex's face.

'Hello. My name is Alex Hyde. I have a reservation with you.'

A half-beat passed before recognition dawned on the old woman's face. 'Och, the Sassenach,' she said in a dancing accent. 'You're just about moving in to stay?'

'That's right,' Alex replied. 'It's an open-ended booking. I'm afraid there's no way of knowing how long I'll be here for.'

'Well, that's just how we like it. Less changing of the sheets for me. Come in, come in. I'm Mrs Peggie.'

Alex followed her through a stone porch – in which coats and boots filled every surface – into a small panelled hallway with doors leading off to the left and the right and a dark brown hardwood staircase leading up at the back. A wicker, rather nibbled dog basket was positioned between further wellies and umbrellas along the back wall. A small mirrored side table to the left was dressed with a cotton lace doily and a shallow bowl which had several sets of keys in it.

'It's getting pretty wild out there,' Alex said, smoothing her hair down. 'Apparently the Met Office has put out a red weather warning?'

'Och, the fuss they make these days with all their traffic-light codes; the animals will tell you soon enough if there's something to worry about. Come this way and I can show you around,' she said, leading Alex into the room on the left of the front door. It was painted a soft mint green, with dark rugs over the floorboards and green- and purple-flowered curtains at the windows. Two small square tables were positioned at forty-five-degree angles to each other, already set with cutlery and dressed with white tablecloths and a small vase of silk flowers. A door in the far corner led, Alex imagined, to the kitchen beyond. 'So this is the dining room. That's Mr P. through there.'

'Hullo,' a voice hailed from around the door and she just glimpsed a thin white face with a patchy beard and Atlantic-blue eyes.

'Hello!'

'You have breakfast and dinner in here, or you can have dinner in your room if you prefer,' she said. 'And if you don't want to take dinner here at all – if you're eating out – just let me know at breakfast so as I know my quantities.'

'Okay. What time is breakfast served from?'

'Six until nine. I'd prefer to stop at eight thirty but you get those who like to have what they call "a lie-in",' she sighed.

'Well, I'll definitely be nearer to the six a.m. end of the spectrum. I'm an early riser,' Alex said, her eyes swinging over the room.

'What is it you do?'

She looked back and smiled. 'I'm a management consultant.'

'Och, you don't look old enough. Is that what's brought you to Islay?'

Alex nodded. 'I'll be working at Kentallen.'

'Like the rest of us then,' Mrs Peggie said with a roll of her eyes. 'So you'll not be doing any sightseeing? Looking for the birds?'

'No.'

'We usually get tourists and twitchers. Arctic terns come all the way here to breed before they head back to the southern oceans. Och, well, it's not for everyone,' she said inhaling deeply, her hands folded across her stomach. 'And is there anything you particularly like for breakfast? Black pudding? Kippers?' she asked, all in the same breath.

'Actually, yes, porridge with honey and banana.'

'We use our own rolled oats.'

Alex brightened. 'And can the porridge be made with almond milk?'

'Come again?'

'Almond milk?'

'Since when have people been milking almonds?' Mrs Peggie asked in bafflement.

'No, it's . . .' Alex decided to let it go. 'It's fine. Porridge with honey and banana, and a cup of Earl Grey would be great.'

'We only have English Breakfast.'

'Fine.'

Alex kept her smile on her lips as Mrs Peggie led the way back out across the hall and opened the door onto a sitting room with a ribbed velour sofa, two armchairs upholstered in a peony print and a small television set on its own stand. On the mantelpiece, as well as another vase of silk flowers, was an art-deco clock, its loud ticking the only thing disturbing the stillness of the room.

'You are most welcome to join Mr Peggie and me in the evenings if you wish. The telly reception can be erratic, especially in this weather, but you can usually get the gist of what's going on. Do you play whist?'

'Whist?'

'The card game. For if the weather's bad.'

'Oh.' Alex pulled an apologetic expression. 'No. No, I'm afraid not.'

'Well, Mr P. could teach you soon enough, I don't doubt.'

'To be honest, I'll probably be working most evenings,' Alex demurred quickly.

'Working at night?'

'I'm afraid so. I have clients in different time zones. Talking of which, what's your bandwidth here?'

'Band what?'

'For the Wi-Fi. Is there enough to FaceTime? I may have to dial in to some clients.'

Mrs Peggie looked back at her blankly. 'Is this to do with the computers? There's a cyber cafe in town,' she said finally. 'Would they know what you're talking about?'

Alex suppressed a sigh. 'Yes, I'm sure they will. Thank you. I'll go there tomorrow.'

'Let me show you your room.' Mrs Peggie turned around, closing the door on the old-fashioned parlour, and, reaching into the bowl on the side table and fishing out one of the sets of keys, started up the stairs. She walked slowly, one hand on the banister and the treads squeaking beneath her weight.

'We've no other guests staying tonight, but we have a Spanish couple coming with their baby tomorrow. I hope it's a baby that sleeps,' she said, puffing slightly as they reached the top of the stairs and turned left. 'Mr P. needs his rest.'

She walked them down to the room at the far end. Floorboards creaked intermittently and Alex resisted the urge to straighten a framed photograph of a black-and-white landscape that had slipped on its wire.

'I've put you in the blue room seeing as you're with us so long. It's got the best views over the water. If it's a particularly fine day, you might even see Ireland, although you'd best not hold your breath. It's also the furthest room from Mr Peggie's so you shouldn't be disturbed when he's putting out the cows.'

'Does he have to be up early then?'

'With the light.' Mrs Peggie unlocked the door and they stepped into a narrow but neat bedroom with dual-aspect windows. It was too dark outside now to glimpse anything of the views but the windows were framed by pretty blue gingham curtains finished with pleated pelmets and there was a window seat in the gable end; a naive but very pretty pastel picture of a lake scene hung on one wall and looked to be a framed amateur print. There was a single wardrobe, a washbasin in the corner and the bed was made up with sheets and a cream knitted blanket; a neat pile of camel-coloured towels was stacked at the foot of the bed. Alex scanned the room with growing unease. There was no duvet (she always froze under sheets). No desk. No multi-plug sockets. No satellite TV. No radio. No ensuite. Something else too . . .

No ensuite?

She looked back at Mrs Peggie with alarm. 'Is there not an ensuite?'

'Aye. There's the washbasin there,' the old woman said, nodding towards the pale blue porcelain Armitage Shanks.

'Yes, but . . . the loo? And the shower?'

'Just down the hall, last door on the left before the stairs. Don't worry, it's only you and the residents of the green room sharing. Mr Peggie and I have our own facilities.'

Alex suppressed a shudder. She had never shared a bathroom with a stranger in her life. But what could she do? This had been the only accommodation Louise had been able to book at such short notice, without having her packing up and hopping all over the island every other day. Plus it was the closest to the distillery, which was key.

'I trust you find everything to your satisfaction?' Mrs Peggie asked, watching her.

'Of course. It's charming, thank you.'

Her landlady nodded but the slight purse to her lips suggested she had picked up on Alex's reservations. 'Well, I'll leave you to unpack, although that shouldn't take long – you seem to travel awful light. Dinner will be ready in an hour. Potato soup for starters, followed by ham, mashed potatoes and cabbage.'

'Uh . . .' Alex felt a frisson of alarm ripple through her as she looked around the room again. She had known there was something else missing. 'Have my bags been delivered?'

'Bags?'

'My suitcases. They were sent up on the earlier train and I understood a cab was going to bring them here directly.'

Mrs Peggie shrugged. 'Jack's not been this way for a week or more, I'd say.'

'Who's Jack?' Alex tried to keep the sharp note from her voice.

'The taxi man.'

'There's only one? There's not someone else who could have picked them up? Perhaps he just hasn't had time to deliver them yet.'

'Well, sometimes his son-in-law helps out if his leg's playing up.' She tutted. 'Terrible thing, the gout.'

But Alex couldn't think about Jack the taxi man's gout right now. She wanted her bags. She needed them. She had nothing but a toothbrush, pyjamas and running kit with her in the overnight bag. 'Is there any way we can find out? Can you ring him and double-check?'

The ferries were stopping – she checked her phone in her pocket – now. They were stopping right now for the next two days at least and there would be no deliveries of any sort from the mainland. Not food or mail, and certainly not purple coordinated T. Anthony bags with the clothes she was going to need out here for the next three weeks.

'I'll call, but Jack's very reliable. If he had them, he'd have delivered them. Is it clothes you'll be needing?'

'Yes.' Alex gestured to her woefully inadequate dress and coat, which were now practically sitting up and begging for a dry clean after that journey.

'Don't worry. I'll put out some things for you. There are still some clothes in my daughter's room.'

Alex hesitated. Mrs Peggie had to be in her early eighties, which meant her daughter must surely now be in her fifties. Very best case scenario, her daughter was also a professional businesswoman who had kept her figure and had a healthy clothing budget, visited often and kept a small capsule wardrobe here, just in case; worst case scenario, the clothes hanging in the nearby room were cast-offs from a 1970s childhood. 'That's very kind, thank you,' she faltered, not wanting to appear rude. 'But you will double-check with Jack?'

'Aye.' She turned to leave. 'Dinner's in an hour, as I said.'

'Actually, I'd like to take dinner in my room tonight, if you don't mind. I have a lot of paperwork to catch up on.'

'As you like. Your key's in the door. You're welcome to leave it in the bowl in the morning or take it with you; I have a master copy for cleaning.'

'Thank you. Very much.'

Mrs Peggie left the room, the door closing with a click behind her, and Alex stood for a moment, feeling helpless and frustrated. Already bored. She wandered to the window and stared out into the blackness, her own reflection the only thing to see. Outside, the wind moaned, making the windows rattle slightly in their frames, and Alex blinked as she saw a flash of white streak past the window. The bed sheet still pegged to the line? 'Oh . . . !' She turned, but Mrs

Peggie's footsteps could already be heard downstairs crossing the hall floor and by the time she turned back it was already gusting away over the fields.

She picked up her phone and went to call Louise – there had to be a tracking number for her bags – but there was no reception. Not even one bar. She tried holding it up, pressing it to the glass, going to the other windows. Nothing. She was in the middle of nowhere and that storm wasn't helping.

Alex sighed, trying to let go of her frustration – there was no point in resisting these events. As she was forever explaining to her clients, what could be more pointless than to resist what already is? She walked back to the bed, unpacking the few belongings she had with her: men's navy cotton Turnbull & Asser pyjamas on her pillow; toothbrush, charcoal toothpaste, Perricone MD skin serum and moisturizers on the sink; her trainers by the window and running kit in the top drawer of the tallboy dresser; and her current reading material: a biography of Aung San Suu Kyi.

She picked up all that was left in there – the report on Kentallen – and, kicking off her heels, sank onto the bed with it, ruminating on this afternoon's introductions. It had been a disappointing start, messy, chaotic and disorganized. On the one hand, it appeared her task here was going to be a lot easier to achieve than she had anticipated: Lochlan Farquhar – flirtatious, irreverent and unprofessional – was out of his depth; on the other, those same qualities meant he was going to be a handful and getting him to the finish line was going to be like herding cats.

She opened the pages and began looking at the numbers again. Kentallen's growth projections had been scaled back by 2 per cent: in part due to losing a key distributor in a vital new growth market in Indonesia; in part due to the single malts sector losing market share to both the blends market and lower-priced whiskies such as American bourbon; but mostly it seemed to be down to their charismatic but feckless CEO making either poor or rash decisions, running the business as though it was his personal playground: kissing the girls and bullying the boys . . .

Alex yawned, the numbers beginning to swim before her eyes as something undefined – a thought, a suspicion – niggled in her mind; it had been tickling her consciousness all afternoon but she couldn't quite reach it. She could feel her exhaustion from the rigours of the day beginning to creep up her weary body. It was tiring always having to be the facilitator in every transaction – the unstinting smiling, the empathetic nods, the steady eye contact – not to mention that the journey here had been a long one, with changeovers at both Glasgow and then the port of Tarbet, and she had been cold for most of it in her unsuitable clothes. Not just that, she was jet-lagged to hell; she had travelled direct to Edinburgh from New York, where in turn she had arrived after an intense week of sessions with a client in Vienna. Her body clock was all over the place. Unable to suppress another yawn, she lay her head on the pillow and closed her eyes; she would allow herself the luxury of a nap. It was something she encouraged all her clients to do and she preferred to practise what she preached. Ten minutes was all she'd need – it had been proven by NASA that cognitive and memory functions were improved after a ten-minute sleep – and then she could get back to the spreadsheets. Just ten minutes . . .

*

She awoke with a start, roused by the sound of the herd protesting as they were moved from the warm dairy to the wind-battered fields. Alex looked around her in alarm. The light was still dim but dawn had definitely broken; she was still fully clothed on top of the bed, but a woollen blanket had been draped over her and the curtains drawn. A tray of long-cold food was placed on top of the tallboy and a glass of water was on the bedside table. On the small chair in the corner, between the tallboy and the main window, was a small pile of folded clothes.

'Oh!'

She had slept through? She couldn't believe it. She blinked several times, trying to clear her head. She never usually needed a prompt to waken her after ten minutes – she had trained herself well – and she couldn't remember the last time she had slept so long, or so soundly. But then she was used to city life and it was the nothingness around here that had lulled her into such deep sleep – no noise, no light pollution.

She swung her legs off the bed and rose gingerly, her body feeling stiff; she wasn't sure she had even moved in the night. Walking towards the gable-end window, she pulled open the curtain and looked out, needing to orientate herself having arrived in a storm and settled in the dark. The view that greeted her was gentle and fierce all at once. On the one hand, the landscape had been painted in delicate watercolour tints – dove grey, storm blue, moss green and smoky white – as a sea mist hovered wraith-like over the fields, the slow plodding bulk of the cows disappearing into its ether, the ancient permanence of the far-off mountains undermined by a gentle haze that wrapped them out of sight. On the other, the wind continued to batter at land and sea like a riled god, flattening the grasses and bending the trees, whipping up battleship-grey waves in the North Channel as though trying to widen the breach between here and the Irish coast. It had been going all night long, the moans of the wind a white noise that had become her sleep's lullaby.

She pressed her forehead to the glass. So much for getting away with pulling on her running kit; there was no sane prospect of going out in this weather. She walked over to the tallboy and lifted the clothes that had been left out for her – indigo flared jeans, an apple-green blouse with pointed collar, a navy Fair Isle jumper and an age-cracked pair of brown leather lace-up boots. They had got to be kidding?

She sighed and reaching for the towels folded at the end of the bed, opened her door and peered out, scanning for the open door that would signify the bathroom. She tiptoed down the corridor, wincing as the floorboards creaked underfoot, and stared in at a salmon-pink bath suite, complete with looped rugs and a limp-looking electric power-shower that was seemingly as old as the jeans.

It wasn't what she was used to – nothing like; she only ever travelled first class and she expected marble in a bathroom as much as she expected towels – but she wasn't seeing it anyway. The niggle that had been itching her mind had finally surfaced, full force, and she spent a good minute standing open-mouthed, staring at the tiles as yesterday's odd tone suddenly made sense.

She got the water running and stepped under it, closing her eyes and letting the windows steam as an old school rhyme played over and over in her head: *Fool me once, shame on you. Fool me twice, shame on me.*

*

57

She was sitting in the desk chair an hour and a half later when the door opened and Rona nosed in first, her owner stopping dead in his tracks. The scowl she remembered from yesterday deepened as he stepped into the room, his light brown hair wind-whipped, thunder on his face.

'Good morning, Lochlan,' she smiled brightly, staying right where she was, in his seat. 'Are you ready to get down to work?'

Chapter Five

'Callum 'fessed up then?' Lochlan said scathingly, after a long pause. Closing the door behind him, he began shrugging off his coat, no apology forthcoming.

Rona, coming over to sniff her hand briefly and finding her to be friend again, not foe, quickly headed over to her water bowl in the far corner and began drinking.

'Callum? Oh, I had assumed he was Torquil. But no, he didn't.'

Lochlan turned to face her again. His expression was suspicious, resentful. As she'd gauged yesterday – hostile 'Then how did you know he . . . ?'

'Was pretending to be you? Body language; and the profile didn't fit, although the state of your desk almost had me fooled, but I sense your chaos may be down to trying to do too much rather than too little,' she said carelessly, dismissing the prank and walking over to the small kettle she had refilled a few minutes before in readiness. Already, the distillery was waking up, the sound of the heavy unit doors being slid back on their rails, voices and heavy boots in the courtyard, the clatter of casks being rolled on the cobbles. 'Tea? Or coffee?'

Lochlan stared at her. 'What are you doing?'

'Making you a drink.'

'No, I mean, what are you doing? Why are you in my office acting the PA when we both know you're nothing of the sort?'

She smiled, deciding he looked as though he needed a coffee and putting a heaped teaspoon into the mug. 'I'm putting you at your ease, Lochlan.'

'Well, it's not working.'

She smiled as she poured in the boiling water and a splash of milk. It was just as Sholto had said: truculent.

When she didn't reply, he added, 'And I don't recall giving you permission to call me by my given name.' Behind her back, she heard him sink into his desk chair, assuming the perceived centre of authority.

'That's because you didn't have the courtesy to either meet me or greet me, much less get on to given names at all,' she said lightly. 'But after yesterday's shenanigans, I figure you owe me this at least.' She walked over with the coffee and handed it to him, a smile on her lips, eyes directly locked on his and ignoring that irksome jolt in her stomach again. She would wear him down with kindness. 'My time is expensive and I don't like wasting it. I've travelled a long way to come to see you.'

He took the mug reluctantly. 'I never asked you to come.'

'No. Your chairman did.'

His eyes darkened. 'Sholto is a dangerous old fool.'

'Dangerous?'

'Because he doesn't know he's a fool.'

Alex nodded. 'Ah. Interesting. Well, that's something we can discuss in the course of our sessions. I take it you've been informed that we're going to be working together?'

'Yes. But I hate to break it to you – you've come a long way for nothing. We're not going to be working together.'

'I'm afraid we are. Unless you want to give me a resignation letter and I'll hand it to your chairman myself?'

'And why would I do a thing like that?'

'Because you're in the Last Chance saloon and if you don't work with me, I would hazard a guess his next step will be to call the board and raise a vote of no confidence against you.'

Lochlan smirked. 'He can't.'

'Oh, there's always a way. Once lawyers start digging they'll find something he can use.'

Lochlan glowered down at her – an intimidating sight – but Alex held his gaze, keeping her expression neutral. He needed her reaction to feed his anger and escalate this confrontation, but the high feeling was all his; she wasn't personally involved in this; it was just business.

'And we could do with another chair in here,' she said calmly as he continued to eyeball her.

'*What?*'

The statement did as she had intended, breaking the deadlock.

'Well, don't you invite people to sit when they come in to see you?'

'No.' He almost spat the word on the floor.

'But what if they have a problem? Something they need to discuss with you at length?'

'A problem?' he scoffed. 'What kind of business do you think we're running here? It's not a counselling practice or a coffee shop. I'm not having people coming in here with their *problems*.'

'Staff morale should be a priority for you. It directly affects productivity. Organizations don't change, people do.

Their welfare is your concern. You're only as strong as your weakest link.'

'Christ, is this how it's going to be? You spouting corporate crap at me all week?'

'Oh, I'm afraid it's going to be a lot longer than that.'

His eyes narrowed; he had a masculine energy that was forceful and unapologetic, his presence filling up the room with every minute that passed. 'And what the hell are you wearing? How am I supposed to take you seriously, looking like that? Is this your attempt at *going native*?'

'These are my landlady's daughter's clothes,' she said calmly, checking the pointy collar was still tucked under the round neck of the jumper, even though the comment stung, her vanity pricked. She had been hoping she could pull off a seventies redux, à la Inès de La Fressange, or Alexa Chung. Clearly not. 'My bags are stuck on the mainland.'

'And there's no ferries for at least another day?' Lochlan smirked, getting the picture immediately. 'How terrible for you. I imagine you must feel pretty ridiculous if yesterday's glamour-puss get-up was anything to go by.'

'It's just for a day or two. Hardly a disaster.'

'It is from where I'm standing.'

In spite of herself, Alex shot him a look, instantly regretting it; she couldn't let him rile her. If he found a single way to undermine her, she knew he would use it. She walked over, adjusting her tone. 'Look, Lochlan, I'm not the enemy.'

His eyes flashed like the swipe of a sword. 'We'll have to beg to differ on that.'

'I'm here to help,' she said, perching on the end of the desk.

He in turn sat back in the chair, hands clasped behind his head – a classic power pose, taking up room. 'Not needed.'

She stared at him, locking him in a gaze again. 'You cannot lead this company and continue to behave as you have been doing. In case you hadn't noticed, you are walking a tightrope at the moment and there's a long way to fall.'

'I have excellent balance.'

'But for how long? For as long as you continue to antagonize the board, you are isolated, and that makes you vulnerable.'

'The moon's none the worse for the dogs barking at her,' he sneered.

She blinked, unfamiliar with the aphorism. 'You need me.'

'No.'

'Okay then, I need you.'

He frowned. 'Unlikely.'

'What if I told you the money from this commission is to help someone in my family who's in desperate need?'

His eyes grazed over her, prickling her skin slightly. 'I'd say that's a lie.'

'Why?'

'You clearly don't need the money.'

'How do you know that? You don't know anything about me.'

One eyebrow arched slightly, mockingly. 'You're wearing a Jaeger-LeCoultre watch, those diamond studs must be three quarters of a carat each, you're tanned – which at this time of year means you've been somewhere tropical – and hair doesn't fall like that anywhere north of Kensington.'

'Very good. So then you're an astute observer,' she smiled. 'Now shall I share what I've observed about you?'

Realizing he'd walked into a trap, he put his feet on the

desk, bigging up the pose even further and throwing in shades of disrespect and contempt to boot. 'I have a feeling you're going to anyway.'

'You're instinctive, confident, dynamic, commanding and I suspect – when it suits you – charismatic.'

There was a pause. 'And the bad news?'

'You're reactive, arrogant, insecure, distrustful and isolated.'

'Surely arrogance and insecurity are mutually exclusive concepts?'

Alex was impressed by his refusal to be distracted by such a brutally direct assessment, overriding any reflexive anger to debate a point of logic.

'You'd think so, wouldn't you, but arrogance usually presents as a deflection to vulnerability; it's a tool that manipulates other people's perceptions of you, so as to protect the ego.'

Lochlan rolled his eyes. 'Jesus, spare me,' he muttered.

'A case in point,' she said. 'Eye ro—'

In a flash, he whipped his feet off the table and got up, coming to stand over her. 'Look, this has been *fascinating*,' he said with sarcastic stress. 'But I'm afraid I *am* going to have to ask you to leave now. I have work to do.'

'Yes. With me.'

'No,' he said flatly. 'Goodbye, Miss . . . whatever your name is.'

She stood up too. 'Hyde. Alex Hyde. And I'm not going anywhere.'

'And I'm not taking instruction from someone dressed as the Milky Bar kid.' With that, he took her by the arm and frogmarched her to the door. 'Thanks for the coffee.' And he set her outside before she could so much as get a word out, slamming the door in her face and bringing their first so-called session to an abrupt and unequivocal close.

'He sounds like an arse,' Louise said in a low voice, flicking her eyes up to make sure the woman sitting by the water cooler couldn't hear her. 'No, I *can't* believe it.' She waited again for Alex to draw breath. 'You're so right.'

She nodded as her boss's stream of fury kept on coming down the line like a pyroclastic flow. She examined her nails.

'Uh-huh.'

Searched for split ends. (As. *If.*)

'I mean, who does that?'

Watched a man bend down to tie his laces outside the window.

'He sounds like a classic Gamma.' She had been working here long enough and had typed enough reports to know the main principles of the Graves model of the change state indicator and this guy – angry, defiant, rebellious, destructive and symbolically throwing himself against the barriers – was a Gamma if ever she'd typed one.

'Oh, absolutely. He deserves everything that's coming to him. You have nothing to feel bad about . . . No, I do mean that. You're just doing your job. You're a professional. Unlike him, from the sounds of things.'

The tirade dwindled to a stop – or Alex ran out of breath – and Louise straightened to attention, knowing her boss's mind would be straight back on point again. These rants never lasted for more than a few minutes; that was one of Alex's great strengths, the ability to forgive, learn, move on. She didn't fester in bitterness or wallow in regret. She always kept moving, always wanted to be facing the light.

'Yes, I texted the tracking number to you but I've already

chased them up: the bags are at the port. I did enquire into getting them choppered over but they're saying the winds are too strong for anything but a Sea King.' She paused. 'Unless you want me to look into that?'

She stared at her own reflection in the screen, narrowed her eyes, pouted.

'Yes, I agree. It does seem a little . . .' She'd been about to say 'extravagant' but in Alex's world, if something was needed, then there was simply no excuse for not moving heaven and earth to make it happen. 'So then they'll be on the first ferry that leaves the port. They've promised to call me the second they slip anchor.'

She could tell from the breathlessness of her boss's voice that Alex was walking again, the wind smacking intermittently against the mouthpiece. It sounded savage up there and more like she was trekking the Antarctic tundra than pacing a Scottish island.

'Yes, I've booked it in for a week today. I explained to his PA you were out of the country on an emergency consultation and would dial in for a Skype session.'

She watched a bus stopping outside, caught in the heavy traffic; the roadworks on Piccadilly were causing long tail-backs all the way to Hyde Park Corner and even up Park Lane and all the cut-throughs in between – including this street – were becoming gridlocked.

'No, everything else is fine. Carlos had to cancel his nine o'clock; I think his car was towed again . . . I know. But Jeanette's been back to back with her clients all day and I've rearranged all yours till the New Year.'

She frowned as the connection crackled, Alex's voice becoming robotic and sporadic. 'What? A *haggis*?' Her frown deepened. 'No, I've no idea what a haggis looks like in the wild. Are they dangerous . . . ? Alex?'

Alex stared back at the wild creature. Or rather, the goat. She'd never seen one at such close quarters before and certainly not one with such long or wild hair as this. (It seemed it wasn't just her that the wind was wreaking havoc upon.) It had given her quite a fright, sneaking up to the wall like that and nibbling her ear with its rubbery lips.

It took a moment for her heart rate to slow again and she was still eyeing the interloper when a door to her left opened and a young woman peered out.

'Is everything okay?' she asked, looking around before settling her gaze on Alex – or rather, Alex's outfit. 'I thought I heard a scream,' she said.

'I'm sorry, that was me.' Alex grimaced as the wind wrestled with her hair again, her New York blowouts a far-off memory now. She pushed her hair back and held it in place with one hand, feeling harassed and humiliated. Exactly how many people had seen her being thrown out by their CEO? she wondered. His office was set slap bang in the middle of the courtyard. All the work houses and units surrounded it, with the maltings, mill house and kiln house at the back, turning to the still house, cooperage and warehouse on the return. Not to mention the long, low canteen on the other side of the square, opposite the maltings. In other words, everyone could have seen.

'I was sitting on the wall, making a call, and I'm afraid this . . . fellow decided to sneak up on me.'

The woman laughed, the action transforming her face from rather wan and serious looking to playful and approachable. 'That's Wet Lips Wendy. She's known for her kisses and absolutely appalling halitosis.'

'Oh.' Alex took another wary look at the creature, its long fringe blowing in the winds, its pale pink, fleshy lips rolling gymnastically as it chomped on the grass.

The woman came further out of the building and offered her hand. 'I'm Skye, by the way. I'm one of the blenders here . . . I think I saw you yesterday, didn't I?' She winced, pushing her glasses back up her nose.

'Hi, yes – I'm Alex Hyde. I'm a management consultant.'

Skye pulled a face. 'Uh-oh. Did we do something wrong?'

'No, no, nothing like that,' Alex smiled.

'What do management consultants actually do?' Skye asked, crossing her hands over her chest. 'Are you . . . like a counsellor?'

'No, but I suppose my job does involve a lot of observing and listening. I tend to highlight and translate my clients' actions and feelings, rather than dictate. I'm a bit like a mirror, reflecting them back to themselves; the most I do is to sometimes angle the light.'

'And are you here for a while or . . .'

'That most annoying of things, I'm here for as long as it takes. It could be three days, could be three weeks. But I *definitely* have to be home for Christmas,' she said, wishing she could be back there this time tomorrow instead. It had been weeks since she'd last had a night at her apartment, running a bath with her favourite Miller Harris oil, relaxing on the sofa in her Bella Freud cashmere tracksuit, watching *Pillow Talk* and sipping a glass of Puligny-Montrachet.

She wondered how old Skye was; she looked only a little younger than her, maybe twenty-seven or so? She had mid-brown, mid-length hair, pale freckled skin, and her fine-rimmed glasses gave her a delicate bookishness. She was wearing a white lab coat and Alex remembered her as the pony-tailed woman she'd seen talking to the group in the visitors' centre yesterday afternoon. 'How long have you been working here?'

'Oh, in various capacities since I was knee high to a grasshopper, really, but I joined the labs formally after uni. My father's the master blender here. He's been training me up since I was wee.'

'I see, so it's not just the Farquhars for whom Kentallen's a family business then?'

'No. My grandfather was master blender here too, and there's plenty other folk like us in the town doing the same jobs as their fathers and their fathers' fathers.'

'Do you enjoy it?'

'Aye. Dad always says the best thing about being a blender is if you make a mistake, it's another generation before anyone finds out.'

'How funny,' Alex grinned, feeling her upset at Lochlan's behaviour towards her begin to wane. 'I wish it was the same for me. Unfortunately, my mistakes tend to be very public.'

'I bet you don't make mistakes, though,' Skye said.

'Everyone makes mistakes.'

'Well, you don't look like you would. In fact, when you came into the visitors' centre yesterday, one of the tasters asked if you were famous.'

'Really? Why?'

'I don't know, I guess you had a very "international" air about you.'

'Heavens. I don't think they'd be asking the same thing

today, do you?' she said, motioning to her get-up with a wry smile.

'You do look quite . . . different,' Sky said diplomatically.

'Needs must. My bags are stranded at Tarbet. These are my landlady's daughter's clothes.'

'Oh. Where are you staying?'

'Crolinnhe Farmhouse.'

'Oh my God!' Skye screeched, her hands flying to her mouth. '*Mrs Peggie?* But her daughter's my mam's age!'

'Well, welcome to her childhood,' Alex said, self-deprecatingly holding her hands out. '1976 called. Apparently it wants its clothes back.'

'I cannae believe it,' Skye laughed. 'She must have been just a teenager when she wore that?'

'No idea,' Alex sighed. 'But I do know reputations have been broken on lesser sights than this. I had been hoping I could pull it off as a Chloé/Marc Jacobs retro/ingénue vibe but I don't think it's working, do you?'

Skye paused a moment. 'You know, if you wanted, I've probably got some stuff you could borrow till you get your bags back.'

Alex hesitated. 'Really?' She couldn't see what Skye was wearing beneath that lab coat but there was not, at least, any sign of a pointy-collared shirt.

'Aye. I mean, it's nothing fancy. No designer labels or anything but they'd sure as heck look a lot more up to date than that.'

'Given that Wet Lips Wendy is looking better than me right now, that wouldn't be hard,' Alex sighed. 'Oh God, are you sure . . . ?' She couldn't quite believe that she'd been on the island less than twenty-four hours and this was the second stranger from whom she was begging clothes.

'Absolutely. Come to mine this evening and we can rifle out some outfits for you.'

'Well, that's so generous. Thank you so much. But only if you're quite sure you don't mind?'

'Of course. In fact . . .' Skye hesitated again. 'Seeing as you're coming over, why don't you stay for supper?'

'Oh no,' Alex demurred. 'I couldn't ask you to do that. It's quite enough that you're kitting me out, without going to the trouble of cooking too.'

'Look, I'm cooking for myself anyway and it'd be nice to get to know you better, especially if you're going to be staying a while. My fiancé lives in Glasgow and doesn't come back till the weekends, so the company would be nice. There aren't many folks my age coming round this way.'

'How old are you, if you don't mind me asking?' Alex asked curiously.

'Twenty-six. You?'

'Thirty-one.'

'Pretty much twins then,' Skye grinned, getting up from the wall and wiping the grit from her hands. 'I'd better get back. Come over for seven?'

'Great. Oh – I'll need your address.'

'Don't worry, Mrs Peggie will give it to you. See you later then.' And with a little wave, she disappeared back indoors.

Alex sighed, the smile fading as she looked back across the courtyard at the little white unit with the puffing chimney stack and closed door. She knew she ought to go back over there and try again but how could she command respect dressed like this?

No, it was better to retreat and make a fresh charge to the enemy camp tomorrow. She had till Christmas, she could afford to take her time. This had been an unfortunate start

– the second such, in fact, after his and his cousin's fun and games yesterday – but it was irrelevant in the scheme of things. She wasn't the best in her business without good reason and in some ways, his behaviour only made her task here easier. Let him have his fun. She knew which one of them would be laughing longest when it was all over.

Chapter Six

SS *Tuscania*, British waters, 5 February 1918

The men's cheers filled every last space as the boxers sparred in the mess, shouts and curses and laughter and gasps lifting them all up as the troopship ploughed through the rearing dark seas. Private Ed Cobb stood against the bulkhead, beads of sweat trickling down from his brow, his own fists drawn into punches as he watched; his money was on Walt Mooney, his bunkie – a Montana boy too, he'd worked as a logger before signing up and had the strength of two men.

There was a roar as a quick 2-2-1 combination allowed Walt to land a sucker punch on Harold Schwartz's chin and the man staggered backwards into the outstretched arms of the spectators who were doubling up as ring ropes. The cheering men rushed Jack Hawkins who was running the bets but Ed stayed where he was. He was feeling hot, unnaturally so, and he pressed a hand to his brow. It came back clammy. He was shivering too and his bones felt leaden. Was it as hot in here as he thought? No one else was sweating.

Leaving the din behind him, he wove a path through the crowd, out of the room and down to the cabins below. It was almost four thirty and would soon be evening mess, the troops settling down afterwards to the quieter pastime of card games.

Chief Kellogg nodded as they passed in the passage outside the turbine room, Ed saluting with a vigour he didn't feel before slumping against the bulkhead again and making his way on to his berth.

He was but two doors away when there was a terrific explosion which threw him off his feet and across the corridor as the ship lurched violently, immediately beginning to list to starboard. The lights had gone out and the momentary silence that followed in the darkness was suffused with fear.

But then the screaming started – the scream of steam escaping the ship's whistle, the scream of a high-pitched voice arrowing through the corridors, and he recognized it as being a kid from Kentucky he was sure had lied about his age.

'They got us!' the boy shrieked, showing the whites of his eyes as he ran for his life. 'They got us!'

Islay, Thursday 7 December 2017

'So you'll no be staying in for dinner then?' Mrs Peggie asked, looking displeased. Her quantities were going to be out.

'No. I'm sorry. It wasn't planned until an hour ago. Skye's very kindly offered to lend me some clothes, you see.'

'But you've got clothes. What's wrong with the ones you're wearing?' Mrs Peggie asked, looking even more dis-pleased.

'Nothing. Nothing at all. They're just a little, uh . . . small.'

'Aye,' Mrs Peggie said, nodding. 'I remember Jane was only a girl when she was in those.' She straightened, heaving her bosom up and folding her arms underneath. 'Well, I hope Skye will give you double portions at least. You need feeding up.'

Alex wasn't sure what to say to that, so said nothing.

'Will you be stopping for breakfast?'

'Absolutely.'

'I've got some lovely kippers.'

'Thank you, but porridge is fine,' Alex said firmly.

'As you like. Oh, and the Spanish family have arrived,' Mrs Peggie said. 'I've had to put a step by the toilet for the toddler – apparently his aim isn't accurate yet.'

Alex tried not to grimace. She was, after all, the one having to share a bathroom with this child. 'Um, fine . . .' she muttered. What else could she say? 'Skye said you'd be able to give me her address?'

'Of course.'

'And I wondered if I could get Jack's number from you. I need to book him to take me over there this evening. And back again, obviously.'

'Och, Jack'll be no good to you. He's on the mainland. Won't be back till the day after tomorrow at the earliest.'

Alex's brow furrowed. How long had he been there for, exactly? Little wonder her bags had been stranded! 'His son-in-law then?'

'No need. Mr Peggie's making a delivery to Euan Campbell this evening; he can drop you on his way.'

'That's really not necessary. I can get a cab. I'll need one to bring me back anyway.' She made a mental note to get Louise to look into booking a car and driver for her; she was going to need more flexibility and freedom over her comings and goings.

'David's in bed by nine, he has such early starts.'

'Who's David?'

'Jack's son-in-law. He works at the fishery. Up by four every morning.'

Alex bit her lip, trying to contain her frustration. So the island's gout-ridden taxi driver was stranded on the mainland and his stand-in son-in-law had to be in bed by nine? Hadn't these people heard of customer service? She didn't expect the 24/7 hours of New York and London, but this was ridiculous!

'Don't you fuss, we'll get something sorted,' Mrs Peggie said, patting her arm. 'In the meantime, can I get you a wee cup of tea? You look awful pinched.'

Worn down, Alex nodded. 'That would be lovely, thank you.'

'And a finger of shortbread?'

'No, thank you. Just the tea, please.'

'Och go on, it won't kill you. You go on up. I'll bring it to you in just a few moments. The water's hot if you want to run a bath.'

Alex retreated, having absolutely no intention of taking a bath in the middle of the day. She had notes to write up, calls to make and she needed to get to this cyber cafe to Skype New York and check that Howard Connolly wasn't doing anything stupid like actually leaving his wife. She would need to take her red coat with her to wear for the call; she couldn't have him seeing her dressed like Karen Carpenter. She might be only a couple of miles off the Scottish mainland, but her day had been curiously warped, like looking at herself in a fairground mirror. Nothing was quite as she expected it to be – there was no Wi-Fi here or corporate hierarchies, no suits or double-shot espressos. Instead, goats nibbled her ear and bras dangled from stag antlers; and as she passed the dining room and glanced in, she saw a set of girdles being stretched on the spoon-back chairs. She felt like *Alex Through the Looking Glass.*

'You found me okay then?' Skye asked, just as Mr Peggie's pea-green tractor rolled past on the street behind her, the trailer rattling over the cobbles. 'Oh! Ew!'

'Yes, I'm sorry about that,' Alex sighed as the wind continued its assaults on her hairstyle and blew in the backdraught of the stench that had accompanied her here. 'My driver is making a manure delivery.'

She tried to smile but in truth she was feeling stretched, her emotions brittle and alarmingly close to the surface. The jet lag didn't help, of course, but then neither did the fact that in the just over twenty-four hours that she'd been on the island, she had lost her bags, been tricked by the local Casanova, manhandled by her client, nibbled by a wild goat and now stank of cow dung. 'I'm so sorry. I smell to high heaven – and you must have such a sensitive nose, too.'

There was a pause and she hoped Skye couldn't read her low mood.

'My nose . . . ?' Skye echoed, a smile twitching her lips.

'Well, yes, you're a blender by profession. You must be very sensitive to smells. Me cadging a lift on the manure delivery perhaps wasn't the best—'

But she didn't get to finish, for the wind took her hair and tipped it over her face like a bucket of water and Skye threw her head back in laughter, an arm strapped across her stomach at the all-round pathetic scene. It took only a second for Alex to join in too, her 'laugh or cry' moment turning into hysterics on the doorstep instead and for several moments, the two of them laughed until they had to clutch the walls for support.

'You've got to come in,' Skye cried finally, wiping tears from her cheeks as she continued to chuckle. 'Or the neighbours will think we're drunk.'

Alex followed after her, smoothing her hair with her hands as she stepped into the warmth. Skye's house was one of the terraces on the waterfront in the heart of Port Ellen, overlooking the jetty and four down from the Co-op. It was white-painted with a window either side of the black door, and a large dog bowl was set at the bottom of the stone steps.

'Oh, this is lovely,' Alex exclaimed, walking into a front room that could have come straight from a Laura Ashley catalogue with duck-egg checked armchairs, a camel-coloured sofa, an oak-lintel fireplace and bookshelves groaning under the weight of books, DVDs and photographs. It wasn't going to be appearing in *World of Interiors* any day soon but the house had an easy intimacy to it and its details spoke warmly of the lives lived within it: the hiking boots drying by the fire, a couple of football trophies on the mantelpiece, a basket filled with fishing rods by the window and stacks of wedding magazines on the floor beside the sofa. And from the kitchen wafted the most delicious aroma of what she guessed was chicken pie.

'Well, it's not much but we call it home,' Skye said, almost shyly.

We. Alex remembered she had mentioned her fiancé lived in Glasgow. 'What's your fiancé's name?'

'Al. Or Alasdair Gillespie to his mam!'

'Skye Gillespie,' Alex smiled. 'It's got a good ring to it.'

'Yeah,' Skye giggled, looking younger now that she wasn't in a lab coat, although to Alex's mild alarm, she was wearing a bibbed, short black denim dress with a plum-

and-custard striped Henley top that was straight off the Topshop home page. 'Oh, let me get you a drink. Where are my manners? Would you like a dram? Or prefer wine?'

'I always say when in Rome . . .'

Skye smiled and disappeared into the kitchen and Alex waited by the fire, peering at the photographs – some of them black-and-whites – arranged along the mantel. They showed Skye as a little girl standing on some rocks in a pair of red-and-black ladybird wellies, her hair plaited into pigtails and heavy pink glasses perched on her nose; Skye and a little boy – her brother? – sitting in a rowing boat together, each holding one enormous oar; Skye sitting on the shoulders of a man with a bushy black beard and kind eyes; Skye as a baby in her christening gown being kissed by her adoring mother; a landscape shot of the port that looked to have been taken in the 1950s, judging by the cars parked and the fashions of the people passing by—

'Here you go.'

Alex straightened up as Skye came back into the room with a couple of glasses, a bottle of the Kentallen 12 and a ramekin filled with a few squares of dark chocolate. 'I was just looking at these photographs,' Alex said. 'You were a ridiculously cute child.'

Skye tutted, grinning as she poured them each a dram. 'Honestly, those ladybird wellies. I loved them so much, my mother says I wore them in the bath, in bed . . . Cheers! Or as we say here, *Sláinte mhath!*'

'*Sláinte mhath!*' Alex echoed, taking the glass with a nod of thanks and moving over to the sofa as Skye curled herself up in the armchair. 'Yes, I feel much the same whenever I get a new pair of shoes, to be honest,' Alex said, picking up the conversation. 'I can't bear to take them off.'

'Aye, but I bet you have the loveliest shoes so why would you take them off. Jimmy Choos, Christian Louboutins . . . ?'

'Well, a few.' All.

'I'm wearing a pair of Louboutins at the wedding. I can't wait,' Skye said with an excited shrug. 'Alasdair almost died when he saw the receipt.'

'Has he seen what you're wearing then?'

'Och, God, no. I'm terrible superstitious, I don't want to invite any unnecessary bad luck in our lives.'

'Yes, right,' Alex agreed, even though she believed you made your own luck. 'So when's the wedding? I see you've got lots of magazines.'

'Aye. It's on the twenty-third.'

'Of December?'

'Mmhmm.'

'You look awfully calm for a woman who's about to be married in a couple of weeks!'

'Honestly, this is the calm before the storm. We're moving to Glasgow straight after the honeymoon so I'm having to pack up the house too. I've pretty much done most of upstairs and now I've got to tackle down here,' she said, pulling a face. 'But I'm getting there. Most of the wedding preparations were organized a while back – the dress, church, vicar, venue, band, cake, catering – they're all done.'

'I'm impressed. Are you having bridesmaids or pageboys?'

Skye grinned. 'Well, now, you're going to think I'm mad when I tell you this but, the ring-bearer is going to be . . . my dog!'

'Huh?' Alex spluttered, almost choking on her drink.

'I know, it sounds so mad but she's the love of my life – apart from Alasdair, of course – so I had to find a way to give her a starring role. We've got her a beautiful new powder-blue leather collar, so she can be my "something blue" as well, and we're going to tie the rings to her collar with a satin bow.'

'Oh my goodness, make sure you double-knot it, whatever you do!' Alex laughed.

'That's exactly what my mam said. She's terrified they'll get lost somewhere between the east door and the altar.'

'Well, it sounds like a lovely thing to do. And highly original! None of your guests will forget it, that's for sure. Where is she, by the way?' Alex asked, looking around the room.

'She's with my ex; we share her. He'll be dropping her back later.'

'Oh. Right. And that . . . works out okay, does it?'

'Mainly. It's getting easier. When we first split up, we had terrible arguments about who got her for Christmas Day, who for Easter, that kind of thing, but everything's a lot more mellow now.'

Alex tipped her head to the side. It sounded like a nightmare. 'How long were you with your ex?'

'Six years. We got together just before I went off to uni. My usual marvellous timing!' she said with a roll of her eyes.

'Was it an acrimonious split?'

'You could say that.' Skye looked down. 'He jilted me. The night before our wedding.'

'What?' Alex spluttered.

'It's . . . it's not as bad as it sounds.' She squeezed her eyes. 'Well, no, it was. I just mean that he did me a favour, the marriage would have been a disaster. I met Al soon after and this time I know it's right.'

'How long after?'

'About a month.'

'Wow, that was soon. How did your ex take it?'

Skye arched an eyebrow. 'He went off on a three-day bender on the far side of the island.'

'So he's allowed to leave you at the altar but no one else can have you?' Alex frowned. 'Sorry, but what a pig. After what he did, he has no right to hold any opinion on what you do or who you see.'

Skye looked back at her. 'Are you married?'

'God, no,' she said, before adding hurriedly, 'I mean, it would be lovely, of course, but I don't get the time. I travel so much with work.'

'I can't believe you've not been snapped up,' Skye sighed.

Alex shrugged. 'It's not about someone else doing the snapping – it really hasn't been a priority for me. My career's my great love.'

'So far,' Skye said with a knowing tone.

'Maybe for ever, we'll have to see.'

Skye rested her chin on her hand, her eyes narrowed with interested scrutiny. 'Are men intimidated by you, do you think?'

'Ummm . . . some, perhaps. Maybe.' Definitely.

'You must work with a lot of powerful men.'

'Yes, I do. And women too. Thirty-five per cent of my clients are women but I wish it was more. I'd love to see more women occupying the roles I'm currently coaching men in. Sometimes I almost feel like I'm part of the patriarchal conspiracy – I'm helping keep those men in those jobs. It's frustrating.'

'But if you're working that closely with that many men, don't you ever—?'

Alex was already shaking her head, already anticipating the question. 'I never mix business with my personal life. Ever.'

'But surely there must have been a time when you were tempted? Just once?' Skye pushed, eyes brightening with the turn into gossip.

'No. I don't even let the thought enter my mind. And besides, powerful men may respect an equally powerful woman but they don't necessarily want to marry one. I'm sorry to say that precious few of my clients have wives whose careers match the heights of theirs.'

Skye sighed. 'God, I'm one of those women. I always mean to put my career first, but somehow I still end up following my men. I came back here after uni because of my ex, even though all my friends moved down to Glasgow; and now, when I'm all set up here with this house and my job and my friends, I'm leaving again because of my fiancé.'

'Well, you're lucky that your job allows it. I'm not saying we should sacrifice our love lives altogether for our careers; it would just be nice to think it didn't have to be one or the other.'

'I guess.'

'So where are you moving to?'

'Oh, not far. It's a place called Killearn, just outside Glasgow. Al works in the city centre and I've managed to get a new job as master blender at the Glengoyne distillery not far away.'

'But that's great news. Master blender is a promotion, isn't it?'

'Aye. I'll be stepping into my dad's shoes. Just not here.'

'So then you haven't sacrificed your career for a man

after all. You've got both,' Alex shrugged. 'I think that's what's called "hashtag winning at life".'

Skye chuckled. 'Maybe. I guess it's just ironic that after resisting coming back, now I don't want to leave.'

'Irony's like that; it likes nothing better than to bite us on the bum.'

'That's a technical term, is it?' Skye grinned.

'Absolutely.' Alex shrugged her eyebrows playfully, surprised that she was having such a good time. She couldn't remember the last time she'd socialized, as opposed to networked.

She watched as Skye brought her glass to her mouth, but before sipping, inhaled it deeply, her eyes closed. She pulled the glass away and then brought it back again, repeating the deep breath in.

'Is that how you're supposed to drink whisky?' Alex asked, fascinated.

'Oh,' Skye said, pulling an embarrassed expression. 'Occupational hazard. I forget not to do it.'

'Well, could you show me how? I've never done it properly before.'

'Sure,' Skye replied, looking delighted and pouring them each a little more. 'The first – or most important – thing to remember is that whisky's not something to be rushed, but rather savoured. It takes a long time to make and it should take a long time to drink, to really allow the flavour to come out.'

'Right,' Alex said, adjusting her grip so that it was the same as Skye's, her fingers on the stem, away from the bowl of the glass. She realized she'd never seen whisky served in a stemmed glass before either – only ever tumblers.

'Now the first thing you want to do is introduce yourself

to it. So you bring it to the nose and say *hello*,' Skye said in a sing-song voice, swirling the glass only slightly, closing her eyes and inhaling the aroma for a good four or five seconds.

'*Hello*,' Alex echoed, feeling faintly ridiculous to be talking to a drink.

Skye then swung her arm away as though it was hinged, before bringing it back in again. 'How are you?' she murmured in another dramatic voice, this time with a light swill of the glass and a deep inhalation.

Alex copied her exactly, right down to her intonation.

'Very well, thank you.' Skye opened her eyes. 'Smell that? See how it's beginning to breathe?'

Alex nodded. It was like the opening of a flower. 'Yes.'

'Now take a good swig but hold it in the middle of your mouth. That's it and we're going to count down from ten . . .' she said, holding up her fingers and counting down. Alex swallowed when she did.

'And now take a bite of chocolate,' she said, handing over the ramekin. 'And then take another swig.'

Alex's eyes widened as the sweetness of the chocolate in her mouth contrasted with the smooth, fiery burn of the whisky.

'See that, how the flavours balance and complement one another? Now take another sip quickly.'

Alex did as she was told, eyes closing with pleasure as the last swig of whisky was drained, to dance in her mouth. She didn't gulp it down but let it play on her palate for a few moments, the different flavours like musical notes. 'Oh my God,' she gasped finally. 'Wow.'

'Yeah? You liked that?' Skye asked, looking pleased. 'You should try the twenty-eight. It's a different level entirely.'

'I'd love to,' Alex replied.

'Yeah? Shall we say hello to it?'

Alex grinned. 'Let's say hello.'

Two and a half hours later, the forgotten chicken pie had been burned and they had greeted the 12, the 28, the 15, a 7 from the new Virgin Oak series and a final slick of the famous Macallan 30.

Skye was wearing her veil and dancing to the Police on vinyl whilst Alex was twirling in front of the fire in one of Skye's curated outfits – a gold pleated midi skirt, pink ankle socks with navy blue dots, gold glittery block-heeled sandals and a navy polo neck. It was fun and funky, and she suspected Skye had spent a lot of time compiling the 'looks' together – she kept apologizing that the labels weren't designer – and if Alex had worked in social media or fashion PR, it might have been perfect. But for an executive coach propping up the morales of some of the biggest bosses of the FTSE 100 and the Dow Jones . . . ? Not so much.

Still, it didn't matter tonight. Those bosses weren't on a little island off the west coast of Scotland, caught in a storm and isolated from real life. They weren't drinking single malts in a cottage with a whisky connoisseur who was going to have her rings brought down the aisle to her by dog.

But she was and she could wear what the hell she liked. She was effectively missing in action, off the grid, with no clothes and no client (well, not one who would cooperate, anyway). For as long as those winds blew, she was a free agent.

The doorbell rang – twice – before Skye, staggering

across the room, got to answer it. 'That'll be my baby!' she cooed, bumping into the sofa en route, her cathedral-length veil trailing over the cushions behind her.

Alex stopped twirling and made her own jagged path towards the record player – the music was really very loud; what if one of the neighbours had called the police? – but as she lifted the needle and 'Roxanne' stopped, she heard the tense silence explode in the hallway.

'Oh, God, I'm sorry, we—' Skye's voice was apologetic.

It was the police? She looked around in panic. Were they going to file a report? Her name couldn't be on something like that. She glanced at the kitchen. Was there a back door? There had to be! She had to get—

She fell over the armchair she had somehow managed not to see, but as she tried to get her feet back on the ground again, she heard the delicate skitter of claws on the slate floor tiles, a tail thumping the coats, and she breathed a sigh of relief. She was overreacting. Drunk. Out of control, for once.

Still, if it wasn't the police . . . Alex made her way unsteadily across the room, curious to see this embittered ex, the jilting jerk . . .

'I had a call from Mrs P. She's asked me to drop back your friend.' The man's voice was terse.

Alex – holding on to the back of the sofa – brightened. Her driver? 'I hope you're not going to be smelling of cow shit too!' she called out, giving a small shriek as she slipped on the LPs which were scattered on the floor and fell over the top of the sofa. 'Bugger,' she muttered, pushing her hair back and taking three attempts to get back up to standing again.

She was almost at the door when the dog rounded the corner and came straight over, nosing her hand.

What? Alex felt a chill run through her.

She got a hand to the door frame and, steadying herself, peered round. The image that greeted her seemed to be on freeze-frame (well, wobbly freeze-frame, like an old-school VHS): Skye was standing there with her hands behind her back, sheepishly bunching up the veil as though trying to hide it. And on the other side of the threshold, looking surprised – and then angry as hell – was Lochlan Farquhar.

Chapter Seven

'Must you drive so fast?' she asked, one hand on the passenger handle, the other on her head.

'I'm doing twenty-five.'

Alex tipped her head back, eyes closed, and groaned. She felt sick. All that whisky and a low-slung roadster on these twisty, hillocky roads were not what she needed right now. She required a hospital bed and an oxygen tank and an IV drip and enough morphine to knock her out for a week, which was roughly how long this hangover was likely to last.

'I didn't know you knew Skye,' he muttered, as he took a corner so sharply that the car rolled onto two wheels. Or so it seemed to her, anyway.

She turned her head on the headrest to look at him. His profile, in the moonlight, looked brooding and defiant, his jaw set half an inch forward, the corners of his mouth slightly turned down. He had surprisingly long lashes, she noticed, seeing how they touched the brow bone, the evening stubble darkening his cheeks. 'I didn't know *you* knew her,' she said knowingly, the words a slur.

He didn't rise to the bait. 'I live here. I know everyone.'

'Biblically, I meant—'

'I know what you meant,' he snapped, his grip tightening on the wheel.

Alex sighed, a tense silence ballooning and filling the small cream-leather upholstered space. She looked ahead again at the singular beam of light illuminating the dark road, the windscreen wipers on max as the rain fell in sheets. Even though she would rather have had anyone but him driving her back, she was glad she didn't have to walk in this. 'I suppose you would have refused if you'd known it was me you were collecting.'

There was a telling pause. 'You're just lucky I had to drop the dog anyway.'

She watched him, her vision as blurry as her words. She still couldn't quite believe he and Skye had had a thing. 'And are you going to throw me out of your car too when we get there?'

'That depends,' he muttered.

'On what?'

'On whether you behave.'

She giggled at his bad mood and he glanced across at her. 'Exactly how much did you have to drink?'

'A *very* nice twelve, followed by a *very* nice twenty-eight, followed by a *very* nice fifteen, followed by a *very* nice seven . . .' she said, counting on her fingers.

'Jesus . . .'

'Followed by a *very* nice Macallan.' She stage-whispered the name as though it was *Macbeth* or a dirty word.

Lochlan tutted. 'You realize you'll be sick from all that.'

'No, I won't.'

'Yes, you will.'

'. . . Oh God, yes, I think I will,' she moaned, clapping a hand over her mouth. 'Oh God.'

Lochlan slammed on the brakes. 'Not in the car!' he barked, reaching over her and opening the door. The wind raced in, rain pelting at her and soaking her in seconds as she spun herself ninety degrees so that she could lean out, away from the hand-stitched leather seats. But she couldn't get up; the car was too low.

'Fuck,' Lochlan muttered, undoing his seat belt and jumping out. He pulled her up by the hand and helped her to stand, being careful not to get too close. She staggered over to the side of the road, putting one hand out onto the stone wall for balance as she dropped her head and waited.

But nothing happened.

The wind, ferocious as it was, had given her enough of a fresh-air boost and the nausea had passed. She couldn't decide whether that was a good or a bad thing.

'I think . . . I think I'm okay,' she mumbled after a minute or two.

'Great,' Lochlan said sarcastically, irritably shaking the rain off his arms and raking his hair back from his face. 'So now we're both drenched. For no good reason.'

'You are not a very gracious Good Samaritan,' she snapped.

'Who said I have any interest in being either? As far as I was concerned, I was dropping back the dog and having a quiet night. Instead, I'm standing in the pouring rain with a woman who's even more of a pain in the arse when she's drunk than she is when she's sober. And that's really saying something.'

The rain fell a little harder, making her squint, and she felt herself sag; she didn't have the energy to fight him right now. She was nauseous, and her clothes so wet, the pleats of her skirt were all but pulled out by the weight of the water dripping at the hem. 'I don't . . . I don't usually drink.'

'No shit, Sherlock.' He stared down at her, seeing how she swayed slightly – and not on account of the wind. He sighed. 'Look, just don't throw up in my car, okay?'

'I won't,' she said, staggering back towards the car again and accidentally bumping into him as he tried to pass on the way back to the driver's side. She staggered sideways and he had to grab her to keep her from falling backwards – it wasn't so very different from how he'd held her this morning, on his way to throwing her out of his office. 'But if I *do*,' she slurred, wagging a finger at him earnestly, 'I'll buy you a new one.'

'You'll buy me a new Aston DB8?' he scoffed, letting go of her arm.

'Sure,' she shrugged, noticing a ring of fire that haloed his irises and suddenly wondering if he kissed as well as he scowled. Because if he could . . . She shook her head, shaking the thought away like a pony tossing flies. She might be drunk but she wasn't *that* drunk. She was never that drunk.

Lochlan looked down at her, watching suspiciously. 'Uh-huh.'

'Any colour you want,' she sighed, feeling herself begin to relax; oblivion was coming. She couldn't keep her eyes open; the rain felt good on her skin. Wet was wet, she couldn't get any wetter now, and it felt cleansing, some-how.

She had a sudden sensation of falling and he caught her, just, grabbing her hard by the arms again. 'Oh whoops, did I fall asleep?' she slurred.

'Just get back in the car,' he said, taking her by the elbow and guiding her around to the passenger side himself; he even protected her head with his hand like a police officer as she ducked – collapsed – in with a groan.

He shut the doors on the storm again and pulled away, Alex resting her head on the headrest; she wanted to sleep but she kept being jolted out of any slumber by the steep bends of the road tossing her from side to side. Or was that his driving again? She wondered if he was deliberately taking the turns too sharply just to keep her awake, but to ask outright was now a command too far. She needed oblivion.

'No, don't go to sleep yet,' he kept warning her, jostling her intermittently. 'It's just another half-mile.'

But her eyes closed anyway and the next thing she knew was the clunk of a car door closing, and she opened her eyes to find the farmhouse fuzzily framed in the beam of the car's headlights. Her door opened, the storm throwing itself upon her again like a bucket of cold water, and Lochlan leaned in to get her out. He pulled her up to standing.

'Can you walk?'

She tried to say something but her voice seemed to have moved from her throat and in the next instant, he had put her arm around his neck and his own around her waist, and was walking her towards the door. The wind and rain did their best to deny them, pushing forcefully against the gate as they struggled to open it, whirling in a fury as they negotiated the gravel path. But a moment later, they were standing under the relative shelter of the porch and a moment after that, Mrs Peggie was there.

'Mother of God,' she exclaimed, taking in the bedraggled sight. 'Did the kelpies get you?'

'The booze did,' Lochlan said, not in the mood for jokes

and walking straight in, to get away from the storm. 'Which room's she in?'

'The blue suite, at the end,' Mrs Peggie said, pointing up the stairs. 'Tch, she's wet through.'

'I'll take her up there, if you could get her a hot-water bottle and a bucket.'

'A bucket? Oh dear, dear,' Mrs Peggie tutted, bustling away busily.

Alex heard the stairs creak beneath their weight as Lochlan helped her up the stairs. The curtains were still open onto the dark countryside, the storm whipping past the window like spectres, as she was moved towards the bed.

'You'll need to change out of tho—' Lochlan pulled his arm away and she swayed dangerously. 'Whoa!' he said, catching her by the elbow and pulling her up to straight again. Her head was a full second behind the rest of her body. 'No, don't sit down. You'll get the bed wet.' He tutted, clearly wondering where to put her. 'Come, sit down here.'

He led her towards the window seat where she plonked down, her head nodding forward like a rag doll's. Balancing her carefully, he took a tentative step back, arms out lest he should have to catch her again.

'Jesus, the state of you,' he muttered, watching as she sagged sideways against the wall instead and slid down it a little. She didn't try to correct herself and after a pause in which it was apparent she was hell-bent on doing nothing other than going to sleep, he bent back down and unbuckled the glittery gold sandals which were even more inappropriate for a Hebridean storm than stilts. 'Why, *why* are you wearing these things?' he asked, holding her leg by the ankle and shaking it frustratedly so that her foot wobbled in his grip. 'You look like a toddler dressed you.'

'And what is wrong with *that*?' she demanded, trying to sound haughty – imperious – but she couldn't pull it off when her head had to be supported by the wall as she watched him, both of him.

He looked up at her but his eyes didn't glitter with their usual contempt. In fact, he looked worn out. 'I knew you were trouble the second I set eyes upon you,' he mumbled, shaking his head.

'I could say the same about you.'

'You didn't know who I was when you set eyes on me.'

'Yes, I did. Somehow, I knew. I felt it here,' she said, punching herself in the gut. 'You fit the brief. Callum was too . . .'

'Dumb?'

'Flirty.'

He stared at her. 'So you're saying I should have flirted with you to get rid of you?'

She looked back at his Libran face: two of him, double the handsome, double the trouble. 'No. Flirt, lie, run – there's nothing you could have done; I'd have found you. Body language always betrays what the mind won't.' The words ran into each other, no commas, no pauses.

'I think you actually believe that.'

'It's a proven fact . . . What? Why are you looking at me like that?'

'I was just thinking it's amazing how you're almost catatonically drunk and yet you're still holding forth on your corporate claptrap like you're the keynote at a conference. I can't decide if you're brilliant or just brilliantly arrogant.'

'The ffffirst one,' she said, jabbing her finger authoritatively.

He said nothing and she realized he was still holding her ankle, her bare foot resting on his knee.

The sound of the door knob hitting the opposite wall made him look back as Mrs Peggie came in carrying what looked like a cottage hospital's matron's kit – hot-water bottle, hot toddy, blankets and a bucket. 'There now, we'll soon have her sorted. Och,' she said in a scolding tone as she saw them sitting there. 'Is she still in those wet clothes? She'll catch her death.'

'I think *you* had better deal with that, Mrs P.,' Lochlan said, getting to his feet.

'Aye,' Mrs Peggie said after a hesitation. 'You're probably right. Will you stay for a bath, Lochie? You're drenched too. I can have it run in a jiffy.'

'No. I'll get out of your way. I'll be home in a few minutes anyway.'

'Promise me you'll have a hot bath when you get in. Don't let the cold get to your chest.'

'I promise.'

Mrs Peggie sighed, satisfied he wouldn't let himself die of pneumonia. 'Well, I'd best get her undressed and into that bed somehow.'

'Are you going to be able to manage it? Is Mr P. around?'

'He's tucked up in bed and I'm not sure, anyway, that this is a sight he'd be much help with.'

'Maybe not.'

'Now you get along. Thank heavens you picked her up. I don't like to think what might have happened if she'd attempted making her own way back.'

Lochlan glanced down at her again. 'No.'

In the silence that followed, Alex was vaguely aware of

the two of them looking at her and she wondered if she was supposed to say something. But where was her voice?

'She's a funny wee thing,' Mrs Peggie said quietly. 'I cannae place her. She turns up here all Miss Uppity Pants but take away the fancy clothes and she's like a lost child.'

'Mm.'

There was another silence and Alex groggily looked up again. They definitely wanted her to say something.

Mrs Peggie bent down and began tugging gently at the sleeves of her jumper.

'I'm off. Good luck, Mrs P.' Lochlan's footsteps retreated across the room.

Alex tried lifting her head, catching his eye as he turned for the last time. She had to thank him. He was a complete arse but she still had to thank him. She opened her mouth to speak.

'. . . See you tomorrow, Farquhar,' she slurred. 'And don't be late.'

Chapter Eight

British waters, 5 February 1918

Water coursed across the engine-room floor, the power sputtering as the sea hit the steam pipes with a vicious hiss. The emergency lights had come on and he could now see the pale, twisted faces of his menfolk as they headed past him for the ladders and the life-boats on deck – friends, men he had played cards with not two hours before, barging past in a frenzy of brawn and staring eyes. It was like the buffalo stampedes back home: the mightiest won through, the meagre and meek were trampled over and left. Self-preservation beat civilization, no question.

On any given day, Ed would have been at the front with the best of them; he was tall and strong for his age thanks to a lifetime logging with his father. But today his head was fogged, the shock slowing down his reflexes, and he had a sense of being suffocated, the air being sucked from the spaces as the water rushed in. It wasn't fear he felt, for he had experienced that several times before in his twenty years; rather a sense of futility that there wasn't a thing to be done. There was no recourse, no way to hit back.

He was alone in the passage when a voice behind him shouted out. 'We'll float for hours, man! Tie a hard knot in your lifebelt and tell the others to keep a cool head.' He turned and saw it was the chief, leaning one arm against the stairs in an almost languid manner.

The words, as well as the way in which they were delivered, stirred him to action and he climbed the stairs, having to hold both handrails to heave himself up as **Tuscania** continued to list. He no sooner stepped through to the main hall below the exit to the deck than the hatch was closed shut behind him, and the crew began to dog it down so as to make the bulkhead waterproof.

The mob had congregated here, thrashing and pleading and fighting as the lifeboats up on deck were launched but as Ed watched, he feared they'd kill each other before the water even touched them.

'We'll float for hours, men!' he shouted as loudly as he possibly could, echoing both the captain's words and his confidence, hands cupped at his mouth. 'Tie a hard knot in your lifebelts and tell the others to keep a cool head.'

His call was met with the same reception as the chief's, the firm manner of experience and authority quelling their panic like water over flames and as the word was passed on, order came out of nothing. The men began to assist one another, calling the names of their bunkies and assembling at their designated exits so that by the time Ed got up on deck himself, the auxiliary lights had come on and he could see them all standing quietly in their assigned meet zones, waiting for rescue. The lifeboats had been launched in the very first moments after the impact and men were shinning down the ropes to the vastly overloaded vessels. He saw the two nurses, the only women on board, being hauled to safety.

The lifeboats pulled away, carried by the current from the failing vessel, her prow already nosing the icy water. A short series of explosions made them start as flares were launched from the bridge and the sky shone a galactic red, illuminating the sea all around.

It would have been almost beautiful were it not for the inky scenes of devastation it highlighted in the black sea – bodies floating, men drowning each other as they fought for scraps of driftwood from those shackled lifeboats that had taken the direct hit of the torpedo.

Ed felt his field of vision contract down, his legs buckle at the knees. It had been only an hour since the strike but he felt aged by it. Changed.

And then suddenly from the gloom, he saw the hulk of one of the British destroyers in their convoy drawing alongside. Multitudes of ropes were sent from the Tuscania *onto her deck, troops sliding down the line, each helping the man after him and making way for the next. The training drills proved their worth as hundreds were offloaded, Ed watching, huddling for warmth by the stack, just behind the bridge. He was sweating and shivering at the same time. It would soon be his turn. . . .*

But the destroyer, brim full in the swelling sea, dared remain no longer and too soon the ship turned away, heading for shore. A boy halfway across on a rope leapt for it – and missed by a foot, plunging into the icy water.

Ed stared at the splash, his comprehension beginning to dim now, shock taking root. The captain issued instructions to the men left behind to cut the remaining long ropes and coil them in readiness for instant use for the next destroyer. The mood was strangely calm as they wound the loops, anxiety cloaked in silence as they worked.

They waited. They waited. The auxiliary lights had gone out again as water flooded the hull, the lit sky faded back to black, and they had only the occasional flash of a pocket light or the glow of a cigarette to see by. The captain rolled a cigarette, making a joke about something. He had survived a previous torpedo attempt and his attitude nerved the men but it did not need to be said aloud, the fate that awaited them: with the destroyer from their convoy gone, it was either a rescue or straight doom as their lot now.

There was a sudden shout. 'Captain! Look.'

The man pointed into the dark and from the night, faint flashing lights emerged, the outline of another destroyer bringing a cheer from the troops. It drew up on the port side and the ropes were thrown over as before. Ed felt hands on his back, pushing him forwards. It was the captain.

'Go on, lad.'

The man quivered as the ships rolled out of time with one another, tautening and flexing like a lion tamer's whip. He took the rope between his hands and legs and began to shin across, feeling how it strained in his grip. The wind whistled as though through a tunnel, the waves rearing up beneath him like the snapping jaws of wolves. He kept moving, hand over hand, his body pleading for relief as every sinew battled gravity. He was almost there . . .

But the destroyer lurched violently on a surging wave, the rope snapping ratchet tight, and his hands opened reflexively. For a moment, his legs saved him, his ankles clamping tighter as his body swung loosely like a trapeze artist's; but his fevered mind was too far from here to react in time. And as his body plummeted to the sea, it wasn't the white rope he saw receding from him in the black sky, but a woman on the snowy steps of their home, a shawl over her shoulders and love in her eyes.

Islay, Friday 8 December 2017

The coffee was already in her hand when the door opened and Lochlan walked in, stopping in surprise at the sight of her standing there. He visibly sagged as she held it out towards him, steam misting the air between them. 'You have got to be kidding me.'

Alex straightened to her full five foot eight height and smiled. 'Good morning.'

He closed his eyes for a moment, as though praying for strength, and Alex took the opportunity to appraise his running kit. From the amount of mud sprayed up his legs, it looked as though he had run through peat bogs to get here. Rona looked half dead and, without bothering to nose Alex's hand, headed straight for the already flickering fire. 'It's like goddammed Groundhog Day.'

'I don't think so, do you?' she asked, gesturing to her outfit of slouchy black wool trousers, Céline trainers and a grey cashmere Chloé sweatshirt. The storm had passed over, just enough for the fishing boats to go back out – though not the ferries yet – and Louise had come through for her, getting her stranded suitcases dropped over from the mainland by the RNLI on a training run, in exchange for a peachy donation. 'One of us is better dressed for a start.'

He looked back at her again, before kicking the door shut behind him and coming further into the office. 'You got your bags back then,' he smirked, pulling his trainers off with the laces still tied and kicking them under his desk as he pointedly looked her up and down.

She rolled her shoulders back, like a soldier on inspection parade. 'Yes.' She was back on top.

He took the coffee from her without a thank-you, and perched on the corner of his desk. 'Well, I guess I should be grateful that it's an improvement on your last get-up. Glittery sandals and ankle socks? What were you thinking?' he mocked, his defiant eyes on hers as he sipped his drink.

They both knew it wasn't her dress sense that she had to account for.

Alex swallowed and took a deep breath. It was the moment she had spent since five a.m. bracing herself for, the one she knew she couldn't hide from if they were going to move forwards.

'Yes, well, about that, I'm glad you've brought it up,' she said, forcing a smile onto her lips. 'I wanted to thank you for last night—'

He cocked an eyebrow.

'It was incredibly kind of you to drive me home.'

He took another long, slow sip of coffee, enjoying this. 'I didn't really have much say in the matter.'

'Well, be that as it may, you went above and beyond taking me . . .'

'Yes?' He watched her, his eyes dancing and enjoying how she stumbled on the detail.

'Taking me upstairs and . . . settling me.'

'Settling you,' he echoed, and she wondered if he could tell that she had no idea how she had come to be in her bed in her Turnbull & Asser pyjamas.

'Yes,' she nodded, sure her cheeks were flaming. 'It was very kind of you.'

He took another sip, never taking his eyes off her. It was like being studied by a tiger from a tree. He seemed to be waiting for something more from her.

'And I'm terribly sorry if the situation was at all awkward for you,' she continued.

'For me?' he grinned.

'Of course, I'm mortified. It was incredibly unprofessional of me and—'

'Why?'

She frowned. 'Why what?'

'Why was it unprofessional of you?'

Wasn't it obvious? 'Well, because you're my client.'

'As I keep telling you, Hyde, no, I'm not. I never hired you and I don't want you here. Hell will freeze over before you get to do your voodoo psychobabble on me.'

His gaze dared her to challenge him on the frankly outrageous slurs on her profession, but she simply stuck her chin in the air and smiled, hoping she didn't look as green as she felt.

'Well, anyway,' she said, ignoring the digs and taking the higher road. 'You will no doubt be delighted to hear that Mr Peggie has very kindly said I can have free use of his old Land Rover whilst I'm here. Apparently there are no car-rental companies on the island.'

He chuckled. 'No.'

'So you don't have to worry about being bothered by me again.'

'Somehow I doubt that.'

'I meant—'

'I know what you meant.' His eyes flashed, showing no mercy, relishing in her humiliation.

She sighed. 'Look, Lochlan, whether you like it or not—'

'Not.'

She cleared her throat. 'Your chairman has made it very clear that you cooperating with me is a requirement or he will be forced into having you charged with gross misconduct.'

Lochlan gave a scathing laugh. 'Nope. Trust me, if he could have done, he would have done by now.'

'He's the chairman of the board.'

'Just let him try.' He looked at her, unperturbed. 'Heavy stones fear no weather.'

Alex looked back at him, incredulous. He really did think he was unaccountable to anyone. 'This war you're determined to wage with him – it's not what he wants; Sholto wants to make it work.'

'What I want has never been something my cousin has concerned himself with.'

'That's where you're wrong. Why else would he have hired me? He wants to make this relationship work. I can help you.'

'No.'

'I can! But you have to work with me, Lochlan. You have to trust me.'

'And I do.'

Alex straightened up, feeling a sudden stab of hope. 'You do?'

'Yes. I absolutely trust you can make your way to the door unaccompanied this time.'

Alex blinked, feeling a flame of fury ball in the pit of her stomach. She had never been met with such outright rudeness before. She had stood here before him with a cup of coffee and a white flag and this – this! – was how he treated her? Did he have any idea of the people she had worked with, the companies she had helped, no, transformed?

'No.'

'No?'

She saw the surprise in his eyes and jerked her chin in the air, defying him to manhandle her again. Just let him try!

'No,' she said firmly. She wasn't going anywhere.

There was a moment of utter silence. A moment in which

both their wills were flexed. A moment which he broke with a cavalier tut.

'Oh, Hyde,' he sighed, getting up and walking over to her. 'You're just determined to do this the hard way, aren't you?' And he caught her by the elbow and firmly led her to the door.

'You have got to be kidding me! No! No!' she cried, trying to wriggle free, but his grip was too firm. 'This cannot be happening again!'

He opened the door and pushed her through it, back into the courtyard.

'I know, right?' he laughed. 'That was exactly what I thought when I saw you this morning too!'

And with a self-satisfied grin, he slammed the door in her face. Again.

Alex stood in the courtyard, feeling conspicuous, feeling small.

But if she was humiliated, no one else seemed to notice. A few men rolled casks past her with a nod that was no more than quizzical; someone else sweeping the cobbles only noticed her when he almost brushed her feet from under her. She turned on the spot, wondering where to hide this time.

It took her a moment to notice the difference in mood about the place. There was a conversational buzz that hadn't been there before. Now that the storm had all but passed and the skies were clearing to a chilly ice blue, people were milling about, lingering on coffee and cigarette breaks where they'd been running for cover only the day before; she could hear radios on in the workshops and units, laughter and bad singing lilting through the open windows. The distillery's energy was completely opposite to that of the muted, downbeat and turgid workplace she had first seen over the last couple of days.

God, she wondered – was this her third day already? Had it been only that?

They'd done zero hours of work together in that time, but how much had happened to *her*? She felt almost unrecognizable to herself, seemingly lurching from one crisis to the next from the moment she'd set foot on this island. Losing her clothes had been the least of it – she felt she'd lost her professionalism, dignity and pride too. Some of her troubles were her fault, some not, but Lochlan Farquhar was feasting on it, drawing strength from her rare weakness.

She straightened up, feeling another wave of nausea rise from her stomach. She breathed it back down – her yoga mentor would be surprised to find her deploying the deep-breathing techniques for this particular scenario – and focused on finding the positives. After all, it wasn't all going Lochlan Farquhar's way. She had allies here already: his ex-fiancée for one, and Mrs Peggie had been a stalwart this morning, demonstrating great charity by bringing up her breakfast – and an Alka-Seltzer – on a tray to her room. Mrs Peggie had even gone as far as running an Epsom salts bath so hot Alex had thought she might faint when she first got in; but the steam had opened her pores and she had sweated out whatever lingering alcohol she hadn't already thrown up, trying to stitch together mind, body and pride, whilst Mrs Peggie had stripped the bed to get rid of the whisky fumes.

She looked back at the dark windows of Lochlan's office. If he was standing in there watching her, she couldn't see him; the lights weren't on. He probably saw this as another victory but she, crucially, knew one thing he didn't: that what separated 'them', her clients, from 'the rest' was what separated him from her right now: adaptability. He had no idea what it had taken her (on a personal level) to come back here and face him, but she had done it nonetheless; her humility was proof in point of adapting her behaviour to the scenario in hand and in so doing, dismantling its power. By squaring up to him, she had put last night behind them now and it was no longer something he could wield against her.

She frowned at the shadowy glass panes. She always told her clients the fastest way past a problem is through it, but she wasn't sure the fastest way past his problems was through them; it was becoming clear that directness wasn't the key, A didn't necessarily lead to B with him. She needed to find another way in.

Lost in thought, she began to walk, heading towards the blending lab at the back of the visitors' centre. There was someone else she needed to face too.

'Hey!'

The shout made her turn; the sight of the man running towards her made her sigh.

'Oh, great, just what I need,' she mumbled under her breath. She waited for him with a patient smile. 'Callum. What a pleasant surprise.'

His face fell as he took in her words. His name. 'Ah. So the cat's out of the bag then?'

She suppressed a sigh. Was he for real? Did he honestly think his joke hadn't been exposed in the intervening days? 'Yes, Callum, of course it is. Well done on your little gag. You completely deceived me.'

'Ah, well now, strictly speaking I didn't actually.'

'Excuse me?'

'Well, if you remember, you came over and introduced yourself and said I must be Mr Farquhar – which of course I am. I didn't so much deceive you as just go along with your assumption.'

She sighed. 'You knew perfectly well I was looking for Lochlan.'

'Did I?'

'Yes. Because you tried to give me a tour of the distillery, even though you barely knew the name of a single person working there or what anything did.'

'It's true it's never been a raging passion of mine, understanding the mashing tuns,' he quipped, hoping his infectiously devilish grin would elicit one from her.

It nearly did; instead, with a brisk businesslike nod, she turned and carried on walking.

'Wait—'

'Callum,' she said as he fell into step with her. 'I realize it was highly amusing for you but I am actually here to work.'

'You can't blame a guy for trying.'

She arched an eyebrow. 'Trying my patience?'

'Trying to get your attention.'

She blinked. 'Here's a tip for you – not all attention is good.'

'But Alice—'

'It's Alex,' she corrected, speeding up to a march.

'What about that dinner?' he called after her as she reached the doors of the visitors' centre.

'There is no dinner,' she called back, flinging them open with a breezy smile.

'But—'

'No dinner, Callum.' And she let the doors swing shut behind her, leaving him standing.

'She's in the sample room, last door at the end of the corridor there.' The young guy at the till pointed towards the double doors at the back. 'Uh . . . is she expecting you?'

'Yes,' Alex assured him, already walking off. With her armour back on, no one dared question her authority. At least – none who hadn't seen her turfed out on her ear from the CEO's office on two of the last three days.

Skye had her back to the door when Alex peered through the glass. Her ponytail was swinging lightly as she moved around a counter laden with small glass bottles, each one filled with whisky of a different hue – some a light caramel colour, others a deep marmalade. She was pouring them into a tall round glass cylinder, about a metre high.

'Hey.' Alex timed it so that she didn't introduce herself whilst Skye was measuring out but still—

'Oh!' Skye cried, whirling round. 'You startled me.'

'Sorry.' Alex gave an apologetic smile from the doorway.

'No, no,' Skye said, shaking her head and putting down the vial, clearly shocked by the sight of her. 'It's my own fault. I get so lost in the process, I . . .' Her voice trailed away, leaving only the blushes on her otherwise pale cheeks and she chewed her lip nervously. 'How are you?'

Alex walked into the room. 'Well, the liver transplant was a success.'

Skye burst out laughing, her hands on her cheeks as embarrassment and mortification blended. 'Oh my God, I am so sorry,' she cried with relief. 'I don't know what I was thinking. I just got carried away. I feel so terrible—'

'You mustn't. I had a great time,' Alex laughed.

Skye's hands dropped down. 'Really?' she asked, grimacing doubtfully.

'Really.'

'I thought you were going to hate me.'

'For plying me with exceptional whisky and reminding me just how good the Police were? I don't think so.'

Skye gave an abashed grin. 'I saw Lochie in the car park. He said you wouldn't be coming in today—'

'In his dreams!' Alex chuckled. 'But he wasn't too happy to see me, that's for sure.'

'Well, if it makes you feel any better, I'm having a nightmare day too. I've got to sample almost five hundred malts.'

'Five hundred whiskies?' Alex asked, astounded.

'I mean, obviously we spit, but still . . .' She gave a shudder.

'You have to sample five hundred whiskies, on a whisky hangover? But that's akin to torture surely?'

'I know,' Skye groaned, dropping her head in her hands. 'It serves me right.'

There was a small, slightly shy, pause as she looked at Alex through her fingers. Her hands dropped down again. 'And you got your clothes back, I see,' she said in surprise, indicating Alex's expensively quiet clothes.

'Yes.' Alex rolled her eyes. 'Finally! I have the best PA in the world. I'm going to have to give her a good bonus – I'm sorry to say I drunk-texted her at one in the morning demanding an emergency delivery. God help me if she ever leaves me.'

'Well, it was worth it, you look amazing.'

'Oh. Thank you. It's a bit dull really,' she demurred, pulling at the six-ply cashmere dismissively. 'Nowhere near as gorgeous as the clothes you had lined up for me; I can't believe I forgot to take them with me when I left. That was the whole point of last night, after all!'

'Well, the starting point maybe,' Skye grinned.

'Listen, I'm afraid your lovely gold skirt got soaked on the way back home. I'm going to have to get it dry-cleaned if you don't mind waiting a bit.'

'Oh, please don't worry about that.'

'The pleats need to be pressed back in. But I'll get it back to you asap.'

'There's really no need.'

'I insist,' Alex smiled.

Skye shrugged, unwilling to argue further.

'So what are you working on?' Alex asked, walking up to the counter.

'Well, this is a custom blend for a Russian client. Or rather, his wife's the client but it's her husband's fiftieth birthday and she wants a blend that will mirror his character.' Alex waved her arm out, indicating the counter laden with bottles.

'He sounds complicated then,' Alex said, arching an eyebrow at the multitude. 'That's a lot of whiskies to choose from.'

'Aye, I'm using fifty.' She sighed wearily. 'Fifty whiskies to whittle down from five hundred.'

'Fifty whiskies to make just one? Hang on, I thought Kentallen didn't do blends?'

'Only for special commissions. And this is going to be my last project for Kentallen so I want to make a good job of it.' Skye smiled, pushing her glasses gently back up her nose and touching the bottles tenderly. 'This one's a fifty-year-old single malt I'm using for the base.'

'How on earth do you know where to begin?' Alex asked in awe.

'Years of experience.'

'But you're so young!'

'Aye, but my father's been training me since I was twelve.'

'He must be sad that you're leaving.'

'I think a little, yes, but he recognizes it's a step up for me. After all, if he's not going to give up the gig here, I've got no choice but to move.' She wrinkled her nose. 'And it wouldn't feel right going to one of the other Islay distilleries. Kentallen's in my blood.'

'That's very loyal of you. They must be really sorry to see you go.'

Skye looked uncomfortable. 'Aye, well . . . some more than others, perhaps.'

'I'm sorry,' Alex said, realizing her slip. In all the fog of her hangover and her own embarrassment, she'd completely forgotten that Lochie had jilted the poor girl. 'I said that without thinking. I didn't mean to—'

'No, it's fine. We've all had time to get used to the idea.'

Alex watched her, suddenly realizing that she potentially had an 'in' here. She was going to need to interview key members of the management team anyway, but Skye was his ex-fiancée – she knew him better and more intimately than any person here. 'Skye, look . . . I'm here to help Lochie as you know; and I know it can't be a secret to you that he's treading a thin line with the board at the moment. But he's being really tricky. He won't even talk to me and I need to find some sort of way in.' She hesitated. 'Can I ask you a few questions about him?'

'Like what?' Skye asked, looking apprehensive.

'Well, I mean, it can't have been easy continuing to work here with him. For him.' Alex found it hard to believe that if he couldn't even bring himself to be professional or civil to her, he could have behaved well to the woman he'd left practically at the altar.

'No, it's been . . . tricky,' Skye sighed. 'It'll be good to go somewhere new and start afresh, you know? No baggage.'

'Has he made things difficult for you? Undermined you? Passed you over for promotion? That kind of thing?'

There was a pause and for Alex, that was telling enough. 'Well, most of the time he just swerves me; he basically tries to avoid having anything to do with me whatsoever,' Skye said diplomatically.

Alex nodded, seeing how she had folded her arms around herself, making herself smaller – a classic low-power pose. How much did his silent treatment have to do with her leaving, she wondered? Skye had self-deprecatingly said she always followed her men, but was it not more the case that she was running from one now? Her ex-fiancé was the big cheese where she worked. Surely the situation was untenable and she was effectively being driven out? Alex had already experienced quite enough of his bullying and harrying behaviour herself, to be able to imagine the full truth of his and Skye's scenario.

'But it doesn't matter,' Skye shrugged – loyally. 'Anything to do with the sampling, he deals with my father. I rarely need to report to him directly; I'm not senior enough.'

'But has he cut you out of meetings, memos?' Alex pressed. 'Because you know, you've got rights. He can't do that.'

'Well, like I said, Dad's the big honcho in this department so he goes to all the senior management meetings and stuff.

No, it's more, if he's looking for my dad, he won't come in here if he sees that I'm in here on my own; and he eats lunch in his office now instead of the canteen. That kind of thing.'

Alex nodded but she still wasn't convinced Lochie hadn't jockeyed Skye from her post. Not that she needed proof of his poor behaviour or inadequate management skills – that wasn't why she was here. 'Would you say he's isolating himself from the staff?'

Skye sighed. 'Aye.'

'Has he changed since your break-up?' Skye was still for a moment, and when she didn't answer, Alex added, 'It's just I've heard he's irritable, short-tempered, unapproachable, unpredictable . . . I get the impression people don't know where they stand with him any more.'

'He's all those things, but I don't think it's down to us breaking up. He was becoming all those things when we were together; when his dad was dying.'

'I see. When was that?' Sholto had said the same at their first meeting.

'A year and a half ago now. He took it bad.' Skye bit her lip, staring into space. 'He was so angry, starting arguments all the time – nothing I ever did was good enough. It was like he wanted to push me away. And then he started doing all this stuff on his own, shutting me out of his life – training for triathlons, mountaineering, kayaking, shooting, stalking . . .'

Before finally letting the blade fall and jilting her, Alex thought, nodding sympathetically.

'What about his mother? Is he close to her?'

'She died when he was sixteen.'

'Oh.' So then the only child had become an orphan, truly alone in the world? 'That explains a lot then.'

'That's what I tried to tell him – all this rage inside him is because he never handled his grief for his mother; he adored her. And then losing his father too . . . It was too much for him.'

'But he didn't want to hear it,' Alex murmured, not surprised in the least. To say he was out of touch with his feelings was like stating that an elephant was heavy. 'This is all really interesting to hear, thanks, Skye. At least it identifies his vulnerabilities. It's proof he is actually human. I've been trying to get some traction with him but he won't even sit down with me, much less talk. This is my third day on the island and so far the only conversations we've had have been arguments.' She pulled a face.

Skye sighed. 'Well, he's a stubborn bugger, all right. You can't make him do anything he doesn't want to do.'

'Right. Which is why I need to find a way to make him want to work with me.'

'I don't know what to say. He's so bloody-minded.'

'Sholto told me—'

'Oh, well, that's your problem right there. He and Sholto hate each other. If he thinks you're working for him, he'll make a point of defying you.'

'Even at the risk of cutting off his nose to spite his face?'

'Exactly so.'

Alex sighed. Usually the hard work came when they *began* working, not beforehand. He was the client from hell – alone and lonely, aloof and remote, isolated and angry. If it wasn't for Alex herself, she'd have said he was his own worst enemy.

*

'Alex.'

She turned to find Callum leaning against the wall. Had he been waiting for her all that time? 'Callum,' she said with a tight smile, feeling inwardly exasperated. Had she not been clear enough? How many times—?

'I've got a proposition for you,' he said, pushing himself off with one foot and sauntering towards her.

'I'm afraid I'm busy. I need to find your brother and have a sit-down with him.'

'Torquil's not here. Off site with the bank today.' He winked. 'By which I mean a day watching the rugby at Murrayfield.'

Great, she silently fumed. What now then? Lochlan wouldn't talk to her and the CFO was on a corporate jolly. She supposed she could pencil in interviews with some of the line managers and start gathering collateral material on him. Hamish could probably help her out with some introductions; she sensed that he commanded respect around here.

'I've just come from seeing Lochie.' He waited for her to stop and turn back – which she did.

'And?' Her voice was low. What exactly had Lochlan told his cousin – had he regaled him with every last detail of their contretemps?

'It doesn't appear things are going well between you,' he said drily.

'No thanks to you. Your little joke undermined me from the off, robbing me of a proper introduction and that vital first impression.'

'It wouldn't have made a difference. He's determined not to have anything to do with you.'

'Yes. Because of your father. If I'm so tainted by association, why should he have more time for you than for me?'

'Blood?' he shrugged, before adding with a wink, 'And the fact that I'm irresistible to everyone.'

'Not everyone.' It was clear he was used to his good looks getting most things, most women.

He smiled, undeterred, walking slowly towards her. 'Listen, I've come up with a plan.'

'I don't like the sound of that,' she said, folding her arms as he stopped within a couple of inches.

'You're going to have to trust me.'

'Well, I don't.' It struck her as ironic that with this cousin, she sounded just like Lochlan, and Callum sounded just like her. Was this how annoying Lochlan found her to be, she wondered, as she pestered him to talk to her?

He chuckled. 'Look, there's a shoot for the board of directors on the family estate tomorrow. It's an annual bonding thing; it's why I'm here. Come as my guest. My father's dropped out anyway so we've got a free peg.'

'Why?'

'Because if ever there's a time when Lochie drops his guard, it's shooting.'

'I'm not sure I want to be around that man when he's armed.'

'Have you shot before?'

'Of course.' She had made it a priority years back to excel at any sport in which clients liked to conduct business and as such was also a competitive tennis player, played golf off a seven handicap, understood the offside rule in football and was up to date on the new scrummaging rules in rugby union.

'Good.'

'No, not good. I haven't got a gun with me and . . .' *Oh God*, she groaned inwardly – *not again*. 'I don't have anything suitable to wear.'

'It's fine, you can wear my mother's stuff. You look about the same size.'

Another stranger's clothes? Borrowing yet again would make it a hat-trick! She checked her watch. It was not even eleven. No, if Louise could buy a plane seat and send up her kit on an afternoon flight . . . ? From the bleak account Skye had just given her of her new client, she couldn't afford to let any kind of opportunity to bond pass her by; she had to find a way to reach him and bring him on side.

She looked back at Callum through slitted eyes. 'You said it's a proposition. What's in it for you?'

He gave a bashful grin. 'Ah, yes. Well, if, as a result of the shoot, you get Lochie on board, you have to come for dinner with me.' He held his hands up defensively before she could speak. 'Just dinner.'

She tried to consider her other viable options for getting Lochlan Farquhar to give her the time of day but he had thrown her out twice now and short of actually training the shotgun on him in his office . . . 'Where?'

'My local pub does a great shepherd's pie. I'm afraid there's no fancy romantic Michelin-starred—'

Across the courtyard, the door to Lochlan's office opened and the man himself strode out – no longer in his running kit but a pair of jeans, a red checked shirt and a heavy navy cable-knit jumper. His stride faltered only momentarily as he caught sight of the two of them standing there talking like old friends, the scorn in his eyes apparent even from this distance to find her still on the premises, making a nuisance of herself.

'Ahey there, Lochie!' Callum called across.

But Lochlan didn't even nod as he continued on his way to the malting house.

Alex could see Callum was right: nothing can get into a closed fist and she could see his cousin had no intention of opening up. If she kept breaking into his office, he would just keep on throwing her out. 'The pub's fine,' she said, looking back at him. 'But only if it comes off.'

'Understood,' he grinned, rubbing his hands together excitedly. 'I'll get the clobber sent over to you. Where are you staying?'

'No need. I'll have my own sent up.'

'Well, where are you staying anyway? I'll need to know when I come to pick you up for dinner.'

'You're getting ahead of yourself,' she said wryly. 'But it's Crolinnhe Farm.'

'Ah, the redoubtable Mrs Peggie,' he said gleefully. 'Have you tried her eggy bread yet?'

'Her what?' Alex couldn't help but wrinkle her nose.

'It's the best on the island. Hell, no, best in Scotland! Ask for it for breakfast tomorrow.'

'Absolutely not, it sounds disgusting.'

Callum laughed as she began walking off. 'Honestly, Alex,' he called after her. 'You must learn to say what you really think.'

Chapter Nine

Islay, Saturday 9 December 2017

'More coffee?' a girl asked, offering to pour some from a thermos flask.

'Thank you,' Alex smiled, relaxed and happy in the brisk morning chill. She was dressed for the weather in her mossy tweed breeks, heather-topped knee socks, a spare pair of Mrs Peggie's wellies, a camel V-neck sweater over a brushed cotton shirt, a matching tweed jacket and a brown felted hat with a woodcock feather at the brim. She could lie face down in the bracken all day and she'd stay warm and dry, which was saying something in these temperatures: yesterday's overly ripe skies had ceded to a peaceful clarity by mid-afternoon and temperatures had plummeted overnight, so that she had been surprised by the hoar frost that stippled every blade of grass this morning. But the hovering mist had quickly cleared as she drove over the moors, the late-rising sun making the sky blush and deepening the purple tint of the far-off hills, the lochans unrippled by even so much as a whispering breeze.

She looked around her at the gathered group; it was high-spirited and gregarious, even at eight thirty in the morning. The beaters had already gone ahead with the dogs to the first drive as the guns (the name given to those shooting) sipped on hot drinks, everyone's spirits high as they milled about on the forecourt of the Farquhar family pile, the gamekeeper making final checks before they set off.

Callum had offered to collect her from the guest house, but she had refused – the less he thought this was a 'date', the better; and besides, she was quite confident that Mr Peggie's borrowed Class II Land Rover and Mrs Peggie's directions would get her here without a problem. As it was, the eagle-topped, stone-pillared gates that heralded the entrance to the Farquhar estate, a straight three miles further up the road from the farm, could hardly be missed.

The carriage drive was extravagantly winding and long, and flanked with mature rhododendron bushes and fir-tree woods that offered only fleeting glimpses of the land beyond, the brownstone laird's house positioned in a high-set clearing with lush lawns and missing only a piper and a grazing stag for the full Highland experience. In the distance, the silver waters of the Sound glittered in the pale sunlight, the boats that sailed on her just specks from here, rooks cawing from the bare-canopied, moss-cloaked birch trees.

She was introduced to Bruce McIntyre, who was not only the master blender at Kentallen and Skye's father but, according to Sholto, the only non-family managing director on the board. He was exceptionally tall, his white hair as silky light as candyfloss and a warming moustache on his upper lip. There was only one other woman in the group – Mhairi MacLeod, a barrister specializing in company law; she had a still, contained manner, never moving or gesticulating unnecessarily and she spoke in a low voice that forced others to lean in and listen. Alex liked her on the spot and they had exchanged cards within minutes of meeting.

They were all chatting with a man called Peter McKinlay, CEO of a plastics company in Perth, and Douglas Fives, the top dog at PWC in Edinburgh, when Callum wandered back over.

'Well, everything's just about set. Feeling ready, chaps?' he asked, rubbing his hands together as the others heartily concurred. He looked handsome in his tweed breeks and jacket, a berry red fleece only just visible beneath his collar throwing flattering colour onto his cheeks. No doubt he knew it too, but for all his self-awareness and vanity, it was also obvious why he headed up the family's wealth management division – he had an easy charisma that was often the difference between sealing a deal and not. 'There's eight guns in total today so we'll all be able to travel in the paddy-wagon,' he said, jerking his head towards the comically adapted stretch Landy with canvas roof and sides that had been fastened down today. They had already drawn pegs; she and Callum were on three and four, but she wanted to know where Lochlan would be. In fact, she wanted to know where he was right now as he hadn't yet arrived.

'Isn't Sholto joining us?' Peter McKinlay asked him.

'Sadly not this time. You know what he's like – never likes to miss a day in the field, but he's in London at the moment. Unavoidable, I'm afraid.'

'Well, it leaves a bigger bag for the rest of us,' Douglas Fives chuckled. 'Your old man gets trigger-happy when he's on a run.'

Privately, Alex was pleased too. Given the flammable nature of Sholto and Lochlan's relationship, it wouldn't help her to have him hanging around; the less Lochlan associated her with him, the better.

Callum glanced over at her. 'All good?' he asked, fixing her with those piercing blue eyes.

'Yes, absolutely,' she said briskly.

'Ready then, chaps? Let's shoot,' he said, laughing at his own joke.

'Don't we need to wait for Lochlan?' she asked him pointedly. That was, after all, the point of her being here today.

'He's going to meet us at the first drive. He's just got caught up with something . . .' Alex bridled, wondering what that could be this early on a Saturday morning. It was poor form to miss the pre-shoot drinks. 'It's in the copse just beside his house anyway. It's easier for him to meet us there,' he added, leading them all over to the shoot bus.

But Alex had spotted another man coming out of the big house and waited as he strode over the gravel with the easy confidence of those to the manor born. She knew who he was by sight alone: he took after his father, sharing the same stocky build, good head of hair and a propensity for bold socks. (Sholto's – at their meeting in Edinburgh – had been orange; his son's today, easily visible at the top of his boots, were peacock blue and purple.)

'You must be Torquil,' she said, extending a hand. 'Alex Hyde.'

'Ah, Miss Hyde, I've been looking forward to meeting you.' His voice was smooth but his manner reserved. He had none of his cousin's abrasive hostility, nor his brother's louche charm – in fact, he seemed the perfect antidote to them both.

'It's a pleasure to meet you too. I'm sorry our paths haven't crossed before now.'

'I'm afraid I've been in Edinburgh with the bank all week but I trust you've been well looked after by my cousin in my absence?'

Alex hesitated, not sure how much Sholto had told his own son about her presence here. 'Let's say it's been an interesting start. And certainly immersive.'

'I'm glad to hear it. We need a strong steer from someone who can see the bigger picture. I'm afraid once relationships begin to break down as ours has, it can be difficult to see clearly and objectively, which is obviously detrimental to the fortunes of the company.'

'Well, I'm here to help.'

'Are you two coming shooting or shall we leave you talking shop? It is the weekend, you know,' Callum called from the back of the shoot bus, a hip flask in his hand.

Torquil sighed. 'I take it you've been introduced to my brother?'

'Oh yes,' she smiled as they walked slowly across. 'In fact, it was he who invited me here today.'

'Ah.'

'He felt it would be helpful for me to meet the rest of the board.'

'Indeed. This is usually one of our more jovial gatherings, but after the way the last AGM ended, it's badly needed. Hopefully this will go some way to restoring civil relations.'

They climbed in, tweed bottoms shuffling up the bench seats to make more room for them, and Callum slapped the side of the Landy hard, twice.

The gamekeeper, doubling as chauffeur, pulled away and they passed the house, following the drive as if to go back to the gates, but hooking a sharp left into the trees instead. In there, the road rapidly became a track, rutted and frozen hard, and the passengers had to grab at anything they could to keep from being bounced out the sides.

They drove like that for maybe a mile or more, the sun making only occasional forays to the forest floor, which was carpeted in pine needles and pillows of moss. Alex saw a red squirrel sitting on a high branch, a fir cone between its paws, watching suspiciously as they passed. Open moorland winked through the trees to their left side, the sea still shining but inching closer now, and when they finally emerged from the trees fifteen minutes later, the vista spread out like a book opened flat. With the sun in their faces, the mud track now gone, they bumped along the moor to the first drive.

'Right, chaps,' Callum said, jumping out first, his gun swinging in the battered leather slip over his shoulder. 'Pegs one to four down to the left, near the tarn; five to eight leading up to the trees there. Alex, follow me,' he said jauntily.

She wanted to say out loud that she wasn't 'with' him – she saw a bemused look pass between some of the older men – but it didn't do to make a fuss; they would only think she was protesting too much.

'Callum, *where* is your cousin?' she demanded as she strode alongside him. 'You promised he would be here.'

'And he will be – yes, he is. Over there,' he said, looking around. 'Ay-ay, and it looks like he's not alone.'

He pointed towards a house, its elegant slate roof and tall chimneys only just visible behind a high flint wall. At the decorative wrought-iron gate, halfway along, Lochlan could be seen bending down to kiss a dark, curly-haired woman – her hands clasping his head as he kept his own arms pinned back to prevent his gun from slipping off his shoulder.

'Christ, she must be *freezing*,' Alex muttered as she saw the woman had just a bed sheet wrapped around her.

'Oh, I imagine he's been keeping her warm,' Callum chuckled. 'My cousin is a dark horse with the ladies.'

'Not that dark,' Alex snipped, turning away as she saw Lochlan pull himself free and make his way across the moor to them. 'His affairs with the staff are well known and recorded.'

They walked along to the pegs and she busied herself filling her pockets with cartridges.

'Morning, cuz,' Callum called as Lochlan passed by. 'Sleep well?'

Lochlan threw him – them – a silent look, and she was glad to see he was riled to find her there too. Throwing him off balance was going to be key with him; a little hole can still sink a big ship.

'What's she doing here?' he snarled rudely.

'*She* is Alex,' Callum said pointedly. 'And Alex very kindly agreed to make up the numbers seeing as Dad's away.'

Lochlan moved off with a low growl and Alex watched as he walked to his peg one along – silhouetted in the sunlight and sure-footed on the rough terrain as though he knew every last clod on this acre, Rona walking to heel off the lead.

'Relax. Your moment will come,' Callum said, watching her watching him.

'Oh, I know,' she said with certainty just as, in the distance, they heard the whistle blow – indicating the start of the drive – and the beaters beginning to flush the game out, hitting the tree trunks with sticks, beating at the grass, blowing whistles and making trilling calls. Putting on her ear defenders, she loaded up the gun and took it off the safety, all poised to point and shoot, her eyes to the sky.

Within a few minutes, the first birds took to the air and she heard the pop-pops of the other guns. She waited for her own quarry to fly ahead, glancing down the line to see Lochlan bag four pheasants in a row and a snipe.

'Here we go,' Callum murmured beside her, his voice low with unusual intensity, as two birds tracked into the sky ahead of them. He brought the gun to his shoulder, Alex doing the same, and in the next moment, they both fired.

'You were fantastic!' Callum exclaimed as they headed back up the moor to the shoot bus.

'Thank you. Although I'm rather offended you sound so surprised.'

'You're always offended by me.'

'True.' She couldn't help but laugh. Perhaps she *had* been a little hard on him, but if he would only stop flirting with her, she could relax and become a lot friendlier. They walked side by side, breath hanging like steam puffs before them, their guns slung over their shoulders and the smell of gun smoke tickling the air. It had been a great start. She felt relaxed and warmed up now that the first drive was done.

'How did you get on?' Callum asked his brother as the group reconvened at the shoot bus.

'Abysmal. I shot like a turkey,' Torquil said, shaking his head.

'Oh, I don't know,' Peter said. 'You did a better job than old Dougie here. At least you remembered to load up,' he said pointedly.

'You didn't?' Torquil asked, looking across at the accountant.

'You promised not to mention it!' Douglas laughed.

'Missed a couple of absolute sitters,' Peter deplored.

'Yes, thank you! As I do recall, you were once guilty of something not so different yourself.'

'Blood under the bridge, old chap.'

'How about you, Lochie?' Callum asked as his cousin made his way over, a closed expression on his face which Alex knew was entirely for her benefit.

'Yes, not so bad.'

Or perhaps it was for everyone else too, she thought, noticing how the light mood dissipated with his presence? She watched as everyone shook hands with him but his absence from the meet-and-greet drinks had clearly been noted as a snub, and the smiles that did break through were stretched and formal.

'Not so bad? You were making out like a bandit every time I looked,' Pip, the gamekeeper's girlfriend, exclaimed. 'Rona's near collapsed from all the picking up she's done.'

Lochlan's hand automatically reached down for the dog and she pushed herself against his legs, her pink tongue lolling from the side of her mouth as she panted heavily on the grass, her eyes bright.

Alex glanced down at Sam, the gamekeeper, picking up the birds that had been laid out in a square in the grass and loading them onto the trailer.

'Well, it appears Alex is a crack shot too,' Callum said. 'She got all the ones I missed, as well as her own.'

Lochlan stared at her as though her success was a personal slight on his own.

'Good for you, Alex,' Douglas said. 'I must say it's nice to have another woman on the shoot for once.'

'What are you trying to say, Doug?' Mhairi asked tartly, but with a smile in her eyes.

'I don't understand why more women don't shoot,' Alex said. 'After all, it's a test of skill not strength.'

'Squeamishness,' Peter tutted. 'My wife can't bear the thought of killing a living creature. It doesn't matter how many times I tell her that it supports the rural economy and strengthens community links; or that the money from shoot days goes straight back into the estates, providing local jobs for gamekeepers, beaters, ghillies, groundsmen and the like; or that those birds are as bred to be killed as chickens and sheep . . . She just won't hear it.'

'You're wasting your breath, old chap. It's all to do with killer instinct,' Douglas said, pulling a fist and shaking it. 'And most women don't have it. They just can't quite bring themselves to pull the trigger.'

Alex was about to argue that it wasn't a question of gender: there were as many men out there as women who wouldn't want to shoot, regardless of the background arguments in its favour, but she didn't get the chance.

'Well, that's obviously not a problem for Alex. I shouldn't think she'd hesitate to shoot anything between the eyes,' Lochlan said darkly, before throwing an arm out and indicating the shoot bus. 'Shall we?'

The second and third drives were a mixed bag – literally. They were shooting partridge as well as pheasant, and the low sun made visibility tricky on some of the lines but she was still pleased with her form. Her hand was steady, her eye keen, her breathing slow. She was bagging eighty per cent of everything she aimed for and she didn't think there was much between her and Lochlan at all, something she noticed appeared to be riling him enormously with every congratulation that was thrown her way.

'You well and truly hid your light under a bushel, Alex,' Torquil said cheerily as they all met back at the bus afterwards. 'I ran out of ammo and watched you. You hit almost everything you aimed for.'

'She's making me look bad,' Callum grumbled with a laugh. 'I wouldn't have invited you if I'd realized you were such a crack shot.'

'Well, it's clear you're the gun of the day,' Douglas said, toasting her with a tot of sherry being drunk from silver caps. 'Congratulations!'

'Hear, hear,' everyone rejoined – all but one.

They had moved to a drive on the outer reaches of the estate – 2,400 acres, according to Callum – the sea just behind them at the foot of the cliffs which rose steeply here. They were on high ground; Port Ellen and the distillery were far out of sight and the two mountains which always appeared so distant from the farm were seemingly within touching distance.

The gamekeeper's girlfriend was walking around and handing out hot sausages to all the guns. Alex was grateful for the warmth. For all the skill and concentration required to shoot, it wasn't an overly active sport and she had begun to lose feeling in her toes. She tried promising herself the reward of one of Mrs Peggie's boiling hot baths when she got in but her power of imagination just wasn't that strong; she tried scrunching up her toes but it was hard in the thick socks; she shifted her weight from one foot to the other, stopping short of jogging on the spot.

'Cold?' Lochlan asked, with a look that suggested it was some form of weakness.

She shrugged. 'A little. I don't have the best circulation in the world.'

'You need to put some weight on,' Lochlan said. 'A bit more meat on your bones would make the world of difference.'

'That's incredibly rude, Lochie,' Torquil snapped.

Lochlan rewarded him with a hard stare that made no attempt to apologize and yet again the tension crackled, as it did whenever Lochlan was holding the floor.

'Oh no,' Alex smiled, brushing off the insult. 'No woman ever minds being told she's too thin. Even when it's not intended as a compliment.'

'Well, even so—'

'Neoprene-lined wellies, they're what you need,' Callum said, coming to the rescue.

'Oh yes,' Peter agreed. 'My wife swears by them.'

'Le Chameau do a very nice style,' Mhairi added, showing off her own olive-green boots.

'Alternatively, you should try proper shooting,' Lochlan said with a scathing tone. 'That would warm you up.'

'*Proper* shooting?' Torquil asked, looking mildly scandalized at the intimation that this driven shoot with full hospitality wasn't 'proper'.

'Yes, you know, walked-up shooting, rough shooting, call it what you will.' His eyes never left Alex, challenging her, trying to intimidate her.

'Oh well, I've done that too,' Alex shrugged, knowing that the calmer she became, the more she enraged him; she was being feted as he was being frozen out and she sensed – somehow – that this was going to be her way through.

There had to be some sort of provocation, a breaking point with him, and there was no doubt he was under pressure here today. 'A lovely estate in Yorkshire. Appleton. Perhaps you know it?' She knew he would; it was one of the foremost shoots in the country.

'No.'

He was lying. 'Oh well, why would you? It's only fourteen thousand acres or so.'

There was a tense silence and it was clear nobody here believed his denial.

'When I say proper shooting, what I mean to say – of course – is doing the MacNab,' Lochlan said finally.

She arched an eyebrow as she sipped the sherry. 'The MacWhat?'

'It's when you stalk, shoot and fish in one day. You have to land a stag, a brace of grouse, and a salmon within twenty-four hours.'

'Sounds fun,' she said lightly.

'It's a lot harder than it sounds.'

'If you say so.'

'I do.'

'Okay,' she shrugged but her body language said 'whatever'. A small smile crept upon her lips. She could see he was infuriated by her – that she was here, that she wouldn't leave, wouldn't lose, wouldn't give in.

'I'm going next weekend, in fact.'

'Oh?'

'To a friend's place in Perth. You should come.'

She pulled an apologetic expression, knowing full well that this was about cowing her, showing her he would win in whatever arena they duelled in. She decided to try a little reverse psychology. 'Well, that's very sweet of you to offer but I'm not sure if I'll still be here next weekend.'

His eyes narrowed as he was thrown off balance again. 'I thought you were here for the foreseeable?'

'Things haven't been going according to plan and I have other clients who need me. I can't keep flogging the proverbial.'

'And if things *were* to suddenly go according to plan . . . ?' Callum interjected, a mischievous look in his true blue eyes.

'Well, then, I'd be here for the foreseeable,' she shrugged with a beatific smile.

'Oh, it would be an absolutely capital opportunity, if you were to take it up,' Peter McKinlay said enthusiastically. 'I tried the MacNab once. Total disaster. I almost blinded my wife with the fly, then she fell back in the river trying to escape and poor thing was half-drowned. It took a holiday to Mauritius and a pearl necklace before she forgave me that one, I can tell you.'

'Well, it's not really my call,' was all Alex would say, but Lochlan didn't take his gaze off her. Her non-committal position was a challenge and he knew it: if he wanted his opportunity to put her in her place, he first had to let her put him in *his* place.

'Right, everyone ready for the off?' Torquil asked, collecting up the sherry tots.

'Absolutely!'

They all marched over the long grass back to the shoot bus, Callum hurrying to her side, a chuckle in his throat.

'I do believe you owe me the pleasure of your company at dinner, Ms Hythe,' he murmured. But she didn't mind his mistake this time.

'Colin, I do believe you're right,' she smiled, sending them both into a fit of laughter that caught everyone's eye.

Mr Peggie was like a bloodhound sniffing the air, surveying the sky with a wrinkled brow as she pulled up into the yard several hours later.

'Snow's coming,' the old farmer said in an ominous tone. 'Heaps of the stuff.'

'It must make life difficult for you,' she said, standing by the back door and pulling off her boots; they were thick with muddy clods.

'Ach, it's not with the first stroke that the tree falls,' he said, sounding and looking like an ancient bard.

They walked into the farmhouse together to find Mrs Peggie standing by the stove, stirring a pan.

'Good evening, Mrs Peggie,' Alex said with a smile, her nose in the air. Her long stay afforded her a special status that meant she was welcome in the kitchen and she enjoyed lingering in here as Mrs Peggie cooked. 'Heavens, that smells delicious. What are you cooking tonight?'

'Mushroom soup, followed by beef stew.'

'Mmmm, I can't wait.'

'It'll be an hour or so yet. Would you like a cup of tea?' the old lady asked, wiping her hands on a tea towel. 'I've got Dundee cake or some tablet.'

'Thanks, that would be lovely, but why don't I get it? You're busy. Mr P., would you like one?'

'Aye. That would be nice.' He was settling himself at the small kitchen table, already in his socks and reaching for the *Ileach* newspaper.

'How was the shoot?' Mrs Peggie asked.

'Very . . . productive,' Alex said with a satisfied smile.

135

'Good.'

Alex wandered over to the small sink and refilled the kettle. 'So, who's in the green room tonight?'

'A Mr Newson, from Sutherland. He's visiting his daughter and son-in-law before the festive break. He comes every year and stays with us.'

Alex switched the kettle on and leaned against the worktop. She liked the sound of him; a quiet sort with an accurate aim who'd sleep through the night – unlike the Spanish toddler. 'Do you get many repeat visitors?'

'Aye, a fair few. Mr Newson every December, and an elderly couple from Dorset come each Easter although his hips are so bad now, I don't think he'll manage the stairs for much longer, do you, Mr P.?' Mrs Peggie asked, seemingly oblivious to her own advanced years.

Mr Peggie made a sound that suggested agreement.

'And then there's our American, Mr Horowitz, who comes every summer to go wreck diving.'

'*Wreck* diving?'

'Oh yes, it's a popular activity here. There's that many ships have been wrecked off the coasts here. They're treacherous waters. The tides in the Sound of Jura, on the other side from here – they race through at almost five knots and there are reefs just below the surface everywhere on this side. It's no place for amateur sailors, that's for sure.'

'But to come all the way from America to go wreck diving *here*? Surely there are closer opportunities at home for him? The Bermuda triangle, for one!'

'Ah, but it's a personal mission. His grandfather –' she frowned – 'great-grandfather . . . ?'

'Grandfather,' said Mr P. without looking up from the paper.

'His *grand*father perished on one of them and he feels this is a way of honouring his memory, to try to salvage possessions off the ship. He's been coming every year for sixteen years now.'

'Heavens.' Alex reached for the cups hanging from hooks on the dresser and placed a couple of teabags in the brown teapot.

'He was that excited when they brought up the bell. Two years ago now, I think it was.'

'Wow. That's incredibly . . . dedicated of him.'

'He's a good man, is Mr Horowitz. There's not many people these days as truly take the time to remember the sacrifices that were made in their name. Which reminds me, when are you going to make a start on those boxes, Mr P.?'

Mr Peggie's eyebrows appeared over the top of the paper.

'You promised you would have it all done and sent to Jackie McKenna before Christmas. You said the bad weather was just the excuse to bring them down and get it done.'

'And I will.'

'You've been saying that for weeks.'

'The weather wasn't bad enough then. There was still too much to do with the walls.'

'Well, they're forecasting a foot of snow in the next few days. Seems like the perfect time, if you ask me.'

'Yes, pet.'

Mrs Peggie huffed, perfectly aware that she was being fobbed off. She looked over at Alex who was watching it all with a patient smile. 'Mr P.'s father was the local sergeant and I'm afraid it was up to him to identify the bodies that washed ashore after a wrecking.'

'Oh God,' Alex frowned. 'How awful.'

'Aye, it must have been, not that he ever talked about it.

The first Mr P. knew about any of it was after his father's death – he found boxes of letters, photographs, logbooks up in the roof. Heartbreaking stuff it was. His father had kept the letters from mothers, widows, all desperate trying to locate or identify their husbands. From the notes he made on them, it seems like he wrote back to them all too.'

'What a noble thing to do.'

Mrs Peggie shrugged. 'The only decent thing, if you ask me. War is hard enough to live through without not having a body to bury at the end of it.'

'You must be very proud of your father, Mr P. It sounds like he helped a lot of people.'

'Aye,' came the voice from behind the paper.

'He keeps promising to donate everything to the museum. They're desperate to add it to their collections,' Mrs Peggie said in a louder voice, just in case her husband should be tuning her out.

Alex swirled the brew with a teaspoon before replacing the lid and beginning to pour. 'Which museum's that?'

'The Museum of Islay Life in Port Charlotte. You should get up there to it. Wonderful displays of times past.'

'I'll make sure I do.'

'It's fascinating seeing everything as it was.'

'Has much changed?' Alex asked, handing out their cups of tea.

'Only the number of cars, really. And people and horses in the fields instead of tractors.' Mrs Peggie stopped from her stirring and sat down at the kitchen table for a moment, resting her slippered feet up on a low, tapestried footstool. 'Oof.'

'I imagine there's some information on the distilleries?'

Alex asked, wrapping her hands around her cup and leaning against the worktop.

'Aye, lots. They've not changed much either. Kentallen sits on the site of an old farm so you can see the old pig-geries and sheep pens.'

'Ah, I did wonder. I thought a lot of the buildings seemed agricultural. Lochlan Farquhar's office is particularly . . . basic.'

'It was a stables, if I'm right?' Mrs Peggie mused to her husband.

'Aye.'

'Mr P.'s great-grandfather sold the land to the Farquhars before the Great War.'

'Oh wow,' Alex smiled. 'So your families go a long way back.'

'All the families round here are intertwined with the Farquhars. Mr P.'s farm supplies barley and peat to the dis-tillery and they sell back to us the grist for the cattle. And my own mother and aunt worked at the big house for the family. My mother was in the kitchens and her sister Morag was one of the housemaids.'

'But not you?'

'I wasnae even born by then, lassie,' Mrs Peggie exclaimed in mock outrage, 'although even if I had been, circum-stances had changed – the wars saw to that. No, within months of war breaking out, almost all the men had gone to fight and the women had to work the fields. The only staff left was Aunt Morag who became the housekeeper and her husband who did the gardens and driving, at least until he was sent to fight too in the final wave of conscription. By the time I was born, knocking on fifteen years later, things were very different; the distillery was barely getting by and the house was still running on a skeleton staff. I expect I could have found work there once I was old enough – poor Aunt Morag had died in the Spanish flu epidemic – but Mr P. and I were married at eighteen and we had this place to run.'

'And here you are, all these years later, still running it. Don't you ever think about retiring?'

'Farmers don't retire,' Mr Peggie said. 'They die.'

Mrs Peggie rolled her eyes and pushed the palm of her hand flat on the table to get back up on her feet. 'Retire? Die?' she scoffed. 'The chance would be a fine thing. I've no time for either.'

Chapter Ten

Islay, Monday 11 December 2017

The mug of coffee was steaming in her hand when the office door opened.

'Good morning,' she said, holding it out.

Lochlan, covered in mud splatters from his run, sighed as Rona treacherously left his side to nose her hand. 'Give me strength,' he muttered.

'Hi, sweetie,' Alex said under her breath, ruffling the dog's soft ears as it looked up at her with gentle chocolatey eyes. 'You're a poppet, aren't you?'

Shutting the door with his foot, he walked in and took the mug from her. 'You don't waste any time,' he grumbled.

'On the contrary, we've already wasted far too much,' she said, walking over to the fire to warm herself. The office was still chilly from the heating being off all weekend. 'How was your run?'

'Fine,' he replied to her back, as suspiciously as if she'd just asked him for his PIN number.

'Do you do it every day?'

'As long as the weather allows.'

A quizzical expression furrowed her brow. 'Tell me, how do you get your car down here?'

'A couple of the groundsmen bring it down for me,' he said distractedly. 'Look, is this what it's going to be? You bombarding me with inane questions?'

'I wasn't aware it was a bombardment,' she shrugged. 'Just being friendly.'

'And where did that thing come from?' he demanded, pointing at the hessian-covered wing chair she had put by the fire. She had found it in one of the farm's outbuildings when she had parked Mr Peggie's Landy after the shoot at the weekend – a long-forgotten upholstery project of their daughter's that was still, after twenty or so years, awaiting a new cover.

'Oh, do you like it? I thought it would be helpful for us to have somewhere more relaxed to talk.'

'It looks like something a cat would scratch.'

Alex laughed. 'Yes, I suppose it does.'

Lochlan looked at her strangely – he wasn't used to her agreeing with him – and there was a sudden silence, this new unspoken arrangement hesitant and unformed, pitfalls hidden below the surfaces as they played to their own agendas.

'So,' she smiled.

'So.' He watched her with knowing eyes and she had that sense again that he was seeing beyond this morning's polish of her Altuzarra armour – a divine charcoal-grey trouser suit and whisper-pink silk shirt – to the drunken mess that had slumped in his car last week. He was going to keep harking back to it, reminding her that her usual authority had been eroded. 'What now? You've got what you wanted.' He shrugged, indicating the room and the small miracle that they were both still in it.

'Well, for one thing, it would be good if you could try to see this as a collaboration, rather than an interrogation.'

'And what is it we're supposedly *collaborating* on?'

'Making you a better leader, helping you steer this ship away from the cliff that is just ahead of you. And before you look at me like that, every leader can become an even better one, even those that *don't* punch one of their board members in the face during an AGM.'

His brow furrowed. 'Sholto told you about that?'

'Of course he did. And about the computer terminal thrown through the window.'

'It kept shutting down and losing my work!'

She merely raised an eyebrow. 'And about the seven-million-pound Indonesian contract you lost because you offended their chairman.'

'*He* offended *me*. The guy wanted us to let them do their own bottling – where they'd have kids working for them!'

She sighed – he'd always have an answer for everything and they couldn't degenerate into argument again. 'Look, I'm not standing in judgement of you. I'm sure you did have your reasons. Why don't we forget about *all* that and start again, okay? We got off on the wrong foot from the start; we never even actually had a formal introduction, thanks to your cousin hijacking proceedings.'

'Yes, well, Callum plays by his own rules too,' Lochlan said darkly.

She walked over to him, plastering a bright smile on her lips. 'Hi. My name's Alex. I'm a business coach, leadership consultant, call me what you will.'

'Hello, What You Will,' he quipped, ignoring her hand until she reached down for his and forced it into her own.

'And so you must be Lochlan Farquhar,' she continued,

pointedly shaking his limp hand. 'Thirty-six years old, CEO of Kentallen Distillery, before that trade director, sales director and head of warehousing operations; unmarried; owner of one very sweet spaniel called Rona; keen athlete, crack shot and man of the people.' She stopped shaking his hand. 'It is a *pleasure* to meet you.'

In reply, he squeezed hers with a firmness that made her want to wince, his eyes still glittering with distrust, and Alex could see how intimidating he might be across a negotiating table. He didn't smile to put people at their ease and he didn't resort to self-deprecation to gloss over awkward moments; he had a straightforward directness that bordered on the brutal and which would be an excellent attribute for a lawyer or banker, but for a boss whose job it was to woo new clients and open up new markets, it was a disaster. He needed to be a diplomat, not a bulldozer.

'The good news is, we can skip the first session where I sit down with you for three hours and you tell me everything you possibly can about yourself. I know all the pertinent points of your personal and professional life, which is all I need as a base mark.'

'Three hours?' he scoffed. 'You think I was ever going to sit and talk about myself for that long? What there is to know about me you could fit on the back of a fag packet.'

'You're not giving yourself enough credit. I think you're a fascinating man and I've been very interested to hear what other people have had to say about you.' It was a lie. She was sick to the back teeth of this man.

'I've already said you can't listen to a damn word Sholto has to say.'

'I haven't just spoken to him. Some of your managers. Callum and Skye too.'

'Skye?' His voice cracked like a teenage boy's. 'Why were you talking to her? What's she been saying?'

Alex looked at him, intrigued by the reaction. 'She was nothing but complimentary; it's clear she holds you in the very highest regard.'

'Oh, I sincerely doubt that,' he muttered, turning away and walking to the desk. He sank into the chair and hunched over, untying the laces on his shoes.

From where she was standing, it looked almost as though he was hiding his face.

'But she thinks you're isolated. That you've isolated yourself.'

'She's entitled to her opinion.'

'And she thinks you're angry.'

He said nothing and Alex inhaled, watching as he fussed over the laces that had been tied in double knots and were now sodden with mud. 'It must be a blow to be losing her.' Her comment was deliberately double-edged, and she was interested to watch his head snap up. 'To Glengoyne, I mean,' she added, wondering why he should be so jumpy about his ex-fiancée when he was the one who'd done the jilting. Did he fear what she was really saying about him? A woman scorned and all that?

'I certainly thought she'd know better than to work on one of the Lowland ladies.'

'The what?' she asked, amused by the moniker.

'It's the name given to the Lowland malts. They're a lighter, more . . . feminine dram,' he scoffed. 'No peat.'

'Ah.' The peccadilloes and nuances of Scotch snobbery were still lost on her. 'Is there no way to keep her?' It was another intentional double entendre.

'And how do you suggest I do that?' he asked, scorn in his eyes as he finally sat back up again.

'How about a pay rise?' she suggested. *Or tell her you made a mistake*, a voice in her head said.

'She's not leaving because of the money,' he said shortly.

No, she was going for love. Alex wondered how easily he said the 'L' word. She suspected it would choke him. 'No, I guess not.'

He turned to face his desk, looking beleaguered as he saw that she had tidied the papers on it. 'Why have you done *that*? You are not the cleaner; you are not my PA.'

'Tidy desk equals a tidy mind – it's way below my pay scale to have to tell you that. But that's beside the point. I want to stay with the PA issue – let's talk about that. Why don't you have one?'

'Because I don't need one.'

'You're CEO of the largest privately owned single-malt distillery in Scotland – of course you need one. How can you possibly stay on top of everything otherwise? Delegation is not weakness, Lochlan, nor is it abdication; it makes you a better, more effective manager.'

'I disagree,' he muttered, rifling through the papers now in a neat pile. 'Where the hell's my finance report? I've got a meeting in twenty minutes.'

Alex leaned over and pulled it from the pile for him. 'Don't you need to get changed first?' she asked, casting a disapproving eye over his damp, smelly running kit.

'Yes, I do, which means I need you to leave. Shall I walk you to the door?' His eyes danced, treasuring the memories of her previous ejections from this room.

Dammit. She had walked into that one. She stuck her chin in the air, determined to make this a graceful exit. 'No, that's quite all right. I let myself in; I can let myself out again.' She rose from the desk, smoothing out the creases of her trousers. 'I'll see you at the meeting shortly then.'

His head snapped up. 'What? *You're* not coming!'

'Yes, I am,' she said calmly. 'If I'm to be of any help to you, I need to evaluate your management and leadership skills – I need to see you in action.'

'Categorically not,' he snapped.

'I'm afraid it's not your call.'

'Those meetings are confidential. You are not a member of staff here.'

She sighed. 'Lochlan, I'm a consultant, not a spy.'

'No. Not happening.'

She shrugged. 'Twenty minutes. I'll be there.'

'On whose say-so?' he demanded.

She tipped her head to the side. Did he even need to ask?

She stepped out into the courtyard, feeling a giddy leap in her chest to have survived – even won – that altercation. These battles with Lochlan drained her more than she wanted to admit, but she knew she just had to hold her nerve. He was coming around, albeit in baby steps. Today had been a definite improvement on their past record.

She wondered whether the canteen did coffees-to-go. She felt in need of a caffeine hit before the next confrontation – playing the benevolent hostess to Lochlan was all very well but he never thought to ask whether she wanted one too.

She turned to hurry over, when she heard someone behind her. She looked to see Torquil poking his head round the door of his office, next door but one to Lochlan's. It was an incongruous sight and she could picture the horses that must have once poked their heads out of these converted farm buildings too.

'Ah, Alex, I thought it was you,' he said, coming out and extending a friendly hand. 'Upping the glamour quotient of our humble yard. How are things?'

'Great. And I must thank you once again for Saturday. I had a great time.'

'Well, we loved having you, even if you did make us look like a bunch of pie-eyed amateurs,' he chuckled, stuffing his hands into his chino pockets. 'What are you up to? Anything I can help with?'

'Um, well, I've just had a brief chat with Lochlan, actually.'

'Oh yes. Helpful?'

Alex wrinkled her nose. 'Well . . .'

'Ah.' Torquil frowned, his gaze sliding over to the closed door of Lochlan's office. 'Hmm. Can we . . . can we talk? Have you got a few minutes?'

'Of course. I'm sitting in on your next meeting anyway,' she said, following him in to his office.

'Great stuff. Coffee?'

'Thanks,' she smiled gratefully, thinking how the contrast to his cousin could not have been greater – not just in manners but their working practices too. Torquil's office was clean and tidy, brightly lit and well organized with filing cabinets along one wall (including in front of the fireplace – indicating this was a workspace, not home). The bumpy right-hand wall adjoining the room between his and Lochlan's had been opened up and a large round table with chairs set in the middle of it. In truth, it looked more like a dining table than a conference table but at least this space was aiming for a corporate feel, unlike Lochlan's office which was more akin to a student's bedsit.

'How do you take it?' he asked, refilling a Nespresso machine. Alex almost wanted to cry at the relief of not drinking instant for once.

'Double-shot espresso, please.'

'Punchy for nine thirty in the morning.'

'Well, it's been a challenging start already.'

Torquil arched his eyebrows. 'Is he coming to heel yet?'

'No. I definitely wouldn't say that. It's a career first having a client who won't even talk, much less engage.'

He nodded sympathetically. 'So you can see what we've been up against then?'

'Yes, I'm afraid I can. And I picked up on the tension with the other board members on Saturday.'

'He's definitely made himself *persona non grata*,' Torquil sighed. 'It's beyond me how he can tolerate being so . . . ostracized. One might almost think he thrived on it.'

'Well, if anger's his driver, you could be right.'

Torquil gave a baffled look. 'I don't know how it's come to this point. It's not just that he's reckless or brash – although that's bad enough – but he's actively jeopardizing delicate client relationships. I've got to spend most of my afternoon, later, talking a key collector down from the ceiling after Lochie blocked the sale of one of our exceptionally rare sixty-year-old reserves – a sale which I'd been personally negotiating for months and which this collector specifically travelled from Hong Kong to buy – all because Lochie didn't like that the man had been photographed with one of our competitors.'

'You're kidding.'

'Sadly, I'm not. It's one thing warring within the company, but when he starts cherry-picking who our clients can and can't fraternize with, well, then we're really in trouble.'

'Quite.'

'Lochie's always had a reputation for being . . . shall we say, rambunctious, but if the press starts to get wind of his tantrums and demands . . .' He sighed.

'How do you get on with him on a personal level?' Alex asked, sipping the rich coffee.

'I won't lie. We've never been close but I've made a point of keeping things especially businesslike between us since the – ahem – incident at the family assembly last year.'

'Oh! It was *you* that he punched?' she asked in surprise. 'I hadn't realized.'

He nodded.

'What prompted it, can I ask?'

'He pulled back on a deal we'd spent months putting together when Robert – his father – was at the helm. Everything was ready to go, the contracts drawn up. Passions were running high on all sides.'

So that excused Lochlan punching him? 'What was the deal?'

'A sale to Ferrandor Group. They've been sniffing around us for years and we've always held back. It never felt like quite the right time.'

'But it did then?'

'Yes, it felt like the right moment. The thing about the whisky business is that it's like playing poker: you're dealing with unseen hands all the time – constantly trying to predict demand twelve, fifteen, thirty, fifty years into the future.' He gave a wry smile. 'It's pretty much guaranteed that at some point, you'll end up with too much or too little. It's all about the long game in this industry – well, it has to be when you've got to wait three years before you can even put the word "Scotch" on the label and sell a bottle!' He laughed. 'Half the time I think we must be crazy for even trying to succeed at this game, but then my father likes to tell me the definition of wisdom is old men planting trees under whose shade they will never sit.'

He smiled and Alex watched him as he talked – his body language was open, relaxed, his tone confiding and inclusive. He behaved like a collaborator, rather than Lochie's dictator.

'So why did Lochie block the sale?'

'Because he could? I don't know. He never gave a wholly convincing answer but his father was gravely ill around that time so he was generally pretty unstable. I think the prospect of more change was deeply challenging to him.'

'And how about now? Do you think Ferrandor are still interested in doing a deal?'

'Sadly, the moment has passed and we're not the hot prospect we were then. Even if they didn't *violently* dislike our new CEO –' he rolled his eyes – 'the truth is we're facing a supply shortage in the next six years; we may have sophisticated forecast modelling now but twenty years ago it was a different matter.' He shook his head. 'And then, of course, trading conditions have changed dramatically.'

'You mean Brexit?'

He gave a regretful look and nodded. 'Ninety per cent of all Scotch is exported – with France being the biggest market – and of the two hundred countries where Scotch is sold, we already faced over six hundred trade barriers in a hundred and forty-three of them. Now, with Brexit in the mix too . . . who knows?' He shrugged, before giving a light laugh. 'And that's not to mention the impending barrel crisis and all that that could entail.'

'Barrel crisis?' she repeated blankly.

'Yes. The oak casks we use for maturing the whisky impart about seventy-five per cent of the character to the finished product. Bruce – whom you met on Saturday . . . ?'

She nodded. Skye's father.

'He says that if the spirit is the child, the cask is the mother. They're incredibly important to us; we mainly buy in two-hundred-litre oak casks from the States which have been used by the bourbon industry, and five-hundred-litre sherry butts from Spain – it's a ninety-five/five split.'

Alex frowned. 'Hamish in the copper shop told me the stills were the most important part.'

'Of the *distilling* process, yes,' Torquil agreed. 'And if you ask them, the malters will tell you it's the barley and the kilnsmen will tell you it's the peat. And of course, all those elements are vital for creating continuity of the Kentallen flavour DNA. You can't make spirit without copper, but you really can't make whisky without oak. It's the barrel that is king.'

She sipped some more of her coffee. 'So, what's the crisis?'

'As the law stands in the States, an oak bourbon barrel can't be used more than once – but they're looking at changing that. The whisky industry needs three million "wet-coopered" barrels a year and Britain can't possibly supply that – we had cut down most of our oak trees by the early nineteenth century to build warships to fight the French, so the industry has been importing them from Spain and France, and then from the States for well over a hundred years – the barrels being cheaper and more plentiful there. But if the Americans do end up reusing their bourbon barrels, supply will become scarcer and prices will go up. They already are.'

'Putting a squeeze on your profits,' Alex murmured, realizing the company was going to be slowly strangled by the triple whammy of limited stock, difficult trading conditions and price hikes eating into their operating profits.

'Exactly. So you can see why the time seemed right to sell. But it wasn't the right time for *Lochie* so . . .' He sighed, a look of bitterness flattening his mouth; Alex couldn't blame him. 'Anyway, here we are, cruising towards a stock crisis and the most challenging trading circumstances of the modern era and there's seemingly nothing we can do about it. We're like an ocean liner heading for the rocks – too big to turn, too fast to stop.'

'But surely Lochie has a strategy? He's the CEO. It's in his job description to lead the company to safety and profitability.'

'He wants to diversify.' Torquil wrinkled his nose as though it was a dirty word. 'We've got an image problem – young people don't want to drink Scotch; they think it's their father's drink. They want vodka, gin, tequila . . .'

Alex felt a twinge of guilt. She was one of them.

'So Lochie thinks we should distil gin and vodka – utilizing our existing operations and resources.'

'And you don't?'

He shook his head. 'Personally, no. Specialism is our USP. We've done very well out of being a legacy brand, producing small batches of exceptional single malts that can hold a premium. Blends account for ninety per cent of Scotch sales, but of our ten per cent market share, we're leading from the front; older whiskies in the super-premium category have grown by thirteen per cent in the past few years and we've benefited from that, not to mention that our twenty is now the official malt of the Houses of Parliament. We won Malt of the Year for two years running in 2014 and 2015 and came runner-up last year. We're never going to compete with, say, Glenlivet when it comes to yield – they produce twelve million litres a year, we produce five million. But market saturation is not our story. And neither in my opinion is gin.' He sighed. 'But it looks like I'm on my own in that viewpoint – it was passed with a sizeable majority by the family council. Lochie scored an important victory there.'

'Well I guess if you need to grow the business . . . Your father told me the business needs a capital investment?'

'That's right, and the board – with the full backing of the family assembly and the shareholders – want to fund it through equity, by issuing new shares.'

'But?'

'But naturally Lochie wants to go another way – raise the money by delaying on dividend payments and reinvesting the profits.'

'Ah.' She winced. 'So everyone's agreed on what to do next, just not how.'

'Pretty much. Not only did the family assembly vote overwhelmingly against Lochie's reinvestment proposal, so too did the thirty-five per cent of non-family shareholders – within that number is a very large consortium made up of employees and former employees, all of whom badly need the quarterly return from their shares.'

'So how has it been left?'

'In limbo. It's on the table for the next board meeting. Lochie is the majority shareholder. He's got a fifty-three per cent stake, but he's not forcing his hand. Yet.'

She frowned, remembering his arrogance and certainty that Sholto wouldn't act against him. 'Do you *need* a qualified majority? Won't a consensus do?'

'No. The Articles of Association stipulate that a clear majority is required.'

'But surely if there's enough family votes and shareholder votes, you would outnumber him?'

'We would – if the family shares were common stocks and not preferred stocks.'

'Oh dear,' Alex said, realizing the problem immediately: the preferred stocks which were issued to the family shareholders, whilst retaining first dibs on dividend payments, came at the cost of one small thing: voting rights.

'Exactly. The vast majority of the family shareholders have no controlling voice in how the company's run.'

Alex thought for a moment. 'But if the family shareholders have preferred stocks, surely Lochie does too?'

'He used to – or rather Robert, his father did – but he converted them to common stocks many years ago. Lochie's mother was from money so Robert didn't need the higher yield of the preferred stocks in the same way. He preferred to have a voice,' Torquil quipped ruefully.

'That was prescient of him.' Alex was impressed by Lochie's father's shrewd business acumen.

'Wasn't it just? As was the fact that Robert also took advantage of the family's "first refusal" rights any time a cousin wanted to sell. He bought as much stock as he could get his hands on and converted it.'

'But even with all that,' Alex argued, 'hereditary shareholdings are usually diluted over the generations.'

'Ah, but Lochie is the only child of a long line of only children leading back to one of the company's founding partners.'

Her head was swimming, trying to work it all out. 'Jesus.' Alex couldn't decide whether luck or brilliance had connived to create Lochie's good fortune. The chances for this scenario coming to pass were negligible and yet he alone now held the veto. The board could neither force through their motion, nor could they remove him from his post, for he was operating perfectly legally. They were caught in an impasse – Lochie the not-so-benevolent dictator making them bend the knee – and Alex was staggered by his arrogance both in single-handedly blocking the consensus vote and refusing to resign. There were precious few leaders, even amongst *her* clients, who had the temerity and ego to bullishly insist theirs was the only way.

'So first he torpedoed the Ferrandor sale, then he blocked the issue of shares?'

'Yes, although perhaps with hindsight it was obvious that he would do that,' Torquil shrugged.

'Was it?' It wasn't to her.

'Of course. If we issue more shares, his stake *will* be watered down and I happen to know for a fact he can't afford to buy up more at the moment.'

Alex's eyebrows shot up. 'So you're seriously telling me he's potentially stalling the growth of this company and disregarding the mandate of its shareholders, *just* to protect his personal position?'

'I'm afraid so,' Torquil nodded.

'But you must be so . . . so angry,' Alex said hotly, feeling utterly indignant herself.

'Furious. Devastated. All of the above,' he said benignly. 'But it's business. Those are the facts. We have to deal with it and move on.'

Alex sighed in disbelief. That bloody-minded man was the limit. 'Why can't he afford to increase his stake?'

Torquil lowered his voice, his eyes flickering towards the

open door. 'He overextended himself on a pet project he was trying to set up as a subsidiary – and which, I should add, was promptly thrown out by the board.'

'What was the venture?' she asked, intrigued and pleased that it cut both ways at least.

'He was trying to develop a trading model for small investors to trade in maturing malts. As you can imagine, we have thousands of barrels of slowly maturing whiskies just sitting around in warehouses and that maturation costs us dearly, as it's years – generations even – before we can utilize it and actually turn a profit from it.'

Alex nodded. 'Go on.'

'Lochie's so-called great idea was to trade on the maturing whisky barrels by buying into the speculation that both the brand and the market will continue to appreciate in value.'

'Sounds like a good idea,' she shrugged. 'If those barrels are just sitting there for ten, twenty years, it's making them work for you until you can actually touch them.'

'In principle it is a good idea. The problem is the matter of scale. We may be one of the smaller producers but we're still producing five million litres a year and every single one of those litres is earmarked for a particular reserve. For flavour continuity purposes, it's clear that these barrels can't be separated or broken up, meaning trades have to be of a very significant size, far out of the reach of most private investors. Simply put, we don't believe the demand is there.'

'But he does?'

'He did, but the proposal was shot down.'

Alex frowned. 'Do you think that could be a factor in him blocking the issuance of new shares? He's angry? This is his revenge?'

'Honestly? Nothing he did would surprise me any more.'

From behind his head, Alex suddenly saw something fly across the courtyard – something round and pink. She looked back at Torquil in alarm.

Torquil swivelled in his chair and looked out the window, following her eyeline. 'Oh, that,' he grinned, getting up and gesturing for her to join him. 'Come and see.'

She walked over and was bemused to see a couple of men in boiler suits playing football in the courtyard with a bright pink ball.

'They've just cleaned the draff pipes,' he said, watching as they passed the ball between themselves.

'What's a draff pipe?' she asked.

'Draff is the barley residue that's left over after the mashing; we reuse it for cattle food. And it turns out a size five football is the perfect size for cleaning the pipes. We just drop it in at the top and it whistles through the chute, cleaning the debris as it goes.'

Alex laughed. 'I've never heard of anything like it!'

He chuckled. 'No, it is one of our more unorthodox working methods.'

'Well, this looks cosy,' a sarcastic voice behind them said, and they turned to find Lochlan standing in the doorway, a bunch of files in his arms. He had changed into jeans and a grey sweater and Alex thought he looked more as though he was going out for a Saturday lunch than heading a management meeting.

'Ah, Lochie . . . I was just bringing Alex up to speed on the *challenges* facing the company,' Torquil said placidly, leaving the window.

'Well, that would explain why my ears were burning then,' he said, walking straight through to the conference room next door. Alex glanced back at Torquil with a know-ing look. After what she'd just heard, if Lochlan was feeling paranoid, he had good reason to be.

Chapter Eleven

The canteen was a cosy affair – a domed single-storey unit behind the mash house – with an old wooden counter and four women in blue housecoats and catering caps standing behind it. The smell of stew seemed to drift down like clouds bouncing off the ceiling, steam from the stainless-steel kitchen behind them warming the space.

'Just a coffee, please,' Alex said.

'A finger of shortbread? Or a scone?' the dinner lady asked.

'No, thanks.'

'It's included in the price.'

Alex smiled. 'No, really, just the coffee, thank you.'

There was a pause. 'Right you are, someone'll bring it over to you.'

She could feel the woman's eye roll as she looked around for where to sit. All but two tables were unoccupied; it was that lag time between elevenses and lunch. Most of the wooden refectory tables were set in continuous rows down the centre of the room, but a few smaller ones had been positioned by the windows and she headed for the one nestled in the corner, furthest from the door and any draughts.

She sat down, thinking over what she'd just seen in the

meeting. It was clear the junior staff were nervous of him, holding their coffee cups high at their chests – a protective measure – and struggling to make eye contact with him. As for the tone of the discussions, Lochlan had been passive-aggressive and argumentative. Nothing was too small to bicker over – not the cost of the embroidery on the new staff shirts, repairing the CCTV system, nor the free biscuits with coffee.

'Here you are.' The coffee was set down in front of her, a little sloshing onto the saucer.

'Thanks.'

Talk of the devil – a shortbread had been put on the saucer and she looked up at the dinner lady who gave an apologetic shrug. 'I figure you've paid for it anyway; and you do look awful pinched. But it's up to you. Leave it if you want.'

Alex watched her go. Why did everyone keep telling her she looked 'pinched'?

She put her hands round the cup and shivered, realizing suddenly that she *was* cold. The temperature had dropped under the clear skies and her outfit – chic and understated as it was – wasn't anywhere near sufficient for keeping her warm in this. She was used to first-class airport lounges and plush climate-controlled offices, not stone huts with cold Crittall windows. The energy involved in engaging Lochlan Farquhar kept her distractedly warm most of the while but even he couldn't cocoon her completely from a minus-five wind chill.

'Hi, Alex!'

She looked up to see Skye coming through the door. 'Oh, hey,' she waved back. 'Join me?'

Skye nodded, placing her order at the counter and making her way over.

'How are you?' Skye asked, sitting down with a 'flump' and unwinding the red knitted scarf from her neck. Her ponytail swung and her cheeks were flushed a wholesome rose tint; she looked ridiculously young and as though she should have been in a school uniform rather than a lab coat.

'Fine. This is a victory coffee! I've just come out from a meeting with Lochlan.' If she found it alarming that her joy lay in not having been thrown out, rather than any great leaps they'd made in coaching, she didn't show it.

'That's great!' Skye enthused, looking surprised as she shrugged off her coat. 'How did you get him to sit down with you?'

Alex blew out through her cheeks. 'Oh, by winding him up, mainly.'

'Huh?'

'I played him – got him to a point where he negotiated with me: he wants to prove his superiority so badly, he's prepared to meet my terms to do it.' She wondered whether he could go through with it though. After his attitude in the meeting just now, was the satisfaction of beating her at the MacNab going to come at too high a cost for him?

'Sly, I like it. Well, congratulations. I must admit I was doubtful you'd get him to listen. He's so bloody stubborn,' she tutted. 'Ooh, are you having the shortbread? It's so good. I'm having to deny myself at the moment. I need to lose another four pounds before the wedding.'

'You do not, there's nothing of you,' Alex protested.

'You're very sweet but it's true. I had a dress fitting the other day and either I've fallen off the diet wagon or they expected me to lose more than I have, but it was tight here,' she said, girdling her waist with her hands. 'They told me *every* bride loses weight before her big day but –' she whistled quietly – 'looks like I'm the exception to the rule.'

'I'm sure Alasdair wouldn't want you half-starved and fainting on your way down the aisle.'

'No, you're right there. He's not got much truck with "faddy diets" as he calls them. But then he's a six-foot-three beanpole who's never known what it's like to have a fat day or not be able to get into his jeans. It's actually really annoying; he eats like a horse whilst I'm nibbling on daisies and I *still* put on weight! He'll be so cross when he comes down this weekend and finds he's having salad for supper again.'

'Oh, he's coming to Islay?'

'Aye. We take it in turns. I went to Glasgow this weekend, now it's his turn to come here – he's got Friday off to help me with packing the last bits. You must meet him.'

'I'd love to.'

Skye looked pleasantly surprised. 'Yeah? Well, how about dinner at the pub on Thursday?'

'Great, where were you th— Oh, wait, I've actually already got dinner plans that night.'

'Friday then?'

'I'm heading off to Perth for the weekend – part of my deal with the devil.' Alex rolled her eyes.

Skye looked disappointed. 'That's such a shame. We're having Sunday lunch with my folks and then Al's getting the last ferry back that evening. And then the next time I'll see him after that will be in the church.' She made an excited squeak.

'Oh, I'm sorry. I'd have loved to meet him.'

'Couldn't you change your dinner plans on Thursday?'

'I'm not sure. Possibly. It's just Callum.'

'*Callum?*' Skye's eyes widened. 'Are you two—?'

Alex groaned. 'Oh God, no! No. No, no, noooo. I just promised to have dinner with him in return for a favour he did me. I like to honour all my debts.'

Skye looked at her. 'Well, you should watch yourself with him. Callum's got quite a reputation with the ladies. He's a bit too good-looking for his own good.'

'And doesn't he know it,' Alex quipped, rolling her eyes. 'Don't worry about me. I can handle him.' She saw Skye eye the shortbread finger hungrily and offered it to her on the saucer. Skye bit her lip but shook her head. 'So where's the wedding going to be held?'

'At St John's, the wee chapel up the road here. And we're having the reception here.'

There was a pause. 'Here? Actually here at the distillery?'

'Aye. In the dunnage.' She closed her eyes and inhaled deeply. 'All that beautiful whisky maturing in oak; we'll be breathing the sweet air of angels' share.' She opened her eyes and saw Alex's expression. 'What? Have you not heard of angels' share? It's the amount of whisky lost to evaporation through the oak casks.'

'No, it wasn't that.'

'What then?'

'Well . . . how did that go down with Lochlan?'

'He was fine with it,' she mumbled, physically retreating.

'Oh.' But Alex wasn't so sure; she had seen his reaction to Skye's name when they'd been talking in his office earlier. It had hurt him, wounded him even – it was the closest thing to vulnerability she had seen in the man since getting here. No, she wasn't convinced he was going to be 'fine' with her marrying Alasdair – right here, of all places – no matter what he might say to the contrary.

Alex folded her hands in front of her on the table, an idea beginning to present itself to her like an image in a dark room. 'Can I ask you something?'

'Of course.'

'Do you miss him?'

Skye's jaw dropped open, her body freezing mid-action. 'What?'

'I mean, just over a year ago you were going to marry him and now, here you are instead on the eve of your wedding to Alasdair. I just wondered . . .'

Instantly, tears stung Skye's eyes. 'Why are you asking me that?'

Her reaction seemed as heightened as his. One tiny scratch of the surface drawing blood. 'I don't know. I just thought . . . Well, that night at yours, when I saw the two of you in the porch, I wondered if . . .'

'If?'

'If there was still something between you?'

Skye looked stunned. 'Me and Lochlan? You have got to be kidding!'

More overreaction. 'Why?'

'You don't understand,' Skye said, shaking her head, her expression closing down. 'I don't want to talk about it. It's too painful.'

'Okay,' Alex said quietly. 'I'm sorry.'

They were quiet for a few moments and both said nothing as the dinner lady came over with Skye's coffee. They waited for her to leave, each of them distractedly stirring their spoons in the cups, Alex knowing that sometimes silence could be as effective in drawing answers as asking questions.

Sure enough . . .

'Why did you ask me that? There must have been a reason for it. Has he said something?' she asked finally.

'No,' Alex demurred. 'He hasn't *said* anything. But then he wouldn't, would he? Tell me, I mean. I'm the last person he'd tell.' Skye stared at her, knowing there was something more. 'It's just how he acts when your name comes up; it got me wondering, that's all, whether there's any unfinished business between you.' She shrugged, and when Skye didn't say anything she added, 'And with the wedding being so close, I wondered if perhaps there might be some benefit in talking before . . . well, before things are done which can't be undone.'

'I love Al.'

'Of course you do! I wasn't . . .' She paused. 'Look, I'm not saying you're not with the right guy; I've never met Al, I bet he's great and that you're made for each other. But if there *are* things unsaid between you and Lochlan, which need to be said . . . ? You don't want to go into married life with question marks hanging over your relationship with your ex, do you?'

Skye blinked at her. 'Are you sure he hasn't put you up to this?'

'Skye, I can barely get him to agree with me that the grass is green.'

'So then . . .' Skye looked flummoxed.

'It was just an observation I made, that's all. I get paid to notice the details and tell it how it is and sometimes, well –' she shrugged – 'it's misplaced, it's unwanted. I'm really sorry if I've spoken out of turn.'

The dinner lady came over again. 'I forgot your shortbread,' she said to Skye, setting down the side plate.

Alex picked up her biscuit at last and took a bite. 'Mmm,'

she said, watching Skye as she stared, unseeingly, at her own. 'Delicious.'

The wind was coming from the north-west, a bleak cold-fingered tempest pushing against her, but she didn't stop. There was no question of quitting. Soon she would get to the headland, and the coast path – what little there was of it – would sweep inland, putting the wind at her back and all this toil would ease. To her left, the battleship-grey sea churned, the storm of the previous week gone but not forgotten, and she wondered what the weather would bring next. It impressed itself upon the daily lives of the island's inhabitants in a way that it didn't in the cities – for the sky was lead coloured and heavy, every so often the sun finding a way through, forcing a crack in the clouds and throwing down dazzling, sharp-edged bolts of light that illumined the grey depths, pointedly reminding her that it was a bright day up there above the clouds.

She checked her Apple watch as she ran: 6.4 miles so far with another 3.7 to go. It had been a steady uphill incline this far, but at least it meant she'd be downhill on the home straight, just when her legs were really beginning to burn.

She passed shaggy sheep and wild-fringed highland cattle in walled fields, and was grateful for the wind breaks provided by the vast moss-covered rocky outcrops that dotted the ground. Digging deeper, she forced herself to sprint a short steep section of one of them – the last before the path moved off the jagged coastline and headed back inland, according to her map – but as she rounded the summit, her feet stopped pounding at last, not from fatigue but from the heart-stopping beauty of the sight that greeted her. The sun was streaming down again in a refracted sheet of light across the sea, the bulging cliffs of the west coast like silver walls, and had the gods started surfing the sky in chariots of fire, she would have believed her own eyes. It had something of the epic about it, this island, alternately bleak in one breath, majestic in the other – all depending on the light.

She stood with her hands on her hips, her ponytail still swinging and her breath coming heavily as she walked slowly over to a weather-battered bench just ahead. She sank onto it with a grateful groan and stared out to sea, taking deep, gulping breaths of the fresh air. The ferry was passing by, looking prettier at a distance than it did close up.

A robin landed on the bench and stared at her. She reached into her pocket and brought out a finger of short-bread that she had hidden from the dinner ladies on one of her coffee runs. Crumbling it lightly, she scattered it along the top of the bench. The robin waited a moment, then hopped once, twice, on its stick-legs. But as it began to peck for the biscuit crumbs, a crack of twigs nearby sent the songbird flying away in a flurry of wing flaps.

'Oh,' Alex murmured, seeing how the crumbs were lost and spying a hedgehog shuffling through the undergrowth. She reached into her pocket for more biscuit offerings but it was mainly lint from her running parka's pockets that she scattered.

As she gave up, her eyes fell to the small brass plaque on the back and she had to brush leaf debris out of the grooves of the lettering, squinting as she tried to read it:

In memory of EC
A view to America, his heart and home.
CF 1918

Almost a hundred years old? How the devil was this bench still standing? She wobbled it gingerly, checking the joints, but it seemed sound enough and she supposed it was quite well sheltered in the shrubbery up here, not to mention that probably no one ever sat on it. Which was a shame, given that it was dedicated in memory of someone who had clearly loved to do so.

America, huh? It was hard to imagine that such a huge continent was the next port of call from this desolate point, its hulk hidden over the horizon.

She watched as the seagulls wheeled in the sky. She had overheard Mrs Peggie at breakfast telling the new occupants of the green room – a retired couple from Leeds – that the wind sometimes blew in puffins from the outer isles, but there were none to be seen today.

No puffins and no Lochlan. She had returned from coffee with Skye earlier to find his office locked and his car gone. According to Hamish, who had been passing, he had left for a 'meeting' but Alex wasn't buying it. He was as likely to be 'meeting' the brunette in the bed sheet as he was an accountant or banker or . . . or peat cutter; he just didn't want to meet with *her*.

But it hadn't been a wasted day by any means. She had taken a proper guided tour for one thing, finally getting to see in practice what she had mugged up on before arriving here. And interestingly, she had stepped outside her direct brief from Sholto and introduced herself to the teams, making a start on interviewing some of the managers. Strictly speaking, their input and assessments of their CEO weren't required; this wasn't a standard 'performance enhancement' commission and it didn't really matter what they thought, just what *he* thought. Nonetheless, if he refused to engage with her, she had to get material on him from other sources; she had to find his pressure points. Skye was clearly one but her conversations with his senior managers had proved to be enlightening too, building on both what Skye had already related regarding his anger issues and what Torquil had highlighted as to his isolation from the rest of the senior executives as they differed on proposed growth strategies.

It was clear that Lochie's wuvictory and there seemed to be a consensus amongst the staff that he was living on borrowed time. Alex was inclined to agree. From everything they had told her, it sounded as though the pressure was already beginning to tell and according to the change state indicator she used for assessing leadership profiles, she – and even Louise – had deduced he was in what was called a Gamma state wherein behaviour becomes frustrated, anti-social and destructive, an open revolt against the status quo. Although she was usually brought in to consult during the preceding Beta state, when first doubts about existing practice start to emerge, she had had a few clients at this juncture before and knew he had two options open to him: turn back to the trodden path or force change.

She thought she could well guess his intended strategy.

Giving a weary sigh, glad this conflict wasn't hers, she pulled her phone out of her pocket and checked for reception. This remote spot was the only place she'd found since arriving here where she could talk without having to shout, where she didn't have to hang from a window ledge for a clear line. She scrolled through her contacts and pressed dial, one hand pulling into a tight fist in her lap as she waited for someone to pick up.

'Hi, it's me,' she said, taking a deep breath and stepping onto her own battlefield. 'How's he been today?'

Chapter Twelve

Islay House, Islay, 5 February 1918

The wind ran laps around the house, making the windows rattle in their frames and fluttering the pages of the book that her mother had left open and unread by the window seat; Clarissa wasn't the only one to spend her quiet hours with her face to the glass.

She reached down to the pile of mending at her feet and picked up another stocking that had gone at the toes. Head bent as she darned, she repeatedly tucked away the loose tendrils of blonde hair that escaped her bun, the pads of her fingers speckled with pinpricks from the needle.

The wireless was off and she worked in silence, her fingers and arms weaving a nimble dance. She could do this in her sleep, the motions as automatic to her body as the in-out of her lungs. Today was Tuesday but tomorrow evening would be exactly the same. And the day after that.

She lifted her head suddenly. 'What was that?'

'Hmmm?' her father asked, from his usual position in his fire-side chair.

'I thought I heard something.'

His eyes swivelled in his head before he shook it fractionally. 'No. It's just the wind.'

171

She frowned but resumed her task. After this, she had to do her father's sweater which the moths had nibbled, and the counterpane on her bed. And if she was feeling really lively, then perhaps pick up her knitting and finish the socks she was working on; she had become so proficient, she could now knit two at once. Her father kept remarking that she and her mother, between the two of them, would single-handedly knit the Allies to victory.

She glanced across at her mother, whose stockinged feet were peeping from under her skirt as she dozed on the chaise longue. She wasn't used to manual work; Clarissa was even less used to seeing her mother with mud on her face. She had always been a mother of the ornamental sort: soft and fragrant, with a staccato laugh and pretty eyes. Having a son at war was too abrasive for her delicate nerves.

She looked back to the fire, her gaze catching in the mirrored glass above the mantel, and she gasped at what she saw reflected there. As she twisted behind her to see for herself, the darning dropped from her lap. She stood and stared.

'Dear God.'

Her father looked up. 'Wha—?' He rose too and made his way to the window.

The sky was red, a ghoulish extraterrestrial light spreading from one point of the horizon to the other and making the heavy sea glimmer darkly.

'Red signifies U-boats in the area, doesn't it, Father?'

He nodded grimly, his hands behind his back as they looked out, unable to make out any detail on the water.

'Should . . . should we go down there?' she asked. 'There might be a boat in distress.'

Her father was silent for a few moments. 'It's a warning signal, that's all,' he said, turning, cane tapping on the floor as he made his way back to the fire.

'*But what if someone's been hit? They might need help.*'

'*You must stop letting your imagination run away with you. It's a warning, I've told you. And besides, what help could we possibly provide in this darkness, in these conditions?*' *he asked, just as the wind picked up strength again and hurled itself against the stone walls. 'I'll go down at first light.*'

'*But Father—*'

'*I've said I'll deal with it. You needn't concern yourself any further with it. Whatever's going on, you can be sure it's no business for a woman. Leave it now,*' *he said sternly.*

Clarissa looked back into the fire, a throb of bitterness at her craw. But she picked up her sewing and let her hands fall back into their mindless rhythm, her mother still asleep on the chair. It was just another night. The same as all the others.

It was still dark when she dressed, the embers still glowing faintly in her bedroom fire. The wind hadn't let up – if anything it was worse – and she clutched her coat tightly to her lean frame as she let herself out through the kitchen door and ran through the herb garden.

Mr Dunoon's bicycle was where he had always kept it: propped up against the stone wall of the potting shed and awaiting his return as though he'd merely popped inside for a cup of tea rather than left for the battlefields of Europe. Grabbing it, taking pains not to brush her finger against the bell and alert anyone, she threw her leg over and – bunching her skirts in one hand – pedalled furiously down the drive. She had barely slept, her dreams febrile and anxious, and she felt propelled by an imperative, an instinct, that she couldn't explain.

Her cloche hat threatened to blow off several times as she sped down the gardens, out of the estate and over the open windswept moors, heading downhill for the port, her eyes streaming as she navigated the increasingly bumpy, rutted track. It was sleeting, the temperature raw and merciless, and she wondered why she was doing this, her soft bed still warm. What would there be to see? Her father had said it was a warning flare to the other ships in the waters, that was all.

But as she drew closer, her breath coming hard as she stood out of the saddle to crest a hill, she could see activity in the little town – horses on the shore and chimneys puffing at a time when most were resolutely dormant. It was still early, far too early for the residents to be up yet. Even the farmers didn't rise at this hour; the sun was barely peeping over the horizon, as though ashamed of what it might reveal.

She felt her gut tighten as she pedalled harder, a gust finally blowing off her hat as she rounded the corner into town, passing the rows of white fishermen's houses. Women were standing in the street weeping.

'What . . .' she panted, throwing the bike down, its wheels still spinning. 'What's happened?'

'An American troopship was torpedoed last night,' Maggie MacFarlane managed, dabbing her eyes with the corners of her shawl. 'Those poor, poor lads.'

Clarissa's insides felt liquid at the memory of the red sky. She had known it! Felt it, somehow. 'Were there any survivors?' she asked, feeling a stab of revulsion at herself for being so easily swayed by her father, warm and bored in the big house.

'See for yourself,' Morag McKenzie said, jerking her chin towards the golden scoop of sand. The tide was out and the beach was littered with long, rubbery fronds of kelp – and bodies. Scores of bodies. Some face down. Some naked. Some, their skin dashed to ribbons from the merciless rocks she herself had grown up scrambling on for mussels.

No.

She ran towards them, towards the men now carefully lifting the perished into the cart that Farmer Kilearan had brought down, his horse tacked up and ready to pull those big wheels from the sand.

'Mr McLachlan,' she cried, flying up to the nearest man as he drew a blanket over the face of one dead soldier. The shore winds lashed the sleet against her, slapping her skin red, her own hair blinding her.

'Get back, lass. This is no sight for you to see.'

She raked her hair back from her face. 'Please, did any survive?'

The ploughman looked back at her. He looked as though he'd been up all night. His face was blue-tinged from the cold and the wet, exhaustion and hunger. She noticed he was in his shirtsleeves and that they were wet. 'Eight. We think.'

'Eight?' she whispered. That was all? From a troopship?

'It was a force ten gale. I don't know how there's even that many as made it.' He jerked his chin towards the far side of the beach where the cliffs and high rocks – so deadly last night – now provided shelter from the wind. A small group of women were doling out hot soup, the survivors hunched and shrouded in blankets, coats, anything that covered them. Several, it seemed, had lost their clothes.

She staggered across, her gaze fixed on the young men who were staring back out to sea with hollow eyes. They were still wet, some of them. Had they been in the water all night? That couldn't be possible, could it, to have survived so long in these temperatures?

'What can I do? Tell me how I can help,' she demanded, grabbing the arm of Amy MacKenzie, one of the quilter women.

'We're just waiting for Old Euan's cart so we can transport these ones up the beach. They can't walk – injuries some of them, but shock and exposure too. They're awful weak and cannae stand. We need to get them off the sand as quickly as possible and in front of some fires. Run up to the hotel and tell Muirne we need water boiled for baths and more clothes. Plenty more clothes. They'll catch hypothermia. Be quick now. That one there isn't looking too good,' she said in a lower voice, glancing at one soldier who was shivering violently, his eyes red-rimmed but his lips a glacial blue. 'And when you're done, go and take over from Molly Buchanan. She's been up all night churning the butter. Her arm will come clean off if someone doesn't help her.'

'Butter?' Clarissa queried.

'For making scones. These boys are going to need feeding if we're to heat them back up from the inside.'

Clarissa felt another burst of self-disgust. All night, she'd slept in a feathered bed, a fire crackling at her feet and these lads . . .

She looked back out to sea. It was menacing still, the waves snarling and frothing, hurling themselves with furious violence against the jagged rocks that peppered the shoreline here, huge sprays of water jetting up to the bleak dawn sky. There was no—

'What's that?' she demanded anxiously, pointing at something pale on the higher rocks, her brow deeply creased as she tried to see through the sleet and gauzy mist.

'What?' Amy asked, trying to follow her gaze.

'It looks like there's something up there. See? About twenty feet up . . . It's a body!'

She felt sick. The man was lying on his back, his bright neck exposed and stretched long, one leg bent double, but outwards at the knee in a terrible angle.

'Oh my God,' Amy cried. 'There's another one! Here!' she cried, gathering her skirts and running towards Donald McLachlan. 'Donald!'

The ploughman looked up. 'Is he alive?'

'We don't know! You must come!'

But Clarissa was already ahead of them, wading through the shallows, holding her coat up but her skirts sodden and weighted, making it difficult to move as the ebb flow tried to pull her off her feet.

'Get out of the water!'

She heard their screams as she waded but she didn't stop. She couldn't go any deeper, she knew that, but if she got behind the rocks that protruded into the water, she could scramble back over them to the cliffs where the soldier was lying. Going in was the only way to get up to him.

It was harder than she'd thought – not that she had thought about it; her legs had carried her here without hesitation or conscious judgement – and the water was shocking in its iciness, the swell monstrously powerful. Her teeth were already chattering, her lower body soaked, but she managed to get a handhold on one of the sharp rocks and timing it carefully, she hauled herself up between the breaking waves. The effort it took was shocking and that was coming from a girl who now toiled sixteen-hour days in the fields, but she staggered onwards, grateful to be out of the water, her skirts clinging like animals to her legs, making it hard to walk.

Behind her, a heavy wave crashed on the guard rocks, sending up a dense spray that fell like bullets on her back and threw her sprawling forwards. The salt water immediately stung the fresh cuts, making her cry out. But there were other cries too, not her own, and glancing round briefly, she saw Donald McLachlan – and others – in the water now too, their arms held high as they shouted at her to get back.

She got to her feet again and kept climbing, her hands growing red raw and cut, numb from the cold. He was just a few feet above her now; she could only see the tips of his fingers splayed and *peering over a rock like lookouts but as she moved round and up, she saw a single hobnailed field boot a few feet away, still tightly laced, and she felt a shiver of fear at the force that must have been required to rip it from him. Time and again she slipped on the wet rocks, the treacherous seaweed lobbying against her as still the waves kept coming, breaking behind her but throwing up great plumes of ice-cold seawater that were all the more shocking for the bitter wind that chilled her wet skin and clothes in the intervals.*

'I'm coming,' she tried calling to him, astonished by the weakness of her own voice. 'I'm almost there. Help's coming,' she panted.

With a final heave, she pulled herself up until she was level with his head. His eyes were closed, his body twisted at grotesque angles, his skin so pale he looked to be drained of blood.

'Hello?' she whispered, suddenly fearful. She'd never seen a dead body before, never touched one. Tentatively, she laid a hand on his cheek. It was so cold, the barest brush of stubble against her skin. He was wearing woollen undergarments only and they were completely wet through; far from providing him with any kind of protection, they would have lowered his body temperature further.

He looked to be not much older than her – twenty, twenty-one? The same age as Percy then, but younger than Phillip, who had barely turned twenty-two when his tank rolled over that land mine. But what did the specifics matter? His was still another young life, lost. She reached out and took his hand still splayed upon the rock and held it between both of hers. 'I'm so sorry,' she whispered.

Donald McLachlan was only a few feet away now. 'Get back here, lassie!' he said angrily, reaching up for her. 'What were you thinking? You could have been killed!'

She looked down at him, tears in her eyes. It had all been for nothing, her hope for redemption as dashed upon the rocks as this soldier's broken body. 'We're too late,' she said quietly, shaking her head.

Donald fell back, his fury switching in an instant to despair. His shoulders slumped.

But against her hand, a finger twitched.

Islay, early hours of Tuesday 12 December 2017

Alex turned over restlessly, her eyes shut but resolutely awake. Sleep wouldn't come, frustration worrying at the edges of her mind. How could she work if the client wouldn't talk to her? She had tried straightforward rapport, she had tried appeasement, she had tried provocation – and they had all barely kept her in the same room as him. The man was a slippery fish, refusing to be caught.

He couldn't know that she wasn't going to go anywhere until this was done, that his games and bullying tactics wouldn't work on her: he could throw her out, shout her down, ignore her, belittle her . . . but she would win because she had absolutely no option not to. Failure wasn't even a consideration. This commission would scale the summit of her career ambitions; it was everything she had spent the past fourteen years working towards and she wouldn't be defeated by an arrogant, egotistical man who felt entitled by mere dint of birthright to put his own interests far above and beyond those of anyone else.

She rolled back over onto her right side with a sigh and stared into the darkness—

Only, it wasn't dark.

Sitting bolt upright in bed, she gasped at the glow that had lit up the room like a lamp. 'Oh my God,' she cried, throwing back the covers and running to the window. The sky was red.

The glow was concentrated in one area just out of sight beyond the moors, but she knew exactly where it was coming from. She knew what it was.

The distillery was on fire.

Mr Peggie's habit of leaving his overalls and boots ready to step into by the door meant they were out of the house in just a few minutes. He was a sprightly man and could move with surprising speed for one in his eighties. They were taking the tractor, in case anything needed lifting or hauling, and Mrs Peggie would be bringing up the rear in the Landy a few minutes behind them once she'd 'got some clothes on'.

Alex sat ramrod straight as they drove as fast as they could in the darkness, down towards the port. In the headlights, she saw that the grasses were flattened and rippling, steady gusts blowing up from the shore. The gods were against them.

'The fire brigade will probably already be there,' she said hopefully, glancing over at Mr P.

His return glance was not encouraging. 'There's a retained unit at Bowmore, ten miles away, but Port Ellen's is a voluntary service. It'll be all hands to the deck till they get there.'

Alex felt her muscles stiffen, fear like concrete setting in her blood as they rolled along, the prongs of the haylift lifted skywards, the cab bouncing over every rut; but being so high up gave them the advantage of a clear view and when they rounded the last hillock before the final straight into town, she gave a horrified gasp. It was an apocalyptic scene: rushing silhouetted figures backlit by a raging sky, flames leaping like delighted devils as the heat billowed and roared, pushing everyone back.

. . . Crackle and snap. Coughing. The air thick . . .

'It's the barley loft,' Mr P. said grimly, his grip tightening on the wheel as he made the sharp right turn off the main road onto the distillery track. People from the town – mainly men and teenagers – were running on foot alongside the path, women with young children hanging back on the bay's shores, mothers' arms grasped protectively over their shoulders, unable to look away from the devastation. Many were crying, hands clamped over open mouths, heads shaking as the sky grew brighter, the flames determined to be seen across the water, to be heard over the wind.

They pulled slowly into the courtyard. Floodlights were on but the sheer number of people gathered there meant they could get no further than just through the decorative wrought-iron gates whose intricate design was markedly at odds, Alex always thought, with the ascetic stone buildings. Mr P. hooted the horn several times, parting the distracted crowds, and they managed to inch through towards the bottling hall, clearing the way at least for the fire service when they arrived. For there was no sign of them yet.

They climbed down from the cab and instinctively took a moment to absorb the heat – even from this distance it was oppressive, sucking the oxygen from the sky . . . *Scorching the hairs in her nose. Rasping her throat* . . . Alex felt her heart rate accelerate, her breathing coming fast and shallow as her eyes darted, taking in the scene – trying to understand. *To escape . . .*

From the chaos of the fire and the wider crowd, there was order of a sort: a line had formed leading from the dunnage warehouse that was one of the original farm buildings and sat nearest to the source of the fire, to the unit where the maltings, mash house and still house were grouped: barrels were being rolled out on their sides, one by one, to the furthest side of the courtyard where others were repositioning them to their all-important final positions, with the seals on top.

'I'm going to see if they want any of them moved on the pallets,' Mr Peggie shouted.

Alex watched him disappear into the mass of bodies, feeling the cry not to leave her stop in her throat. She was alone . . . *she was alone* . . .

She scanned the crowd. She could see Hamish, the coppersmith and her taxi driver that first day here, amidst the men rolling the barrels, a vein bulging at his forehead, his complexion puce with the effort; he was no young man. Torquil was there too, his shirtsleeves rolled up, face blackened with soot, frantically issuing orders to the men as they passed each other on the runs.

'Alex!'

She turned to find Skye running over to her.

'Oh my God, are you okay?' Alex asked, seeing how her eyes were red-rimmed, her skin blackened as if with coal dust.

'Aye. We've been frantic, trying to move all the rare and historic bottles from the visitors' centre and the sampling labs.' She was breathless, the flames reflected in her glasses. *Flickering, leaping, lunging, reaching for her . . .*

'What can I do to help?' Alex asked.

'It's all done. We got them in the back of Dad's car and he's had one of the men drive it up to MacLennan's farm on the other side of the bay, against the wind,' she puffed, her hands on her hips as she took in the sight. Tears gathered in her eyes as she looked back at the burning malting house. 'I just can't believe it.'

Alex stared at it too, wanting to press her hands against her ears and drown out the sound of the fire as it bayed and bellowed, billowed and roared. People always talked about the colour of the fire, the heat, but for her it was the noise of it that terrified her most, like a creature from her childhood nightmares.

'When did it start, do you know?'

'An hour ago, they reckon. The alarm was raised by a nightwatchman at Lagavulin.'

'An hour? But then why aren't the fire brigade here?' She looked around in panic . . . *Terror rising. Despair* . . . 'I thought they were only ten miles away. That's, what, fifteen minutes?'

'The road's blocked at Glenegedale. A logging lorry jack-knifed on some black ice and has jammed across the road. There's no through pass until it's moved.'

'You're kidding!' Alex exclaimed, her eyes wide with fury and sheer indignation that chance could have taken these opposing elements of fire and ice to wreak such havoc in the middle of the night on a tiny island. Chance, that was all it was. Sheer, rotten bad luck. No one's fault.

'Do you think they'll be able to save the stock?' Alex asked, struggling to remain calm. In control. She was shaking, she realized.

. . . *Red haze blooming. Black smoke creeping. Under the doors. The slow groan of glass cracking* . . .

'I'm not sure. The heat could affect the ABV – the alcohol content; and the smoke will probably permeate the casks.' Skye's tone was grim. 'We won't know immediately. They may have got there in time.' She bit her lip, looking doubtful. 'Maybe.' She chewed a fingernail anxiously, watching as the flames danced as though for an audience. 'But it's the still house they really need to contain; it's the most hazardous environment because of the ethanol – we don't even let the tour groups take photos in there because of the spark hazard . . .'

. . . Explosion. Glass shattering and splintering. Gases whirling in the heat. The air a fan, bigging up the flames . . .

'But the stills themselves are our most vital asset; they're what give Kentallen its unique flavour profile. If we lose them, it will affect our market supply ten, fifteen, even twenty years from now.'

. . . Sirens far off. Blue lights flashing . . .

A sudden noise made them both start. It was a noise that was unnatural for this scene. A noise that shouldn't be anywhere near here. A bark.

Skye shrieked. 'Rona!'

Alex turned to see the dog barking in the courtyard further up nearer the seat of the fire, outside Lochie's office; she was jumping agitatedly at the flames as they swayed hypnotically through the windows of the maltings.

'Rona! Rona! Come here, girl!' Skye cried, running over and throwing her arms around the dog's neck as it trembled against her, its tail between its legs. 'My baby! What are you doing here? Where's . . . ?' Her voice trailed off and she stood up abruptly, a look of abject horror on her face. 'Where's Lochie?'

'Lochie?' Alex repeated, turning in circles, over and over like a child trying to make herself dizzy. Yes. Where *was* he? Everyone else was helping, mucking in. But he was nowhere to be seen.

'Lochie!' Skye shouted, panic in her voice, the whites of her eyes showing. She ran over to the nearest group of people, grabbing them by the arms. 'Have you seen Lochie?'

One of the women pointed towards his office, behind them. Skye ran over to it, Alex following after; Rona stayed where she was on the cobbles, jumping on her front paws, growling and snarling, barking at the flames, her head and tail down low.

'Lochie?' Skye cried, flinging open his office door. But there was no one in there. She whirled round. The maltings was only four metres from here and the heat was ferocious, forcing them both to raise their hands protectively. *Melting. Burning. Raging. Dying* . . .

'Where is he?'

Skye ran back into the courtyard, Alex close on her heels, just as a sudden shattering of glass made everyone gasp – one of the windows had blown out and Rona whined, running back to their feet and cowering on her belly as a gust spewed billowing black smoke in their direction. They were bent double from coughing. *Choking. Suffocating* . . .

Alex felt her arm grabbed, saw her feet moving as Skye dragged her and Rona back to the office. She slammed the door shut, blocking out some of the heat, the smoke, the noise. But none of the horror. It was in here, out there. They were part of this story. It was already part of them.

Alex fell to her knees, coughing. *Lungs clogged shut. Soot and toxins like a dirty fog inside her, speckling her from the inside out. Eyes watering. Blind. Her hands on the floor. Carpet backing melting* . . .

She heard water running and saw Skye at the basin, pouring a mug full of water, downing it in one go herself, before refilling it and bringing it over to her.

'Here. Drink that,' she said, putting the mug in Alex's hands.

She looked out of the window as she drank – dropped the glass.

Her body wouldn't move, even her heart had paused its tireless work, her eyes trained on that upper window where she'd seen a flash of movement. She waited.

And saw it again.

Her mouth opened in a soundless cry . . . *A scream. Falling past the window . . .*

'What?' Skye asked, seeing her, watching her. And then understanding. Her eyes swung over to the flames. 'No . . .'

Blue whirling lights spun on the white walls and Skye gave a shout . . . *Savage. Desperate . . .* She ran to the door and flung it open. 'Over here!' she screamed, waving her arms wildly. 'Over here!'

A few people turned to look, the pitch of her screams marking out a new desperation.

'Over here! He's inside!'

Expressions changed, mouths falling open as the word spread, moving through the crowd so that the fire officers – jumping down from the red cabs – headed straight for her, outstretched arms in her direction pointing the way.

'He's in the malting house!' Skye shouted as a masked fireman stopped in front of her, before nodding and giving the order for two others to follow him into the blazing building.

Bug eyes. Aliens . . .

Skye gave a cry as they were swallowed up by the smoke. 'He can't be in there. He can't,' she sobbed. Alex put out an arm to touch her shoulder but the gesture was mechanical. Robotic. She felt . . . far away. *On the ceiling. Looking down . . .*

Skye began to cry, huge heaving sobs wracking her shoulders, moans and wails escaping her as she struggled to get free every few moments, but Alex held on tight, her gaze never leaving the malting house. Everything was colour. Heat. Rage. Chaos. The flames growing bolder with every minute, the wind whipping them upwards as more firefighters ran over with high-pressure hoses and began training them on the building.

'Oh my God, oh my God,' Skye moaned, as the minutes ticked past. 'Why aren't they coming out? Where are they? Have they found him? Why can't they find him?'

But Alex had no voice, the tension in her keyed as tight as a garrotting wire. Everything had gone silent, the world on mute as she saw an indistinguishable shape emerge in the fiery haze. A moment later, it stepped free from the building and she saw what it was – two firemen, each with one arm linked between Lochlan's, his head dropped, his feet dragging behind him.

'No!' Skye screamed, rushing forwards, and this time Alex couldn't contain her, her grip as weak as ribbons . . . *Dead. Lifeless. Broken . . .*

Skye threw open the door of the office as the firemen ran him in, seeking refuge from the smoke and the heat, laying him out on the floor. A paramedic came through and immediately began making checks – for breathing, opening his mouth for obstructed airways, beginning CPR.

Useless. Helpless. Hopeless . . .

'It'll be all right,' someone said as Skye sobbed.

'You don't know that!' she cried. 'You don't know that. He's not breathing!'

She stared at him from the corner of the ceiling, so far away from the dirty body stretched out on the floor, inert, unresponsive; watching as they breathed and blew and pumped. *Airless Lifeless* . . . The man who had done nothing but torment and sneer and humiliate her from the moment they'd met. The man she could say in all honesty she disliked more than anyone she had ever met. But that didn't mean he could die.

'Come on, Lochlan! Fight!'

The voice was a roar – savage. Hers. As though he'd revive – survive – simply to spite her.

Dead. Dead. Dead.

Dead . . .

And then she saw a finger twitch.

Chapter Thirteen

Kilnaughton Bay, Islay, 8 February 1918

The procession moved through the town, the tread of boots on the cobbles the only sound below the mournful lament of the bagpipes. The survivors walked up front, those that could, their heavy coats and buzz-cut heads a distinction from the tweeds and caps, skirts and shawls of the villagers. Rifles were pressed against the shoulders of the local men as they marched, one British and one American flag flapping in the winds as they moved through the town to the small cemetery along the bay that the menfolk had been preparing ever since the terrible night of the tragedy.

The ground was firm underfoot, for in spite of ferocious winds and attempts at snow, it had not rained much in recent weeks and the vicar led them sedately to the newest graves that lay empty and waiting. Nearby, the freshly heaped soil of yesterday's burials was slowly drying in the air, the heather posies that had been laid atop already loosened and scattered from their bunches by the wind.

The vicar's words carried amongst them, telling them of 'peace' and 'everlasting sleep', 'honour' and 'glory', just as a skein of barnacle geese flew overhead in a V formation of – fittingly enough – almost military precision. And when it was time for the fallen to be released to the peaty soils of this windswept Scottish

Isle, rifles were pointed to the air and a three-volley salute pep-pered the sky, that could be heard for miles around.

Islay, Thursday 14 December 2017

After the flames came the snow, transforming the bleak, bare, storm-battered landscape to a pristine and pillowy picture-postcard setting; the sheep huddled in flocks against the crumbling walls; deer tracks dotted the moors; and the sky, milky and opaque, offered no sightings of the sun or moon for two days.

Even with the snowfall, it had taken that long for the maltings to stop smoking, the blackened and charred roof struts like exposed ribs, some caving in on themselves. The Chief Fire Officer had confirmed the fire had started on the top floor in the barley loft (where the dry grain was stored), moving rapidly downwards through the building, aided by the chutes from the steeps down to the maltings floor below, and dancing quickly across towards the kilns. The flames had been licking at the kiln room walls when the first hoses had been turned on.

Within hours of the alarm being raised, journalists had begun lingering at the gates, trying to 'get an angle' and interview the staff as they came and went, but Torquil had issued a mandatory silence order as the investigation into the cause of the fire was still ongoing and 'foul play' hadn't yet been ruled out. In his opinion though, they'd been 'lucky'. The lost barley stores could be replenished easily enough by buying in from an external maltings; the old stone walls and slate roof of the malting house had done much to hinder the fire's speed and they were hopeful that the stonework of the building at least would be salvageable; the maturing whisky stock had been rescued (although tests were still ongoing to ascertain whether it had been affected by the heat and smoke) with the dunnage warehouse now sitting all but empty. And critically, the stills were undamaged.

The distillery had taken a hit, but it wasn't fatal and the most pressing concern for the management (besides how this had happened in the first place) was getting the maltings division back in operation – as stage one of the distillation process, nothing could proceed without it. With Lochlan still being held against his will in hospital, Torquil had stepped into the breach and Sholto was flying back from his annual pre-Christmas jaunt in Mauritius to survey the damage for himself; even Callum had stepped up, driving through the dark hours to get the first ferry over from the mainland.

The fire brigade had cordoned off the area around the malting house, but the staff had mobilized their own recovery system, washing down the walls and floors of the other units, trying to get rid of the ash and soot and smell, taking inventories and checking whether any of the operating or venting systems had been damaged.

Alex herself had sprung into action with an energy that surprised everyone but her. She had been here once before and she knew that shock was the enemy. Sitting around weeping and staring at walls – it helped no one and changed nothing, and if they wanted to be rid of the burning reek and the smoke stains on the walls and the carpet of ash on the floors then they had to sweep and mop, scrub and polish; so when the fire brigade had handed back the site yesterday – having put out the last of the embers and checked the surrounding properties for signs of structural damage – and the staff were allowed back in, she had been one of the first down there, swapping her Narciso Rodriguez dress and heels for a spare distillery uniform of black work trousers and a red polo shirt with the Kentallen crest on the chest, her towel-dried hair pulled back in a ponytail. She had seen the looks some of the staff had exchanged among themselves as she'd grabbed a mop and bucket and set to work with a Cinderella-esque zeal, but she didn't care; she didn't consider herself too grand to help with the clean-up, even if others did. She needed to be part of the recovery process for reasons they would never know. And anyway, what else was she supposed to do? With Lochlan in hospital suffering from smoke inhalation and with the distillery's operations suspended, no one else was working to their job descriptions this week either. So she had helped brush the courtyard cobbles with Sheila, Liz and Flossie from accounts; she had joined Torquil in carrying wheelbarrow-loads of ruined draff and mash to the bonfire that was being built in the adjoining field; she had laughed with Callum as he'd helped her hose down the outside of the kiln house. And when the three-metre Christmas tree, which had been ordered a month previously, arrived that afternoon when the embers were still smoking, she had been part of the team hoisting it into position in the nearside corner of the courtyard, just inside the gates.

'Isn't it trivial – disrespectful – to erect something as frivolous as this in the immediate aftermath of what could have been an unspeakable tragedy?' Torquil had asked her in his usual earnest voice.

'People need hope and reassurance during the darkest hours, not the brightest,' she'd replied.

And she'd been right. As the tree was being erected, the ladies in the canteen had brewed up some hot toddies and scones, someone put on a playlist of carols and, as the sun had set on their first day 'back in' and they had switched on the lights, a cheer had gone up, the tree suddenly totemic of the community's resilience.

The only person missing – apart from Lochlan, of course – had been Skye; she had remained by his side ever since going in the ambulance with him to the Bowmore hospital, keeping up a vigil that, according to reports from some of the staff who'd paid him a visit, was wholly unnecessary: Lochlan was in his usual fettle, they said, and driving the nurses mad in his restlessness to get out. Apparently, he had been decoupling the dust collectors in the maltings to prevent the fire from propagating back through the entire plant system, thereby saving the whole distillery from the risk of an explosion. It was unthinkably brave. And stupid. He could have been killed. *He* didn't know what the fuss was about.

Alex scrubbed his office windows a little harder – being so close to the maltings, it had absorbed the worst of the smoke and she'd been airing it with the windows open almost constantly for the past couple of days, keeping the little fire going in the hearth to keep out the damp and the cold as the snow continued to fall in sporadic showers. There were no soft furnishings in the room besides the hop-sack wing chair she'd brought in from the farm – no curtains, no rugs – which made the job a little easier at least, but she must have mopped the stone floor five times by now and it still kept turning the water black. After the fourth time, she'd taken his spare suit, shoes and trainers back to Crolinnhe and left them airing there in the stone porch of the farmhouse.

She stepped back from the windows to assess her handiwork, the scrunched-up newspaper she'd been using with vinegar blackened in her hand.

'Very impressive.' The voice was wry. And hoarse. 'We're not looking for any business coaches right now but I believe there's an opening for a cleaner if you're interested.'

Alex spun on her heel to find Lochlan standing in the doorway. His eyes were still reddened and in spite of his heightened complexion and berry-coloured lips, she saw exhaustion in his features.

'You're out!' she exclaimed, feeling an unexplained rush of relief to see him standing there, still testy, still sarcastic as hell.

'I made a bid for freedom when the nurses were changing shifts.'

'You didn't.' A question mark hovered in the statement – one could never be quite sure with him – and a hint of a smile curled his lips as he slowly made his way into the room, heading straight for the chair.

She watched him. His movements looked laboured. 'How are you feeling?'

'Tickety-boo.'

'You look tired.'

'So would you if you'd just had forty-eight hours' enforced rest.' He sat down in the chair, coughing a little, and she went over to the sink to get him some fresh water.

'Here,' she said, handing it to him.

'A nurse too, they could have done with you at Bowmore,' he quipped, one eyebrow hitched as he sipped it.

'Thanks for visiting, by the way. Much appreciated. I could have died, or so they keep telling me.'

'My pleasure.'

It was a joke, or at least she had intended it as such, but as he stared at her with his usual expression, she saw not scorn but questioning and she found herself adding, 'Given how you can't stand the sight of me, I didn't think your recovery would be hastened by having me sitting at the end of your hospital bed.'

'On the contrary, you deprived me of the pleasure of having security throw you out; it would have cheered my spirits no end.'

His eyes glittered wickedly – he was in a rare good mood – and she found herself smiling back for once. 'I'm sure it would.'

A small silence bloomed as she recalled the memory of him lying on this very floor and the deep panic it had rent from her: the urgency in her voice, the minuteness of his reply, and she felt . . . exposed somehow, as though the mask had dropped.

He blinked, his eyes travelling over her. 'The uniform actually suits you. Maybe we really should find you a job.'

'Ha-bloody-ha,' she said, bracing herself for the next onslaught of sarcasm.

'What? Clearly this place is getting under your skin.'

'It wasn't like there was much else I could do whilst you were resting in hospital.'

'You could have gone home.'

'You wish,' she quipped, thinking how she sounded more like her twelve-year-old self than the thirty-one-year-old version with a flat in Mayfair and a private banker.

'Hey.'

They both looked across to find Skye at the door.

'Hi!' Alex said brightly. 'How are you?'

'Oh my goodness,' Skye grinned, taking in the sight of her in the uniform. 'I almost didn't recognize you.'

'Well, I'm not sure I've worn a ponytail since school.'

'I can't believe they've got you helping out.'

'I offered. There was nothing else for me to do whilst Lochlan was off harassing nurses.'

Skye groaned. 'Och, you heard about that? He's a nightmare! I don't think they've ever been so glad to see the back of someone.'

'I know how they feel,' Alex agreed.

'I am sitting here,' he protested, swinging the chair round to face the desk – and Skye. 'What is it, anyway?'

'I'm just checking to see you've taken your meds?'

'I was just about to.'

'Remember, every four hours—'

'Uh-huh,' he nodded impatiently.

'Even if you feel fine. It's important to be consistent in the first week and stop any inflammation from getting out of control.'

'Thank you, but I can deal with it.'

'Yes, but will you, though? I know what you're like—'

'Skye, I said I'll deal with it. I'm not a child and you are not my—'

He stopped short and Alex saw how Skye had held her breath. She was not his what? Fiancée?

'You are not my mother,' he said with forcible calm.

'I'm sorry. I was just trying to help,' she said in a quieter voice.

'And you have. You've been very . . . supportive. But I am fine. I just want everyone to stop fussing.'

She nodded. 'Okay.' She glanced briefly at Alex and managed a tiny smile. 'See you later.'

'Yes, see you,' Alex smiled back, feeling embarrassed on the one hand to have witnessed the spat. Intrigued on the other.

Skye slunk away and there was another silence, one which Alex didn't dare to break as she watched Lochlan watch her go. His defensive body language – jutted jaw, hunched shoulders, dropped head, small angry movements – warned her against saying a word and she pretended to concentrate on balling up another sheet of newspaper for the next window; there was absolutely no point in trying to work with him today; even she wasn't that bullish. It was clear he should still be resting and besides, Skye's appearance had popped his good mood and sent him back into his usual taciturn self.

Behind her, she heard the metallic tear of pills being popped from a packet and the agitated tapping of his keyboard.

'Jesus, mother of God,' he said under his breath a few moments later.

'What is it?' she asked, turning to find him watching something intently on his screen.

His eyes flashed up at her coldly. 'Nothing.'

The word was a rebuke and she turned back as he continued to mutter vicious expletives under his breath. After another minute, he angrily got up from the desk – but too quickly, prompting another coughing fit – and she stayed quiet as he gulped down the water. He hesitated before moving again and she could feel his resentment at his invalided state. And more besides.

'If anyone needs me, I'm going to inspect one of the old stores,' he said in a croaky voice.

'Okay,' she replied, thinking he should be sitting down; thinking he should put on a coat. But she carried on rubbing the glass panes as she watched him cross the snow-cleared cobbles and turn the corner out of sight, the hunch which had come to her before the fire beginning to grow into a potential plan now that she had seen first-hand his anger and frustration. Because for all that Skye had done for him, weeping in the ambulance and sitting by his bedside, at the end of the day she was still engaged to another man. And in just over a week's time, she'd be that other man's wife.

Lochlan Farquhar was running out of time and he knew it. He just didn't know what to do about it.

Sholto's arrival was not inconspicuous, the helicopter's jud-jud-jud-jud vibrating in her chest as it landed in the field between them and the chapel, all the staff stopping their chores to watch as the chairman leapt tentatively into the snow and ran in a crouch out of the downdraught. Alex heard several sarcastic mutterings – about his shiny shoes in the snow and his still-warm tan – before the crowd scattered, everyone running back to their posts and looking busy.

For a moment, she felt her own shot of panic at being seen by one of her clients dressed like this; but there was no way to avoid it. And these were exceptional circumstances, to say the least.

She was working on the final window when he popped his head in the door and she turned.

'Don't mind me, I'm just looking for Lochl—' He stopped dead. 'Alex?'

She smiled and walked over, shaking his hand. 'Sholto, how are you? I heard you'd be coming.'

'I barely recognized you!' he exclaimed.

'Well, cometh the hour . . .' she shrugged. 'It's been all hands to the pump the last couple of days.'

'Indeed, indeed, but I'm sure that didn't require you to get your hands dirty.'

'I've found it's best for morale if hierarchical divisions are blurred at times like these. And I must say, there's been a great sense of camaraderie amongst your staff. Everyone's really pulled together. You've got a very dynamic team here.'

'Under Torquil's strong leadership, I heard,' Sholto said knowingly. 'Apparently he was responsible for getting the stock moved from the dunnage warehouse in just a couple of hours?'

'Yes, he's been great. He's a natural leader. If only he was my client.' She rolled her eyes.

Sholto chuckled. 'If he was, I wouldn't need you!' He frowned. 'Where is Lochie, anyway? I heard he'd been released from hospital but I can't track him down.'

'He got back here about an hour ago. He's just inspecting an old storage unit.'

'And how does he seem?'

'Frail, although don't tell him I said that. He should still be resting.'

Sholto tutted. 'Another of his foolhardy moves, running into that fire. You've seen the headlines, I expect, painting him as some sort of have-a-go hero?'

'Yes.'

'God knows what he thought he was doing,' Sholto muttered.

'I heard he went in to decouple the dust collectors, to stop an explosion moving through the ducting systems and taking out the rest of the distillery. All things considered, we might be wise to consider this one of his finer moments,' she said generously.

'But imagine if he'd been killed. Imagine the headlines then. We'd probably have been closed down on some Health and Safety point because of it and all those people's jobs would have been lost. There are trained professionals to deal with that kind of thing.'

'You're right, of course.'

He sighed. 'I doubt he'll have learnt any lessons from it, though. I expect he'll continue in the same vein as before, thinking he's untouchable and unaccountable.'

Alex, feeling inexplicably defensive of Lochlan for once, decided not to say anything further as Sholto came deeper into the room and perched on the end of the desk. Whether or not Lochlan's actions had been correct or brave or justified was beside the point.

'Where did you say he's gone again?'

'Something to do with inspecting an old storage unit, he said.'

'So then we're at liberty to talk freely for a few moments?'

'I should think so.'

'Tell me, how's it going? I've been eager to know but as I mentioned at our meeting in Edinburgh, I think the less contact between you and me, probably the better.'

'I have to agree. Lochlan has been incredibly resistant to the idea of even talking to me, much less working with me, and I think it's partly because he feels that as you hired me, I must be in the enemy camp.'

'Mmm. I can't say it surprises me. He's a stubborn beggar. Probably doesn't help that you're a woman either.'

Alex wondered whether that was strictly true – had her being a woman stopped him from ejecting her from his office? Or would he simply have thrown her further if she'd been a man?

'So, you've not had much luck then?'

'Not much, I'll be honest. I did think I was beginning to make *some* headway with him earlier in the week, but I'm afraid with the fire intervening I've most likely lost that little momentum now. And even if I haven't, I'm not sure when he'll be well enough to sit down and work with me. He inhaled a lot of smoke.'

Sholto looked concerned – though not by the report of Lochlan's health. 'Can you still meet the target?'

She inhaled deeply, thinking over the events of the past few days, even the last hour: Skye's fretting over him, Lochlan's frustration that she remained off limits . . . Increasingly she was beginning to think that his former fiancée was his only area of vulnerability, in which case, did this business problem have a personal solution? Could the fire have opened their eyes to their true feelings for one other? Could it even have hastened things along a little? 'I think so.'

'You think so?' Sholto echoed sceptically.

'I'm quietly confident—'

'Confident about what?' Lochlan asked, suddenly appearing at the door and stopping at the sight of Sholto on his desk.

'Ah, Lochie,' Sholto said, rising and walking over to him. 'Miss Hyde here was just telling me she's confident you'll be up on your feet again in no time. Is that true? We need to find a way to get back into production before Christmas.'

'Before Christmas? Christ, that's punchy,' Lochlan laughed mirthlessly. 'In case you're not up to speed, we lost all the malt stores in the fire so that's a two-week time lag even if we got a new delivery in the steeps today – which we won't because the lead in the steeps buckled in the heat so we need new ones to be cast first. And then of course there's the small issue of the barley loft being completely destroyed so there's nowhere to actually *do* the malting,' he added with no small amount of sarcasm.

Sholto shot him a stern look and there was a long pause as they waited for him to calm down.

Lochlan – so ready to anger – took a deep breath and put his hands on his hips. 'However, I've just scouted one of the old hay units,' he said in a more conciliatory tone. 'It's not really big enough but it's not like we've got any other options: the floor's sound and it's well ventilated. It wouldn't take much to get it cleaned up and fitted out; and if I can get the copper shop to knock us up some new steeps, the best-case scenario would mean we could get a first batch in by next week – that could then steep over the festive break and it'd be ready to go in the kilns straight after New Year.'

'But that's still three weeks from now,' Sholto said with a tut.

'Well, what else do you suggest we do?' Lochlan replied, impatient again. 'It wasn't like the fire was planned. None of us saw this coming.'

'And what has it exposed? That we have no backup, no contingency. This simply highlights the case that I've been making for years now, that the site is too small. We don't have enough stores.'

'And as I've been telling you, there's no point in having

more stores if we can't fill them. We are hamstrung by our peat stocks. That peat is what makes Kentallen unique. We can't ship it in; we can't replicate it. I'm no happier about it than you are but the facts are the facts: our greatest strength is also our greatest limitation. When will you accept that we can be small and still be the best?'

'And when will you accept that there's not just profit in consolidation but security too? Something like this would never have happened if we—'

'What?' Lochlan snapped. 'Sold out?'

Sholto's cheeks flamed. 'The site is too small, the buildings too old and the technology inadequate,' he said in an ominously quiet voice. 'We have to move with the times. I would have thought that you – as a young man – would see that more than me.'

'Oh, I do. I see that diversification is the answer, not consolidation. We can grow and still be our own masters.'

'How? With what?' Sholto scoffed. 'We don't even have the money to get the bloody CCTV working!'

'You know how. Reinvest the profits.'

Sholto held his hand up. 'Stop right there. The proposal was unequivocally thrown out.'

'Not unequivocally. Bruce supported it. And I think Mhairi could be convinced . . .'

Alex, watching the dynamic closely, saw Lochlan's jaw pulse: he was barely keeping his temper in check. That anger, always there.

There was a knock at the door behind Lochlan.

'Yes?' he asked, whirling round, his expression changing as he saw it was Skye again. 'Oh, for Christ's sa— Look, I've taken them,' he snapped, shaking the pill packet at her.

'It's not that,' Skye said, looking startled. Hurt. 'Dad's asked if you can join him by the rack warehouse.' She looked at Sholto. 'All of you.'

'What, *now*?' Lochlan asked, clearly eager to get back to his argument.

'He says it's urgent.'

At Sholto's insistence – no doubt to use her as a buffer between him and his combustible CEO – Alex was obliged to join them. They walked across the courtyard past the canteen and the copper shop, to the warehouse, where the barrels had been restacked outside the night of the fire. Fresh snow had settled on top of the tarpaulins that had been cloaked over them, and Torquil was already there, talking to Bruce.

'Sholto,' Bruce said, shaking his hand as the men met. 'How are things?'

'You mean, apart from the obvious?'

'Och well, aye . . .' Bruce murmured, his gaze snagging on Alex in her worker's uniform.

'You've met Miss Hyde, I assume?' Sholto asked courteously.

'Of course. She put us all to shame on the shoot last weekend. Although I barely recognized you, I must say,' he said with a smile.

Alex looked down at the worker's uniform and her bare arms, suddenly feeling the cold. It had been fine when she'd been working up a sweat in the office, but standing here in the softly falling snow, she gave a shiver. She wouldn't be able to stand out here for long. 'Admittedly, I don't usually go undercover. I do prefer to wear my own clothes,' she smiled.

Lochlan gave a derisive snort and she shot him a look – although perhaps he had a point.

'Well, thanks for coming. I'll make it quick seeing as it's perishing. Do you want the good news first or the bad?' Bruce asked, rubbing his hands together briskly as the snow continued to flutter and they all lightly stamped their feet.

'More bad news?' Sholto asked grimly. 'Haven't we had our share?'

'I'm afraid it's all connected.'

'Let's lead with the bad then. Get it out of the way.'

'Well, as we feared, the fire *has* affected some of the stock. I'm afraid the first few batches we've sampled of the seven-year-old virgin oak casks have shown fizzing upon pouring.' He sighed. 'Now, they were at the very back of the warehouse, closest to the fire, so this could be as bad as it gets, but worst-case scenario? The whole lot could be unusable.'

Lochlan winced, physically turning away and planting his hands on his hips, and Alex remembered what Torquil had told her about their upcoming stock squeeze six years from now: someone a generation back had miscalculated and numbers were tight enough as it was, without a fire depleting the rest of their reserves. These virgin oak casks – though doing well for some other brands – had been a new and untried category for Kentallen, but Torquil had told her it had been their only chance at riding out this supply crisis.

'But look, we knew they might be the worst affected,' Bruce said, trying to mollify. 'Everything else was thankfully sufficiently far from the blaze at that point as to not suffer too great a change in temperature, and the snow has helped to dissipate the smoke stench in the dunnage; I'm hopeful that if we can start getting the casks back into the dunnage in the next few days and regulate temperatures again, no lasting damage will have been done to the rest.'

'But the seven is our cash cow – lower price point, easier palate,' Lochie said abruptly. 'She's bringing in the new business, she's where we need the numbers as we come up to the shortfall.'

'Aye, and it's a blow. But the good news I've got for you may actually compensate for it. In fact, in a funny way, the fire may just have done us a favour.'

'You think?' Lochlan muttered sarcastically, one arm in the air indicating the charred wreckage behind them.

'In all the reshuffling that night, we unearthed a few barrels of a malt which was in the furthest corner from the fire. It was buried right away behind the '67s, deliberately hidden behind a wooden board. Unless you knew it was there, you couldn't see it.'

'And what is it?' Lochlan asked.

'That's just it – we don't know. It wasn't on the inventory system and never has been, as far as we can tell. No one's ever seen it and there's no record of it. I certainly had no idea about it and I've been here almost fifty years.'

There was a brief pause.

'What are you saying, Bruce?' Sholto frowned. 'That we have a malt no one knew about?'

Bruce grinned, rubbing his hands together vigorously and not just because of the cold this time. 'Aye, exactly that. I'm saying we've hit on the holy grail – a hidden malt. An eighty-five-year-old hidden malt.'

'Eighty-five . . . ?' Torquil spluttered as an audible gasp went round.

Alex looked around the group: they were all open-mouthed whilst Skye was grinning from ear to ear. Clearly, this was a big deal.

'But . . . the angels' share,' Torquil spluttered. 'Surely there's nothing left.'

'That's what we thought too. But all I can say is your grandfather must have had an excellent cooper back then. Not to mention, the particular area where it was sitting on the earth in the dunnage was damp – we think there must be a water source close by. Either way, it's meant it created a little humidity pocket which slowed down the rate of evaporation. We need to look into it more closely, but our estimates at the moment are that we'd have enough for sixty, maybe sixty-five bottles.'

'Of an eighty-five-year-old malt,' Sholto breathed, saying the words over and over and looking as though he'd been hypnotized. 'What's the oldest that's gone to market?'

'The Mortlach seventy-year-old Speyside,' Lochlan said without hesitation. 'Fifty-four bottles at ten grand each and a hundred and sixty-two smaller bottles at two and a half.'

'Worth considering,' Torquil nodded, locking eye contact with his cousin and nodding intently, both clearly on the same wavelength for once. 'More at a lower price point opens up the market.'

'We should have new bottles designed for it,' Lochlan replied. 'It's going to generate massive interest when it comes out – it needs to be special. In fact, I had an idea a while back for the upcoming private reserve sixty to have its labels punched from copper but it would be even better suited on this.'

'Ho!' Sholto held up his hands. 'Let's not get ahead of ourselves, gentlemen. This must be strictly confidential until the say-so. There can't be any talk of limited-edition bottles and special labels. It's bad enough having the press still crawling about the place; if the wrong ears were to get wind of this, we'd have people robbing us in the night.' He turned to face their master blender. 'And besides, the most pertinent question of all has not yet been asked. Have you drawn any off yet, Bruce? How does it actually taste?'

Bruce shook his head. 'I thought we should do that together. It'll be a special moment.'

'We hope,' Torquil said cautiously. 'What if it's gone too far?'

'Well, there's only one way to find out. I'm going to get these barrels moved over to the sampling lab; security's tightest there and we certainly can't leaving them sitting out here. Shall we all reconvene there at eight tonight? I realize it's late but it's best to be cautious and let everyone go home first; we don't want a crowd.'

'Quite right,' Sholto nodded. 'Eight it is, everybody.'

The group dispersed, all of them walking away with decidedly more spring in their steps than when they'd arrived.

'A hidden malt, huh?' Alex asked, going over to Skye and walking alongside her. 'It even sounds exciting. I imagine this is a blender's dream come true, isn't it?'

'God yes, as Dad said, it's the holy grail for any distillery. I've heard of hidden malts before, of course, but usually they've been deliberately hidden when a master blender hasn't wanted them to be used in a blend, when he considers a malt to be too good for that.'

Alex wrinkled her nose in confusion. 'But . . . Kentallen doesn't produce blends.'

'Aye. And we don't let anyone use our malts for their blends either.'

Alex stopped walking. 'So then why would it have been hidden?'

'I've got no idea,' Skye shrugged. 'But Grandad must have been up to something. He taught Dad everything about Kentallen; Dad could identify every vintage in here blindfolded. It's inconceivable that one could have been hidden all this time and he not know about it. It must have been put away for a damned good reason.'

'But if your father didn't know *his* father had hidden it, we'll probably never know what that reason was.'

Skye nodded and gave a hapless shrug. 'No. I guess not. But if it tastes as good as it should do, after eighty-five years –' her eyes gleamed excitedly – 'who really cares?'

Chapter Fourteen

She could smell the coal smoke long before she reached the house, or could even see it from the moor. She pulled off her boots with her feet and left them in the porch, returning to the small box on the windowsill the snowy bobble hat and home-made scarf that Mrs Peggie had loaned her 'for the duration'. Burberry it wasn't, but Alex found she rather liked its homespun charm. Hanging her coat on the peg in the hall, she glanced through to the dining room and kitchen; but the voices came from her right.

'Hello?' she smiled wanly, seeing Mrs Peggie through the open crack of the sitting-room door and popping her head through.

'Miss Hyde, you're back.' Mrs Peggie was sitting in her husband's wing chair, the fire flickering nicely, boxes scattered at her feet. A small Christmas tree had been put up in the corner; it must have been freshly cut for it still smelled of the outdoors – peat and pine fragrancing the little room and mingling with the alder coal smoke.

'I am,' Alex nodded. It didn't matter how many times she asked Mrs Peggie to call her Alex, she accepted now that she never would.

'Would you like a wee cup of tea?'

'That would be lovely. But I'll get it.'

'No, no, you come in and warm up, you look perished. I need to check on the beef anyway. I take it the snow's falling again?' the older woman asked, taking the box off her lap and setting it down on the low coffee table to her side. She pushed herself to standing with a groan.

'Yes, pretty hard. Here, do you need a hand?' Alex asked, coming further into the room and holding out a hand to pull her up.

'Och, you're kind. It's dashed annoying being so stiff.'

'You put people half your age to shame.'

'Well, my foot's playing up so I thought I may as well take advantage of a quiet house, rest it and get on with sorting out these boxes.'

'You look very busy. Sifting through that lot will take hours, surely.'

'Aye,' Mrs Peggie sighed with a weary shake of her head. 'You take a seat and make yourself comfortable while I go and get us some tea. Feel free to have a look if you like.'

'What is it?'

'Mr P.'s father's boxes. For the museum. I reckon if he can't make a start, I will. Though it's awful haunting to read some of it. I'm beginning to wonder if this isn't why he's been putting it off.' She tutted, sadness in her eyes. 'Just terrible what those poor families went through.'

And with a shake of her head, she left the room.

Alex wandered over to the small two-seater fringed sofa and looked down at the boxes. There were three large ones and several more shallow ones. Tentatively, not at all sure she did want to see any of it if it really was that upsetting, she flipped the lid of the nearest box.

A small navy leather book lay on the top of a heap of

papers. She reached for it and opened it, her eyes skimming the first entries:

'*Logbook: Sergeant James Peggie; 156795*' had been written in brown ink.

6TH FEBRUARY 1918

Physical description: White male. Weight 10st 2lbs. Height 5ft 9 ½. Estimated age 18–25. Light brown hair. Brown eyes.
Clothing: One black leather boot (left foot); tan trousers.
Identifying features: Moustache. Gold tooth (right molar). Kidney-shaped mole on the upper left arm. 1-inch scar on the left knee.
Injuries: Right side skull fracture. Broken nose. Multiple lacerations to both cheeks. Upper front teeth missing. Broken right arm. Broken fingers, right hand.
Suspected cause of death: Blunt force trauma to the head.

Physical description: White male. Weight 13st 4lbs. Height 6ft. Estimated age 18–25. Dark blond hair. Green eyes.
Clothing: White vest. White underpants.
Identifying features: Tattoo: 'Mary' on inner right bicep. Appendix scar on abdomen.
Injuries: Compound fracture to right thigh.
Suspected cause of death: Drowning.

Physical description: Black male. Weight 13st 9lbs. Height 5ft 11 ½. Estimated age 18–25. Black hair. Brown eyes.
Clothing: None.
Identifying features: Tattoos: Black swallow above left shoulder blade; barbed wire around right wrist; large jaguar inked on the lower back.
Injuries: Left leg missing.
Suspected cause of death: Blood loss.

She frowned, her eyes moving faster over the words: *'Drowning . . . bone crushed . . . 4-inch scar . . . internal trauma . . . 19 . . . broken neck . . .'*

Alex closed the book decisively. No. She didn't want to read that. Not today. Not ever. There was enough ugliness in the world and she was still shaken from the fire. She hadn't slept well since and it had turned a key deep inside her, the one she always kept locked.

She reached down into the box again, pulling up a mustard-coloured card folder; inside was a sheaf of papers. Letters.

February 12th, 1918

Dear Sgt Peggie,

I have been given your name by the war department regarding the sinking of SS Tuscania *just off the shores of Islay. I am the mother of Private Harold Cooperson. He is eighteen years old and my eldest boy. He is six feet tall and last weighed 156lbs. His hair is light brown, like a thrush's back, and everybody always says he has such a handsome, strong jaw. His eyes are dark brown and he has freckles over his nose, but not the cheeks. He doesn't have any birthmarks, but he does have a long scar above his right knee from where he fell against a saw in his father's mill, when he was eleven. He's such a distinctive man, I'm sure you must know who I mean? We pray his injuries are not severe and that you will be able to communicate our love and concern to him. Everyone at home calls him Harry so if you could please call him by that name, I'd be much obliged? It might make him feel a little more at home. I know he looks big but he only graduated high school in the summer and before he signed up, he'd never spent a night away from home.*

We send our deepest thanks to you and your townsfolk; we have

*heard of your rescue efforts and all you have done for our boys, and
pray our son is the happy recipient of your beneficence. If you were
able to put our minds at rest and write back as to his welfare, we
would be for ever indebted.*

Sincerely yours,

Kathleen Cooperson

Alex pressed her fingers to her lips as she saw the nota-
tion that had been added to the bottom of the letter in that
brown-inked neat cursive: *'Drowned. Body washed ashore 6th
February. Mother notified by letter 14th February. Gold watch
returned. JP.'*

February 12th, 1918

Sir,

Word of the SS Tuscania *disaster has reached American shores
and I write to you in the hope that you may set my mind at rest as
to the welfare of my husband, Lieutenant John Grantley. He is a
squadron leader for the Sixth battalion, 20th Engineers and is a tall,
strong man – twenty-nine years of age, 177lbs, six feet two inches
tall. His hair is blond, his eyes are blue and he has a rose tattoo on
his right shoulder. He holds himself very well when he walks and he
will look you in the eye when talking to you. His favourite song is
'Delilah' and our daughter, Ella, beseeches me to send on her great
affection for him.*

*It would give me great comfort to hear from you and know for
certain that my husband is safe and well and recovering in the great
care of Islay's people.*

Faithfully yours,

Mrs Lavender Grantley

Note: Safely offloaded to HMS Pigeon. *Taken to Buncrana, Co. Donegal, Ireland; transferred to Wiltshire Best camp on 13th February. Mother notified 16th February. JP.*

Alex sank against the cushion as she flicked back and saw that the letters kept coming – and in all of them, a tangible despair marbled with the vain and desperate hope of these poor women, thousands of miles from their husbands and sons fighting in a European war.

In spite of herself, she read on.

February 11th, 1918

Kind Sir,

I have been supplied your name in my efforts to track the well-being of my son Private Edward Cobb. He is just nineteen years old and my only child. He signed up on December the 22nd, 1917 and marched not a week later to Camp Washington in order to serve his country on this mission. Though he is a timberman by trade, he is proud to call himself a soldier and felt an urgent need to prove himself in the fighting fields of France. But I have heard the reports of his troopship being sunk by the Germans and now I must ask – did he even make it that far?

I feel sure you will recognize him from this description for he is a noteworthy and handsome young man: five foot ten, slight build, approximately 169lbs. He is pale-skinned with dark brown hair and hazel-green eyes and a bewitching smile. You will notice there is a gap between his two front teeth but it is a charming flaw and he certainly has the easy manner to go with it. He is earnest and kind, humble and respectful; to know him is to love him, for sure.

I have sent with this letter his boyhood bear Berry. I realize how this might look – a soldier, being sent a toy. Indeed, he would not take it with him to Camp Washington, saying his pack had to be light, but I cannot help myself – if he is injured I know, in the way that only a mother can, that it will comfort him and raise his spirits to have a little piece of home by his side.

I pray you have him on your beautiful isle and that he is safe and well in your care. Any tokens you could offer as to his well-being would by deeply appreciated, as I'm sure you can imagine.

Yours, in humble thanks,
Dorothy Cobb

Note: Found washed ashore by town rescuers 6th February. Broken leg. Multiple fractures. Serious case of influenza. Transferred to Islay House for recuperation. Contents of letter: one toy bear with orange glass eyes. Mother notified 9th February. JP.

February 17th, 1918

Kind Sir,
I trust that this letter reaches you swiftly and that you can bring a conclusion to the agonies we are suffering here, after learning of the—

'Well, Mr P. was right again,' Mrs Peggie said, coming back in and setting down a tray on the small pouffe. 'It looks like we're going to be sitting pretty for a couple of days or so.'

Alex looked up in alarm. 'What?'

Mrs Peggie handed her a cup of tea. 'The weather's setting in again. The drifts are already deep in some parts and much of the road is impassable down to the town. It's as well you're no trying to get to Kentallen.' Mrs Peggie sighed. 'Och. And to think you arrived in a storm too. You've no had much luck with the weather here.'

'No.' She frowned. 'What's the *Tuscania*?'

Mrs Peggie's expression changed. 'That was the name of the ship that went down in these waters. SS *Tuscania*. So many boys on it.'

Alex saw the dates. February 1918. 'They were soldiers?'

'Aye, American lads. Sailed all the way from New York in terrible weather, only to be hit out there, seven miles away in the Channel. Many of them never even got to set foot on Europe's shores.'

'What happened? Was there a storm?'

'The Germans,' Mrs Peggie said with pursed lips. 'They fired a torpedo from one of their U-boats and sank it.'

Alex winced. 'Did anyone survive?'

'More than should have done. There were over two thousand two hundred troops on board and it was only two hundred or so that perished – and mostly they were the ones who panicked and jumped too soon, straight into the sea, or overcrowded the lifeboats. As if that wasn't bad enough, there were terrible gales too that night. Just like now, in fact.' Alex looked out of the window to see the snowflakes, so tame just an hour ago, beginning to dance wildly against the panes. 'Most of the men were picked up by our destroyers on patrol and taken to Ireland but those that perished . . .' She was quiet for a moment. 'Their bodies were washed up on the beaches here. And the men who thought they were safe in the lifeboats were dashed upon the rocks. It was as terrible a day as ever there will be in Islay.'

'That's just awful.'

'It was. It fell to the poor islanders to retrieve the bodies, bury them . . . They did manage to rescue some survivors, but not many.'

Alex frowned, trying to think back. 'Wait – is this the

wreck you were telling me about? The one your American guest's grandfather was on? He does the dives?'

'Aye, that's the one. And he's not the only member of his family to have come here to pay his respects. His grand-mother – the widow – she came over as part of the Gold Star Pilgrimage in 1932, to see where her husband perished.'

'The Gold Star Pilgrimage?' Alex echoed, as Mrs Peggie came and sat on the sofa beside her. 'I've never even heard of that. What is it?'

'It was a state-sponsored trip organized by the American government for all the mothers and un-remarried widows of American soldiers killed in the line of duty in the Great War, so that they could see where their loved ones had fallen. All their expenses were paid – the ship over, hotels, food. They even arranged for chairs to be put beside the graves so that they could sit without tiring. And they took a photograph of each woman beside her loved one's grave which she could take back home with her – because remember, these were the days when you couldn't just . . . photograph your toast, or whatever it is you young folk do these days. A photograph meant something.'

'That's amazing that they did that – the US government, I mean. Nothing like that would ever happen now.'

'No, but then there's no honour in war these days. All this fundamentalism and extremism . . . it's just barbarity.'

She was looking upset so Alex let the subject drop.

Mrs Peggie rifled through the box again, pulling out a wad of small, no more than five-by-three-inch black-and-white photographs. 'Ah, now that's more like it.'

Heads bent together, their eyes grazed the photographs as Mrs Peggie passed them over to her, one at a time, giving a commentary on the black-and-whites of people long since dead, wearing fashions of petticoats and cloche hats, boots and tweed coats. They were a jumbled mix of different dates and scenes: Alex saw the old General Stores in Port Ellen, now the Co-op, but the modern sign above the door was the only tangible change; she saw small, rigged fishing boats moored alongside the quay, a photo of a couple of fishermen in heavy jumpers and caps, one of them puffing on a pipe as they mended their nets. Some of the photos had names, places or dates ascribed below them, others were left blank. There was a picture of the school house, maybe fifteen children gathered in an orderly group in the playground, tunics to their knees; she saw a young woman holding the hand of a child outside a church, her hair set in Charleston waves beneath a felt hat.

There were agricultural scenes – men working in the barley fields, one farmer guiding the cattle down the lane with a long prod, a group of workers burning the peat – women picnicking in a field, a game of cricket on the beach, a donkey nodding over a garden gate, a graveyard scene with a crowd in shirtsleeves and guns pointed to the sky . . . It was a remarkable history of the island, of its people. She saw some of the same faces several times.

'Is that the distillery?' Alex asked, holding up a black-and-white photograph of the distinctive maltings and the pagoda-topped still house.

'Aye, and . . . That's *my* father there, second from the right.'

Alex examined the image – five men were standing in the courtyard where the copper still now sat so decoratively, four of them in rolled-up shirtsleeves and knitted tanks, shovels held in front of them like ceremonial swords, the man in the middle in a wide-shouldered dark suit.

'And the one in the middle is Archibald Farquhar, the eldest of the founding brothers of Kentallen whisky. He was Sholto's grandfather – and Lochie's great-great-uncle.'

'I think I can see a bit of a resemblance,' she said, taking in the reserved expression and intense eyes, able to glimpse her taciturn client in his ancestor even three generations back. 'It's amazing, it really doesn't look like much has changed at all,' she said, her eyes taking in the familiar layout: only the loss of the maltings, so recently destroyed in the fire, now separated the skyline in the photograph from the one still standing two miles down the road from here. 'I mean, I know the technology has been upgraded but in terms of the actual buildings and the landscape around it, it's exactly the same.'

Mrs Peggie picked up the next photo and Alex saw Islay House, recognizing the broad sweep of steps and the gravel drive where they had drunk coffee before the shoot and she had introduced herself to Torquil. There were several shots of the house taken from the grounds, florid rhododendrons in full flower, a couple of Gordon setters sitting majestically on the lawns at the foot of a man in tweed breeks and Norfolk shooting jacket; she saw a young woman sitting on a terrace in a hooded wicker chair, a man of similar age sitting beside her with a bandage around his head and a vacant look in his eyes. Then they came to a later photo – Mrs Peggie's wedding day – and Alex saw that she had made a lovely bride with a slim, wiry figure in cotton lace and a bunch of heather in her hands, her cheeks fuller then but the set of her jaw as purposeful and resolute as it was now; Mr Peggie, though shorter than his wife, had stood broad-chested on the church steps in his best suit, his hand proudly over hers and his shoes polished to a high shine that matched his eyes.

She saw a group of nurses standing beside their patients in dressing gowns and pyjamas. It didn't look like a typical hospital on account of a large oil portrait hanging from wires on the wall behind them and a grand fireplace poking into the corner of the image. The patients – all men – looked thin and pale, their eyes slightly too big in their sockets, but their smiles were genuine enough. One had his leg in plaster and a teddy bear comically tucked under one arm.

Alex felt her eye drawn to him. To them. For he and his nurse had smiles wider than the rest, as though sharing a joke no one else was in on. She didn't think it was the comedy effect of the bear. She held the photo closer and realized the woman looked familiar. Had she seen her somewhere else?

'Who is this, do you know?' she asked, holding up the photograph and showing it to Mrs Peggie.

The old lady squinted. 'Aye, that's Miss Clarissa. Clarissa Farquhar. Archie's sister – and Lochlan's great-grandmother. She was quite the beauty.'

'Clarissa Farquhar,' Alex echoed. She quickly flicked back through the photographs in her hand, stopping as she found the one of the young woman holding a child's hand outside the church. 'That's her there too, isn't it?'

'That's right. With her son George. She adopted him after the war.'

Alex looked at her. 'Adopted?'

'Aye. There were so many poor wee orphans after the war ended. Her own fiancé – Phillip Robertson I think was his name, he was from another of the important families – he had been killed early on in the war and I think she believed she would never marry; she must have felt it was her only chance to become a mother. After all, so many of the young men had left for war and precious few returned. Archie came back unscathed but the younger Farquhar boy, Percy, was one of the fallen. Their mother never recovered from it.'

'God, no. How would you?' Alex asked, feeling drained. She knew all too well that no mother every fully recovered from that loss. She looked back at the picture taken in the hospital. 'So is that Clarissa's fiancé in the picture?'

Mrs Peggie looked at it more closely. 'No. I believe those men are the American soldiers that survived the *Tuscania*.'

'Looks like this poor chap broke his leg.'

Mrs Peggie peered at it again carefully. 'Yes, probably when he was thrown onto the rocks. In fact, if I'm remembering correctly, *she* was the one who found him,' she said, pointing to Clarissa.

'Really?' Alex asked interestedly.

'Yes, that's right,' Mrs Peggie said, rembering now. 'Everyone said it was a miracle. No one knew how he survived it – being out there in those conditions all night; especially since he was already half dead with the Spanish flu before he even hit the water.'

'The Spanish flu?'

'Surely you know about that? It was a terrible epidemic in 1918 and 1919 – as if life wasn't bad enough! It just decimated the troops. Mr P. tells me more American soldiers were killed by that than by enemy action.' She tutted, looking back at the photo. 'Aye, everyone knows of that poor fellow – he was ill for weeks; stayed long after his comrades were sent on to England. He wasn't expected to pull through but Miss Clarissa didn't leave his side. She was just determined he would survive.'

'Wow, so . . . he got off a torpedoed boat, was thrown onto the rocks, broke his leg, survived exposure, and pulled through from Spanish flu? He sounds the luckiest man alive.'

'Not that lucky. He stayed here for four months, recovering. But as soon as his leg was mended, he was sent to France and killed nine days later.'

'Oh God.' Alex's jaw dropped open. 'That's so awful.'

'Everyone here was deeply upset when they heard. My mother spoke of it often. She said he had made many friends during his recuperation and was fondly remembered by the folks round here.'

Alex looked back at the photograph. 'Clarissa must have taken it really badly, surely, having saved his life and nursed him back to health?'

'Aye. She became very reclusive after that. I think it was too much after losing her sweetheart and brother as well.'

'That's understandable. I suppose it must be awful to be the one who keeps being left.'

'I suppose so, yes. She left the island for a time. I think it was too painful for her to stay in a place where no one ever came back.'

Alex sipped her tea. 'But she came back eventually?'

'Aye, when she adopted the boy, she came back to her roots. After all, there's no place like home, is there?'

Alex suppressed the shiver that ran up her spine. There was certainly no place like *her* home. 'Exactly so,' she murmured. 'No place at all.'

Chapter Fifteen

Twenty-four. Twenty-five. Twenty-six . . .

She burst up through the water, panting but feeling clean at least. She dropped her head back against the salmon bath, her stiff muscles softening at last in the Epsom salts, and examined her toenails. Ordinarily she would be due a pedicure this weekend but clearly that wasn't going to happen. Would the polish hold for another week? she wondered, looking for chips.

The knock at the front door made her jerk in the water and stare at the wall in alarm. What time was it? She and Mrs Peggie had been looking at the photos downstairs for well over an hour, but she hadn't been up here for long; surely she had more time? She stretched over to check her phone on the wicker laundry basket, water drops splashing all over the floor. Seven forty. She frowned, certain he'd said he'd collect her at eight.

Scrambling out of the water, she had just wrapped the fresh lilac bath towel around her when she heard Mrs Peggie's distinctive voice at the bottom of the stairs. 'Miss Hyde?'

Alex stepped out of the bathroom. 'Yes?'

'You have a gentleman visitor.'

'Dammit,' she hissed below her breath, feeling a growing sense of panic. 'Er . . . I'm not ready. Could you tell him he's early?' Didn't he know it was rude to show up before time?

There was a pause and then . . .

'You're early,' she heard Mrs Peggie say in a prim voice.

'No, I'm not. We need to be there for eight,' replied a hoarse one.

Alex straightened up. What? She tiptoed down the corridor and peered her head round the corner. She looked down the stairs – just as Lochlan looked straight up.

'Oh!' she said, recoiling quickly and holding the towel even tighter, wondering what to do next. She wanted to stay hiding behind this wall, but that would be farcical; besides, she wasn't showing anything in this towel besides her shoulders and legs; strangers saw more on the beach. With a deep breath, she came downstairs, her most dignified smile on her face. Mrs Peggie made a discreet exit, but not before looking mildly scandalized by Alex's attire.

'Lochlan, I wasn't expecting you.'

'Why not? Bruce asked us all to meet at eight.' He appeared not to notice that she was wearing just a towel and to her surprise, she felt mildly offended by the fact.

'Bruce?'

His eyebrows hitched. 'The tasting? The potentially most exciting discovery in the company's history?'

Alex's jaw dropped. 'You expected me to go?'

'Well, he did say "everyone".'

'Yes, but he wasn't including *me*. I'm not . . . I'm not a connoisseur of whisky.'

The look that came into his eyes then told her he was remembering that she had at least been an enthusiastic amateur the week before. 'Well, trust me, you'll know this one's good.' His eyes caught on something. 'Is that . . . my *suit*?' he asked incredulously, taking a step back and fingering the dark grey wool flannel currently dangling from a hanger on a coat hook in the porch.

'Oh . . . yes,' she said, shivering a little as a slice of wind whistled in through a cracked window.

He looked back at her. 'Please don't tell me you're wearing my clothes too now.'

The quip made her laugh out loud. He could be very amusing when it suited him. 'No! I brought it back here to air after the fire. It's probably . . .' she leaned forward to sniff it, grazing him slightly as she did. 'Yes, it's almost gone now. The smoke smell, I mean,' she added, noticing he was looking at her strangely. 'I . . . I brought your shoes back too, and your trainers,' she said, pointing to them with one foot but inadvertently highlighting her bare legs.

It was a moment before he replied. 'Very thoughtful of you, Hyde.'

'Well, you ran into a burning building. I saved your shoes. I thought it was the least I could do,' she quipped with a lackadaisical shrug that she hoped covered up more of her awkwardness than the dratted towel.

There was a pause, his look growing impatient. 'Well, what are you waiting for? You'd better hurry up and get dressed.'

'I'm really sorry,' she sighed. 'Of course I'd have come if I'd known . . . but I can't make it.'

'What do you mean you "can't make it"?' he asked, in a tone that implied her words didn't make sense. It was a Thursday night on the isle of Islay. How much could there be to do?

'I've got plans.'

'So, then, change them. This is a once-in-a-lifetime opportunity.'

'I can't.'

His eyes darkened. 'What could you possibly be doing that's so important you can't ditch it for this?'

'Knock, knock, anybody home?' a voice called from the path outside. The door – pushed to – was opened gently and a blond head peered round. 'Wahey!' Callum beamed, taking in the sight of her in her towel.

Alex pulled it tighter again. 'For God's sake,' she muttered under her breath.

'Oh hi, cuz, how's it going?' Callum asked, stepping fully into the porch and finding Lochlan glowering behind the door. 'Thought I recognized the wheels outside. What are you doing here?'

There was a silence as Lochlan glanced over at her, an anger in his eyes she couldn't explain.

'I came to pick these up,' he said finally, reaching for the suit and scooping the shoes off the floor – only to prompt another coughing fit.

'You do not sound good, Lochie,' Callum said, managing simultaneously to frown and smile. 'Sure you shouldn't still be resting up?'

'I'm fine,' Lochlan muttered, looking anything but. 'See you tomorrow.' And with his eyes on the floor, he stalked from the porch, his suit slung over his shoulder.

Callum gave a shrug. 'So,' he said, turning to her, delight in his eyes. '*Please* tell me you're coming out dressed like that.'

*

He was good company, she'd give him that. And surprisingly well read. Plus, he actually seemed to listen to her, which wasn't what she'd anticipated at all.

The pub he'd brought her to – the Stag – was cosy to the point of cuddly: giant and ancient stone flags blackened with age clad the floor; the walls were painted a deep Prussian blue and a lively fire in the corner threw out a beautiful amber light. Outside, by the path, a fir tree had been dressed in white fairy lights, from the glow of which she had just been able to make out the low stone building's grassed roof. It was a 'black house', Callum had explained as he'd taken her arm ('in case of ice'), leading her into the warmth.

The Stag was primarily a drinker's pub, with a bar at the back and a mix of battered leather chesterfields and tweed armchairs in various groupings in the middle of the floor; tall-backed wooden booths flanked the perimeter of the room and were so small and intimate as to make the knocking of their knees against one another unavoidable and Alex had quickly taken to sitting at an angle.

The journey over had been relaxed. Callum was easy company and whilst she brooded over the calamity of Lochlan's unexpected arrival – what had he been thinking? Even if she had been planning to attend the tasting, they had never discussed him collecting her – he navigated the icy roads with a local's ease. The half-moon light was dim, the snow clouds still sitting heavily above the isle, as they had quickly tracked away from the coast, taking her into countryside she hadn't even begun to explore on her runs: she sat, hypnotized, as the full beam of Callum's smart Audi R8 swung with every turn to pull from the darkness a fairytale-like pine forest or a heather-clad moor. They'd only passed a few hamlets and the occasional lone croft, so when she saw just one booth was free, it was a wonder to her as to where all these people had come from. 'You always have to book,' Callum had said as they'd taken in the sight from the door.

'Come here a lot then, do you?' she'd asked, rather more tartly than she'd intended, but if he'd caught the gist of her dig, he didn't show it.

They'd ordered Old Fashioneds – with Callum specifying the Kentallen 15 for theirs – and he had gone for the venison stew, whilst she'd been very pleased with her black truffle risotto.

Now they were back on the whiskies again, this time just a finger of the amber nectar, and Alex was feeling very relaxed; she was well fed and warm in the drowsy heat of the fire and enjoying the Christmas carols that were on low at the bar. Sitting side-on in her booth, her legs outstretched on the bench, she was watching Callum as he regaled her with a tale about boarding-school antics – lowering a stash of Jaffa Cake biscuits to his friend in the dorm below by tying them in the belt of his dressing gown.

It had been a long time since she'd had dinner with a man that wasn't a business appointment. Not that this was a date – in a way, it too was work-related: she had struck a deal and was simply keeping up her end of the bargain – but she hadn't anticipated actually having a good time.

He really was very handsome, she mused, as he laughed at his own joke – so ready to smile and find the light side. There was no darkness in him and seemingly no black-hearted ambition; he was simply the archetypal rich kid: born to money with nothing to prove. Why would he have? He lived in a world where his name opened doors, and his face opened hearts.

He was so unlike his brother and as for Lochlan . . . what was it she detected in him? He had a defensiveness that bordered on chippy, forthrightness that masked an anger, making him blunt, intransigent, closed, fixed. This afternoon had been revelatory on many levels – aside from witnessing his relationship with Skye, it was also the first time she had seen him face to face with Sholto and it was clear the relationship had disintegrated to the point where they would simply disagree with each other on principle. In her experience, once—

She caught herself, realizing she was thinking about him, her client, working again when she was supposed to be having a night off. *Focus on Callum*, she told herself, sipping the dram and tuning back in. He was talking about – oh, he was talking about her.

'Huh?' she asked, straightening up. 'Fairytale of New York' was playing quietly in the background.

He smiled, leaning in on his elbows, his concentration trained entirely upon her. It was a flattering technique and something which she advised her clients to do in meetings when they wanted to indicate connection and empathy. 'I asked, why the devil aren't you married? You're successful, ambitious, witty, great company – and if you don't mind me saying, a stone-cold fox.'

'Not every woman wants to get married, you know. Believe it or not, the whole white-dress, big-wedding thing is a nightmare scenario for some of us.'

'Sure, I get that,' he murmured. 'You're a modern woman. What's marriage really going to give you? You don't need a man. You're financially independent, intelligent—'

She laughed. 'Stop. Enough with the flattery already.'

'So are you seeing anyone . . . exclusively?'

'No.'

'Are you seeing anyone, non-exclusively?'

'That's my business.'

He clicked his tongue against the roof of his mouth. 'See, that's what I like about you. No BS. Very few women say what they really think.' He paused and a smile came to hover at his lips. 'Tell me what you like about me,' he said in a lower voice.

Your eyes. She arched an eyebrow. 'Who said I like anything about you?'

'You are brutal,' he laughed, shaking his head and looking delighted. 'But don't think I haven't noticed how you deflect anything personal at all. I have, and it only piques my interest all the more. I want to know what makes you tick, Alex, and I do intend to find out.'

Alex smiled – deflecting again – knowing he could never possibly guess; knowing that even if she told him outright, he probably wouldn't be able to believe it anyway. Some stories were simply too terrible to be true. She began to tap her fingers on the table. 'So how often do you come over here? It seems a lot,' she asked, not so subtly changing the subject. 'Surely you've got a life in Edinburgh?'

'That depends whether there are any beautiful women trapped by the storms over here.'

She shot him an unimpressed look.

He put his hands up in surrender and laughed. 'Fine. Most of the time, I get over every other weekend, but with all the extra family assemblies recently it's been more frequent than that – luckily for me, or I'd never have had the joy of meeting *you* last week.'

'Extra family assemblies?' she queried, her antennae up.

He shrugged. 'More than usual. No biggie, though.' He

took a sip of his drink and she refused to acknowledge how golden his hair looked in this light. 'And how are things going with that cousin of mine? Did the shoot help?'

'It might have done if the fire hadn't happened.' She sighed. 'No, whatever momentum I may have had went up in flames with the barley loft. What with dealing with the fire service and the police and the press, and the clean-up and trying to get production going again and now this hidden malt, I'd say he's got the perfect excuses to get away from me.' She dropped her head back on the booth, exposing her pale throat. 'Honestly, I don't know what it is about this job. It feels like I take one step forward, only to take another three back.'

'That's how it is with him. Don't take it personally. He confounds everyone.'

'But *I* should be unconfoundable.'

He arched an eyebrow. 'That's not a word.'

'I know,' she grinned. 'But you know what I mean.'

'Yes.'

She wrapped her hands around her glass, lost in thought again. 'I don't know. He's impossible.'

'Well, what do you usually do with difficult clients?'

'Sit them down, talk it out.'

'Talking? Really?' Callum looked sceptical. 'Well, look, I'd better put you out of your misery and stop you now then. Lochie's never going to talk about his feelings.'

'I mean Socratic talking. It's a probing questioning method that gets to the root of any issue. The theory is that we all of us know the answers to our dilemmas, it's just a question of knowing how to access them.'

Callum took another sip of his drink, still looking dubious. 'Is there a Plan B?'

'The one-eighty.'

'What's that?'

'When the path you're on isn't working and you can't go forward, switch back and go in the opposite direction.'

'So with regards to Lochie, that means what exactly?'

Alex was quiet as Skye flashed into her mind. Did getting Lochie to perform a U-turn on his life mean getting him to go back to her? Was jilting her the biggest mistake he'd ever made, as she suspected? Or was there something else he had to revisit? Something worse? After all, Skye had told her he'd been rejecting her for months beforehand. 'I'm not sure yet, but if I ever get him to do more than insult me, I'll let you know,' she said non-committally.

'Well, I really hope you do. Don't repeat this but I miss the bugger.'

Alex was surprised. 'You were close?'

'You'd never know it now, would you? But yeah, we were more like brothers than cousins – way closer than I was with Tor; there's only eight months between us so we were in the same year at boarding school, same dorm even. We were inseparable.'

'So what happened?' she prompted.

He shook his head and stared into the bottom of his glass. 'Things were tough at home for him. He was pretty messed up – kept running away from school, acting up. Then his mum died and he didn't come back after the funeral. I didn't see him for years after that and when I did, he might as well have been a stranger.'

Alex watched him. His demeanour had changed completely, all his happy-go-luckiness gone. 'Have you ever tried talking to him about it?'

'Christ, no. You've met the guy! Try talking about *feelings* with him and see where it gets you. He'd launch me into the loch if I so much as opened my mouth.'

'So silence is better?' It was her turn to look sceptical.

He looked up at her, seeing the sympathy shine from her eyes. 'It's the preferred option. Lochie can't help being this way; it's who he is now. Sometimes, we just have to accept that pain changes people, you know?'

Pain changes people? She nodded, feeling the hairs lift on her arm. Yes, she did know that.

They were both quiet on the journey back and Alex felt that something had shifted between them, almost as though something in her had weakened. That high wall of hers that was usually so hard to scale felt a little lower tonight; ropes could be thrown over the top – and it felt so lovely to just let go a little, just for once, to allow herself to imagine she was like other people, free to play, free to fall.

She stared out of the window as they rolled through the undulating moors, the pinprick lights of far-off dwellings like fallen stars from the night sky as they wound their way back to the barley fields and the coruscating shimmer of the sleeping sea.

When they got to the farmhouse, he jumped out before she could stop him and took her arm up the garden path – 'in case of ice' again. She could feel the muscles in his arms through his coat, she could smell the subtle musk of his scent in the breeze. She felt as though she was waking up from a deep sleep.

'Thank you for dinner,' she smiled, standing in the porch. 'I actually had a good time.'

'Well, unlike you, I knew *I* would.'

She smiled and she felt her stomach give a flip as he bent towards her fractionally, then paused.

'Just checking whether there's a right hook incoming,' he murmured, his eyes locked on hers.

She laughed and he swooped in, kissing her softly on the cheek. The laugh died in her throat as their eyes met. 'Would you be horrified at the prospect of dinner with me again? Sometime next week?' he asked, his eyes on her eyes, lashes, lips, hair . . .

She shook her head. 'Surprisingly, no.'

He grinned, chuckling softly. 'You *must* learn to say what you really think, Alex Hyde,' he murmured, pulling back and straightening up with an amused shake of his head. He turned and walked up the path, glancing back one more time before he slid into the car. It was a cold night, the snow crystallizing the island's hush, but she stayed where she was and watched until his red tail lights had disappeared over the last hill, looking just like any other woman on a date, wanting to be kissed.

Chapter Sixteen

Islay, Friday 15 December 2017

He had beaten her to it. The kettle was still steaming and the coffee in the red Nescafé mug still untouched but he was at his desk, his head down when she opened the office door, Rona sleeping at his feet.

'Oh!' Alex exclaimed. 'You're here.'

His eyes switched up but his head didn't move. 'It is my office.'

She stepped in, trying to gauge his mood. His colour was better than yesterday's and his eyes looked brighter. 'Bear with a sore head' seemed to sum it up best. 'How are you feeling today? You look a lot better.'

'Funny, that, I thought you were going to look a lot worse.'

'Thank you, I shall take that as a compliment,' Alex said in a sunny tone, refusing to be riled by his insistence on revisiting over and over the scene of her humiliation. She was perfectly capable of drinking whisky without getting hammered.

Her tactic worked and he watched sullenly as she wandered over to the kettle and made herself a cup of coffee. 'Oh, by all means, make yourself at home,' he said sarcastically. 'Come in. Have a coffee.'

'Thanks,' she smiled, even sunnier.

'So how was your *date*?' he sneered after a long silence, as she busied herself with washing a cup and sniffing the milk.

'It wasn't a date,' she said, not bothering to turn back.

'It looked like a date.'

She shrugged, stirring with the spoon and taking her time before walking over to the hopsack chair. She noticed that his suit was hanging on the hook behind the door again. 'Tell me about *your* night,' she smiled, warming her hands around the mug and peering over the rim at him. 'Everything you hoped for?'

There was a drawn-out pause, before he threw down his pen and swivelled in the chair. He sat back in it, his hands clasped behind his head – taking up space, assuming his role. He stared at her with an inscrutable expression, as though debating whether to trust her with the verdict. '. . . Sublime.' The word sounded almost treacherous as it escaped him and she could tell it was almost a physical effort for him to throw off his bad mood to admit to something good.

She gasped, her eyes wide with delight. 'Really?'

'Single best moment of my life.' He grinned suddenly and it was as though he'd been lit from within – his edges softened, his eyes gleamed and that invisible carapace, that was like a force field around him, simply dropped away. 'Shame you missed it. That was a slice of Scottish history last night, right there.' He closed his eyes, remembering. 'God, it was better than any of us could have hoped for – it's got such incredible body and richness, with orange and peach notes, and hints of toffee,' he said. 'I thought Bruce might die on the spot; it's never going to get any better than that. Not for any of us.'

'I'm so pleased,' she said, watching this new anima. He was like an entirely different person, one she'd never met before – this passion, enthusiasm. If she could just harness that positivity. 'Well, what an incredible turnaround. Who would have thought, when we saw those flames in the sky on Monday night that the week could be ending on such a high? It's like a phoenix rising from the ashes.'

She smiled and he smiled back and just for a moment, things felt easy between them. Her phone buzzed and she glanced at it.

Would it be wrong to admit I dreamt about you last night?

Her mouth parted in surprise but she couldn't keep from smiling. As much as anything, she wanted to know how he'd got her mobile number. His father?

She put the phone away and looked back up but Lochlan had already turned away and was hunched over the desk again, reading a document. She watched him as she sipped her drink. 'And how's it going with the new maltings floor? Can you press ahead with it?'

'It's all in swing,' he murmured as he picked up the pen and signed something. 'The team are flat out getting everything cleaned and ventilated and I've got some of the guys constructing some new steeps and couches. I'm pretty hopeful we can start operations again as soon as we come back in the New Year.'

'You sound on top of things.'

'You sound impressed.'

'You do impress me, Lochlan,' she said, tipping her head to the side. 'Why? Did you think you didn't?'

'I've got no idea what you think,' he said flatly.

His tone suggested he didn't care either. She watched him as he worked, seeing the tension in his face.

'You know, now that you're able to tolerate my presence for more than five-minute intervals, perhaps you could think about actually working with me? There's only so long I can continue drinking coffee in the canteen and cleaning your office.' She leaned forward, her elbows on her knees and a beseeching smile on her face. 'What do you say? The sooner we work, the sooner you're rid of me. Short-term pain, long-term gain.'

It was actually the most compelling argument she had to make and there was a long silence – she knew he was only pretending to read the spreadsheet he had picked up.

'What exactly does it involve?'

'Talking to me,' she said, to his profile.

He said nothing.

'Come on,' she cajoled. 'If nothing else, it'll get Sholto off your back. Refusing to play ball with me is only playing into his hands; you're confirming his worst fears. I know I can help you. You keep telling me there's a million reasons why things between you won't work, but you only actually ever need *one* reason why it will.'

He looked at her, unresponsive.

'Think of it this way: the sooner you cooperate, the sooner I'm out of your hair. Imagine –' she smiled, holding her arms up in the air, conjuring an image – 'coming into this office and I'm *not* here. How great would that be? It's something to aim for, isn't it?'

He cleared his throat, reaching for the tall glass of water on his desk; his throat was still bothering him. 'Fine.'

It was enough to make her almost fall off her chair. He'd actually agreed to it? Finally agreed to work with her? 'Great!' Instinctively, she got up and turned on the spot, not quite sure what to do or where to go; it was nought to sixty in three seconds. 'Well, then, I'd better get prepared. Umm . . . meet me at . . .' She didn't know where to meet him. 'Agh, I need space. And chairs.'

He arched an eyebrow. '*Chairs?*'

'Yes, lots of them.'

He groaned. 'Oh dear God, what am I signing myself up for?'

She smiled as an idea came to her. 'Any chance you can have the canteen closed for us for a few hours?' She put her hands up placatingly at his expression. 'I know, I know. But just . . . trust me, please?'

He blinked, looking at her as though she was mad. 'Fine, three o'clock,' he sighed. 'For *one* hour.'

'Two,' she said, quick as a flash.

His eyes narrowed. 'One and a half.'

'Deal,' she beamed, practically dancing her way to the door.

She stopped as she got to it, turning back to face him, her hand on the doorknob. 'You know, I think you're going to surprise yourself and end up liking it.'

He looked up at her. 'No.'

She shook her finger. 'I think you will, in the way that you *like* disliking me; it's a new hobby for you. A distraction.'

He sighed and picked up his pen. 'It's true you are very distracting,' he muttered, looking back at his paperwork as she stepped out into the snow.

He was early, curiosity getting the better of him. 'What's all this?' he asked in a suspicious tone. She had pushed the canteen tables to the walls so that there was a space in the middle of the floor and she was sitting on a chair – one of several – on the periphery.

'*This*,' she said proudly, 'is called a constellation.'

His expression darkened. 'If you even think about talking to me about horoscopes . . .'

'Relax,' she smiled, beckoning him in. 'It's nothing to do with horoscopes. This is a tried and tested technique and it's widely used, not just in a business context.'

'Widely used for what?' he asked, moving slowly from the door.

'Identifying tensions and resolving conflict.'

'Is the UN aware of this? There's a little conflict that needs to be resolved in the Middle East. I'm sure they could do with a *constellation*.'

Alex smiled, almost enjoying his sarcasm. 'Come over here.'

He came over, weaving through the tables and chairs like a child told to sit on the naughty step. He sat on the chair beside her.

'So far so good,' she said, noticing how he was fidgeting his feet – a sure sign of nervousness, his body telling him quite literally to flee. 'So, all I want us to do today is talk through what *you* consider to be the problems you're facing in your role and how you think we might go about resolving them.'

'That's simple. The problem is Sholto and the resolution is to get a new chairman.'

She tipped her head to the side. Let him bait. 'And why is Sholto the problem? Was he the one who made you throw the computer through the window?'

'No—'

'Was he even there at the time?'

'No, he was in Edinburgh, where he always bloody is.'

'Was he there when you called the Indonesian trade minister – and I quote – "a fucking idiot"?'

'Well, no, but—'

'But you think Sholto's the source of your anger?'

Lochlan blinked at her. 'I think he's a dangerous fool.'

It was a deliberate echo back to their first ever conversation, a pointed reminder that nothing had changed in the almost two weeks that she had been here.

She straightened in her chair, her hands clasped on her knees. 'Lochlan, you know the phrase "no man is an island"?'

'Please don't trot out clichés to me.'

'It's a cliché because it's true. We all move and operate within multiple relationship systems – business, personal, cultural and family circles. Each one has its own loyalties and different ways of how they make us feel about our place in the world. But they also all intersect.

'Now, the needs of each system push us towards "balance" – we often call it the work–life balance: we want our days to be productive, but we also want to see our friends or our families, or have time to ourselves, right? Getting that balance right makes us feel whole, or fulfilled, but when we lose just one aspect of it, everything else suffers. And that's because within each of these relationship systems, there are three elements at work: the Me, the We and the It. Try to think of them as three overlapping circles. If one of those elements of a system is out of balance, it creates blockage or dissent or resistance and the system fails. For example, say I worked here: *I* (the Me) cannot perform to the highest of my abilities for you (the We) if I'm depressed, or being passed over for promotion or my husband's cheating on me – and that means the company (the It) suffers.'

'I've already told you, I am not going to be an agony aunt for the staff.'

'And no one's asking you to. But right now, this session is about you. Who do *you* go to when you lose the balance?'

He stared at her as though the question was a stupid one. 'I don't. I go for a run.'

She nodded, watching him closely. 'Okay, good. We'll come back to that. Let's return to Sholto. Do you think your problems with him are from the business sphere, or family?'

'Business.' He hadn't hesitated.

'You're sure about that?'

'I said so, didn't I?'

'Do you think you would feel such anger towards him if he wasn't a relative?'

'Yes.'

'You don't think that intimate relationship – whether consciously or not – allows you to express a negativity that you couldn't if he was merely a colleague?'

'No.'

'Do you feel it towards Torquil?'

He snorted. 'Well, I *didn't*.'

'What does that mean?'

He sighed, the shutters coming down. 'Nothing.'

She watched him, blinking slowly as she remembered that it was Torquil he had punched at the family assembly. She made a mental note to also come back to his problems with his CFO. 'How about Callum?'

'No.'

'You don't feel any negativity to him whatsoever?'

Lochie shrugged.

'He said you used to be close—'

Lochlan's eyes flashed. 'Tell you that on your date, did he? What else did he tell you about me?'

'Nothing. We weren't talking about you specifically,' she lied. 'It just came up in conversation. He said he misses how close you used to be together.'

Lochlan looked away. 'Yeah, well, people change.'

'That's kind of what he said, although *his* exact words were, "Pain changes people." Are you in pain, Lochlan?

Lochlan glanced at her, putting his hands on his knees with a sigh of impatience. 'Look, what exactly is the point of this? I'm flat-out frantic. We've just had a freaking fire, production is stalled, we've got the biggest discovery the company's ever had needing to be managed and you've got me sitting here in a bunch of chairs talking about your date with my layabout cousin. I don't have time for—'

'You do have the time and shall I tell you why? Because this company cannot run effectively with its two figure-heads at war. It doesn't matter what you do: you can get production going again or commission fancy new bottles for the hidden malt or locate a new maltings, but none of it will count for anything if there are problems at the top. The "It" will fail if you don't sort out the "We" between you and Sholto. You cannot keep clashing antlers. I saw the two of you together yesterday – you don't even hear what the other's saying, you just spout your own agendas. You hear only what reinforces the story you've told yourself to be true, locking you in a pattern that is destined to repeat until—'

'Until?'

'Until one of you loses.'

'Well, it won't be me.'

'Almost the entire board and family assembly is against you, Lochlan.'

He said nothing in reply and after a moment she added, 'Would it make you feel better if I told you this kind of dynamic is actually quite common in family-run businesses?'

'Not especially.'

'How about if I told you we can actually break the deadlock between you both?'

'I'd find that hard to believe.'

'Well, I'm going to show you right now.'

'How?'

'We're going to make a living map,' she said, reaching down for a pile of papers and a pen on the floor.

He tipped his head back, closing his eyes. 'I should have known. You're basically a shrink.'

'No. I'm not interested in hearing you talk about your childhood; I'm better than that. I can give you *solutions*. Don't you want that – for the good of the company?'

'Don't play that card on me. I am the *only* one who cares about that. The rest of them are just about profit,' he snapped.

'But Kentallen is a business, not a family.'

'Wrong. It's both. They don't see it and neither do you.'

'Look, I've been here less than a fortnight and it's clear to me what this company means to you. No one runs into a blazing building for anything other than love. This company has been your entire world, your identity, I get that. It's both your future and your parents' legacy. You grew up knowing you'd one day take over from your father—'

'Do *not* start on him,' Lochlan said in a warning voice. 'If you think I'm going to listen to you put the blame at my parents' door, I'll take you down to the ferry right now.'

She looked at him, wondering as to his overreaction. She had scarcely mentioned his parents. 'Okay. Tell me, in the most basic of terms, why you think Sholto has brought me in here?' she asked, changing course to calm him down again. 'What's the root cause of the problem?'

He sat back in the chair, his legs crossed at the ankles, his arms folded over his chest. He wasn't conscious of doing it, but he was physically blocking himself off from her. 'Supposedly my anger?'

Alex was surprised, but pleased. She hadn't expected quite such an honest response quite so soon. She wrote the word 'anger' down on a sheet of paper in her lap.

'Okay, so the problem is the anger. And what is the goal you think we should work towards? If you and I were to achieve anything together, what would it be?'

'Well, I guess, in the words of every great beauty queen, that would have to be peace,' he said, sarcasm dripping from every word.

She scribbled it down. 'Okay. So do you mean a peaceable working relationship? Peace of mind?'

'Both.'

'So anger is the problem; peace is the goal,' she murmured, looking at his profile as he stared resolutely out of the high-up canteen windows, as though he was wired to electrodes and being sporadically shocked. 'Do you have any resources that can help you achieve this goal? A support system. It doesn't just have to be a skill or an attitude—'

'I run.'

'Yes, you mentioned that earlier. But what about a person, someone you could consider an ally, someone you could confide in and trust? Is there anyone like that for you?'

'Yes.'

'Who?'

'Rona.'

It was her turn to be quiet now. 'The dog?'

He shrugged. 'She listens.'

Does she talk too? Alex wanted to ask. Instead she blinked, hiding her true feelings. 'She's the one you confide in?'

He nodded and that's when she saw it, the laughter in his eyes again, mocking this, mocking her. She felt her anger spike.

'What about Skye?'

He frowned, looking baffled by the suggestion. 'No.'

'Why not? It's clear you're still close.'

'We're not close.'

'How can you say that? She sat with you in the ambulance. She didn't leave your bedside for two days and nights.'

'I never asked her to be there.'

'She obviously still cares deeply for you.'

He snorted with contempt. 'No. She doesn't.'

She stared at him, trying to get at least one handhold on this man, but it was like rubbing at granite with sandpaper. 'You expect me to believe that nothing remains between you when she does all that for you? You share a dog together; you were going to spend your lives together.'

'Yes. And then we didn't.'

No, Alex mused. *You jilted her; abandoned her the night before when her dress was already hanging at the end of the bed and her nails had been done, the flowers were cut and the guests all arrived.* 'Why not?'

'That's none of your business,' he said bluntly.

She tried a different tack. There had to be another way in. 'Fine. Let's talk about trust, then. Who would you trust with your life?'

'Rona.'

She'd never slapped a client before, nor had she ever been more tempted. She forced a smile. 'What I mean is, if your life was hanging in the balance, who would you place your trust in to save you?'

'Rona.'

'Lochlan, you cannot keep mentioning the dog! It has to be a person. Give me a name.'

He shrugged.

'You're honestly trying to tell me there's not a single person in this world that you trust?'

He looked at her with hard eyes. 'Trust is overrated.'

'No,' she disagreed. 'Trust underpins everything.'

'I've got my dog. Deal with it.'

Alex inhaled irritably. 'Fine! So for ally we'll put Rona,' she said through gritted teeth, scribbling the dog's name on another piece of paper.

She got up and placed a sheet of paper on each of four chairs just as her phone, which had been by her feet, buzzed with a new text.

Lochlan automatically glanced down. His expression changed as he saw the name on it and picked it up. 'Oh look, how sweet,' he sneered. 'My cousin can't stop think-ing about you. How's tomorrow for dinner?'

'Give me that,' Alex said, snatching it from his hands. 'It's private.'

'I thought you said it wasn't a date.'

'It wasn't.'

'Then why are you blushing?' he asked as she pocketed

the phone without reading the message. 'Isn't it incredibly unethical for you to date a client?'

'He's not a client,' she said. Before realizing the pertinent point. 'And it wasn't a date.'

'So you're *not* seeing him again?'

'That is none of your business.'

'I don't see why not. You seem to think you can ask whatever you like about the state of affairs between me and my ex-fiancée but whenever the questions turn to *you* . . .'

'That's different.'

'How?'

'Because we're not here to discuss my life or my job. And because in my professional opinion, I think you're a wreck. Your private relationships are in disarray – with your family, your ex-fiancée – and it is affecting your ability to do your job.'

'That is a crock of shit.'

'It's not and I'm going to show you. Come and stand over here,' she said forcefully, getting up and standing by the chair in the centre of the space.

He glared at her for a moment, both of them barely keeping a lid on their true emotions; but he did as he was told, for once, his expression betraying his evident scepticism.

She took a deep breath, grateful that she'd meditated before breakfast this morning; it always helped her dissipate her own high feelings. 'We're going to create a living map – a physical symbol of you and the system you're currently locked within, so that you can actually see the dynamics at play. Now sit down here. This chair represents you. Okay?' she said, showing the sheet of paper on the seat with his name on it.

'If you say so.'

'Now I want you to tell me where, in relation to your chair, you'd like me to put the problem, which we identified just now as anger.' She stood behind the chair upon which she'd put the piece of paper with '*Anger*' written on it.

'Right here,' he shrugged.

'Where? To the left? Right? In front of you? Tell me exactly.'

He got up and, taking the chair from her in silence, stacked it on top of the chair upon which he'd been sitting. 'There.'

Alex was quiet for a moment; actually a little stunned. '. . . Okay. Good. Now where should I put the goal we're working towards, which we just identified as peace? Where do you see it as being in relation to where you are now?'

He jerked his chin forward.

'Over there?' she asked, taking the chair and walking it several spaces ahead of him. 'Here?'

'Further.'

She took another three steps. 'Here?'

'Further.'

'Tell me when.' She lifted the chair again and walked away, getting closer and closer to the stacked chairs by the walls, getting nearer to the double swing doors.

'There.'

Alex put down the chair and looked back at him. She was almost out of the room; he was almost out of sight.

'And finally, your ally, Rona,' she sighed, walking back and lifting the last remaining chair.

'Here,' he said, pointing to the space in front of his feet.

Alex positioned the chair and looked back at the arrangement they had made. 'Okay, so we've got you here, with the anger, or the problem, literally stacked upon you; you've got your ally at your feet and the goal . . . well, almost outside.'

She blinked, staring at the arrangement. She'd never seen anything close to this before. It was as bleak a picture as *The Scream*, the prospect of resolution quite literally a distant hope.

'How do you feel, seeing the dynamics mapped out like this?'

He looked around at it, getting up and walking round the space slowly, his eyes tracking between the different chairs and the claustrophobic proximity of some, the distance of the others. She could see he was absorbing what it said – his shoulders slumped, head low, feet shuffling on the floor. He looked back at her. 'I feel vindicated.'

'Vindicated?'

'Yes. I told you it's hopeless,' he said, his voice flat. 'There's nothing you can do. Maybe you'll listen now.'

'Lochlan, there's always a way—'

'No, there isn't; not always. Give up, Alex, go home. This isn't your problem. You can't do anything here.'

'I am the best in the business, Lochlan!' she said fiercely. 'I am the *only* person who can help you.'

'I'm afraid I don't believe that. How is your success even quantified?'

Alex knew she could prove it – her work with the president of a giant telecoms group in the States had reset his patterns of thinking so that within a year he had led the company from a profit warning to an IPO; she had helped the chairman of a German bank rebuild after an insider-trading ring had brought the company to near-collapse. But this wasn't about her work. It was about her. He didn't rate her because he didn't trust her – not that he trusted anyone, but in her case, it was also because he didn't respect her.

And could she blame him? From the moment she had arrived here she had, for reasons both within and without her control, lost her dignity and, by extension, her authority. And for a man like him – isolated, angry, untrusting – that made her inconsequential. Attempts at empathy – smiling, mirroring, doing favours such as making coffee – made no impact. Callum had been right; she wouldn't get through to him by *talking*. That was like trying to crack a frozen pond by blowing bubbles and for as long as he didn't want to do this, she could force no change.

She put her hands on her hips and walked over to him, pinning him with her eyes. 'What's it going to take, Lochlan, to make you believe in me?'

'You can't. You don't have what it takes.'

'Why not?'

'You're too young, for one thing.'

'The average age of my clients is fifty-eight and none of them have had a problem with it.'

'No? Well, perhaps they like that you make coffee and "chat", or that you play with chairs and make shapes in a room. But I don't see anything in you that makes me think you understand what is required to be in the game at my level.'

'And what is, exactly?'

'Drive. Fire. Cut-throat ambition. The killer instinct.'

Alex felt herself steam at his withering assessment, as though she spent her days arranging flowers and learning dance routines. He thought she was a flake, just some hippy-dippy counsellor preaching love and kindness in the workplace. Every instinct in her wanted to tell him what was really going on here; he had no idea who he was dealing with or what he was up against; when it came to the wolf in sheep's clothing, she was the archetype. But the retort stuck in her throat. It had to.

'Sorry, Hyde,' he said with a decisive look. 'You've given it your best shot but this isn't going to work. I can deal with Sholto on my own. Just get the ferry and go home.'

He walked out without so much as a handshake, the door swinging shut behind him, and she kicked out at the closest chair, sending it clattering across the floor. He made her want to scream.

She walked around the room in tight circles, squeezing and releasing her hands, forcing herself to breathe deeply. Yes, she would dearly love to get the hell out of here too and return to the plush silence of her Mayfair flat. She would love never to see that man again or have to make him coffee, she would love not to have to force a smile on her face when she felt contempt in her heart. But for all the reasons there were to go, there was a far more compelling one to stay.

She watched from the window as he walked towards the burned-out maltings and began talking with the last remaining fire officers still conducting their investigations. Yellow tape cordoned off the area, flickering gently in the onshore breeze as she saw him gesticulate with his arms – his movements large and dominant, always so sure of himself.

But he had underestimated her at his peril. She had tried doing this the nice way, but if it was killer instinct he wanted, it was killer instinct he was going to get.

*

'Miss Hyde's office?' Louise asked, suppressing in her voice her annoyance that the caller had rung just as she was leaving the office. 'Oh hi, Alex.'

It was dark outside and raining, the long beams of headlights moving up the walls and past the windows. She walked back to the desk and perched on the corner, her coat still on. She'd been hoping to get to the 6.30 p.m. Barrecore class.

'No, no, it's fine, I was just finishing up some notes . . . Yes, it's all been great here, no problems. Carlos just left and Jeanette went early to get to the carol concert at St Martin-in-the-Fields. How are things with you? Any progress with Mr Charisma?'

She tilted her head to the side as she jingled the office keys lightly in her cupped hand. 'He did what . . . ? His *dog*?' She tutted. 'Christ, he is such a moron,' she sighed. 'Honestly, I don't know how you put up with it. What are you going to *do*?'

She rolled her eyes and shrugged off her coat, balancing the phone between her chin and shoulder as she booted the computer back up again. 'Yes, of course I can . . . No, it's no problem. I was still working on some stuff.'

She noticed that the orchid needed watering as she threw her coat over the back of the chair and began typing. 'So you want me to go over there now . . . ? Yes, I pass by yours on my way to the station anyway.'

She cleared her throat as she listened to the list of orders. 'So can this go by bike? It'd be quicker . . . Okay, I'll book a car . . . Yes, they can collect in an hour so it should be with you before breakfast . . . Uh-huh, if you could text me the address.'

She stopped nodding, her fingers hovering above the keyboard. And her voice, when she spoke, had risen an octave. 'Sorry – did you say you want your *gun*?'

Chapter Seventeen

The blades had only just begun to slice the air when she crouched low and ran across the field. Sholto's arrival the day before had meant much of the snow cover had been blown away, leaving a radius of exposed yellowy grass like a sort of crop circle.

She grabbed the handle and opened the door with force.

'Holy mother of God!' Lochlan shouted, slapping a hand across his chest. 'You almost gave me a heart attack!' He frowned. 'You can't just run up to a fucking helicopter when the blades are going! What if I had begun to move?'

'Relax. It's hardly my first time in one of these things. I know when to step back.'

'What . . . what the *hell* are you doing?' he demanded as she stepped up and in, depositing her small overnight bag at her feet. She waved blithely to Mr Peggie as he drove off again, only the top half of the grey Landy visible over the stone wall. It had been a tight turnaround getting back here in time for this.

'I'm coming with you, of course. Torquil told me you were using this for the weekend. I had assumed we'd drive.'

'I'm not going to *London*,' he scoffed.

'Well, of course not, I know that,' she shrugged. And

then when he continued to look at her with open-mouthed disbelief, 'The MacNab, remember?'

'*What?* You're not coming!'

'Of course I am, we had a deal. If you would cooperate, I would do the MacNab with you.'

'But I haven't cooperated!'

'Yes, you have. I mean, I realize we haven't covered as much as I'd hoped – not with the fire to contend with – but our session earlier was hugely . . .' She took her time considering the correct word. 'Illuminating. We're getting somewhere, Lochlan, we really are.'

'No, we're not!'

She tipped her head to the side. 'Don't you think *I* should be the judge of that?'

'No!'

'I suppose you would say that,' she said lightly, making no move to leave. She sighed, shrugging her shoulders excitedly. 'Well, I am really looking forward to this, although – I'll be honest – I am a little nervous too. What's the forecast like for the weekend, do you know?'

Lochlan stared at her in disbelief. 'You can't honestly think that I meant for you to come to this?'

She blinked. 'Why not? You asked only last weekend.' She smiled. 'There were witnesses and everything.'

'But with the fire . . . We haven't discussed it since.'

'I wasn't aware we needed to.'

'Fuck's sake . . .' he muttered, looking defeated. Worn down. It was clear if he wanted to get her out of here, he was going to have to climb down and physically wrench her out. (Not that she would put that past him.) He turned back to the controls with a furious expression, before whipping back to her in the next moment, looking delighted.

'Wait! What are you going to wear? You can't wear that,' he said, indicating her skinny jeans and belted Burberry jacket, the leather tassels still swinging on her Penelope Chilvers Spanish riding boots.

'Well, of course not,' she chuckled. 'Don't worry, my kit is being couriered up; it should be with me before breakfast.'

'But I do worry. I know all too well just how loosely acquainted you are with your own luggage and I'm telling you now – I'm not giving you anything of mine.'

'I wouldn't dream of even asking,' she smiled. 'If I have to shoot in my pyjamas, then so be it.' She smiled but she fervently hoped that even joking about it wouldn't provoke fate; she was on a sticky wicket with the travel gods at the moment.

He looked away with a tut and she felt herself relax a little that she appeared to have got away with her bluff. They lapsed into silence as he began concentrating more closely on the apparatus, the blades beginning to whir into invisibility. She buckled up and slipped on the headset that made it easier for them to talk in the air.

'I didn't know you could fly,' she said, impressed.

'You still don't know that I can,' he mumbled, his eyes dead ahead.

'Touché,' Alex smiled. She figured she could hate him and still laugh at his jokes.

They rose into the air, the nose of the chopper pointing slightly down, Lochlan's expression intent as they rose above the distillery – they swept above the smokeless kiln chimneys, the slate-topped buildings hemmed in by the stone walls becoming a random pattern beneath their feet, the grey sea nudging at the shore on the other side of the field. She saw the swell and curve of the island, saw how the land rose and fell beneath the different treeless terrains of heather moors and barley fields and peat bogs, the coastline a corrugation of merciless sharp rock and gold-fringed sweeping bays. She saw Port Ellen and the road that led up the island, past the guest house (Mr Peggie was parking the Landy in the yard, she saw), to Bowmore and Loch Indaal. They moved out onto open water, over the neighbouring isle of Jura, the ferocious tides of the Sound visible even at height. She lifted her eyes to the horizon. Beyond this narrow slip of sea lay Scotland, the Highlands like stern sentries guarding her shores, white-capped and ancient mountains furred with dense fir forests at their feet.

She looked across at Lochlan, his concentration absolute as they skimmed purple clouds, chasing to the horizon before the sun dipped from view.

'Everything okay?' he asked without turning his head, his voice surprisingly clear in her ear defenders.

'Mmhmm. When did you qualify?'

He looked bemused. 'If I told you last month—'

'I wouldn't believe you, no,' she chortled.

'Don't worry. I won't stall it.' He paused. 'I hope.'

Alex smiled and looked back out of the window again. She loved flying by helicopter; apart from the obvious convenience, it was a more intimate, immediate experience than flying by plane, more visceral somehow. She loved looking down and seeing the country laid out like a picnic blanket.

'You ever flown in one of these before?' he asked.

'An AgustaWestland Grand? Sure,' she shrugged. It hadn't been what he'd meant and she knew it, but it was time to start giving him some clues that she wasn't the walkover he assumed. 'But I prefer the Bell 430.'

She could feel his glances coming her way like heat probes. 'Travel by chopper a lot then, do you?' he asked.

'Only for short hops.'

He was silent for a moment. 'Well, I guess that would explain why you were underwhelmed by the Aston.'

'Astons are beautiful. They are never underwhelming.'

'Yes, well, you enjoy the distinction of being the only woman to ever sit in my car and not spend the journey caressing the leather like it's a dog.'

Alex shot him a bemused look. 'Then perhaps you should reconsider the kinds of women you're driving in your car,' she quipped, wondering exactly how many he *had* driven around in it. She remembered the woman in the bed sheet from last weekend. Who was she? Was it serious?

She added after a moment, 'Besides, your car should not feel slighted; as we both know, I was not in a position to show appreciation for anything that night.'

'I don't know. You'd clearly shown a lot of appreciation for the whisky.'

Alex chuckled again. 'I guess that's true.'

He was silent for a moment. 'Which did you like best? Or can't you remember?'

'The Macallan thirty,' she said, no hesitation.

He nodded. 'It's a fine malt. Almost as good as ours.' Another pause. 'Even more of a shame you missed the hidden malt last night then. If you like the Macallan thirty, you'd have loved that. And it was probably the only chance you'll get to ever try it. The oldest matured malt whisky in the world,' he sighed.

'Unless I buy a bottle.'

'We're putting them on at forty grand a pop.'

'Oh,' she said, nodding as if in agreement. 'Then I'd better get two.'

He smiled and shook his head, his eyes dead ahead. 'I can't work you out. I do not get you.'

'No, you've made that quite clear,' Alex drawled. 'I'm positively Sphinx-like to you, I know. If it's any consolation, you're an enigma to me too, so at least we can be in the dark together.' She frowned as she heard how that sounded; she hadn't meant it to come out like that. 'You know what I mean.'

She looked down at the landscape rumpled by their feet – the long glassy waters of Loch Lomond stretched into the distance, flanked on all sides by steep-sloped mountains, and the blocky silhouette of Glasgow's industrial skyline smudged the horizon.

'So who's in the group?' she asked.

'The usual crowd, ten in all, I think. The hosts are uni friends – Ambrose Arbuthnott and his wife Daisy; his family owns the estate, Borrodale Two and a half thousand acres, twelve miles from Perth.'

'Are you going to be up to much walking?' she asked. 'You were in hospital two days ago.'

'Don't remind me. Besides, this is exactly what the doctor ordered. Plenty of fresh air and gentle exercise.'

Alex looked down at the dramatic up-hill-down-glen landscape. It didn't look terribly gentle to her. 'So who else? Ambrose and Daisy . . .'

'Max Fischer and his wife Emma. He's a cardiologist, she's a nurse.'

'Ooh.'

'Mmm.'

'Did you meet them at university too?'

'Him; but pretty much everyone coming is ex-Stannies.'

'Stannies?' she queried.

'St Andrews.'

'Oh.' Her stomach tightened. 'What did you read there?'

'Economics and politics.' He rolled his eyes. 'To please my father.'

'What did you want to read?'

'Geography.'

'Really?' she asked, interested.

He gave a bemused glance. 'I've always had a strange fascination with fluvial systems.'

'That *is* strange.'

He shrugged. 'Where did you go?'

'I didn't.'

There was a shocked pause. 'You didn't go to uni?'

She always hated this question. 'No. I wanted to get work experience instead and I'm glad I did. As far as I'm concerned, I got a three-year head start.'

'Well, I guess that explains the improbable youth–experience dichotomy,' he said after a moment.

'Quite,' she said shortly. 'Besides, I read the degree syllabus myself. I'm as qualified as the next social psychologist, just without the graduation photo.'

'You read the degree syllabus?' he asked incredulously.

'Mmm-hmm.'

'Who does that? Why would you *not* go to uni and yet you'd do the work?'

'Well, clearly I was a very dull teenager,' she said, using self-deprecation to deflect from her awkwardness as she looked out of the window, trying to look relaxed; people usually reacted like him – stunned and then embarrassed. The image she presented now of glossy hair and cut-glass vowels suggested a defined pedigree and well-worn life course: private school and a gap 'yah', university and then work experience with a friend's father's bank. But unlike him, she hadn't been born to this lifestyle; she had made herself in this image through grit and graft. He had no idea what she'd come from and what it had taken to get here.

'So Ambrose and Daisy,' she said lightly, rescuing the conversation – and herself. 'Max and Emma . . .'

'Uh, Sam and Jess. He sold an app and retired at the grand old age of thirty-one. She illustrates children's books. Um, who else?' His brow furrowed as he tried to concentrate, fiddling with a few controls at the same time. Dusk had given way to darkness and she became aware of the lights flashing outside, markers to those on firm ground that they were in the sky. 'Oh, how could I forget: Anna and Elise. They're . . .'

Alex watched and waited. 'Together?' she prompted.

'Exactly.'

'Wow. Lesbians. How revolutionary,' she said, her voice dripping in irony.

'What?' he asked, sounding defensive.

'You can say the word, you know. It's not exactly a taboo.'

'Yes, well . . .' he huffed. 'I was trying to be discreet.'

Alex rolled her eyes. 'My best friend at school was gay. It's not a big deal. Don't be such a duffer.'

'A what?' he blustered.

'You heard me. So, if I've got this right –' she began counting off her fingers – 'there's Ambrose and Daisy; Max and Emma; Sam and Jess; Anna and Elise . . .'

'And me,' he shrugged, before adding, 'and you. Me and you.'

'Oh,' she said, shifting awkwardly. 'I see.'

'What?'

'Nothing.'

'It's clearly not nothing. What is it?'

'Well, I wish you'd said; I thought this was a corporate thing. I didn't realize it was a jolly with your university mates.'

He gave a sudden disbelieving laugh. 'You didn't give me a chance, leaping into the cab like Rambo back there!'

'You had invited me!' she retorted.

'Once.'

'*Once?* How many invitations should I have expected?'

'You know what I mean! A lot's happened since then, what with the fire . . . Besides, you know I only said it in the heat of the moment.'

'What heat? What moment? I thought it was a friendly offer post-shoot.' It was a disingenuous comment, her tone too innocent to be credible, but she wanted to make him say it, to own up to the momentary jealousy that had prompted him to make a spontaneous – and unwise – offer; didn't he see that as a CEO, he couldn't afford to be so rash and impetuous?

'You know perfectly well that I just—'

'Just . . .' she echoed, watching him closely. His jaw was pulsing again.

'Forget it,' he muttered.

There was a tense silence and she wondered why every conversation with him turned into a battle. Was he this exhausting with everyone, or just her? '. . . So are they going to mind, these friends of yours?' she asked.

'No.' There was another pause. 'They'll be surprised, though.'

'Sorry about that.'

He shrugged. 'They'll probably jump to the wrong conclusions too so . . . I'm just warning you now,' he muttered.

'You mean they'll assume we're . . .' She could scarcely bring herself to say the words. 'An item?'

He shrugged again. She watched him. 'Probably. I don't usually bring anyone to this.'

'What about the women who stroke your car?'

'No.'

'And the one last weekend?'

There was a short silence as he frowned. 'How do you know about her?'

'Well, she was hardly discreet, standing at the bottom of your garden in just a bed sheet!'

He looked annoyed. 'She's just a . . . friend.'

'Mm, she did look friendly.'

He shot a scowl her way. 'It's nothing.'

'If you say so.'

'I do. It's just an agreement, a casual thing whenever she's over. Her husband plays golf here occasionally.'

'Husband? Oh, nice,' Alex said sarcastically, looking away with a tut.

'Hey, she tells me the marriage is dead, I believe her. Frankly, I don't care one way or another – it's not like either of us want anything more. And I'm the free agent anyway, I don't pretend to live like a monk. Not that it's any of *your* bloody business – unless of course you think I'm going to screw up the future of the company if she doesn't respond to my texts.'

Alex's cheeks burned in the darkness but she didn't reply, lapsing into a cross silence. He really was contemptible.

The ground glowed red as they floated back to earth in

stony quietude twenty minutes later, bare-headed flower beds bending in the downdraught as the helicopter landed on the lawns of what looked to be a large stone house, complete with a square turreted tower, and a fountain – its water frozen – in the carriage drive. There was no snow here but a hard frost was already glittering the garden, the blades of grass standing rigid in their stiff white coats.

Whilst Lochlan ran through the wind-down checks, she looked over at the big house. Lights glowed from various rooms on all three floors, the front steps dramatically flood-lit, a wreath the size of an ice-truck's tyre on the front door.

They were just jumping down from the cab, the blades at a standstill, as the door opened and a man came out, sandy-blond curls springing from his head with more bounce than a cocker spaniel.

'Farquhar!' he hailed, arms stretched wide as they walked over the lawn, the grass crunching underfoot, their bags – and Lochlan's guns – slung over their shoulders.

'You'd better call me Lochie,' Lochlan murmured to her as they approached.

'Why?'

'Because they'll think it odd if you don't. Only my mother ever called me Lochlan; I feel like I'm being called to the naughty step whenever you say it.'

'If it made you so uncomfortable, I wish you'd said so earlier.'

He shrugged. 'I didn't think you'd be around long enough for it to matter.'

'Well, sorry about that,' she said with a sarcastic smile. 'Hashtag not sorry.'

He chuckled.

'My man!' their host – Ambrose, she assumed – said,

enveloping him in a bear hug. He was huge, at least six foot three with a chest almost as broad as he was long.

'Butthead,' Lochie said, slapping him hard on the back, apparently in affection.

They pulled apart. 'Well, hello,' Ambrose said, looking over at Alex with a bemused smile and outright curiosity. 'Ambrose Arbuthnott.'

She shook his hand. 'Alex Hyde. Pleasure to meet you.'

'The pleasure's all mine,' Ambrose said, looking between the two of them quickly.

'Uh, Alex is doing some management consultancy work with us,' Lochie said quickly, clearing his throat only to trigger another small coughing fit.

'Trying to whip him into shape, are you?'

'Something like that,' Alex smiled, trying not to shiver in the below-freezing temperatures.

Lochie was still coughing.

'Dear God, man, have you taken up a fifty-a-day habit?'

Lochie tried to smile, his eyes watering. 'You didn't hear about our small fire then?' he rasped.

'A fire? At Kentallen?' Ambrose asked, his easy smile disappearing.

Lochie nodded. 'Christ – you really didn't hear?' he asked as Ambrose's eyes dimmed with alarm.

'Quick, let's go in and get you out of this cold air; it can't be helping. Everyone's waiting,' Ambrose said, shuffling them in. 'And to think I thought the disaster story would be you landing that thing.'

'Disaster story?' Alex asked, ears pricked.

'Aye, Daisy's been fretting all day he was going to crash the thing and scorch the lawns. He only got his licence last month.'

Alex's mouth opened in disbelief as Ambrose led the way, Lochie's shoulders shaking with laughter as he followed behind him.

Chapter Eighteen

They walked through into an impressive panelled entrance hall, a thirty-foot Christmas tree set up in the middle and a red-carpeted winding staircase hugging two walls with thick bushy garlands of eucalyptus wound around the handrails. Portraits of wigged gentlemen and ladies in lace caps bore down with dour expressions, interspersed with a few twelve-pointer stags' heads and a collection of pewter jugs grouped on a medieval wooden chest. It had probably looked exactly like this for the last three hundred years, Alex mused.

'I love what you've done with the place,' Lochie said drily as they walked over the creaky old oak floor, towards a corridor at the back.

Ambrose laughed, leading them through a succession of richly coloured, darkly wooded rooms. 'You sound like my wife. What she wouldn't do for a magnolia wall.' He glanced back. 'Where do you live, Alex?'

'London.'

He nodded as though he'd expected as much. 'Of course, pretty hamlet. Which corner?'

'Mayfair.'

'Ooh, you're in the Manor House,' Ambrose teased with

enlivened eyes. 'I think you may be punching above your weight there, Lochie, old boy.'

'No, it's not . . . we're not . . .'

But they had walked into a room and the buzz of conversation came to an abrupt halt at the sight of them. Her.

Alex scanned the group without moving, seeing how the women were grouped together, sitting on one of the turquoise velvet sofas and the pocketed ottoman that doubled as a coffee table, their elbows on their knees as they hunched forward in intimate conversation. The men were largely standing by the fire, whisky in one hand, the other casually stuffed in their trouser pocket. Ordinarily she would have made a beeline for them – in a balance of probabilities, it was more likely they'd be potential clients. But this wasn't work, she reminded herself. Or at least, it was, but she had to pretend to them it wasn't.

'Everyone, the evening is saved,' Ambrose announced. 'Farquhar has managed not only to not kill himself in his flying machine, but also to persuade this fantastically rare and gorgeous creature, Alex Hyde, to accompany him.'

God, there was an introduction to live up to, Alex thought to herself as she gave a smile. 'Hi.'

A woman with dark curly hair got up from the ottoman and approached with a smile.

'Hi, Alex, I'm Daisy, this one's long-suffering better half.'

'Hey.' She watched as Daisy reached over to hug Lochie too. She saw how he squeezed her affectionately, his features softened from their usual flint-like solidity like melting butter. 'I'm glad you made it up okay. I was worried.'

'It was *fine*,' Lochie reassured her. 'Although it's nice to know that someone would care if I went down in a ball of flames.'

'Talking of flames, did you hear they had a fire?'
Ambrose called from across the room, where he was serv-
ing out some more drinks.

'No.' Daisy looked alarmed. 'What happened? Is everyone okay? Was anyone hurt?'

The others got up and came over, murmuring their concern as Ambrose came back with the drinks and handed
them to her and Lochie.

'It's fine. The maltings is burned to a crisp but . . . all
things considered we got off lightly.'

'Seriously?' one of the men asked.

'Christ. That was the extent of it?'

'Yep,' Lochlan nodded.

'Only thanks to Lochie, though,' Alex said, taking a sip
from her drink. 'He stopped a bigger explosion from razing
the place to the ground.'

They all looked back at him open-mouthed again; in
return, Lochlan shot her a look, seemingly annoyed to be
credited as a hero.

'What did you *do*?' a blonde-bobbed woman with a slight
accent asked, looking rapt.

'Nothing—'

'He ran into the burning building and shut off the venting system, to stop it from blowing through the pipeworks.'

'Mate!' a man with a stubbly beard said, looking both
concerned and impressed at once.

'He was incredibly brave,' Alex nodded. In spite of his
glares warning her to the contrary, it never hurt to big a
man up in front of his peers. 'He could have been killed. If
the fire service hadn't arrived when they did—'

'Oh my God,' several of the women gasped.

'Lochie!' said another, throwing her arms round his neck

before punching him on the arm. 'You damned fool! I can't believe you put yourself in danger like that.'

'It was fine. It wasn't as dangerous as Alex is—'

'The fire chief said he couldn't understand how Lochie had been able to withstand the heat,' Alex added.

Lochie stared at her as the other women threw punches at his arm.

'You crazy fool!'

'I always knew you were a dumb-arse! A brave one but still a dumb-arse.'

'I'm Elise, by the way,' said the white-blonde woman with the accent; she was slight, with perfectly symmetrical features and owlish eyes.

'Anna,' said the one with long frizzed hair and an athlete's physique, who had instigated the arm punching.

'I'm Emma,' said the one with dark bobbed hair.

'Hi,' Alex smiled, ticking them off mentally and wondering where the other one was – Jess, was it? 'Alex.'

'Top-up?' Ambrose said to one of the men – tall, broadshouldered, long legs.

'So do they know how it started?' the man asked Lochie as they followed Ambrose back to the bar and the fire, leaving her alone with the women. Clearly, she wasn't Lochie's 'responsibility'.

'This is so thrilling. New blood in the group!' Emma said excitedly. 'I didn't realize Lochie was bringing anyone this weekend. I mean, he never does, does he?'

'Not to these gatherings, no,' Elise agreed. 'Well, not since you-know-who. How long have you guys been together?'

'Oh, we're not together, we're . . . colleagues, I guess you'd say.'

'You guess?' a voice behind her asked, and she turned to

see a striking woman with long, dark hair and a blunt fringe, holding out a tray of blinis.

Alex smiled, seeing in the other woman's eyes a steady coolness. 'I'm consulting for them at the moment. You must be Jess?'

'Yes.'

'Hi. Alex.'

'Hi, Alex,' Jess said. 'Hungry?'

'No, I'm fine, thanks.'

'You sure? We all need to keep our strength up. Tomorrow's going to be a long day.'

Alex took one, hoping to God her clothes arrived in time in the morning. She was not shooting in her pyjamas in front of *this* woman. 'You've done the MacNab before, then?'

'Well, every year I *try*,' she said. 'Once I missed it by forty minutes.'

'How about the rest of you?' Alex asked the group, covering her mouth with her hand as she chewed.

'Nope,' Emma sighed. 'I'm afraid I just keep Max company and watch. Killing a perfectly healthy animal for sport isn't my thing.'

'Their numbers have to be controlled, darling!' the heavy-set man with strawberry-blond hair called from across the room. 'At least these culls generate revenue and create local jobs.'

Emma rolled her eyes. 'Like I said, not *my* thing.'

'Well, I would have managed it a couple of years ago if they'd accepted my brown trout instead of a salmon,' Anna pouted.

'Not that we're refusing to let that little grudge go,' Elise chuckled, rubbing her hand playfully.

Alex glanced over at Lochie. He was standing by the fire, deep in conversation, a flush on his cheeks although Alex still thought he looked tired.

'Lochie pulled off the double last year; he's going for the hat-trick,' Elise said, catching her gaze.

'Really? Do you think he'll manage it?' Alex asked.

'Knowing Lochie. Once he sets his mind to something, he doesn't give up,' Jess said, taking a sip of her whisky. Alex noticed the bespoke semi-precious cocktail ring on her left hand, the subtle but flawless diamond studs at her ears; her skin was lightly tanned and she looked as though she had an expensive personal trainer. Alex wondered what the app was that her husband had sold – and retired on; she wondered which of the men was Sam, her husband, and she wished they weren't standing across the room in two separate groups, like teenagers at a school disco.

She also tried to imagine Skye standing here – part of this group. She would have been so much younger and less sophisticated by comparison. It was hard to visualize.

'Well, he's neck and neck with Ambrose, but I'm afraid that husband of mine is determined to regain his crown; family honour rests upon it, apparently,' Daisy said with a roll of her eyes. 'He says it simply wouldn't do for the first Borrodale MacNab hat-trick to be won by a "rank outsider".'

'Can a Farquhar be considered rank?' Emma asked with a chuckle. 'They're one of the grandest families in the country.'

'Clans,' Anna clarified.

'Listen, forget the MacNab, all I really want to know is what the lot of you are wearing tomorrow night?' Elise asked, smoothing her hair back with small hands. 'Because I really don't have anything black or tartan.'

Alex felt a bolt of panic arrow through her stomach. What? What was happening tomorrow night? She slapped a smile on her mouth and kept it there as the women detailed their outfits – a black crêpe column dress for Jess; a black silk butterfly-sleeved dress for Anna . . .

'Do you think it's okay that my dress *isn't* black and *isn't* full length?' Elise asked, her round blue eyes wide with apprehension.

'Well, what's it like?' Emma asked.

'Silver three-quarter length; strappy with a pleated skirt.' Elise bit her lip. 'Black just washes me out – doesn't it?' she asked Anna.

'I think you look great in black,' Anna said.

'No, it washes me out.'

Anna shrugged, as if to ask, why bother?

'It sounds gorgeous,' Daisy sighed. 'I, on the other hand, am in my usual Bride of Frankenstein monstrosity. Black Watch taffeta.'

Jess giggled. 'Stop it. I love that dress. It's so eighties and yet it seems to get more *right* every year.'

'Ugh,' Daisy groaned. 'It's an abomination. Never marry a clan chief, that's all I can say.'

'How about you, Alex? What are you wearing?' Emma asked.

'Um . . .' Alex decided to come clean. She pulled a face. 'What exactly is happening tomorrow night?'

Elise gasped; Anna frowned. 'Didn't Lochie tell you?'

'Well, he . . . I mean, I . . . it was all a bit last-minute,' she blustered, not wanting to admit she had practically hijacked her way over here.

'Tomorrow's the Keepers of the Quaich,' Anna said.

She might as well have said it in Ancient Greek. 'The *what*?'

'It's a society for whisky aficionados. Very exclusive for those who care about such things. Lochie's being made a master, which is a massive deal,' Anna explained.

'Maybe that's why he didn't mention it,' Jess said. 'He's never liked people making a fuss.'

'Yes. Maybe.' Alex finished her drink.

'I can't believe he didn't tell you,' Elise said sympathetically. 'Men. No forward planning.'

'Do you need to borrow a dress? I'm sure we could find something to fit you,' Daisy offered kindly. 'Although you're so tiny, it would probably have to be something from my thin era, 2006 to 2009 when I dieted to get into Ambrose's grandmother's wedding dress. A twenty-four-inch waist, I ask you!'

'Oh, you are kind,' Alex demurred. She was not-not-NOT borrowing someone else's clothes again! 'But luckily I always pack a black dress. You never know when you might need it.'

It was a half-lie. She did always pack a silk-jersey full-length Amanda Wakeley dress with a twist knot below the bust; it was sculptural, elegant and could be rolled up into a ball for the smallest carry-on bag. But coming up for a job on a tiny island off the Scottish west coast? She had thought, for once, it was surplus to requirements. She hadn't bargained on some exclusive ceremony at a castle on the other side of Scotland.

'Sorry, would you excuse me for a minute?' she asked, putting her glass on the nearest table.

'Straight down the corridor, third door on the right,' Daisy said discreetly.

'Thanks.'

Louise was in third position, her feet turned out to improbable angles and her thighs screaming, when she heard her phone go in her bag. She scrambled over the piles of furry parkas squashed into the corner to get it.

'Yes?' she panted, only just getting it before it went to voicemail. 'Oh, Alex.'

She sagged, sliding down the wall and staring at her reflection in the mirrors opposite.

'Is everything okay? The car left an hour ago.'

It was eight thirty on a Friday night. She was meeting Jago at the pub at nine thirty.

'Black dress?' she asked, scrambling to her feet and mouthing an apology to the Barrecore teacher as she tiptoed from the studio. 'The one with the jet beads, the lace one or the one with the chiffon overlay? . . . Oh, good. Because I sent up the lace one.'

Her phone pressed between shoulder and ear, she carried on with her *pliés* as she watched the class continue through the small window in the door. She smiled as she heard Alex's surprise. 'Well, I figured if you were going to be shooting, there was a good chance there'd be a dressy dinner afterwards too. The car will be with you before breakfast.'

She rolled up onto her tiptoes and continued with her *pliés* in second position. 'No, it's fine, of course I don't mind. I'm not doing anything special,' she said, reaching one arm up above her head. 'You've got to do whatever it takes. Just get him, Alex.'

*

She lay in bed, staring at the upholstered button that formed the centrepiece of the four-poster's dramatic canopy. Every pleat was exactly the same size as its neighbour, the pattern of the blue-and-white toile lost to an abstract melange. The wood was heavily carved and the bed must have weighed the same as a family car, even though her toes reached to the bottom of the mattress.

The walls were papered in the same pattern as the curtains and the soft furnishings on the bed, colour and pattern layered up in a dizzying celebration. It wasn't to her taste; she preferred a more 'restful' scheme, but it suited the house. History oozed from its bones. Aside from the ceremonial swords crossed on some of the walls, and even – yes – a suit of armour standing guard further down the corridor, the very fabric of the building belonged to the past: the walls were lathered in a bumpy limewash, the carpenters and joiners and stonemasons had never been introduced to a right angle and the walls had to be two feet thick if they were an inch, with mullioned windows and deep stone sills. Every door was so heavy it creaked on its hinges and the floorboards were thirty inches wide. She had glimpsed a keystone above the front door on the way in that had read 1546 and she could well believe it.

She turned over with a weary sigh and looked out of the windows. She hadn't drawn the curtains – a habit of hers; she liked to rise with the sun and make her days productive – and she could just make out the shadow of the helicopter on the lawn, its blades drooping in the stillness like wilted wasp antennae. Lochlan's studied concentration made sense now that she knew he was freshly qualified.

It had been a long day and already felt like a week since the disastrous constellation in the canteen, not *eight hours* ago. But dinner had been interesting and she sensed that her hunch to come had been right. He was a different person here – softer, less defensive. He laughed readily and was at the centre of most of the jokes; they had their own language, his group, talking in shorthand about the pubs they used to frequent as students, the disastrous dinners they would cook when they'd shared a house just outside the town, and she felt those familiar pangs of regret to have missed out on the opportunity herself: the friendships she might have had, the memories it would have given her that would make her smile even now, even when she was on her own. Whatever she might have insinuated to Lochie, that three-year head start of hers rarely felt like the clever win she claimed it to be.

She resolutely closed her eyes, pushing the thoughts – feelings – away. Going to university herself had never been an option and it was the very definition of wasted energy to regret something that had never even happened. 'What could be more futile, more insane, than to create inner resistance to what already is?' It was one of her favourite Eckhart Tolle quotes, one that she used time and again on her clients. She repeated it to herself, trying to make the lesson truer.

She felt her muscles relax, giving up the day and letting the night come, sleep on a stealth mission creeping up her body as she sank deeper into the soft mattress, her long hair splayed on the pillow behind her. She needed to rest well tonight and be up with the sun in the morning, because tomorrow they were going to hunt. And it wasn't just the salmon, the grouse and the stag she had in her sights.

Chapter Nineteen

10 February 1918

Dear Clarissa,

Was very glad indeed to get your letters. I hope you are all well as I am myself. I had a bit of a knock at Barisis as you know but have quite got over that now and am in the best of health and spirits. I am sorry I did not write before but opportunities are hard to find and we've had a fairly trying time of it. We've been 'in' since the 8th but the 9th and the day following have been difficult, although we have reinforcements now; just as well, we were down to our last two hundred. I don't know how long we shall keep it up. Had a dirty time yesterday dodging damned great bombs the blighters were presenting us with. It's a noisy business as you might imagine. One shell landed in the middle of some corned beef tins, scattering them and their contents quite around so we proceeded with boiling water for tea to show the Huns we were still there. I have enclosed a copy of my will for you to keep, in case I can't get round the corner in time, though they can be seen descending in the air so don't fret.

We managed a game of football two weeks ago, sorely tested by the pitch which I think was a cabbage patch. Haven't bumped into Frostie or Kit Oakham yet but Billy Wilkes has not been with us the past eighteen days. He broke his glasses and would not buy new ones and so got left behind with the Transport. Don't know whether he worked the ticket and got a safer job further back. Shouldn't blame him if he has. His nerves have been in a shocking state and he'd brood a lot which is absolutely fatal in a dirty job like this.

I must close now to get this letter away. Give my love to Mother, and tell her by God's help I shall come home safe. I hope Father is quite well and please remember me to Mrs Dunoon.

Your loving brother,

Percy

Borrodale House, Perthshire, Saturday 16 December 2017

Breakfast was hot kippers and scrambled eggs, strong tea that looked as though it had been made with brick dust, and toast so thickly cut, it could prop open the doors. Alex had been the first up, naturally, standing by the window and waiting to intercept the car as it came up the drive at first light. The house was set upon a knoll, the grounds more beautiful and landscaped than she had been able to see in the twilight last night – wide level lawns rolling away from the house, old tiered fir trees on the periphery framing the view as they dropped down in a series of terraces towards the wild, unbrushed textures of the open moors. A gentle mist had drifted, wraith-like, over the gardens as the reluctant sun was nudged into the sky, soft colours of blue, grey and green beginning to bud hesitantly. When she had seen the car crunch over the gravel, she had torn silently through the house in her pyjamas and dressing gown and managed to catch the driver before he could knock on a knocker or ring a bell. And as she had turned to go back inside, she had been surprised to see that half the house –

the other side from her room – was covered in scaffolding. It had been obscured in the darkness when they'd arrived last night.

It was barely brighter now, a pale strip of daylight pushing weakly against the night clouds like a saucepan with its lid askew, and everyone apart from Ambrose and her looked half-asleep.

'We've got to eat as much as is humanly possible,' Elise said, helping herself to a huge bowl of cranachan – a traditional breakfast made of a blend of oats, whisky, cream and raspberries and which looked to Alex more like a pudding. 'It doesn't matter how full we think we are, we must push through,' she said grimly. 'We're going to be standing in a river in two hours.'

Anna gave a shudder. 'Remind me why we always agree to this?'

'Because you like Ambrose's whisky,' Sam – the tall, broad-shouldered, long-legged man with sandy hair – replied in a knowing tone.

'And Mary's cooking,' Elise added. 'No one does cranachan like Mary.'

'Thank you,' Daisy smiled. 'I'll tell her you said that.'

'It looks freezing out there,' Jess said, eyeing the dark vista beyond the windows suspiciously.

'How are you feeling, Alex? Nervous?' Daisy asked, passing down the salt and pepper to Max who seemed not to be a morning person and had so far managed to communicate via a series of grunts.

'I'm nervous about the fishing. I've only done it once before.'

'You'll be fine – just be careful where you stand. Lochie's a good teacher.'

'Lochie? But aren't we . . . aren't we competing against each other?'

'Ordinarily we do, but with the Quaich on this evening we don't have the time to push through the night so we're working in pairs.'

'Right.' Alex wondered if Lochie had been appraised of the situation yet. He wouldn't be happy about it. The whole point of inviting her had been to assert his dominance in the field, to beat her. Partnership wasn't on the cards; if he couldn't work with her in an office, she didn't see it working out on the moors either.

'And how are you with a gun?' Daisy enquired.

'Well, I love shooting but I've never stalked before.'

Max broke his morning's silence to chuckle. 'But apart from that, you're raring to go.'

'Exactly,' she laughed, just as Lochie walked in looking as rumpled as bed pillows. He hadn't shaved, his hair was sticking up at angles and he had deflated airbags beneath his eyes. It was clear he hadn't showered and she could suddenly imagine what he had been like as a hungover housemate at university.

He – like everyone else – was wearing a shirt and jumper, tweed breeks, thick knitted knee-length socks with garters and chunky brown walking boots, and only the newspapers on the table could have informed a passer-by that the date was 2017 and not 1917.

'Morning, mate,' Ambrose said brightly. 'Sleep well?'

Lochie rolled his eyes in reply and Ambrose chuckled to himself.

'Hungry?' Daisy asked as he grunted his greeting to the table in general and headed straight for the sideboard where the breakfast was being kept hot on platters under silver domes. Alex didn't say anything as he came and sat down opposite her but one, beside Jess. There had been a space to Alex's right side – considerately left by Sam for Lochie's late arrival, as she was after all his guest, or 'plus one' – but it clearly hadn't occurred to Lochie to go along with the charade that they were friends, or that she was his guest.

'Straining at the leash, I see,' Ambrose said delightedly as Lochie tucked into his breakfast with silent efficiency, head dropped and shoulders hunched as he tried to wake up. 'Well, this bodes well for me,' he said, rubbing his hands together in anticipation of victory.

Lochie arched an eyebrow in reply but didn't stop eating to speak.

'So, you know the drill for today – we're breaking with tradition and going in pairs,' Ambrose said, pouring himself some more tea.

Alex saw Lochie pause eating for a moment, his eyes swivelling around the group as though checking it was a joke.

'The packs are all ready in the hall – maps, compasses, flasks, the lot. And there's house waders in the boot room. First back here with fish, bird and photographic evidence of the stag, wins. And remember to make a map reference of the deer kill so that the ghillies can retrieve them after,' he said, pointedly eyeballing Max. '"The tree on the hill past the river" doesn't cut it.'

Max groaned. 'You promised to let that go.'

'Alex was just saying she doesn't fish or stalk,' Sam said to Lochie, devilment in his eyes.

Lochie stopped eating – his fork paused at his lips. 'What?' He looked at her in disbelief. 'You never said . . .'

'You never asked,' she replied, feeling embarrassed. Oh please, she thought, please don't let them have another of their arguments in front of all his friends. 'I didn't . . .' She cleared her throat. 'I'm sorry, I hadn't realized we were working in teams. I wouldn't have come if I'd—'

If she'd known she was going to be such a liability? She could see the accusation in his eyes.

'Oh, but it's not taken seriously!' Elise said quickly, looking alarmed. 'That's just the boys being competitive. We don't give a damn, do we?' she asked the girls.

'Of course not,' Emma smiled.

'Actually, I do,' Anna said apologetically.

'Just so long as I don't get blisters,' Jess drawled. 'I cannot wear those heels tonight with fucking great blisters on my feet.' She shot a warning look to her husband and Sam sighed.

Lochie didn't say anything but resumed eating in even louder silence. Alex smiled benignly to no one in particular but she felt his irritation across the table. Different crowd, different place, but it was Groundhog Day once again.

They were the first pair to stride out – Lochie finishing his breakfast at speed once he realized how hindered they were going to be by Alex's novice status – Jess and Sam looking to follow soon after with Ambrose left hamstrung by his hosting obligations and unable to crack on until Max and Emma, and Anna and Elise, had left too.

'We'll start with the shoot; you should be quick with that at least,' Lochie said ungraciously, taking long strides over the lawn and heading towards the open countryside with easy familiarity – over breakfast she had learnt they had done the MacNab every year but two since graduation thirteen years earlier.

'Okay,' she said, grateful they weren't going straight into standing waist deep in freezing waters as Max and Emma had planned. She pushed her gun further back on her shoulder and glanced around, seeing the dark, deep impressions of their footsteps sunken into the frosted lawn. Their packs were light but it was an unwieldy process as they had to deal with shotguns, rods *and* rifles.

They walked for the best part of an hour, Lochie leading as if by instinct over the moors. Alex didn't bother asking where they were. It was beautiful here but after the first hundred acres or so, it all started to look the same. For the most part, they didn't talk; Lochie had insisted on it in case they spotted any deer. The hardest part of stalking was actually tracking the beasts in the first place – a tall order with only a few hours to play with – added to which, they were going to need the wind on their side; if it came in when the animals were downwind, they'd be gone before she and Lochie could even unslip the rifles.

'I bet you wish you'd got Rona here, don't you?' she asked, breath coming hard as they trekked up a particularly steep hill.

'I usually do. She loves it. This is the highlight of her year.'

'So why not this time then?'

'Because it's Skye's weekend to have her, for one thing.'

'Couldn't you have asked her to change it?'

'Maybe,' he shrugged.

'Surely she wouldn't have minded having her next weekend instead?'

There was a short pause. 'She's away next weekend.'

Alex thought – and then realized. Honeymoon! This time next week, she'd be Mrs Alasdair Gillespie. 'Oh. Yes.'

They were silent for a few moments and Alex stole a glance at his profile but he was looking dead ahead, eyes reading the landscape.

'Besides, I've not taken her in the chopper yet. I'm not sure she'd like it. And until I can be sure I'm not going to kill us both . . .'

Alex chuckled at the intimation that it was fine to take the risk with his – and her – life, but not the dog's!

'What?' he asked, seemingly baffled by her amusement, which only made her laugh harder.

'Nothing. Nothing at all.' Maybe he really hadn't been winding her up during the constellation session when he'd said the dog was his confidante.

He stopped walking and looked around them. She realized that the ground beneath their feet was blackened, with young shoots pushing through, yet fifty metres away, the heather was bushy and thick. 'See that?' he said. 'It's muirburn, the heather-burning that stimulates new growth and protects the birds' habitat.' His eyes keenly scanned the variegated moorland around them. 'Which means this is an active grouse moor.' He shrugged off the backpack. 'Shall I beat first?'

'If you like,' she said, pulling her shotgun out of the slip and grabbing a couple of cartridges from her coat's deep pockets.

'They fly fast and low so be ready,' he said. 'And bag only one. Wait for my whistle,' he said, walking away, carrying just the carved-headed cane.

'Yes, sir,' she said under her breath as she put on her ear defenders, broke, checked and loaded the gun. And waited.

It took him several minutes to reach the spot he wanted but soon enough she heard the whistle. She stood ready, weight forward, gun down as he beat about the long grasses, issuing warbling whistles and cries, anything to agitate the birds from their roosting spots.

Nothing happened for a while and she was beginning to think they'd chosen the spot unwisely when a sudden flurry of squawks and wing flaps brought the gun stock instinctively to her cheek. She slowed her breath, took aim and fired.

And missed.

What? She barely ever missed! But these birds were fast. Faster than the pheasants she was used to bagging.

'Dammit,' she muttered under her breath as she saw Lochie clock her fail and begin beating again.

She was successful on the fourth attempt. Creditable for some, perhaps, but not her, and as her chosen grouse hen plummeted to the ground and she cocked the gun, Lochie raised his arm in some sort of command.

She didn't know what he was intending to convey, but then she saw his own gun – already out of its slip – point to the sky.

'Do you want me to beat for you?' she called.

He didn't reply as he inserted the cartridges into the barrels, before kicking his legs through the grass.

Infuriated by his arrogance that he could single-handedly rough-shoot without either a dog or beater, she watched him work – instinctive and sure-footed. She knew the point he was making – by driving the birds for her, he had given her 'easier' shots, making his own trickier by comparison and thereby edging his points against her where he could. Winning in the very field in which he knew she excelled.

She saw a rock nearby and went and sat on it, her arms folded across her chest. Even though she heard the gun crack not two minutes later, it was still going to be a long day.

They walked for several miles without stopping, the river tumbling alongside them for at least two of those miles, as Lochie scrutinized and examined and judged a stretch before moving on with a tut or a stern shake of his head.

'What exactly are you looking for?' she asked finally, beginning to feel delirious for a coffee. Elise's advice to fill their stomachs at breakfast had been wise indeed and she was beginning to wish she'd had extra toast.

'I know the beat I'm looking for,' he said distractedly, never taking his eyes off the water. 'The dry autumn means water levels are low and the fish are late this year. I remember there's a deeper pool somewhere near here – there's a chance they'll be more likely to take the fly there. It had a . . . like, a split tree by one of the rocks. You could push your arm through the trunk . . . Dammit, I know it's near here.'

Alex looked around them. There were trees everywhere, of course – some bent double, drooping their branches towards the water, other clinging to the banks . . . 'Like that one?' she asked, pointing ahead to a small ash tree where the trunk had cleaved a third of the way up, creating a sort of porthole.

'Oh. Yes.' Without a word of thanks, Lochie marched over, scrambling over the rocks and clearly expecting her to follow. He stood with his hands on his hips and inspected the beat. 'Aye, this is it. Drop the pack on the bank there and get the waders on. I'll attach the fly for you.'

'Aren't you going to instruct me? Surely it would be better for me to learn how to do it myself?'

'There's no time.'

'But wouldn't it be time saved in the long run, to show me once and then I won't have to keep bothering you?' She smiled. 'Remember, it's called delegation, not abdication.'

It was intended as a joke but he shot her an unimpressed look. 'This is not a workshop and you are not in charge.'

'Well,' she said under her breath, watching as he pulled his waders from the backpack. 'That's me told.'

She copied his every move, climbing into the supplied waders – not a good look – and standing in silence as he coupled the fly to the rod.

'We're going to be Spey casting. Heard of it?'

She shook her head, looking warily at the broad, fast-flowing expanse of water. Did they really have to stand in that? 'Can't you catch two salmon and we'll just say I caught one?'

'No.'

'Why not? I'm clearly nothing but a hindrance for you.'

He didn't disagree. 'It's called principles. I'm not sure if you've come across them before?'

Alex sighed at his sarcasm as he finished with the fly and handed the rod to her. 'Come and stand over here.'

She made her way uneasily to the edge of the water, following him in to knee depth. She could immediately feel the coldness of the water against the rubber of the waders, even though she remained dry. The current was strong, pushing against the backs of her knees.

She felt scared but she didn't say anything.

'Now watch me,' he said, wading deeper out to waist height. 'We're fishing right shoulder out, parallel to the bank, and we want to be landing the fly in that pool of still water over there. See it?'

He pointed to a calm area, sheltered just beyond some rocks, and she nodded.

'We start with the forward cast so you need to hold the rod with both hands wide apart, right hand uppermost, left hand at the bottom of the rod,' he called, having to raise his voice to be heard over the water. 'Energy comes from the hands, okay? The top hand has about sixty per cent of the power and the bottom forty per cent and if you snap them at the same time – locking the right elbow too – you get a push-pull tension and maximum power for the cast. Yes?'

She nodded. 'Yes.'

'Now you need to get a forward casting motion – you're aiming for a flat straight path with the rod tip directed at the target.' He pointed towards a clump of trees on the opposite bank. 'Cast out, trying to get a big D loop – that's the shape you get between the straight rod and the line as it bellies over the water. The bigger the D, the less amount of line is in contact with the water – or water stick as we call it – and you get a more efficient cast because you're not having to rip it off the water film. So, a big D, then lift the rod to put tension on the line.' She watched as he threw the line overhead, the fly landing in the water downstream. His enunciated intonation reminded her of Skye when teaching her how to drink the whisky. 'Then sweep it back upstream over the right shoulder and rotating the body, launch the line,' he said, moving his body and line as one in a gentle, rhythmic, fluid movement. 'Remembering to stop the rod high.' He looked across at her. 'Got it?'

'Sure.' It had to have been the quickest fishing lesson ever but he made it look easy enough.

She took a deep breath and tried to repeat what he had just shown her – except that as she flung the rod back for the first cast, the fly got caught in the branches of a tree behind her. There was a loud silence and then she could hear his curse under his breath as he waded over to her.

'Wait! Don't try to pull it!' he demanded crossly as she tried to rattle it free.

She handed the rod to him. 'Sorry,' she winced, feeling uncharacteristically useless.

He glanced at her. 'No. It's fine,' he sighed heavily. 'I'm sorry. I didn't mean to snap. I'm just tired. I didn't sleep well.'

She watched him as he cut the line and began fiddling with a new fly he'd got in a box in the chest pocket of his jacket.

'You mean because of the fire?' He surely must have been having flashbacks, if not nightmares, of that burning building. She certainly had.

'It hasn't helped. There's just a lot on at the moment.'

Skye. She knew he was referring to her, even if he wouldn't say it. Up close, she could see the tension in his jaw; he looked hard-wired with stress.

'There, try again,' he said, handing the rod back to her. 'But maybe come in a bit deeper and keep the line shorter.'

He held out a hand to help steady her as she walked deeper into the water, her fear ratcheting up another level. His grip tightened around her fingers as she gave a small gasp, her foot slipping on a loose rock. His hands were warm compared to hers and significantly bigger.

'It's okay,' he murmured. 'I've got you. Try to get to that

bigger stone there. It looks pretty flat,' he said, directing her as best he could with his own foot.

She settled herself on the rock and he moved out of the way again, wading back towards the bank.

'Now just remember what I showed you: cast the line, lift up, sweep upstream and launch. The whole point of the Spey is that it allows you to cast when there's no ground area behind you to get an overhead cast. You can go to the side so it doesn't matter if you've got high banks or trees. But you must rotate the body. It's called the hundred-and-eighty-degree principle.'

Alex arched an eyebrow. She had one of those herself.

'Point yourself to where you want the fly to cast. Remember, it's an art form, not a science. You've got to feel it.'

And she did. 'I did it!' she cried excitedly, jiggling in the water a little, as the fly landed without mishap downstream.

He watched, bemused. 'Although you might want to give the river dance a miss. The fish aren't fans, apparently.'

'Oh yes,' she laughed, biting her lip excitedly. 'And so I just keep doing this?'

'Yep,' he said, watching her do it a few times before beginning himself.

'This is quite relaxing, actually,' she called after a little while, feeling proud of herself as she found a rhythm.

'Stop talking!' he scolded. 'You're scaring off the fish!'

'Oh. Yes. Right.' She bit her lip and concentrated again, casting forward and—

The line resisted and she tugged again, feeling the tension carry through the rod. Rigid. Immovable. It was caught on something. 'Oh God,' she murmured, a rip tide of panic flooding her as she looked over at Lochie moving in an unbroken rhythm, looking perfectly at peace for once. 'Um, Lochie . . . !'

They sat on the mossy riverbank, their hands wrapped around the plastic lids of their thermos flasks as they sipped on the oxtail soup with which they'd been provided. Lochie was looking out over the water, his elbows on his knees.

'I'm sorry,' she said for the hundredth time. 'I'm completely messing this up for you.'

'It doesn't matter.'

But she could see it did. 'I wouldn't have come if I'd known I was going to handicap you.'

'Well, as you said, I had invited you.'

'Lochlan, we both know you only invited me because you wanted to put me in my place. You wanted to show me what you could do and I couldn't.'

The truth – plain and simple as it was – sat like a red coal between them, too hot to touch.

'Yeah. And see how well that's turning out for me,' he said finally.

She bit her lip, sensing an opportunity, but bracing herself for the slap down that would inevitably come with it. 'You know, one thing I go into with my clients is the abundance mentality.' She paused, waiting for him to turn away, walk off, take her by the arm and throw her into the river. Instead he just stared. 'Have you ever heard of that before?' she asked, tentatively.

He shook his head, looking too weary to argue for once.

'A lot of us – well, most of us – grow up with a belief system which propounds the idea that for me to win, you must lose. People in my line of work call it a zero-sum game. We prefer to find win-win scenarios which are mutually beneficial to both parties; you know, trying to be coopera-tive, rather than competitive.'

'Good in principle,' he said. 'I don't suppose you've worked out how to make today a win-win scenario?'

She pulled an apologetic expression. 'I'm afraid no, not for this.'

'But you have for something else?' He arched an eye-brow. 'I suppose you've got a long list identifying all the things I'm doing wrong.'

'It's not a matter of you doing anything wrong; it's just a question of finding methods to be even better and at the moment, you're overextending yourself. You feel besieged and embattled, and as a result, you're trying to do every-thing alone.'

'You mean you want me to delegate. Your favourite word.'

She smiled. 'Yes, that. But also synergize – you need someone you can debate and discuss ideas and problems with. It's not weakness to look for other perspectives. You'll go mad if you can't externalize all the problems and issues you have to deal with on a daily basis – and, before you say it, I know you talk to Rona, but she can't talk back!' She paused, not wanting to rush him. 'Is there *anyone* who fits the brief for you?'

He shook his head.

'What about Torquil? He seems solid.'

He looked away sharply. 'No.'

'Why not?' She remembered how he had closed up when she had brought up Torquil's name in their meeting yester-day too. What exactly had happened between them to make Lochie assault him at the family assembly?

He was quiet for a long moment. 'We're too different.'

'Is that a bad thing? People mistake uniformity for unity, sameness for oneness, but they're very different things.'

He shook his head. 'The guy's a robot.'

So one of them had too much emotion, and the other not enough? 'Okay, how about Bruce? He seems level-headed and vastly experienced.'

He shook his head again. 'We used to be close, but ever since—' He stopped abruptly and Alex realized the problem: ever since he'd jilted his daughter. 'I just can't. It would be an intrusion for him.'

'Okay, I can see that would be difficult,' she said, her heart beating a little faster as she got to the point she'd been wanting to make. 'So then, what about Skye?'

His eyes darted quickly, defensively. 'What about her?'

'Well, I know things have been . . . tricky,' she said quickly, seeing how he began to move his feet, straightening up and holding his drink higher as though he was protecting his heart. 'But couldn't you reach out to her, as a friend, a colleague?'

'No.'

'Why not?'

'Because she's not a senior manager for one thing – it would be inappropriate.' His voice was snappish again.

Alex stared at him. 'Are you sure that's what it is?'

'Of course I'm sure.'

She paused for a moment. 'Do you remember yesterday, when I suggested the root of your problem with Sholto might be a personal problem rather than a business one?'

'Vaguely.' She was losing him now, she could see it in his eyes; they were becoming guarded, blank.

'What if it's the same with Skye? You and I both know it's not because she's junior to you that's the problem. It's that your personal situation is unclarified. There's unfinished business between you both.'

He was looking angry now. 'You don't know the first thing about what happened between us.'

'But I do. I know you jilted her the night before the wedding. And I've seen with my own eyes how you are around each other: you're both jumpy and nervous as hell because you literally don't know where you stand with one another.'

'I'm not listening to this,' he said, getting to his feet and throwing the remains of his soup into the grass behind him. But where was he going to go? He couldn't get away from her, not out here.

'Do you know what I think?' she persisted, calling after him as he went back to get his rod from where it lay in the grass.

'I don't care!'

'I think you still love her,' she said to his back. 'You love her and she loves you, but she's about to marry another man because she has no idea that you still have feelings for her. And that's why you're so angry and rash and impetuous: leaving her was the worst decision of your life and you are fast running out of time to make it right.'

He was in the water now, wading furiously over the rocks.

'I know you can hear me, Lochlan!' she called after him. 'You're running out of time. This time next week it'll be all over. You'll have lost her for good and your lives will have changed for ever. Can you live with that?'

But there was no reply. He was facing downstream and casting into the water, the top hand pushing sixty per cent into the current and the bottom hand at forty per cent pulling back against it, a tension that might make the line fly – but the rod was stuck in place.

Chapter Twenty

The hours passed. The soup had had a brief warming effect that enabled her to momentarily feel her toes again but standing motionless up to her waist in cold rushing water was taking its toll and she was beginning to shiver. It didn't help that Lochlan, still not talking to her, was now sitting on the bank with a face like thunder and making her ever more nervous. He had landed his salmon an hour ago but they were at an impasse – it was more a lesson in pique, rather than chivalry, that he flatly refused to move from the spot until she caught hers too. It didn't matter that they both knew she was never going to catch a fish today. He knew he couldn't win without her but if he was going to lose, he was going to make sure she knew it was her fault. So much for that abundant mentality.

Not that she was leading by example, for she had just as stubbornly refused to come out of the water for lunch, almost weeping with hunger as he tucked into the beef-and-horseradish sandwiches without her.

Their silent war continued even though her teeth chattered and her arms ached, but she remained where she was, casting the line out, over and over. It had become automatic now, the rod and line part of her own body. The sun had moved round to behind the trees, its low angle in the sky sending thick rays through the bare branches, straight into her eyes.

She cast out again, angling her body slightly more to turn away from the light when she felt a sudden tug. It was so surprising, so unexpected, that her first instinct was almost to drop the line.

'Oh!' She pulled her arms up, lifting back on the rod.

Lochie heard the surprise in her voice and his head snapped up. 'What? What is it?'

'I . . . I think I've got one!' she cried, sounding more alarmed than anything.

He was on his feet in an instant. 'Okay, okay, just stay calm,' he said, running down the bank and over the rocks towards her, the big fishing net in his hand. 'If it wants to run, let it run. Don't resist. Let it tire itself out. But if it's coming in, reel it in, you hear me?'

'Uh . . .' she cried, feeling flustered as she felt the tugging become more frantic, the tension ratcheting up on the rod.

'Let him go, let him go. That's it . . . Now lift the rod a little – no more than that,' Lochie said. But he was running downstream, away from her. 'Come towards me.'

She took hesitant steps downstream. Why did she have to go down to him? Why couldn't he come up to her, she wondered in frantic silence?

'That's it. There's no rush. Now when you feel the rod bend, let him out. He's fighting the rod and the current. He's going to tire.'

She tried to calm herself down – the excitement and sur- prise, not to mention the struggle, had left her almost panting.

'Whatever you do, don't lock the reel,' Lochie cautioned, standing only knee deep by the water's edge with the net.

'Aren't you going to get it?' she cried. Why wasn't he going further out with the net?

'Lift up the rod. Lift up the rod,' he said, his eyes on the water. 'He's not ready yet. He's about a foot away.'

She felt the tension stiffen the rod again and she lowered the tip, feeling the line run. 'Oh God, I'm going to lose it,' she whimpered. Her arms were tired, her muscles cramping. She hadn't eaten, she hadn't rested. All of this and the damn thing was going to get away. It would all have been for nothing. She wanted to cry. To scream. 'My arms . . .'

But Lochie wasn't looking at her; his eyes were on the water.

'Take another step towards me,' he said in a calm voice, taking a step deeper himself.

She stepped, just as the reel stiffened again, the fish thrashing as it surfaced momentarily and Alex felt a violent jerk on her arms, the rod almost torn from her grasp. Lochie lunged, swooping the net and catching the fish within the big hoop.

'Yes!' he yelled, the fish flipping and flopping about as he held it high above the water. It was big – bigger than his! 'You actually did it! I don't bloody believe it!' he cried.

'Oh my God!' Alex cried, jumping up and down on the spot as much as she dared, actual tears falling from her lashes as they waded out of the water as quickly as they could. 'I did it? I actually did it?' She felt hysterical with relief. Delirious.

'You bloody did it!' he laughed, holding the net up high so that she could see it properly.

'Oh my God, that was . . .' She was open-mouthed, not sure what it had been. It had been so awful, standing there for so long braced against that cold, rushing water. But now it felt exhilarating. 'It's amazing,' she gasped, her hands on her cheeks, her eyes bright.

'*You* were amazing!' he laughed, beaming down at her. 'I can't believe you stuck it out. You're just amazing.'

His words made her look up at him. He'd never said anything nice to her before.

There was a pause, both of them as surprised as the other to not be arguing for once and as his gaze fell to her mouth, she felt a sudden drop in her stomach. What—?

'Hey, you're shivering. Your lips are blue. We need to get you warmed up,' he said, putting down the net and, opening his jacket, wrapping its sides and his arms around her.

Alex went very still as suddenly his warmth and smell enveloped her and she felt her stiff, frozen muscles instinctively soften. She closed her eyes, grateful for the reprieve from the cold as his hands rubbed her back, moving quickly, getting the blood flowing. 'Is that better?' he asked after a few minutes, his voice a rumble against her ear.

She nodded and he moved back a step. 'Thanks,' she said quietly, tucking her hair behind one ear.

'Hmm, your lips are pinking up again,' he said. 'But you need to eat. Have the sandwiches whilst I get this lot sorted,' he said, and he walked over to the net to disentangle the hook from the salmon's mouth.

Alex stared at his back, still trembling. But it wasn't the cold she was feeling.

Her haul had energized them both and after a brief look at the map, Lochie led her purposefully away from the river, towards the uplands. Though the shadows were lengthening, they suddenly had hope again. They knew she was a keen shot, and tracking and sighting a stag in time was the only obstacle in their way now – Daisy and Ambrose had booked the coach to leave Borrodale at half six and whether Lochlan had considered it or not, she (as a female of the species) was going to need time to get ready beforehand.

The packs were lighter now that they'd eaten and drunk their provisions, although the game bag – which Lochlan was carrying; it hadn't even been up for discussion – was heavy with two salmon on the inside and the brace of grouse swinging outside.

They stopped every so often for Lochie to look through the binoculars, but her blue lips were quickly replaced by flushed cheeks as they marched at speed, rifle and shotguns on their shoulders, nets and rods in their hands. The ground was uneven and rutted, hidden rabbit holes a constant peril, but before too long, the heather-striped moors were behind them, the ground becoming craggier, with rocky outcrops and swathes of dense woodland. Lochie spotted some deer droppings that he said looked fresh. To her they just looked like deer droppings.

They continued on, Alex wondering how many miles they had covered today and how long it was going to take them to get back to the house. She didn't think she would be capable of going to a black-tie event tonight; she felt physically broken and wanted to have a bath and be in bed by eight—

She felt Lochie's hand on her arm, stopping her. 'Shh,' he hushed, motioning with the other hand for her to crouch down.

She did so, squatting on her haunches and wondering what he'd seen and where. Without a word, he pointed to an area north-north-west of where they were positioned. The light was beginning to fade and she struggled to pick out anything against the pale camel-coloured moors. Only a slight movement caught her eye.

She felt her heart quicken as her eye attuned and she thought she saw a stag with three females. But it had to be three hundred metres away.

Lochlan took the rifle off his shoulder and unzipped it from the slip, his eyes never leaving their quarry. 'Lie down,' he whispered. 'Take this.'

She took the rifle from him. 'Me?' she hissed.

'Only one shot for this,' he whispered back. 'It has to be you.'

Why? Why did it have to be her? She lay down on her stomach and propped herself up on her elbows, feeling the adrenaline begin to surge again – it had been up and down like a yoyo all day.

The ground was damp; they were lying in a peat bog and she could feel the coldness of the earth through her tweed layers.

'Check the scope,' he murmured, the binoculars up at his eyes.

She looked through the telescopic sight – and was amazed. Suddenly, a magnificent red stag was beamed to her through the lens: it was surely twenty stone, its antlers a six- or eight-pointer.

Her heart rate increased. It was beautiful.

'Got it?' he murmured.

'Yes.'

'Now you need to aim the crosshairs halfway up the body, right behind the shoulder.'

'Crosshairs . . . behind the shoulder,' she repeated, feeling herself begin to tense, her hands to tremble. She tried to slow down her breathing.

'That's where the vitals are – it's about a five-inch circle. You need to get a good clean shot.'

'Okay,' she whispered, swallowing hard as she watched the stag grazing, intermittently stopping to nose the air.

She kept staring at it.

'Got it?' he asked again after a few moments.

'Mmhmm.'

'Take the shot when you're ready then.'

She could hear the suppressed urgency in his voice. Tension overlaid with enforced calm.

'. . . You okay?'

'Uh-huh.' But she wasn't. Her hands were shaking and her breath was coming too fast. Panic was making the deer swim before her eyes and she had to keep alternating eyes, opening and closing one, then the other.

She heard him turn his head to look at her. 'Alex, there's over a million and a half deer in the UK,' he said. 'Their numbers have to be controlled. We have to cull. They can devastate the countryside if they're left unchecked.'

'Yes, I know,' she murmured.

'So then take the shot.'

'I am. I will. I'm just . . .' She took a deep breath. Cull, not kill. She refocused on the scope; she could see the animal's brown eye moving in its socket, its ears twitching for untoward sounds – for them. It wouldn't hear the bullet speeding towards it and by the time the gun-crack got to it, it would already be lying on the ground. Her finger twitched by the trigger.

'This is our only chance, Alex. We'll never find another in time.' Lochie was sounding anxious now. She could hear the urgency in his voice.

He was right. It was almost four o'clock and the light was fading fast. Hat-trick.

Come on. She could do this.

But a tear blurred the stag from sight and she dropped her arm down. She looked across at Lochie, already scared of what she'd see, as she held out the rifle for him to use. 'I'm so sorry,' she whispered. 'I can't do it.'

Chapter Twenty-One

WEEKLY MONTANIAN
February 9th, 1918

THOMPSON FALLS MAN IS AMONG MISSING TUSCANIA TROOPS

Edward Samuel Cobb, of Thompson Falls, Montana, enlisted in the forest reserve unit of the 20th Engineers on December 22nd, 1917. He was sent to train at the American University Camp in Washington DC, and assigned to company E, 6th Battalion. He was one of the men aboard the SS Tuscania *which was torpedoed by a German U-boat five days ago. The troopship, bearing 2,197 American soldiers to the war zone, was sunk off the coast of Scotland. 267 men are missing.*

Borrodale House, Perthshire,
Saturday 16 December 2017

'Family honour is restored!' Ambrose cried, holding up his sherry glass and raising a toast to the Arbuthnotts' MacNab hat-trick. They were all sitting in the library in their finery. Alex's dress had arrived with her shooting kit this morning although she rather wished it hadn't, for it would have given her a perfect excuse to get out of coming tonight. It wasn't that she was exhausted – her hot bath and a power nap had restored her energy – but it was almost more than she could bear to see Lochie's disappointment.

He'd been gracious, in the circumstances. Something – instinct? – had startled the deer as she had handed over the gun and it had been gone from sight by the time they had looked back. She had been conflicted by how it made her feel – on the one hand, she was glad it had escaped. It was too beautiful an animal; she couldn't bear to see it killed, culled, whatever it was. On the other hand, she had wanted Lochie to get his hat trick; his desperation on the river bank had been palpable and when she had miraculously landed the salmon, he had been euphoric; she had been so swept up in his delight, it had done what the river had not, and almost lifted her off her feet. So to have let him down when victory had been within their – her – grasp . . . she had done the very thing she had stood in a river for four hours to avoid: she had made him fail.

He was standing by the bar, one hand in the pocket of his tartan trews – all the men were wearing them – and looking a different man to the vision they'd all seen at breakfast. He had showered and shaved, his skin still flushed from a day out in the elements, and his body was looser-limbed than it had been for days. The doctors had been right – fresh air and exercise was just what he'd needed. But though he smiled and joined in the conversation, she could see the disappointment beneath the surface. He was a true stoic, keeping his feelings to himself, but she alone knew she had ruined his weekend and for what? He was no closer to either listening or talking to her about Skye, but his over-reaction again had only convinced her that she was right and she felt certain now that this had to be her principal strategy for getting into his head. If they could be reunited, Alex was sure it would be a case of mission accomplished for her too.

'That dress is to *die* for,' Elise said, coming to sit beside her on the velvet sofa. 'I wish I could wear black.'

Alex smiled, grateful for the compliment. It was Dolce & Gabbana corded lace, with no sleeves and a deep V neckline, a black ribbon beneath the bust. Its long, slim – but not tight – silhouette was flattering but also easy to wear. 'I would have thought you'd look lovely in black.'

'No,' Elise sighed, looking radiant in silver. 'It really washes me out.'

Alex met Anna's eyes and they shared a smile. 'How was your day?'

'Another bloody trout,' Anna sighed. 'It's becoming my nemesis. We were only twenty minutes behind Butthead, apparently.'

'Such a shame.'

'How about you?' Elise asked.

'Well, I did manage to get a salmon although I almost had to contract pneumonia first.' She took a weary breath. 'No, I'm afraid it was the stalking that did for me.'

'I thought Lochie said you were a crack shot?'

Did he? It surprised her to think that he had been talking about her in any positive terms at all. 'Well, it was more of an . . . emotional issue. I wussed out.' She bit her lip. 'I just couldn't do it.'

'Oh, but you mustn't worry about that,' Elise said kindly, seeing she was upset.

'I just feel so bad.'

'I can totally sympathize. They're such incredible creatures. You need to be really committed and understand what it is that you're doing. Otherwise, you just feel like you're killing Bambi.'

'Exactly.' She bit her lip again. 'But Lochla— I mean, Lochie's just so disappointed. He seemed to really want the hat-trick.'

'Look, I know it was a nice idea but it's not like his dad is going to care *now*.'

Alex frowned. 'His dad?' She looked over at Anna – she was a grounded, steady sort. She could explain, surely?

'Lochie promised his father he'd get the hat-trick,' she shrugged.

'But . . . his dad's dead, isn't he?'

Anna gave a reluctant smile. 'Yes. He promised him . . .'

She didn't need to finish the sentence. Alex gripped her cheekbones with one hand, feeling even worse. He'd made a deathbed promise.

'Apparently it had been an ambition of his father's.'

Elise patted her knee. 'But you mustn't worry. He can always do it next year.'

'But it won't be the same, will it? This would have been three on the trot. It's not a hat-trick in the same way.'

'Oh God, don't tell Ambrose that,' Daisy groaned as she came through with a bowl of olives.

'Hey,' Emma said, joining them and looking lovely in her dress. She had twisted her hair up, revealing an elegant neck and beautifully creamy skin. 'Everyone recovered? My legs are still throbbing,' she said, joining Anna on the ottoman.

'Well, thank God you're wearing long then,' Anna smiled. 'That could look alarming in a mini.'

Jess – who had been in the kitchens with Daisy – came

back through, clapping her hands. 'The coach is outside,' she said. 'All good to go?'

Everyone murmured their assents, draining their glasses and smoothing out their clothes with their hands. Alex's eyes slid across to Lochlan and she was surprised to find his were already on her. She gave another sorry smile. It was his big night tonight; he was no doubt wondering whether she was going to ruin that for him too.

The last time she had been on a coach had been on a school trip, but this vehicle was a world away from that experience – just a 'baby' size, it nonetheless had tinted windows and extra-wide quilted leather seats, multi-entertainment screens and a fridge stacked with gold-topped bottles. It was the private jet of the coach world and Ambrose kept everyone in champagne – and strong voice, instigating a singalong, mainly of Scottish rugby songs – as they sped up the A9 in luxury.

Lochie was looking nervous, his leg jigging more and more quickly as they approached Pitlochry, his smile matching everyone else's, but he kept looking out of the windows to see exactly where they were.

Soon enough, in the village of Blair Atholl, they turned into a tree-lined lane and passed through a set of grand – and towering – stone-flanked gates. Everyone stopped singing as they looked out of the windows at the magnificent park-like grounds, the lawns clipped and pristine with a nearby lake shimmering in the moonlight, groupings of full-skirted fir trees stopping the eye from seeing everything in one sweep. To her dismay, Alex saw they were driving through a deer park of all things, and as they passed close by a standing herd, she kept her eyes down on her hands in her lap.

They drew up before a grand white castle and even before the doors had opened, she could hear the haunting sound of the bagpipes; it always gave her goose bumps. They stepped out, one by one, onto a red carpet flanked on each side by soldiers in full ceremonial dress, with kilts and sashes, feathered caps and muskets by their sides.

Alex was the last off and she was surprised to see Lochie waiting for her, the others already walking ahead in their pairs. He held out a velvet-jacketed arm for her to take, looking down at her with unreadable eyes.

'Shall we?'

If she had thought Borrodale House was grand, Blair Castle was positively regal with a double-height entrance hall that was almost armour-plated, such was the density of historic weaponry hanging from its walls. Waiters stood in the same rigid lines as the soldiers outside, but they were holding out silver trays with champagne on them and she and Lochie each took one. She could feel his nervousness.

'It sounds like a big deal, being made a master,' she said to him as they waited in the short line that had bottlenecked at the entrance to the ballroom.

She felt his torso stiffen against her arm in reply. 'It's just a ceremonial thing. It doesn't mean anything.'

'Except that you're highly regarded by your peers,' she countered.

He looked down at her but didn't reply.

'You know, you should learn to take a compliment,' she smiled.

'I could say the same about you.'

'Excuse me?'

'You look very beautiful in that dress.'

Alex whipped her head up, looking at him in astonishment; she didn't know what to say.

He chuckled and looked ahead. 'See?'

The line moved and they began walking again, Alex emitting a small groan, the sound imperceptible above the bagpipes, as she saw a stag's head mounted over the entrance to the ballroom above them. Really? Was she to be faced with her failure *all* night?

Lochie must have felt the vibration through her body, her arm still linked through his, for he looked down at her and then followed her eyeline. 'Just forget about it,' he said in a low voice.

'But . . .' She didn't know what was wrong with her. What had happened to her out there? She wasn't sentimental about country sports; she understood the economies behind them and the agricultural livelihoods they supported. What had made her flake? 'I'm just so sorry.'

'I know. You've said it a hundred times now.'

'But that was before I found out about the promise you made. To your father, I mean.'

He looked down at her again, that suspicion always in his eyes.

'Anna told me.'

He inhaled, clearly irritated. 'It was just a . . . challenge. A dare even. It doesn't mean anything in the scheme of things.'

They were quiet for a moment.

'Besides, it was fairly enlightening,' he said, his eyes dead ahead, the words scarcely more than a murmur.

'What do you mean?'

'Well, I guess it proves you have a heart.'

'What?' She frowned, knocked sideways by the comment.

'I was beginning to wonder,' he shrugged. 'But it looks like you don't have it after all, the killer instinct.'

'Yes, I do!'

He looked straight at her. 'No.' His voice was calm, almost too calm. 'You had him in your sights and you could have taken the shot. But you didn't. You couldn't do it.' His gaze was piercing, so direct she felt he could see straight through her.

Whether his remark had been intended as a compliment or an insult she wasn't sure, but she took it as the latter. Offended, she tried to remove her arm from his but he clamped his elbow in to his side – effectively trapping her – as a photographer suddenly pointed his lens at them; they both flashed fake smiles and the camera snapped.

The bottleneck had cleared now and they walked into the ballroom. In spite of its great size, it was packed and their progress through the crowd was slow as Lochlan was back-slapped and greeted by almost everyone they passed, the great and the good of the whisky industry clamouring for their moment with him. Alex smiled and went through the motions as introductions were made but for once, she wasn't storing names or clocking the non-verbal cues that always alerted her to prospective clients; she felt distracted and unlike herself, off her game, his words replaying over and over in her mind, and it was a relief when she spotted Ambrose's curls springing a half-head above everyone else.

'God, I hope they feed us quickly. I am *starved*,' Emma said, looking around the room restlessly. 'I brought cake up to our room with tea earlier and Max ate it all whilst I was in the bath! Honestly, and he's the one telling his patients to cut out hydrogenated fats.'

Alex knew she should be hungry too but her appetite felt dampened. Lochlan's words still cut like blades, drawing blood. What was wrong with her? Why *hadn't* she taken the shot?

'Lochie's looking nervous, don't you think?' Anna murmured to them as the guys began to tease and heckle him about something.

'Mmm, but handsome though,' Elise smiled, looking – for some reason – at Alex.

'He always did look nice in those trews,' Jess said, sipping on her champagne and looking over at him with studied concentration.

'Oh-ho,' Daisy laughed, slapping her playfully on the arm. 'Don't let Sam hear you saying that!'

'Why not?' Jess grinned. 'It's just an honest observation.'

'Honest observations are not allowed about your ex. We all know Sam's convinced Lochie thinks you're the one who got away.'

Alex looked at Jess in surprise. She was his *ex*?

'They were together at university,' Elise said, seeing her surprise. 'Didn't you know?'

Alex shook her head. 'No. We, uh . . . well, we don't talk about our private lives.'

'Oh no, that's right – you're just *colleagues*,' Emma said, a wicked glint in her eyes.

'Yes.'

'If you say so,' she grinned, one eyebrow cocked.

Alex looked puzzled. 'We are! There's not – there's not anything like that between us.'

314

'Oh, come on!' Anna laughed. 'We've all seen how he looks at you.'

'We've all seen that he doesn't *stop* looking at you!' Elise rejoined.

'That's not true,' Alex protested, feeling her colour begin to rise. They didn't know the first thing about it; they hadn't heard how he'd just spoken to her and the things he'd said. They didn't know that this supposed 'friendship' was just a charade, a brave face in front of his friends whilst they battled it out, each with their own agenda for rescuing their professional pride. They didn't know that he hated her, that he couldn't stand the sight of her, that a week from now she would be home and they'd never have to see each other again.

The sudden realization of it almost winded her with relief. A week from now, life would be back to normal: she would return to her pristine flat and early-morning Pilates sessions; she would be able to wear heels again and have her chef-developed lunch delivered to her desk. There would be no more borrowing strangers' clothes and sharing a bathroom; there would be no more biscuits with her coffee or cabbage with everything. She could finally get out of that westerly wind that kept wrecking her hair and she wouldn't have to kill a living beast just to prove she was good at her job.

She sagged, feeling suddenly exhausted. The emotional and mental toll of going through this, dealing with him, had depleted her more than she had realized. It was too much, living and breathing it, with no respite, 24/7.

'Hey, are you okay?' Elise asked, putting a hand on her arm in concern. 'We were just messing around. We didn't mean anything by it. If you say it's just professional between you, then it is.'

'No, it's not that,' Alex said, trying to smile. 'I've just realized how . . . bloody exhausted I am. I haven't stopped for weeks and with today too . . . it's all just caught up with me. I feel a bit faint, actually.'

'It is hot in here,' Emma said, looking up at the barrelled ceilings as though steam would be collecting there.

'I think I'm just going to go and . . . get some air,' she said, looking around for the exit again.

'Sure. Do you want one of us to come with you?' Daisy asked, looking concerned.

'No, it's fine. I'm fine. I'll only be a minute.'

'Okay. We'll wait for you here,' Daisy smiled.

Alex turned and left, but she was still within earshot when she heard Elise's voice. 'Ow! *What?* He *is* always looking at her.'

Her hands were sore from clapping. The ceremony and speeches had gone on for over an hour now and the tension was radiating from Lochlan beside her. She hadn't seen him like this before; he was so good at always presenting a bluff exterior and hiding any emotion or vulnerability behind a rhino hide and quick temper. But he was up next, the man on stage delivering a rousing speech in praise of Lochlan's apparently numerous achievements – it had been news to her that it was he who had managed to get the Kentallen twenty as the official malt of the Houses of Parliament. A man on the next table leaned over and whispered to him.

'Where's Sholto? I thought he'd be here tonight.'

'No, he couldn't make it,' Lochie said, fiddling with his bow tie, and when the other man looked surprised – he was after all being honoured for services to the industry; his chairman ought to be here – he added, 'The fire.'

'Oh yes, yes, of course,' the man said, remembering the headlines and patting his arm apologetically. 'I was so sorry to hear about that.'

'Thank you.' Lochie sat back in his seat, his eyes already on the speaker on the podium.

'You didn't even invite him,' Alex said quietly.

'How do you know?'

'Because you covered your throat, your voice changed and you blinked more rapidly when you were speaking – all classic non-verbals for lying.'

Lochie looked at her for a moment as she stared ahead at the speaker. 'Huh. Well, it was for his own safety.'

'Safety?'

'Of course. He would have choked on his own bile having to sit through these plaudits for me.'

'I think you're being a little harsh.'

'I'm perfectly aware of what you think,' he said brusquely. 'Your loyalties are quite clear.'

She looked away, refusing to get into another fight with him. Today had already been quite hard enough.

Everyone started clapping again, looking their way, and she heard him clear his throat as he rose to his feet, a smile on his lips. He was up.

He wound his way past the large circular tables and the delicate gilt chairs, faces upturned to him with admiring smiles as he walked by, his eyes on the stage. He and the other man shook hands and then Lochie turned, facing back to them all – his hands on the podium, elbows splayed slightly, chin up.

Alex frowned as she saw it for what it was – a power

pose. He was bigging up, establishing himself as dominant, reminding everyone that he was the CEO who had run into a burning building to save his company and its employees' livelihoods.

'Thank you, ladies and gentlemen,' he said, waiting for the applause to die down. 'Thank you very much.' He wasn't using notes; it was all in his head.

He surveyed the crowd, a faint smile on his lips and from here – at a distance – she could suddenly see his similarity to his cousin: his darker hair was such a contrast to Callum's blond thatch and their demeanours such polar opposites, that she had never stopped to notice it before, but under the lights, she could see they shared the same good cheekbones, squared chin, deep-set eyes; but whereas Callum was quick to smile, revelling in his beauty, Lochie was quick to scowl, seemingly oblivious to it.

'Ladies and gentlemen, it is a privilege to stand in front of you all today to accept this honour. As most of you know, I have not blood but the amber nectar running through my veins and my entire life and career have been devoted to trying to spread the love that we here all share for it, to as many people, in as many countries, as possible.'

He cleared his throat. 'That's not always an easy mission to accomplish. This industry has many pitfalls. Who else has to wait out three years before they can even get started? Who else has to try to predict demand for a product up to fifty years in advance? Who else has to create a DNA from just water, barley and peat – and then, when they have cre-ated a unique flavour fingerprint, repeat that alchemy exactly, over and over again?'

He smiled. 'The answer is no one. No one else has to face the unpredictabilities not just of demand but of supply, in the way that we do. It cannot be replicated, in spite of what some quarters may try to tell you; not all whisky can be Scotch – they need our water, our air, our soil, our *passion*. But we need Spanish sherry casks and American oak bourbon barrels; we need India to drop its punitive import duties so that an entire market is allowed access to us; we need Chinese companies to stop corrupt business practice so that Scotch is not tainted with the stigma of bribery.

'And what about the news that sales of white spirits have continued to outpace us for the second year running, that sales of vodka and gin are where the new profit margins are to be found, that diversity is the key? Surely in the face of such challenges, our cycle of boom and bust is destined to be repeated for ever more? We all remember the whisky lake of the eighties when demand crashed, prices plummeted and distilleries across the country were left with worthless stocks. Many distilleries closed; Kentallen certainly teetered on the brink on several occasions and my own father risked personal bankruptcy to keep operations going when the banks pulled their support.' He paused, taking a breath and looking around the room, unhurried, in his element. Every bit the CEO.

'So how do we continue in the face of such odds? How can we *thrive* against so many competing problems?' He smiled, looking perfectly calm, and Alex felt her ears prick. He was building up to something. She could hear it in his voice, see it in his eyes. He looked . . . excited, and she realized it hadn't been nervousness she'd seen in him earlier; it had been restlessness, impatience. He had been waiting for this.

'We thrive, ladies and gentlemen, because we know that these elements are not a collective disaster for our industry

– but the perfect storm. Rarity and legacy bottles are achieving record prices at auction, and diminishing supply coupled with increasing demand – even in the face of competitive sectors and closed key markets – means there has never been a better time to invest—'

What? That word— She heard the faint echo of Torquil's voice . . .

'And so I am delighted to announce to you today, that Kentallen Distillery Group has established a new subsidiary company, Scotch Vaults; a company in which private and even small-scale investors can for the first time invest in our maturing malts—'

A collective gasp whistled round the room, only making him smile all the more. Alex felt herself freeze. No. He couldn't be doing this.

'For the past two years, we've been developing a revolutionary collective trading platform in which the individual can buy by the *litre* – not per cask as was only available in the past; small investors can now buy as little or as much one-, two- or three-year-old maturing malt as they want; they can sell *when* they want with no minimum holding period. And by investing in these young whiskies which are already stored in our bonded warehouses, they are exempted from all the hassles and costs that bog down the industry's end product – namely re-vatting, transportation, marketing, bottling and of course duties and excises.

'Up till now, the huge scales required by the industry to produce a consistent product couldn't dovetail with the needs of the small-scale investor – but Scotch Vaults will change that; Scotch Vaults will aggregate high numbers of private stockholders into consortiums whose investment needs can mesh with the long-term, large-scale quantities required by the trade.

'Lairds, ladies and gentlemen, as of now, Scotch whisky maturation investment can step into the light and take its long-awaited, rightful place alongside the investment fine-wines market. High market returns need not be confined to those rare, top-of-the-market legacy bottles but to young stocks too, nor shall the market remain closed to the elite few, and I actively look forward to holding talks with those distilleries interested in adding *their* maturing stocks to the Scotch Vaults lists.' He beamed as he looked around at the rapt expressions staring back at him. 'Ladies and gentlemen, whisky's historic boom-and-bust cycle has just become a tradeable, open-market commodity. We are open for business. Let's all enjoy the ride.'

People were on their feet before he had even left the podium, the room vibrating with cheers and whistles, arms outstretched to shake his hand so that it was several minutes before he made it back to the table, Ambrose whooping and refilling everyone's glasses, and the guys all enveloping him in bear hugs.

'You crafty bugger!' Max laughed. 'How the hell did you manage to keep that under your hat?'

'It's called discretion,' Lochie laughed. 'You might like to remember that next time you're in Soho.'

'But how did you go about developing the software?' Ambrose asked. 'You run a distillery, for Chrissakes. Who did you know to—?'

He stopped talking as Lochie grinned, his eyes sliding across the table.

'*Sam?*' Jess cried, almost dropping her glass.

'Well, I had to find a new project, darling,' he grinned.

'But you never said—'

'I couldn't. He was incredibly James Bond about the whole thing and said it was top secret.'

'But not to say anything in two years? I'm your wife! You could have told me!'

'Yes, but then I would have had to kill you. Forgive me?' he asked playfully, leaning over to kiss her on the cheek as she continued to gawp.

Lochie took his seat beside her again, but Alex couldn't laugh like the others.

'Are you completely mad?' she whispered, staring at him with desperate eyes as he finally deigned to look at her.

'Quite possibly,' he chuckled as Ambrose dropped a whisky shot in his champagne.

'You cannot do something like that – *and then* announce it to the entire fucking industry,' she hissed, as he downed it, vigour in every movement, 'when you haven't got the mandate of the board.'

'How do you know I don't?' he asked in a low voice, coming to look at her, the smile still on his lips but his eyes becoming hard.

'Because Torquil told me. It was thrown out.'

'Well, lucky for me then that I used my own money and that Sam's working on an equity basis.'

'You *know* Sholto's not going to take this lying down.' Her eyes swivelled round the table but no one was looking at them; they were all talking to each other excitedly and seemingly 'leaving them to it'.

'It's *my* money,' he reiterated darkly, his good mood beginning to evaporate. 'It's nothing to do with Kentallen.'

'Yes, it is!' she cried, only just keeping her voice down. 'You've just used the Kentallen name as the primary brand;

you're going to be using Kentallen's stocks! You cannot do that without a majority vote.'

'Actually, if you take a moment to think back, you'll see I never said we'd be using Kentallen stocks. I simply said it would be a subsidiary company to the group. Of course, if you want to infer from that that Kentallen stocks will be traded, then that's up to you. And I certainly hope that once the shareholders see *this* response –' a sweep of his eyes indicated the room – 'they'll reconsider and sign up too.'

'Don't play games with me. You know exactly what you did up there.'

'Look,' he hissed, eyes glittering. 'I can't force the board to be a part of this venture; but they can't force me to relinquish it either. The technology's in place, the patents are pending. And as of tonight, the entire industry is going to be clamouring to sign up.' He gestured with a nod to the people at the tables around them, conversations buzzing.

'It's career suicide, you know that. Sholto will push you out for this. You cannot go around making binary orders. There is a board for a reason!'

'No, the board is redundant, don't you get *that*?' he snapped, making her recoil. 'We're at an impasse. Checkmate. No one can move. *Something* has to happen.'

'And so this is your answer?' she asked incredulously. 'This is what you're going with? Out on a limb?'

'Yes,' he snarled, reaching for another whisky cocktail from Ambrose. 'Deal with it.'

Chapter Twenty-Two

The party continued back at the house. Lochie's mood had ignited the place, everyone forgetting their exhaustion from a day spent on the moors as he gave vent to his triumph. Champagne was chased with shots, music blasting through the Sonos system, which was about the only thing Ambrose had added to the house during his young reign as the clan laird.

Daisy – who had changed out of her taffeta monstrosity and into an eye-popping little black dress – led the dancing on the island in the kitchen, which in turn had led to a conga through the hall and around the Christmas tree, and the guys holding an ill-advised body-popping dance-off in the drawing room.

Alex, watching them from the chaise longue, was drunker than she wanted to be. She didn't want to be drunk at all, she wanted to be in bed, far, far away from here; she knew she needed to think about the ramifications of Lochie's actions and what it meant for her – but her glass had been repeatedly topped up when she wasn't looking, so that without intending it, she was as far gone as all the rest.

But if they were happy drunks, she was angry. Her frustrations of the last couple of weeks had boiled to the surface: it had all been for nothing – wearing other people's clothes, living with strangers, dealing with his insults and abuse day in and day out. And for what? If Sholto could boot him out for insubordination or gross misconduct or some other technicality – and he most likely would – then she was as much out of a job as he. He had absolutely no idea of the real consequences of what he'd done and what it meant for her. This wasn't just a case of hard luck; it was a full-blown catastrophe. In blowing his own trumpet on that stage, he had unwittingly blown up her life. And the most galling this was he would never even know it.

She threw back her whisky shot, pressing the back of her hand to her mouth, feeling how it burned down her throat. Her stomach felt on fire. She felt as though she might spontaneously combust into flames. All her anger was becoming heat, her heat in turn stoking the anger.

Daisy and Max were dancing a flamboyant tango, crossing the room from corner to corner, cheeks pressed together and mouths pursed in outrageous comedy pouts, the others whooping as they stalked, stopped and flung out their ankles, Daisy wrapping one of her – extraordinarily good – legs around Max's. It was all going well, until he tried to do a double turn and they lost what little balance the whisky had left them, falling in a tangled heap over the low ottoman to a rousing chorus of cheers.

'My turn!' Sam cried, slamming down his glass and – to Alex's slow dawning horror – making a beeline straight for her.

'Oh. No . . .' she protested, as he grabbed her by the hand and pulled her up to standing with such power, her feet almost left the ground and she found herself chest to chest with him. There was a momentary pause and as she caught her breath, he grinned – and immediately dipped her low.

She shrieked with surprise, her long hair touching the ground, the room upside down in her vision – and Lochie too. She saw him for a fraction of a second, leaning against the bookcase, his long legs crossed at the ankle in that louche way of his, one hand in his pocket, the other around a glass. But in the next second, he was snatched away again; or rather, she was; Sam's arm rigid around her ribcage, holding her firm and sure, his eyes glittering with merriment, one leg between hers as he spun her round and round and round. She was astonished to realize the man could actually dance, really properly hold her in position and lead . . . It didn't matter that the room was spinning or that she had no idea where to go or what to do next. He simply put her where she needed to be, and if he spun her out, sending her spinning off like a top, he easily caught her again in the next beat and pulled her back in.

She laughed, feeling delirious and helpless all at once, her hair flying around as she vaguely heard everyone's whoops and cheers; they were clapping, stamping their feet. All except Lochie who hadn't moved a single muscle, not even his drink to his lips.

She laughed harder, something in his demeanour spiking her defiance as she realized that her good time seemed to be at the expense of his. It might be a petty revenge but it was the only weapon left in her arsenal. So much for abundant mentality.

On and on they danced, Alex letting herself relax and Sam leading. If he wanted to dip her, he could; spin her, he could; lift her off the ground and twirl her, he could – and did. She couldn't remember the last time she'd felt so free and when the song finally ended, the two of them jumped up and down on the spot, cheering with everyone else, their arms wrapped around each other as though they were old friends.

'That was amazing!' Elise cried – she was, of course, the happiest of happy drunks – as Alex, still dizzy, gingerly made her way across the room towards where everyone was standing.

'Well, it was nothing to do with me,' Alex demurred, looking over at Jess. 'Your husband is an *incredible* dancer!'

'I know. He learnt to dance for our wedding.'

'Uh-huh. Well, wow,' Alex laughed, still breathless, one hand on her chest. 'It totally paid off. That was . . . exhila-rating,' she puffed. 'I'm not sure I've ever danced with anybody like that before.'

'No.'

Alex caught her breath, her smile freezing in place. Was it just her, or was Jess's manner . . . cool? 'Are you going to dance?' she asked. 'I think you should. I don't see why Daisy and I should be the only ones to be flung about. Phew . . . I think my head's going to be spinning for days.'

'Well, I can't dance with my own husband. How dull would that be?' Jess quipped, putting down her drink and scouting the room for her ex. 'Where's Lochie? He used to have a few moves on him, I seem to remember.'

Alex kept her smile firmly on her lips, even though the mere mention of his name now brought about a visceral reaction. She was so mad with him right now she didn't even trust herself to look at him.

She heard the text buzz on her phone, lying on the arm of the sofa, and saw the blue light flashing. 'Oh,' she mumbled, swaying slightly as she reached over to it. 'Christ, six messages. Who . . . ?'

'Oh, Lochie! There you are. Come over here,' Jess demanded.

A smile grew on Alex's lips as she read the messages. 'How far's Edinburgh from here?' she asked, a plan forming. Why the hell not? It was all over now anyway. There was definitely no conflict of interest any more. And she felt so angry, so reckless suddenly that the very 'wrongness' of it thrilled her.

'Oh, not far,' Anna said. 'Forty miles or so.'

Lochie came over, his movements oiled, heavy and easy like a panther. 'What is?'

'Edinburgh,' Anna said, hiccupping. She put a hand over her mouth, looking cartoonishly surprised. 'Ooh, excuse me . . . ! It's about an hour from here, right?'

'Yes. Why?'

Anna shrugged. 'Alex was asking.'

'Lochie, dance with me,' Jess purred, holding out her hand and beginning to sway her hips sexily. 'Seeing as you made my husband keep secrets from me for two years, the very least you can do is fling me round this room.'

'What's in Edinburgh, Alex?' Elise laughed, detecting mischief.

But Alex bit her lip and winked. Not what, who. 'I'm just going to make a call,' she grinned, not lifting her head as she wove her way unsteadily across the room.

'Where are you *going*?' Ambrose asked, the words plaintive, as she passed. 'Not to bed?'

'I'm just making a phone call,' she laughed. 'I'll be right back.'

'But it's half past three in the morning!' he called after her.

'Precisely. I'm coming back!'

She staggered out into the hall, heading for the front door – she had had to lean half out of the window this morning to get any kind of reception. It was chilly away from the fire-lit drawing room and her bare arms goose-bumped in the cold as she tried to open all the various locks and bolts of the enormous door, her fingers fumbling and slow.

'Fuck,' she hissed under her breath, breaking a nail as she struggled with the last bolt. It was ancient and stiff and only released with a sudden action. She opened the door, gasping as the dead of night drifted in—

'Who are you ringing?'

The voice was hard and she turned in surprise. Lochie was striding past the Christmas tree towards her. He had taken off his velvet jacket – unsurprisingly, given all their earlier boy-band antics – and his bow tie had been pulled loose, his shirt part untucked. She felt her stomach contract at the sight of him. He moved around this place as though he owned it.

She was confused. Why was he here? Hadn't Jess snaffled him for a rhumba? 'Why aren't you dancing?'

'Answer the question,' he snapped. 'Who are you ringing?' He had stopped dead in front of her, trying to intimidate her with his size, the fact that this was his turf – his friends – and not hers.

'That's none of your business,' she said, feeling her happy buzz of a few moments earlier begin to fade.

'It is my business when you're ringing my cousin.'

'*What?*' she cried, unable to believe her ears. 'You honestly think you have the ri—'

'Give me that.' And before she could so much as blink, he had snatched the phone from her hand.

'How dare you!' she shouted furiously, reaching up for it,

but he only held it higher, stretching away from her. 'You have no right to interfere with my private life.'

'Private . . . ?' His expression changed as he looked at the screen and saw the name on it. 'I thought you were . . .' His voice faded into a deafening silence.

Sholto? He'd thought she was calling Sholto, a spy giving the chairman the heads-up on what had gone down at the dinner? Ha! As if he didn't know already; his phone would have been ringing off the hook all night.

His arm dropped down and she grabbed the phone back from him.

'You said there was nothing between you.' His voice was low. She couldn't read him – she never had been able to and it was no different after a skinful of champagne whisky chasers.

'Did I? Well, maybe there wasn't, but let's face it, everything's changed now. Thanks to your stunt tonight, all bets are off,' she sneered. 'Now that you've most likely lost us both our jobs, we can do whatever the hell we like,' she said, throwing her arms into the air drunkenly. 'I don't even have to pretend to like you any more.'

He stared at her. 'So that's . . . that's your great plan. You're going after Callum?'

'*Going after?*' she sneered. 'Please! I haven't had to do a damn thing. He's made it perfectly clear that he's right there. All I have to do is say the word.'

She saw the ball of his jaw pulse as he clenched his teeth. 'And obviously you realize you're just one of many. I mean, you know what he is, right?'

'Yes. He's fun. And funny. And charming. And about as opposite to *you* as it's possible to be,' she taunted. 'In fact, I can hardly even believe you're relate—'

'That's enough.'

'No, actually, it's not,' she said, determined to defy him. She hadn't been able to turn him to her way of thinking, she hadn't been able to beat him in the field, but she could and would defy him now, for as long as she had to spend time in his company – she would no longer be the patient, long-suffering, rising-above-it professional, because he was no longer her client. She could do what she liked. She could behave just as badly as him if she wanted. The gloves were off. 'You are the most obnoxious, arrogant, pig-headed man I have ever had the misfortune to meet. These past two weeks have been the worst of my career. Every single day with you has been under sufferance. I cannot wait to get back to that island, pack my bags and *never* have to see you again.'

'Great. I'll fly you there myself. Make it happen that bit sooner,' he snapped.

'Great!'

'Great!' He glared at her, his breath coming as fast as hers. 'It's not been a walk in the park for me either, you know, having to deal with *you* when there's been a shit-storm flying round my head. The fire, that fucking deal – and yet everywhere I look there you are, getting in my face. I can't get away from you. Not at work, not at the weekend, not even at night. I close my eyes and there you are! I come here and here you are! You're dancing with my friends, making a booty call to my fucking cousin—'

The sound of the slap – of her hand on his cheek – was so loud, it stunned them both, the surprise in both their eyes only growing in hers as she saw her handprint bloom on his skin. He looked so angry. Angry and devastated.

'Oh,' she gasped, her breath held high in her lungs, her

shoulders up by her ears as she realized what she had done. She had never hit anyone before. She wanted to tell him she was sorry. She wanted to undo what she'd done. She could see, from the dark look in his eyes, the instinct to slap her back and it stopped every word, every thought.

Until in the next instant, he kissed her instead, anger switching to passion, his mouth on hers, her back pushed against the door frame, the cold forgotten as he pressed himself to her. For a moment, she couldn't move, she couldn't catch up, but her body instinctively stirred beneath his touch, her tongue to his lips, and their mutual frustration exploded into a hunger she had never known. Every cross word that had passed between them, every insult they had traded, was now swapped for a counterpart kiss, a parrying touch, his body solid and firm against hers.

She wanted to know every inch of him, her hands winding through his hair, her leg hooking around his, pulling him in to her, holding him closer. She wanted this moment to hold through time; she wanted it to – but somehow she still found herself pushing him away.

'Wha—?' he panted, confused.

'I can't do this.'

'Alex—'

'This is a mistake.' Her voice was thick, the words a struggle, a blatant lie, for it was more right than anything she had ever known. She couldn't believe she hadn't seen it, all this time. Even two minutes ago, it had been veiled from her, but now – now it was like trying to hide an elephant behind a throw cushion.

'No. It's not.' His eyes were locked on hers in a rare moment of honesty between them. No more games or power plays – they both felt it, both wanted it, their longing shimmering between them like a white heat. 'It's the only bloody thing that's right.'

She shook her head, using her hand to keep him back as she edged away from him, putting space between their bodies which only moments before had been intertwined, as one. But still the words came from somewhere deep inside her. Not him. It couldn't be him. 'This is a mistake,' she repeated, her voice shaking. 'It never happened. Do you hear me? It never happened.'

Chapter Twenty-Three

Borrodale House, Sunday 17 December 2017

Breakfast was a subdued affair. Everyone was hung to hell, unable to look their sausages in the eye and slurping the strong tea in broken silence. Some didn't even make it downstairs at all, Lochie being one.

Alex, for her part, got through it with a resolution she didn't feel. She hadn't slept for more than a couple of hours as she lay in that enormous four-poster bed, tossing and turning, trying to unpick the events – to determine how and when exactly things between them had changed. The slap was the obvious moment, but was it really the first? What about the way he'd stared at her as she danced with Sam? The way he'd held her arm in his along the red carpet, or how he'd complimented her on the way into the castle? Or maybe it was before then too: his arms around her after she landed the salmon, blue-lipped and shivering; his relentless jealous probing the morning after her dinner with Callum; his unexpected arrival at the farmhouse to take her to the tasting of the hidden malt like a date; the way his finger twitched when she cried out his name as he lay inert and lifeless on the floor; the shock of even laying her eyes upon him that first day in the visitors' centre when Callum was him and he was late.

Had it started right back then, in the first moment? How could it have done? She was trained to read human behaviour, to pick up the non-verbal cues people didn't even know they were giving. It was inconceivable she couldn't have seen this in herself.

No, they had warred from the start, *that* was their natural state; last night's passion was just a momentary, fleeting by-product of too much whisky, a wrong turn in the confusion of the chaos that ensued whenever they were together.

She went back to her room after breakfast and took a long bath. Daisy had suggested elevenses at the village tea rooms, with the men supposedly booked for a round of golf, 'if they can manage to swing without falling over,' Emma had tutted.

She dressed and met the others by the front steps, noticing for the first time, as she passed through the doorway, a dense bunch of mistletoe hanging above. It made her stop in her tracks as though it was a poster showing everyone their secret passion. Had it been there last night? she wondered, staring at the back of the door as though expecting to see their imprint there.

To her relief, they got away before the men had organized themselves and everyone chatted easily in the car, in spite of their hangovers; Alex felt it was natural she should be the quietest – she was the newbie, the interloper, after all. Lochie had never even invited her here, not really, not properly – and she sat with her elbow on the windowsill, her chin in her hand, looking out the window as they drove through the sweeping rhododendron-dotted grounds to the village.

The tea rooms themselves were pretty – a small white-washed building with bow-fronted windows looking onto the village square – and they managed to get the table in the window, a small scented candle flickering prettily in the middle. Daisy and Emma went up to the till to look at the selection of cakes at the counter.

'We're lucky,' Elise sighed, shrugging off her coat. 'Usually we get here just after the church service and can't get a table.'

'Lucky us,' Alex smiled, her voice toneless as she pretended to read the menu. Just a few more hours and this would all be behind her.

'The scones look like they could revive a dead cow,' Daisy said, plonking herself down heavily. 'I'm having two.'

'I'm going to treat myself to an éclair,' Emma said, eyes brightening. 'It's been *years* since I've had an éclair.'

The waitress came over and took their orders. 'And you don't want anything with your tea?' she asked Alex as she double-checked the requests.

Everyone looked at her expectantly.

'. . . A shortbread would be great,' she said finally, wondering how she'd be able to swallow it down. Far from last night's debacle beginning to recede from her mind, if anything it was beginning to swell, like one of those vacuum-packed towels placed in water. Tears pressed behind her eyes and her throat felt closed, her mouth drooping at the corners every time she actively forgot to smile.

How could she have let this happen? How could she face him again?

'The sugar will perk you up. You look awful peely-wally this morning,' Emma said kindly.

Alex still didn't know what peely-wally was, though

Emma's tone suggested it might be something along the lines of 'peaky', her other main description this side of the border. Clearly sixteen per cent body fat and a resting heart rate of sixty-four bpm weren't the desired state here that they were in New York.

'So what are you up to for Christmas, Alex?' Elise asked brightly, as though sensing her discomfort.

'I'm just having a quiet one at home.'

'Are you doing the turkey?'

'Oh, no. No, it's just me so I'll probably just have a salad.'

There was an astounded silence.

'A *salad*? On *Christmas Day*?' Daisy blustered, accidentally blowing out the candle.

'Oh, now look what you've done,' Elise pouted.

'Are you fucking mad? You can't do that! Come and spend it with us!' Daisy continued as Alex reached into her bag and pulled out a tab of matches, a small silver-clipped wad of business cards coming with it and dropping to the floor.

'Oh God, no, I couldn't do that,' Alex protested to Daisy, who was still looking flabbergasted. She pulled out a match and struck it, but it broke. And the next one. She was all fingers and thumbs, her grip clumsy and heavy-handed.

'Here,' Emma murmured, reaching down to pick up the wad of cards. She frowned as she handed it over. 'Cereneo?'

'Why not?' Daisy continued. 'This lot do.'

'Do you?' Alex asked in surprise.

'Sure!' Anna shrugged. 'Max is usually working or on call so poor Emma's left on her own otherwise and Elise's family . . . well, they're so blinking far away in Uppsala, we prefer to go over in the summer. As for my family – Christ, you wouldn't. You just wouldn't. And as for Little Miss

Suntan over there, well, they don't usually come. You're usually on some tropical island, aren't you, sweets?'

'Not this year,' Jess sniffed. 'The weather's becoming too unpredictable. I'd rather wait till January.'

Anna shrugged.

'Well, that's really nice of you to offer but I'll be flying out to join my dad on Boxing Day. He lives in Switzerland,' Alex said.

'Whereabouts?' Emma asked.

'On the edge of Lake Lucerne.'

'Nice,' Emma smiled.

'Well, the offer's there if you want it,' Daisy said earnestly. 'I mean it. You could always fly to Geneva from here.'

'Thanks,' Alex smiled, but with no intention of ever taking up that offer.

'Look, forget about Christmas for just a minute,' Jess said impatiently, pulling her chair in closer. 'Now that it's just us and we don't have the boys hanging around and making a nuisance of themselves, why don't you explain to us exactly the deal between you and Lochie? Because *we* don't get it.'

'I'm not sure there's anything *to* get,' Alex rebuffed. 'I've come in as a consultant to the company. I've done a couple of weeks of work with him and I'm leaving . . . well, tomorrow probably.' The words sounded shocking when she said them aloud.

'Yeah but, you see, you say that,' Jess said. 'Just like he did. We get that that's the official line – but we still don't buy it. There's definitely something going on between you two.' She looked at the others. 'Don't you think?'

'Yeah.'

'Mmm.'

'Definitely,' they chorused.

'I mean, it's not normal – even for Lochie – to come in and punch the wall.'

'Excuse me?' Alex asked, startled.

Jess nodded. 'Oh yeah – last night. He went into the library and punched the wall.'

'I didn't know that!' Anna chuckled, looking thrilled.

'Well, I only heard him because I was going through to the kitchen to get another bottle. I put my head round, thinking he must have tripped over the bed or something – I mean, we were all pretty wasted, let's be honest – and there he was, bent double, holding his fist and swearing like a navvy. Emma had to check he hadn't broken anything, didn't you?'

'Mm-hmm,' Emma sighed. 'He's fine, though.'

'It's the bloody wall I'm worried about,' Daisy muttered.

Alex stared at them all. She didn't know where to start: that Lochie was going around punching walls; or that there was a bed in the library. She went with the latter; it seemed safer and bought her time.

'Why is there a bed in the library?' she asked.

Daisy looked sheepish. 'Ah well, there was a little mis-communication on his part and I'm afraid he hadn't exactly told us he was bringing you this weekend. So when you guys turned up on Friday night, well . . .' She pulled a face. 'We gave you his room and put him up in the study. Ordi-narily it wouldn't matter in the least – there's so many blinking bedrooms in that house – but what with all the building works going on, half the house is out of action,' Daisy shrugged. 'But it's fine. I told him if he couldn't organ-ize himself at his age then what could he expect? We've got a little camp bed he's using. It's not the most comfortable mattress ever but no one's ever died from a cricked neck.' She glanced at Emma. 'Have they?'

Emma shrugged. 'Not that I'm aware of.'

'Emma's the expert on cricked necks,' Anna grinned.

'Why did he punch the wall?' Alex asked.

'Well, we were hoping *you* could tell us that. I think you'd just gone up to bed, which may be coincidence. Or not.'

The waitress came over with the pots of tea and set them out on the table with mismatched vintage cups and saucers. 'The cakes are just coming,' she said.

'Thanks,' Anna murmured. But all eyes were on Alex.

'I'm sorry,' Alex said, buckling beneath their scrutiny. 'I don't know what you want me to say. I had no idea he'd punched a wall.'

'So nothing happened between you two then, just before?' Jess pushed.

'Nope.' Alex shook her head, keeping her eyes down as she lifted the lid of her teapot and stirred the brew.

The others all sighed.

'Well, that's just really weird then. I don't get what could have upset him so much,' Anna said. 'I mean, he's usually a pretty level guy.'

Alex couldn't help but snort. '. . . Sorry.' She pressed her hand to her mouth apologetically.

'What? You disagree?' Emma asked.

'Well, yes,' she said, looking back at their astonished expressions. She was silent for a moment, wondering whether she should say another word; then sighed. What did it matter? She'd be gone from here in a few hours and would never see any of them again. 'If you want the truth, he's one of the most volatile people I've ever worked with.

I mean, I know you all know him far better than I do – you go way back as uni friends – but in the workplace? I'm sorry but "level" does not begin to cover it.'

They all looked between one another; it was as though she'd called him a serial killer.

'You'll have to back that up with some evidence,' Jess said, ever the gate-keeper, stirring her own tea.

'Fine. Well, I'm sorry to say he's physically abusive for a start. Not only did he punch his CFO at the family assembly but he has manhandled me too, actually throwing me out of his office on two occasions,' she began. 'He's erratic and unprofessional, pulling out of deals without warning or explanation. He has completely inappropriate relationships with some of his staff . . .' And when they frowned at her blankly, 'Affairs. He has affairs with his female employ-ees—'

'Whoa, now hang on a minute,' Jess said firmly. 'Skye doesn't count. He loved her. They were going to get married.'

'No, you're quite right, Skye doesn't count,' she agreed. 'But what about the girl in accounts? And apparently there was another one in the maltings. He's CEO of a small, tight-knit community. It is completely unacceptable for him to cut a swathe through the staff like that. It creates resentment, forms divisions, undermines his authority . . .'

'Well, quite frankly, after what he went through with Skye, I think he can be cut a little slack, don't you? It's called the rebound for a reason. His dad had just died and then he finds that out? Christ, who wouldn't go a bit crazy?'

Alex frowned. 'Wait, finds out what?'

'That she'd been having it off with his cousin,' Emma said, looking surprised. 'Didn't you know?'

341

Alex was thunderstruck. Skye had cheated on him? 'But she told me he'd jilted her.'

'Ha! I bet she did – that makes it sound like she's the victim, doesn't it? Like he left her waiting at the altar?' Jess asked disdainfully. 'And he *could* have done that to her, perhaps he even should have: let her get dressed up, the church fill up – and then tell everyone exactly what she'd done. Who would have blamed him, when they'd found out the truth?' She shook her head. 'No, that girl got lucky. He called the wedding off the night before and spared her the humiliation and shame, keeping what she'd done a secret – even though he must have known they'd all hear the word "jilted" and assume *he* was the bastard. Like you did.'

Alex sat in silence, feeling duped, stupid. Skye had cheated on him? Jess was right – she had made exactly those presumptions. 'But it doesn't make sense . . . I don't understand why Lochie would be so prepared to come across as the villain of the piece?'

'Oh, don't get me wrong. I don't think he just did it for Skye's benefit. He was very close to Bruce, her dad; I think he knew how ashamed Bruce would have been if he knew what his daughter had done – it's a small community up there, after all,' Jess said. 'Plus, if nothing else, the whole thing was straight-up humiliating for him. Can you imagine if word got out round the distillery that his fiancée had been having it off with his cousin?' She shook her head. 'Nah, if there's one thing Lochie will always have, it's his pride.'

Alex bit her lip. The world felt as though it was spinning just a little too fast, her footing no longer certain. She felt angry and disappointed. Skye had lied to her, deliberately misrepresenting herself to gain Alex's sympathy and good opinion. Alex thought back to everything Skye had told her about their relationship and wondered where the truth lay, for Skye had squarely put the blame at his door, pointing the finger at his anger after his father's death, saying he'd pushed her away.

And perhaps he had. Perhaps that had been her reason for straying – straightforward neglect.

But even if it was, what excuse did Callum have for seducing his cousin's fiancée? Jealousy? Or a complete inability to respect boundaries, either personal or professional? Did he believe that his wealth and family name meant he could do whatever he wanted, have whoever he wanted – even if that meant betraying his own blood? No wonder Lochie had been so furious when Callum had got to Alex first on her arrival here, when she'd gone on her date with him, when he'd seen Callum's texts, when she'd tried to ring him last night . . . No wonder they were no longer 'close', as Callum had said at the pub that night. Lochie must hate him with a living, breathing passion and from where she was sitting, Alex couldn't blame him.

'It was all for the best in the end though; Lochie dodged a bullet there,' Anna agreed. 'The balance was never right between them.'

'You know she's engaged to that other guy now?' Emma said, smiling up at the waitress as she set down the plates of cakes.

'Christ, no, I didn't! She didn't waste any time,' Anna said, reaching for a scone.

'Hey, those are mine,' Daisy said, slapping her hand away.

'You can't possibly eat two,' Anna smiled, taking it anyway. 'No hangover is that bad.'

'What do you mean, "the balance between them"?' Alex asked, completely uninterested in the food as she watched Elise begin to pull apart a blueberry muffin and eat the crumbs.

'Well, I always kind of thought Skye was using him; you know, she liked the "idea" of him, landing the big boss.'

'You make him sound like a salmon,' Daisy chuckled.

'*Don't* mention salmon,' Anna groaned.

Alex stared down at the fan of shortbread untouched on her plate. The sugar sparkled in the morning light. She felt sick. Oh God. She rubbed her face in her hands. 'I wish I'd known this,' she mumbled.

'Sorry, we assumed you did,' Daisy said.

'Well, why would she?' Jess asked. 'Alex is there to work with him on a professional level. The break-up of his engagement is hardly relevant.'

'Actually, I work with people holistically, I *should* have known this, it changes everything. It's my fault.' She was angry with herself. Deprived of any opportunity to hold a detailed debrief of his life with him personally, she had been too ready to take Skye's account at face value.

'Come again?' Daisy asked. 'I thought you were a business coach, not a psychiatrist.'

'I'm not, but there are elements of social psychology that I use. I look at the person's whole being and identify the areas of imbalance. None of us operate in vacuums and what happens in our personal lives will always leak into our professional lives too. Sometimes it can be a positive thing, making us more compassionate, or patient. Or conversely, as in Lochie's case, it can make us angry and volatile.'

'Poor bugger, of all the people for it to happen to; it was *just* what he didn't need,' Daisy sighed. 'It's not like he didn't have trust issues to begin with.'

'Trust issues?' Alex asked, feeling her stomach dip again.

'Yeah, you know, with his folks.' And when Alex continued looking at her blankly, she added, 'His mother's suicide?'

What? Alex went cold. *Another* lead she hadn't followed up? Skye had put all the emphasis on his father's death. How could she have omitted something as devastating as suicide? 'When?' The word came out as a whisper.

'He was sixteen. She'd suffered from depression for years, made numerous other attempts. The doctors kept saying they were just cries for help but Lochie knew otherwise; he kept on running away from boarding school – one time he escaped during a cross-country run, another in the middle of the night, or going down to the village shop for tuck. They had to physically restrain him to get him in the car each time they took him back and every time he would be hysterical, knowing his father believed the doctors and didn't take the attempts seriously; Lochie was frantic, worrying about her being left on her own. Until one day he was proved right and she did it. Walked into the sea.'

Everyone had gone silent. Alex felt as though she'd been tranquillized. Everything seemed heavy and slow. She wanted to cry. For him, for the desperate young boy he'd been, trying to save his mother, no one listening. Was it any wonder he didn't trust anyone but his dogs?

'God, it's so sad,' Jess whispered, her eyes tearing up.

'We were together for four years at uni and I don't think a week went by when he didn't wake up screaming.'

Alex stared at her, feeling a strange mix of anger and resentment and jealousy. 'Why did you two break up?'

A look of hurt cracked Jess's usual composure. 'It was his decision, not mine.' She hesitated, clearly not wanting to say the words. 'Basically . . . he punched me in his sleep one night and gave me a black eye,' she sighed. 'Obviously it wasn't his fault. *Obviously.* I didn't blame him at all. But even though I kept telling him that, he was so devastated by what he'd done, nothing I could say would make him change his mind. He said he wasn't safe to be around, that he had to be on his own.'

'Jesus,' Alex whispered as the others shook their heads, well familiar with this story.

'I begged him to reconsider. Properly begged. I couldn't bear the thought of him alone but he wouldn't have it. He just wouldn't forgive himself.' She rubbed her face in her hands, looking pained. 'Eventually, I met Sam and . . . moved on,' she shrugged. 'But I still feel responsible for him, even now.'

'I can understand that,' Alex nodded, seeing the strength in Jess's manner, picking up the trace of threat in her words as the two women's eyes met. Did she know that Alex could – would – hurt him?

'I thought Skye was exactly what he needed when they first got together,' Jess continued. 'She had an innocence about her that I think he found reassuring. She felt uncomplicated, safe. I think after everything he'd been through with his parents, he needed that.'

'Until he found out she was anything but innocent,' Emma said darkly.

'Yeah, but you know what?' Jess said, fingering her teacup. 'Being really honest, even before that, I think things were going wrong between them. His father never got over his mother's death; he blamed himself for not taking Lochie's pleas seriously and I think Lochie would admit now that deep down, he blamed him too. They were both so angry and so sad and neither of them knew how to deal with it; and when it became apparent his dad was drinking himself to death, right in front of him too, Skye wasn't strong enough to help him handle it. It wasn't her fault necessarily – she just wanted a nice quiet life but instead she found herself in a terrible situation like that. Maybe I wouldn't have done much better either. He needs someone stronger than both of us.'

'Poor guy, it's frying pan to fire when it comes to women and him,' Daisy murmured.

Alex felt her heart gallop to a staccato beat, remembering the passion that had exploded between them last night. He was more like her than she had ever thought to see – both closing down their feelings, compartmentalizing their mothers and fathers and lovers into individually sealed boxes they rarely opened. Was that why they clashed? Was it why the kiss had been so good?

'Well, thank God he's got Alex in his corner now,' Anna said, toasting her with her dainty teacup. 'It's about time his luck changed.'

'Hear, hear,' Elise cheered, raising hers too as the others followed suit.

'To Alex, may she save his soul!' Anna said dramatically.

'Or at least his job,' Emma grinned.

Alex smiled as Elise reached over and gave her a friendly hug, but inwardly she felt sick. They all thought she was a friend, or at the very least, an ally. It simply hadn't occurred to any of them that she was anything but – a snake in the grass, slithering on her belly and just waiting for the right time to strike.

Chapter Twenty-Four

Lunch, suitably, was a haunch of venison that seemed to assuage the worst of everyone's hangovers. The guys had managed only four holes before the wind – 'nothing at all to do with their heads,' Daisy had scoffed – drove them back indoors, and they settled down to a lazy afternoon of reading the papers, Spit – a card game craze they'd all had in school – and watching films from the sofas in the living room. Lochie – looking unshaven and unkempt in his jeans and socks, wearing just a faded black T-shirt that occasionally pressed against rocky abs – had managed not to look at her once, as though he could track her shadow or detect her spirit, positioning himself away from her or moving off outright; she could see from the way he involuntarily turned away whenever she was in range that he was angry, blocking her physically and mentally. Thankfully no one seemed to notice; the women certainly appeared to have accepted her assertion that they were just colleagues, and the banter and jokes that bounced around the room were mainly confined to historic uni references and Ambrose's pathetic attempts at a beard.

She was flicking through the *FT* magazine when his mobile rang – again – and he hauled himself off the sofa with a self-pitying groan as he picked up to yet another distillery contact wanting in on the Scotch Vaults venture. She watched him leave, his heavy sensuous tread like a big cat on the parquet, his phone pressed to his ear, voice croakier than ever now that it had smoke damage *and* whisky to contend with, as she reminded herself with moving lips: a kiss changed nothing.

'Anyone want tea?' she asked, determining that she ought to do something to be a good guest given that she had turned up empty-handed for the hosts on Friday night and Mary, the housekeeper, was now off duty for the rest of the day.

'Oh yes, please,' they chorused, with varying degrees of desperation and gratitude.

She walked down the long-panelled corridor and into the kitchen at the far end of the house. Outside the back windows, plastic sheeting flapped around the scaffolding and whilst the kettle boiled, she texted Louise to arrange to have a Fortnum & Mason hamper sent up as a thank-you gift the next day. Walking over to the front of the house, she stared out of the mullioned window at the grand gardens, her arms spread on the cool countertop. Fairy lights which had been strung on the closest topiaried-box balls were beginning to twinkle as dusk crept in and she knew that meant they would be leaving soon. They couldn't avoid each other then; whether they liked it or not, they would be sitting side by side in a giant metal balloon, his thighs just centimetres—

She remembered again the feeling of his legs against hers last night and she dropped her head, trying to push the memory out. No.

No.

She shook her head clean of the thoughts, like an Etch A

Sketch board, and walked across to the walk-in pantry – and almost screamed.

'Oh my God!' she gasped, smacking one hand to her chest. 'I didn't . . . I didn't know anyone was in here.'

Lochie blinked back at her, holding out the phone in his hand. 'Best place for a signal,' he said quietly, his eyes like sniper dots upon her.

'Oh.' There was a pause and she felt her body change at the sight of him; whether they chose to acknowledge it or not, things were different between them now – his hands had caressed her, his tongue tasted her; she had felt his hair between her fingers, his leg between her thighs. She couldn't unknow his physicality, any more than she could erase her words last night, *'This is a mistake.'*

She looked away, unable to hold his gaze. It had been easier to stare him down, to hate him, when she'd believed him to be all those things Sholto had told her he was – renegade, dangerous, reckless, maverick. And maybe he was, but he was more besides: alone, isolated, abandoned, great kisser . . . She shook her head again, pressing her eyes shut.

'What?'

'Nothing,' she murmured, reaching to the fridge beside him and pulling out the milk.

She heard his footsteps follow her into the kitchen, felt his eyes on her back as she lifted the kettle and poured the water, steam flushing her already pink cheeks. 'Would you like a tea?' she asked politely, without turning.

There was a pause. 'I guess.'

'You don't have to have one. I'm not going to force you to drink it.' She poured the milk into the cups.

'Really? You usually try to make me do things I don't want to do.'

'Well, we all know you never do anything you don't want to do.' Her voice sounded snippy and she turned to take the mil—

He was standing right behind her. 'That's right. And how about you? Do *you* do things you don't want to do?'

She swallowed, knowing he was referring to the kiss. 'All the time.' If he only knew how true that was. 'It's called compromise.'

'Is that what they call it?' His gaze was on her mouth. 'So what are we going to call last night, then?'

'A mistake.'

He shook his head. 'Mistakes don't feel like that.'

She willed her voice not to betray her. 'We were both hammered,' she said slowly. 'It had been a long day; I was feeling emotional after the whole stag thing, you had that massive adrenaline rush from unveiling the new business . . .'

He looked at her as though she was talking gibberish. 'You don't really think that.'

'Yes, I do.'

He took a step closer, so close she could almost feel his toes nudging hers. 'Alex, alcohol doesn't *make* people do things against their will. It simply lowers their inhibitions to allow them to do the things they've already thought about.'

Her pulse skyrocketed as memories of the heat between them began to colour the air again, colour her cheeks. 'Well, I had never thought about it. You are my client and I never get emotionally involved.'

'How about physically?'

The retort was like a slap. 'That's just the kind of comment I'd expect from you,' she said hotly, pushing past him, returning the milk.

'Shit, Alex, I didn't mean tha—'

'No. We're done here.' She lifted the tray but he stepped in front of her, blocking the way.

'Wait. We have to talk about this. You can't pretend it didn't happen. You don't seriously expect that we can work together now?'

'No, well done, Lochlan – if you hadn't already done such a fine job of sabotaging your own career, I don't suppose we could have done. But you *did* do it, so congratulations, you're rid of me at last.' She tried to step past him again but he caught her elbow.

'What are you talking about?'

'What do you think?' she asked, giving a short, tight, humourless laugh, tears pressing behind her eyes, her emotions alarmingly close to the surface. 'It's over. Do you honestly think there aren't going to be repercussions for what you've done? Whatever you choose to believe, there's no way Sholto will take that lying down. You're going to get back there tomorrow and find you're out. And that means I am too.'

'No, you don't get it. You don't know the detail.'

But she shook her head, refusing to listen to any more of his arrogance that he was untouchable. 'I know that you are everything he said you were.' It wasn't true. Thanks to his friends, she had the full lowdown on him now and she knew that he was just like her – a jumbled mess of the good and the bad, a man who had been hurt, abandoned and let down by almost everyone he had ever loved. He wasn't the cartoon villain Sholto had pitched in his Edinburgh office, or at least, he wasn't *only* that; but it would have made no difference anyway. Even if he was the world's greatest Samaritan, she would still have had a job to do, and there was no option for failure. Yes, it was regrettable that her success would have had to come at his expense, but she had no doubt that if their places had been swapped, he wouldn't have hesitated to do it either. But now, it was all gone. Without even realizing it, his actions had ruined everything for her. He had hit upon the only way to rid himself of her. 'You're a liability and a bloody joke. You haven't just messed things up for you, you've messed them up for me too.' Tears stung her eyes but she immediately blinked them back. She would *not* cry in front of him. 'You have absolutely no idea of what you've done. None at all.'

'Alex—'

'Leave me alone, Lochlan,' she said, pushing past him. 'We're done.'

Everyone stood on the front steps, waving, their hair flying back and upwards in the downdraught of the blades as the helicopter tenderly rose into the air. They had swapped mobiles and email addresses but as Alex smiled her fake smiles, she knew she would never see any of them again; as much as she liked them, they were his friends, his allies.

They changed direction, Borrodale at their backs, and gained height quickly, the lights flashing in the endless darkness as the garden became mere space and the land became a map.

They didn't talk. Instead, she looked down at the cities below them – the long lines of street lights delineating motorways and residential streets, floodlights picking out football stadiums and tennis clubs, tail lights and headlights marking out journeys being taken, lives being lived.

He flicked a few switches and she felt his glance bounce her way every few moments. She could hear his breath in her headset. She looked out of the window even harder, the Cairngorms crumpled at their feet. It was a long time before either of them spoke.

'Alex.'

She pointedly turned away, the silence that swirled round the cabin louder than the drone of the blades.

'Alex, I know you don't want to talk to me. I know I crossed the line last night and I was a jerk back there earlier. I'm sorry, okay? But just listen to me: you haven't lost your job. And the reason I know you haven't is because I haven't lost mine. He can't fire me. All I've really done is jump the gun. He'll be pissed off, yes, but he can't kick me out.'

She turned back to him. There it was again – that cocksure arrogance that he was untouchable. How could he not see the consequences of his actions? 'You've just given him the *perfect* opportunity to raise a motion of no confidence.'

He blinked. 'And if he does, there's still no legal imperative on me to resign as a result of it.'

'But *how* can you possibly hope to continue without any shred of support or respect if that happens?' she demanded. 'I don't know why you can't see how doomed your position is.'

'I'm sticking it out because I have to, not because I want to.'

'*Why?* Why do you have to stay? How can you live like this?'

He was quiet for a long time. '. . . Because I'm the only thing stopping the distillery from being closed down.'

Alex stared at him, baffled. 'Wha— Why should it close down?'

'Because they want to sell.'

'The *Ferrandor* deal?' she asked in surprise.

'You know about that?'

'I know you torpedoed the deal a few years ago.'

'Damn right I did.'

She waited for an explanation, having to prompt him when none came. 'Because . . . ?'

'Look, you know enough about Kentallen by now. You know we don't buy anything in and we don't sell anything out – we don't distribute our maturing malts to another distillery for them to use in their blended whisky; we own and manage our own peat bogs on the island, we buy barley from the local farmers, like Mr Peggie; we store and bottle everything on the island . . . We may not be competing with the production capacity of someone like Glenfiddich or Macallan, but we're still the biggest single employer on Islay.'

'And why would selling to Ferrandor change that?'

She saw the ball of his jaw pulse. 'Because they'd take practically everything off the isle – they'd move the bottling and warehousing to Speyside, take branding, marketing and advertising in-house, ship in the barley, ship in the peat . . . They'd basically mothball operations here and kill the Islay infrastructure.'

'They wouldn't do that,' she said quietly, thinking of Mr Peggie; his family had farmed that land and supplied the distillery for almost a century. She looked out and saw that they were crossing over the Northern Channel already, the hulk of Jura and behind it Islay, like a giant's stepping stones in the sea.

'Wouldn't they? Would you still be so loyal to them if you knew that when my father was dying, when he was literally on his deathbed, delirious and out of his mind on medication, they brought him the contracts and tried to get him to sign them?' He glanced over at her, fire in his eyes. 'Are you hearing what I'm telling you? They tried to manipulate and deceive a dying man, for their own profits. If I hadn't happened to come in and stop them—' His voice broke and he fell silent.

Was that really true? Sholto had tried to con a dying man? Alex stared at him, at the determined set of his jaw as he surveyed the dark skies. 'Torquil told me the deal was off the table.'

'Torquil says a lot of things.'

'He said it would create three supply-chain jobs for every direct-line operative employed.'

'Ha. Did he now?'

She couldn't stop looking at him, so defiant even in profile. 'So you think that if you go, they'll push the sale through?'

'I don't even need to go. Their current plan is paving the way for a hostile takeover, with or without me at the helm.'

Alex looked at him in bewilderment, hardly able to keep up. He was paranoid. Properly paranoid. He had to be. 'Current plan?' she questioned, thinking back to what Torquil had told her in his office that day. 'You mean the move into white spirits?'

He gave a bitter laugh. 'Trust me, they have absolutely no interest in diversifying into spirits and growing the company.'

'Yes, they do. It was sanctioned at the AGM. Torquil said it was the first time everyone's been in agreement with your proposal in years.'

'Only because it greases the wheel for their real ambition.'

'Which is?' she pressed. The lights of Port Ellen flickered

ahead of them like the flames of hurricane lamps in the dark.

'In order to fund growth for a move like that, we have two options: either reinvest our profits – as I want to do – or release more equity, which they're pressing for. But it's a Trojan horse. They know that issuing more shares would mean my holding becomes diluted and my majority erased; they also know that all my money's tied up in the Scotch Vaults venture at the moment so I can't buy more to protect my stake. And once they've neutralized my majority, it's a straightforward proxy fight.'

Alex stared at him. It tallied with what Torquil had told her and she knew perfectly well what a proxy fight was: the acquiring organization persuaded key shareholders to use their proxy votes to install new management who could approve the sale.

Alex caught her breath as she realized what this meant. If what Lochie was saying was true, Sholto wasn't merely the antagonist in this dog fight but a mole too, there to connive in the best interests of a hidden third party. And she had been working for them. She was his deadliest weapon.

She felt suddenly sick. Sickened by herself.

'Who else knows about this?'

'No one who believes me. Peter and Doug for starters. I've tried telling them. Mhairi, I'm not sure – I think she has her doubts. As for my many cousins, there'd be no point—' He snorted contemptuously. 'They couldn't give a damn what goes down, so long as they get their paycheques every quarter.' He sighed. 'Look, I'm only telling you this because . . . well, I think you might actually be the only person who does get it. Maybe you really are the only one in my corner

– and I don't want what happened last night to drive you away.'

'It wouldn't,' she replied hotly, resenting his words and the implication that she'd run. Like Skye.

'Like you said, it was a . . . heat-of-the-moment thing,' he said, looking dead ahead. 'We were drunk, that was all.'

Did he really believe that? She looked out of the window as they lost height, as though being dropped on a rope. Beneath them, the giant copper still in the courtyard gleamed under the security night lights, the plush Christmas tree a contrast to the thin black ribs of the maltings' charred rafters. The place was locked up and deserted, the weekend almost over.

His concentration on the landing was absolute now and she didn't say another word until the power had been cut and the blades began to slow.

'Home sweet home,' she mumbled, undoing her harnesses and taking off the ear defenders. 'Thanks for the ride.'

'My pleasure,' he said, watching as she reached back to retrieve her small carry bag from the space behind the seat.

She twisted back and stilled at the sight of him. He was staring at her, his body tense, his face unmasked, and she had that feeling again – almost violent in its intensity – that she got whenever they were too close, those brown eyes the dice that could ruin her future – or make it?

She blinked, refusing to let the moment bloom to its natural conclusion, and turned away, getting ready to jump out.

The snow hadn't budged over the weekend; if anything there had been fresh falls, the staff footprints in the car park all but obscured under the crisp new cover, and it took

Lochie several minutes to heat up the car and clear the windscreen as she sat in the passenger seat, blowing on her hands.

'I can't believe the difference in temperature,' she said as he finally got back in, his shoulders hunched around his ears.

'Aye, it's bitter,' he said, blowing on his hands too. He turned on the ignition and the car started up first time.

'You really don't have to do this. I'm more than happy to wait for Jack to drop me back.'

Lochie snorted. 'With his leg? It'd be a long bloody wait. They'd find you as a frozen statue when they came to unlock the gates tomorrow morning. Besides, I'm passing anyway.'

They pulled away and she tipped her head back against the headrest; the buttermilk leather was as soft as her new Connolly gloves, the smell reassuringly expensive and reminding her of her real life, the one to which she actually belonged, even though it had receded from sight the first moment she'd stepped off the ferry in that approaching storm. It was this world here that wasn't real: him, Callum, the Peggies, Skye . . .

Her hands fell to the seats, gripping them lightly as they wound their way along the slippery country lanes, her thumb rubbing against leather. Maybe she would buy herself one of these when this job was all done and behind her – a memento, a souvenir, a private joke in which she was laughing at herself for the many errors of judgement she'd made on this tiny isle.

They rounded the steep hillock and she saw the lights of the handsome farmhouse set back from the road, the only inhabited building for the next two miles. It looked as though Mrs Peggie had another guest in the green room, not that she cared about making small talk tonight. She couldn't eat anyway. She wanted bath, bed and a bloody great pillow. She needed to think, to regroup. Nothing and no one was as she had thought and she felt dangerously adrift.

He pulled on the handbrake and turned off the ignition, jumping out to get her suitcase and gun before she could stop him.

'Here, it's icy,' he said, holding out his arm, as unthinkingly chivalrous as his cousin had been a few nights before.

She took it and together they trod carefully along the path, her heart already hammering in anticipation of what would happen at the door, in remembrance of what had happened at last night's door. Was he thinking it too? Did their kiss prey on his mind as it did hers? To her dismay, she saw Mrs Peggie had trussed up a hearty bunch of mistletoe too. It was like some sort of conspiracy!

'Well, goodnight,' she said, trying to sound brisk, her hand already on the door knob.

'Alex, wait—'

She turned, sure he must be able to hear the blood pounding through her veins like raging rapids.

'I just wanted to say that . . . in spite of everything, I'm glad you came this weekend.'

'Oh.' She tried not to acknowledge the massive flood of disappointment as he made no move to step closer to her. 'Yes. Me too. It was fun.' *Fun?*

'And I know I've behaved badly. Believe it or not, I'm not in the habit of throwing beautiful women out of my office—'

He thought she was beautiful?

'But I guess what I'm saying is I know I can trust you

now. I'm sorry it's taken me so long to realize it. I've been an arse.'

'Yes. You have,' she said, her mouth drying up as she realized she had manoeuvred him – finally, accidentally – to exactly where she'd wanted him. Only now . . . everything had changed. The players had changed roles.

'So, as of tomorrow, you'll get the full charm offensive, I promise.'

Her smile slipped. She wasn't sure she could manage that.

He grinned. 'Who knows, perhaps you really can help me.'

She shrugged. 'Maybe.' How could she do what had been asked of her, knowing what she knew now?

For a moment, his gaze caught hers, scooping it up and holding it high, and she felt her stomach contract just as it had in that moment before he'd kissed her last night, just as it had in that moment in the helicopter before she'd leapt out. He grinned again and began to walk backwards up the garden path.

'Maybe you're gonna be the one that saves me.' He chuckled suddenly, as light-hearted as he had been with his friends. 'Maybe you're my wonderwall, Alex Hyde. '

Alex watched him, wanting to cry. Wrecking ball was more like it.

Chapter Twenty-Five

Islay, 14 March 1918

Everything was coming back to life again. The trees were in bud, crocuses and primroses dotting the banks like spots of sunshine as she wheeled past, her hair flying off her shoulders. The highland cattle were grazing the ocean-side fields, their low, reverberating moos swaying through the gently tossed air as the sun began its slow descent.

Part of her wanted to stop and pick flowers – their colour and scent would cheer the ward; she wanted to bring spring in with her. But to stop was to lose time and that was the one thing she never had enough of now. Her day in the field had been arduous. With the ground softening and the daylight hours growing more numerous, they were working for longer trying to sow the crops; on the other hand, her father would not hear of her returning home in the dark. She was squeezed at either end, the long day and the equally urgent night rushing towards each other and leaving her scant time to see him, to read to him, to hold his hand.

He had only begun taking food in the past week and was now almost as slight as she; the delirium from the influenza had taken weeks to pass and numerous times, Matron had braced her to prepare herself 'for the worst', to not 'become too attached', but she didn't understand. No one did.

She, Clarissa, had saved him. He had been more dead than alive on those rocks, almost hidden from sight, the tide fast rushing in towards him again, and his survival – against all the odds – had reawakened her own urge to live. Her fiancée was dead. Her beloved brother was dead. Death defined life for the living now – everyone was marked by it – and she had grabbed at this soldier's survival as though it was her own. For there had to be more to being alive than sleeping with the sun and waiting for the post as she had done, passing the small, quiet hours with worrying hands and a knitted brow; there had to be hope of beauty and peace, of laughter and love.

So she had read to him as he languished and held his hand while he slept, feeling every day his grip growing stronger in hers, seeing the colour return to his flesh as the virus died back, his broken bones knitting together strongly as the soup and the rest and the warmth of a soft bed played their parts.

She sped into the town, seeing from the angle of the sun that she had an hour at best before she would have to leave again. She rang the bell gaily before rounding the corner into the main street.

'Good evening, Mrs McPhee,' she called as she appeared at speed, her petticoats flashing her stockinged legs.

'Good evening, Miss Clarissa,' the woman called back, stepping out of the way with a shake of her head and a smile as the girl streaked past the General Stores and continued on apace to the Port Ellen Hotel, which had been given over as a temporary hospital.

She threw her leg over the bar and freewheeled, standing on the pedal for the last fifty yards, almost throwing the bike against the wall as she hurried in, smoothing her skirts.

Matron cocked an eyebrow at her flushed cheeks and wild hair, her eyes shining brightly – too brightly – as she hurried over for today's news.

'Well?'

'He managed a few steps today—'

Clarissa gasped, her hands flying to her cheeks. 'That's won-derful!'

'But it has depleted him, Miss Clarissa. He needs to rest.'

'Is he . . . is he sleeping?' She strained to see in through the glazed doors to the makeshift ward that had once been the lobby. 'Can I see him?'

Matron sighed. 'He's in there. He's been asking for you. But he is still very weak—' she called, as the girl burst into another sprint. 'Only ten minutes!' she said, the doors already swinging open and closed, open and closed in diminishing returns.

Islay, Monday 18 December 2017

'They found a what?'

'A teddy bear. I mean, it's only a tiny one but still . . .' Skye giggled, pulling out her phone and showing a photo of a badly worn golden bear with one orange glass eye and a bald stomach. 'Right at the bottom of the cask. An empty cask, obviously. It wasn't floating around in the whisky.'

'A bear was hidden in the hidden malt? But who put it there?' Alex asked, examining the picture with forensic scrutiny. 'And why?'

'I don't think we'll ever know,' Skye shrugged. 'I wonder if the baby died and the mother couldn't bear to hold on to its things.'

'God, that's so sad. And it's been sitting there all that time?'

'Aye. Since 1932, they reckon; that's what the cask was

stamped with, anyhow – along with the rest of the hidden stuff.'

'You mean there was more, apart from the teddy?'

'Aye, there was a wee baby's blanket in there too, so sweet it was: blue and white chequerboard with little red stitches around the sides.' She put her phone back on the table. 'We're holding a vote for what we should call the bear; they're going to announce the winner at the party.'

'Party?' Alex asked, sipping her coffee.

'Yes. The Christmas party's on Thursday – didn't you know?'

'No.'

'Och, you must come,' Skye said emphatically, splaying her hands across the edge of the table.

'I don't think so. I don't work here, remember.'

'But you've been here for nearly three weeks now. That's longer than most coopers last, I can tell you.'

'I'm just a contractor.'

'But it's a ceilidh,' Skye said beseechingly, as though that would swing the vote.

'And I can't reel,' Alex said firmly. 'It's sweet of you to ask but I'm not in the least bit bothered. I am beyond tired; I need to sleep for a month. It was an eventful weekend,' she said meaningfully, pinning Skye with a direct stare; she had been trying to get the girl on-topic since she'd got here – it was the reason she'd suggested this coffee – but Skye was seemingly oblivious to Alex's muted mood.

Skye smacked the table with her palm, clearly not hearing her. 'It is also, unofficially, doubling as my leaving party.'

'Skye—'

'You have to be there; I insist upon it.' She leaned in a little closer. 'We're friends, aren't we?'

366

Were they? Did friends lie to each other? Even if everything Skye had told her had been factually correct, she had still lied by omission; she knew that the reason why Lochie had jilted her changed the complexion of everything. 'Of course . . .'

'Then it's agreed, you're coming.'

Alex gave an impatient sigh. 'Fine, I'll look in but only for a few minutes.'

Skye looked at her, finally keying in to Alex's resistance. '. . . Alex, are you okay?'

'Why do you ask?'

'You just seem a bit . . . remote. Have I done something?'

Alex hesitated. Was this even any of her business? Skye cheating on Lochie changed everything, yes – not just who she thought this woman was and what her lie said about their so-called friendship, but most importantly it sabotaged her plans: she knew there would be no reconciliation now; Lochie was too proud to ever forgive or forget something like that. Skye wasn't the answer she'd been looking for.

But her fractional pause was enough to make Skye gasp, covering her mouth and nose with her hands. 'Oh God, they told you!'

Alex held her breath, wondering whether to lie, to spare her the humiliation – then nodded. If nothing else, she – personally – wanted to know why she'd done it. 'Yes.'

'I knew it!' she cried. 'As soon as I heard you'd gone up there, I knew they'd tell you.' Her wide eyes blinked back at Alex in horror over the tops of her fingers. A deep frown puckered her brow, hurt and shame swimming over her face. 'I bet they couldn't wait! They never liked me!'

'That's not true.'

'Isn't it?' She sat up defensively. Defiantly. 'Did they call me a slut?'

'No! Nothing like that.'

'Because it's not like they think.'

Alex looked at her. '. . . How was it then?'

'He was pushing me away, like I told you. I was so confused, I didn't understand what I'd done wrong. And then when—' A sob escaped her and she hid her face in her hands. 'Oh God. I thought all this was over with. But I can see it in your eyes. You think I'm a monster.'

Alex reached out to touch her arm pityingly. 'Skye, look. No one thinks you're a monster. He did the same to Jess; he pushed her away too. He didn't know how to process grief, not for his mother and not for his father either. And he still doesn't.' She gave her a sympathetic look, squeezed her forearm. 'It must have been an incredibly difficult situation. No one blames you.' She shrugged. 'And anyway, things have all worked out for the best in the end, haven't they?'

Skye studied her fingernails. 'Have they?'

What? Alex looked back at her. 'What do you mean?'

'Well, ever since the fire and what you said . . . you know, about things being unfinished between us.' Skye looked at her with wide eyes. 'I can't stop thinking, what if we *were* too quick to give up?'

Alex felt the floor drop a foot below her chair. She felt giddy, disoriented. Skye was saying this *now* – after admitting she'd cheated on him? 'But what about Alasdair?'

'Al?' Skye looked pained. 'Al's lovely. He so sweet and tender with me, you know? I mean, he doesn't have the fancy car and the beautiful house and the grand name but . . . we fit. We understand each other. It's just easy.'

'Well, there you are—'

'But then Lochie . . . he's so . . . glamorous and adventurous, you know?' she interrupted, her cheeks flushing, her eyes brightening. 'Life feels bigger with him somehow. He's like Heathcliff, striding about in a mood on the moors. And he's exciting and sexy and ohmigod, he's so good—'

'Uh-huh,' Alex said quickly, not remotely wanting to have that discussion.

'I mean, being with Al is like slipping on my old pair of favourite slippers, but ever since you said Lochie's got feelings for me, I can't help thinking: do I really want to spend the rest of my life like that? Where's the energy? Where's the vigour? Twenty years from now, won't I be going out of my mind?' She reached for Alex's hands, desperation on her pretty face. 'Alex, you've got to be straight with me: am I about to make the biggest mistake of my life?'

'Skye, I can't possibly answer that.'

'Please try. You're the one who's stirred the pot after all. I thought it was all done. Dusted. *Dead*. But then you said all those things . . .'

Her voice faded out as she pinned Alex with a bewildered stare, holding her to account.

Alex took a deep breath, trying to calm herself down as much as Skye. The girl had a point. She *had* stirred the pot. She *had* seen the thickness of longing and regret between them both, hadn't she? 'Okay, look, don't panic for a start. You're not to do anything. You need to take some time and think – properly think – about what you want and who it is you want to be with. Marriage is a big deal. It's for ever. But you have to be honest and you have to be brave.' She swallowed, feeling her words become smaller, tighter, harder. She couldn't believe she was saying this. Now now. 'If

Lochie is the man you want to be with, then you need to tell him that.'

'But when? Al's arriving on Friday and the wedding's the day after that.' Hysteria tinged her voice. It was clear she had been brooding on this for days.

'Friday's four days from now.'

'But . . . but everything's organized. It's already happening. I'm getting my tan and my nails done tomorrow. And my bikini line. And then Mum's picking up the flowers . . .'

'It's plenty of time, Skye.'

'No, it's not. Not when Lochie's in Edinburgh. God only knows when he's coming back.'

Alex's head snapped up. *Edinburgh?* It was the first she'd heard of it. She looked outside, scarcely able to believe she could have missed something so glaringly obvious on her way in but sure enough – the field where the helicopter had landed only last night was empty.

She felt a rush of anger. They had had a meeting scheduled for this afternoon; she had thought she was getting somewhere with him after that spiel at the front door about trusting her and wonderwalls. She thought she'd broken through at last, but he was just back to his old tricks – messing her around again. She had been deluding herself – the kiss truly had meant nothing for him – it really had been the whisky talking.

'Alex?'

She realized Skye was staring at her, wanting answers. Needing direction. 'Look, anything before "I do" will do,' Alex said calmly. 'But let's not let it come to that . . . If it's going to happen, the sooner you tell Alasdair the better.'

Skye nodded – nodded frantically, like that dog in the insurance adverts. 'Oh, but how can I do to him what

Lochie did to me?' She dropped her face in her hands, vacillating between one man and the other. 'It was so awful; I thought I'd never get over it. His face that night, he was . . . broken. It was all I saw whenever I closed my eyes.'

'It's not the same situation.'

'But I betrayed him, Alex. And now I'm going to do it again – to Al?'

Alex tried to mask her frustration. She didn't need this right now. Her head was spinning, trying to work out what Lochie was doing in Edinburgh, but there was only one scenario she could realistically envision: Sholto had called that board meeting; Lochie had got it wrong, he'd overplayed his hand after all. 'No one's saying you will. If Al's the one you love, then everything goes ahead as planned.' She tipped her head to the side. 'Look, you said it's the party on Thursday, yes?'

'Uh-huh.'

'So spend some time with him there. He's bound to be back by then . . .'

Was he?

'He can hardly miss his own company's Christmas bash . . .'

Would it even be his company by then?

'It'll be a relaxed setting, everyone will be letting their hair down . . . talk, maybe dance together, see how you feel. Give him the chance to talk to you. There may be things he needs to say to you that he hasn't had the opportunity to do; or it may be he simply doesn't feel he can; perhaps you need to offer him some hope.'

'Hope,' Skye murmured.

'Exactly.'

Skye reached over for her hands again. 'Oh God, you will

come to the party, won't you? Say you will. I don't think I can do it without you.'

Alex nodded, suppressing her sigh. Now wasn't the time to mention she might not be here by then either. 'Of course I will.'

'You promise?'

'I'll do my best.'

Alex stayed at the canteen table, staring out through the window. Skye had left forty minutes ago now and the coffee cup was cold in Alex's hands. A few of the coopers across the way were challenging each other to a barrel-rolling contest – it was something of a Christmas tradition according to the canteen ladies who, still in their blue coats and hair caps, were huddled at the windows, other workers also coming out from their units or leaning from the windows, cheering them on as the burly men stripped off their shirts and flexed their muscles. In the snow.

'I like Mungo,' she overheard one of the women say – Mary, Alex thought her name was – arms crossed over her bosom as she watched the shenanigans with a keen eye. 'It sounds right somehow.'

'Who says the bear's a boy?' the middle woman asked indignantly; she was the one who could never hold back Alex's free shortbread.

'My Euan thinks it should be Archibald, after the founder,' said Eileen, the older woman standing to her left. 'After all, if it's going to be a company mascot—'

'Ach, it wasn't just Archie as started the company, it was his brother Percy too,' Mary protested. 'If you're going to go down that road, you'll only give them's in the suits another reason to fight – *which of the original brothers gets the principal claim?* – and it's not like they're not at loggerheads already.'

'Well, I don't see why there should be any argument over that,' Eileen snipped. 'We's all know it's Archie's direct bloodline as has the truest claim – Sholto and Torquil are blood; Lochie's side of the family, charming though they may be, are buy-ins.' And when the other women looked at her with buckled brows, she clarified: 'Adopted. Surely you know that?' She tsked. 'Everyone knows that, it's no secret.'

No, it wasn't a secret. Alex had known it too. Mrs Peggie had told her, that day in the farmhouse. Torquil too.

Why hadn't she given more thought to such an important fact? Alex sank into her thoughts, forgetting all about the high jinks in the yard. She didn't hear the cheers, she didn't even hear the rest of the women's conversation. She just heard two words over and over: Adopted. Bear. Adopted. Bear.

She didn't know why they had stuck in her mind or why they mattered.

She sensed only that they did.

Chapter Twenty-Six

Islay, Wednesday 20 December 2017

'Mrs Peggie, is the water hot, do you know?' Alex stuck her head into the little kitchen to see her landlady chopping swede. The breakfast tables had been cleared and preparations for dinner were in full swing.

'Of course,' the old lady smiled, the superior temperature of the water clearly a source of personal pride. 'Are you wanting a bath?' She put down the knife and wiped her hands on her apron.

'If that's okay. I'm pretty chilled from the walk.'

'Och, you and your daily constitutionals. You've been out there in all weathers and now it's snowing footballs. You're hardy, I'll give you that.' She walked towards Alex with a fond smile. 'You help yourself, pet. I'll go and turn on the immersion in case the lovebirds come back cold too.' A couple of Norwegian honeymooners were in the green room for the next few nights, bagging Munros by day and creaking the bedsprings by night.

They walked together into the hall, where swags of red tinsel were draped over the paintings. 'I've put fresh towels on the bed for you.'

'Thank you,' Alex smiled, thinking how much she was

374

going to miss living here. It would be Christmas in less than a week and in just a few days she would be home again; it had been two days now since Lochie had left for Edinburgh and she hadn't heard from him at all; even Sholto hadn't returned her call. Whatever they were doing, they were as locked in as a papal conclave, no outsiders admitted. It was over. She had lost.

But it wasn't just the unfamiliar bitterness of failing at something that wounded her; she was taken aback by the sorrow she felt at the thought of leaving this proud, weather-battered farmhouse with its salmon-pink bath and balding velour sofa with the fringing coming away at one corner, the circular Chinese-style rug, the onyx ashtrays that hadn't been used for forty years, the small, shallow fire which threw out a drowsy heat. But more than that she was going to miss the Peggies, with their quiet, no-fuss ways and stalwart routines, moving in tandem like figures in a Swiss clock around the strangers who came to stay in their home, around the sheep and cattle that needed moving from the fields and pens according to the winds.

She climbed the stairs, stopping at the bathroom to start filling the bath, before going into her room and sinking onto the window seat. The distant grey water had a cold hard glaze to it this morning, the wind like a whip on its surface, and the sky was bellied with snow. She dropped her forehead to the glass and watched as fat flakes parachuted down like silent armies. Had she really been out walking in this? It looked foolhardy from this perspective, but it wasn't like he had any choice in the matter. She could never let a day go by without checking in: every day that dawned presented a fresh opportunity for something to go wrong; what would be a nuisance for anyone else could be potentially fatal for him.

A cold gust made her shiver and she saw that Mrs Peggie had left the window open fractionally to air the room. She got up and closed it, staring out of the window for another moment as the snow whirled in a giddying dance. At least she didn't need to drive down to the distillery in this; it would be another afternoon learning to play whist with Mrs Peggie for her today. She went to turn back into the bathroom to check the water, when her eyes fell to the pastel painting on the near wall. It wasn't to her taste but it had charm and a 'confident' use of colour and was signed in the bottom right corner. She squinted to read it. *'Morag Dunoon, 1928'.*

She began pulling her socks off when she stopped – and looked at the painting again.

What?

Islay, Thursday 21 December 2017

'Oh Christ, the horoscopes thing again.'

She looked up in surprise at the wry voice, feeling a physical jolt at the sight of him standing there, as though he'd never been gone, as though it was perfectly fine to leave without a word and remain incommunicado for three days, seemingly never thinking she might be wondering what was happening, or if he'd be coming back, or if she'd ever see him again.

'You're back.' Her voice was quiet and she made a concerted effort to keep her arms and feet still, to not betray herself with those non-verbal cues that tripped up everyone else. Because she wasn't everyone else. She couldn't be.

'You're here. I wasn't sure if you would be.' He walked into the room, her eyes tracking him.

'Of course,' she swallowed. 'I have a job to do.'

He gave a rueful smile. 'You still believe you can save me?'

She forced herself to meet his gaze. 'I don't know. Can I? Or has Sholto let the axe fall?'

'He gave it a good go. And I'll admit, my neck is pretty sore – he landed some of the blows.'

'. . . But?'

He was standing in front of her now. 'But it's like I told you. For as long as I hold the majority, he can't touch me.'

She could only imagine the pressure he would be under now, though. Alex looked away, feeling the quickening of her pulse rush to colour her cheeks. The game was still in play. She wasn't dead in the water yet. 'Congratulations.'

'Alex—'

She whipped her head round to face him, ignoring the look in his eyes. 'So then we have work to do. I'm glad. I don't want my heavy lifting to have been in vain.'

She felt his eyes upon her as she readied the last details. His unexpected text, not an hour ago, had left her practically no time to prepare but she had managed to get all the tables and benches pushed back against the walls; and although the dinner ladies were still tidying up and cleaning the kitchen after the lunch rush, they had pulled down the metal shutters and Alex was satisfied they wouldn't hear anything over the carols on the radio and their own chatter.

He stepped back, receding from whatever it was he had wanted to say. 'Okay. So talk me through the science of this then,' he said, clearly feeling generous from his victory and playing ball. 'I assume there *is* a science to it?'

'You're funny,' she quipped, before forcing a smile on her lips. Because this was it. Phase one of everything she had come here to do. It was time for her to work at last.

'In short, by creating a physical experience that you have to stand in and walk through, it makes the problem somatic, i.e. it brings it *into* your body and *away* from your rational mind,' she explained. 'It's a brilliant technique for problems where there's no apparent solution, when a pattern has become established and the mind is simply reinforcing the existing belief; but by making it a physical experience, it brings fresh perspective to the story. I've used it numerous times when I've felt there's something in the client's system that is affecting the way they manage or perform.'

'I see.' He came and stood beside her in the middle of the space. 'So how do you want me?'

She swallowed. It was best not to think about that. 'Well, today, we're not going to focus on the "We" – i.e. you and Sholto. In fact, I don't want us even to mention his name after this point.'

'Fine by me.'

'We're going to focus on the "I". Come and sit with me here.'

He groaned but she led him over to two chairs, where she had left a stack of paper and some pens. They sat down and she inhaled deeply, looking over at him with what she hoped was an innocuous, impersonal gaze. 'We'll start with the problem – as you see it. What's the biggest problem that you feel is rooted in you?'

He looked at her but his cocksure demeanour was already fading fast. Agreeing to do this with her – letting her be his wonderwall – might have seemed flippantly easy in principle but he was already challenged. And she hadn't even started yet.

He fell quiet, his Adam's apple bobbing in his throat as he stared at a spot on the floor, and she knew he was trying to think of something he could say that sounded plausible without being the truth. 'Uh . . .'

After a minute or two of heavy silence, she said, 'Would you like me to make a suggestion for you? The problem as *I* see it? You can of course correct me if you think I'm wrong.'

He shrugged.

'It's as we discussed last week. Trust.' The way she said it – such a little word; she saw him relax.

He nodded. 'Yeah . . . I guess I probably do have trust issues.'

You think? she wanted to shriek. But they were off.

'Okay, so you are Lochie, obviously,' she said, writing his name on the topmost sheet of paper, and beside it an arrow. 'And the problem is trust, or rather lack thereof – distrust,' she said, writing 'trust' on another sheet, again with an arrow. 'Great. Good start.' She smiled at him encouragingly. 'Honesty is good.'

'I think so.' His eyes were steady upon her, flipping her stomach over with ease.

'And what would you want to be the goal of resolving your trust issues?' she asked.

'Um . . .' He swallowed, his hands gripping his knees in a subconscious display of tension. He brought his fist to his mouth and coughed. 'Better relationships?'

'Okay, great. So you feel that if we can resolve the trust issues, you can move towards better relationships.'

She bit her lip as she wrote the word on the paper, aware of his gaze on her as she worked.

'And who or what do you think you could rely on, that could help you get from the problem to the solution?' She arched her eyebrows. 'And before you say it, don't say the dog. You cannot put the dog.'

He grinned. 'Well, who would you recommend?'

'What about Ambrose, for instance? You're clearly very close friends.'

'Yes, when it comes to banter and the rugby score. We don't . . .'

'Talk?'

'Men don't.'

She sighed. 'How many times do I hear that?' she asked, shaking her head sadly. 'How about Jess then? She's very protective of you.'

He shook his head. 'Too much history. She can sometimes . . . blur the line.'

His eyes held hers and she felt her neutrality colour into something stronger; she had detected Jess's complicated feelings for him, herself. 'I see.'

'It's best to keep it simple.'

'Yes,' Alex agreed, wondering if they were going to end up with Rona after all.

'How about you?' he asked.

'*Me?*'

'Why not?'

She blinked. 'Because I drive you up the wall? Because I won't be here much longer? Take your pick.'

'Well, can't I call you if there's a problem? I thought you said you FaceTime clients when necessary?'

'Yes, but it's generally considered better to have someone who can be physically around for you, someone you feel genuinely at ease with.'

He sat back in the chair and shrugged. 'Well, there's no one else. It's literally you or the dog.'

'Wow, that makes for a compelling argument,' she quipped, trying to hide behind a breezy smile. 'Okay, well then, for the sake of putting down something constructive, let's put me as your ally.' She scribbled her own name down before looking back at him. 'Is there anything else you want to bring into the dynamic, any elements that aren't covered with those bases?'

She fanned out the sheets in her hands for him to read. 'No. I think that covers it.'

'Okay then,' she said, rising and motioning for him to do the same. 'Now as the first step, I want you to take these sheets and place them in the constellation that best represents how you feel right now about the issues we're discussing here. Use the arrows to point which way you feel the energy of the dynamic is flowing. Or if it's not, use the arrow turned away, like a blocking force.'

Lochie stood in silence for a few moments, staring at the cards, before he went to the centre of the space and set down his name.

Alex watched as he took a few paces forward and set down 'trust', with the arrow pointing back at his name. Three paces on from that, he set down 'relationships', the arrow pointing away from 'trust'. Alex watched closely as he held the last sheet with her name on it, deliberating where to set it down. He finally settled on the space beside 'trust'.

Alex walked over, assessing the constellation in silence. Her pulse was up. She'd never seen her own name on the paper before.

'Okay,' she said finally, looking back at him. 'You're happy with that? You feel it represents the current state of affairs?'

He nodded.

'Good. Now come and stand by the paper with your name on it,' she said. He came and stood by her. 'I want you to breathe deeply, close your eyes and tell me exactly what you feel when you step on each element. You need to *become* that energy, talk to me in the first person, stream of consciousness, okay? Don't overthink or try to analyse, just say the first thing that comes to you. Do you understand?'

'Sure.'

'In addition, whilst you're talking, I want you to try to feel the energy in your body as you talk through each element. Try to focus on where you feel it – your throat, gut, stomach, heart? We all have energy centres or chakras, for the dispersal and flow of energy or prana or chi. It doesn't matter what you choose to call it, it's the same thing: our feelings are literally rooted in our bodies.'

'Okay.' He looked sceptical but she reasoned at least he wasn't sneering or kicking chairs about.

'So close your eyes and tell me what you feel when you're Lochie?'

'I feel . . . uh . . . strong. Confident.' She watched as his eyes moved behind his eyelids. 'Pretty powerful. Successful . . .'

He opened one eye. 'Should I say bad things too?'

'Say whatever occurs to you.'

He exhaled. 'So then, angry too, I guess. And a bit . . . I don't know, foggy?'

'Interesting,' she murmured. 'And where are you feeling that when you acknowledge those emotions? Can you feel, like a heat, anywhere? Show me with your hands.'

He waited for a moment, then raised his hands to his solar plexus.

She nodded, touching him lightly on the arm so that he opened his eyes.

'That was great,' she said. 'Now I want you to do the same here on the problem spot. Close your eyes and go back into your body. What do feel when you think about trust? How does your body react?'

He closed his eyes again. 'I feel . . . empty. Blank.' He sounded surprised. 'I can't feel anything . . . It's like everything's been taken. All my energy. I can't move.'

'And if you were to put your hands anywhere, to signify one place in your body—'

His hands went straight to his heart.

Alex looked at him, making the notes before she got him to open his eyes again.

'Okay. Let's go to the goal: relationships.'

He inhaled sharply but followed her. She turned him so that he was facing in the direction of the arrow on the paper.

'What do you feel here when you think of having a relationship?'

He closed his eyes. '. . . Frustrated. Restless. Stuck.' He raised his hands up. 'It's . . . sort of here,' he said, touching his throat.

'Okay, that's good, that's good,' she said, making a note and getting him to take a step over to the final sheet.

'And lastly your ally, the solution to your goal,' she said, not wanting to say her own name out loud. 'What's happening here?'

'Hot. Cold . . . Irritation. Jealousy.' He opened his eyes. 'Why would I feel jealous of you?'

She put a hand on his arm. 'Don't think about it now. Close your eyes. What else? Just stream of consciousness.'

'Powerful . . .' He frowned. 'Hel . . . helpless.'

Alex bit her lip as she wrote down the notes. 'And where are you feeling it?'

He hesitated. 'There.' He pressed his hands to his navel.

He opened his eyes and looked at her. 'Don't tell me any of that made sense to you?'

'Actually, yes,' she said quietly, trying to smile. 'Shall we sit?'

She cleared her throat. 'Right, so that was a really interesting exercise. Basically, what we started off with was creating a spatial representation of your situation.'

He was watching her with a studied concentration she hadn't experienced before.

'Now, if you look at the cards as you've placed them on the ground, you'll see you've got the arrow for trust pointing back towards you – indicating you trust yourself, but no one else. The goal of better relationships is set *behind* that element, away from you, as though blocked by it. And then finally there's your ally, me, the mechanism supposedly there to enable the pattern to come together. Now you've placed me next to trust, suggesting you trust me.'

'Well, I do.'

She drew a breath, wishing he'd look away, stare at the cards – something, anything other than her.

'So that was your subconscious imaging of the pattern. Then we moved through it quickly and instinctually. Now your feelings about yourself – when you stood on your own name or identity – and when taken in isolation, were highly positive: you're dynamic, energized, confident, but you recognize you've got anger too. You mentioned fog – as though you can't see the path and when I asked you about where you felt that energy, you pointed to here,' she said, showing him on herself. 'Which completely corresponds to what you were saying, because the solar plexus is the root of energy from where we take our action – it's our central vibration, if you like; it's where we feel the ability to be confident and in control of our lives. But when energy is blocked, we feel it as heat.'

'And why exactly does one get an energy blockage in the solar plexus?' he asked. He was trying not to look sceptical but she could see it in his eyes.

'That's what we're going to find out, but it can come from fear of rejection, for example. It's actually the most common centre for suppressed desires and freedoms.'

He stared at her with an expression that didn't reveal whether he thought she was completely mad or the wisest person he'd ever met.

'Don't worry, this will make more sense when we've gone through it all.' She glanced back at her notes. 'Anyway, then we moved on to the problem in hand, namely trust – but I'd like to come back to that one at the end, so let's go next to the proposed goal of better relationships. Here, when I asked you how it made you feel, you said frustrated, restless and stuck. Again, your body tallied with what your instinct was telling you because a blockage of the throat chakra – which was what you identified there – points to an inability to communicate, of literally the words being held back. So, in other words, the language of relationships is not something you can put voice to.'

He crossed his arms and folded his legs. 'Right.'

She smiled and leaned over, unfolding his arms. 'And your legs, please. You're physically blocking what I'm saying to you. I need you to be open and receptive to what we're learning here.'

He did as he was told but he looked as uncomfortable as a teenage boy in a pole-dancing class.

'Now with "ally", you actually spoke in opposites: hot versus cold. Powerful versus helpless.'

'Didn't I say jealous too?'

'That's right.'

'Well, what does that mean? I'm not jealous of you – although you do have a fabulous shoe collection,' he drawled.

She laughed. 'It doesn't mean you're jealous *of me*. Again, these negative feelings point to a blockage in that energy centre. The sacral chakra which you pointed to relates to our fundamental sense of self and our relationships – connection with others, our ability to accept others. So when that's blocked, it might manifest as jealousy or a need for control, power play, a fear of betrayal.'

'So the fact that you're my ally . . .' he frowned.

'It's suggesting you're *not sure* you can trust me. You want to but you have conflicting feelings about me.'

He blinked but said nothing.

'Let's go back to trust.'

'Oh, good.'

'This was where you had the most dramatic reaction. It was almost as though you completely shut down – you said you felt empty, blank, that you had no energy, you couldn't move.' She bit her lip. 'And when I asked where you felt the heat, you pointed to your heart.'

'Am I actually dead?' he deadpanned.

She grinned. 'The heart chakra, contrary to common perception, isn't about love. It's actually the source of empathy, self-love and forgiveness. You've heard the phrase "a heavy heart"?'

'Of course.'

'This is where it comes from. A blocked heart leads to guilt, anger, resentment.' She tipped her head to the side. 'I've noticed you very often roll out your shoulders.'

He shrugged. 'It's where I hold my tension, according to my masseuse.' He gave a look that suggested the masseuse's theories were as 'alternative' as hers.

'Well, stiffness between the shoulders is another manifestation of blocked energy in the heart chakra. But what your body is telling you, loud and clear, is that your issues of trust stem from guilt and anger about something, seemingly something for which you have yet to forgive yourself.' She dipped her head, trying to make eye contact with him. 'Is there something that instinctively comes to you when I say that?'

'Nope.'

The answer came too sure, too fast.

'Really?' It was her turn to look sceptical. 'Because according to what we've just walked through, I've got sitting in front of me a confident, empowered man who can't trust people – even those he wants to – and who can't put a voice to love, even though he wants that too. And his body is screaming out – when he listens to it – that he needs to let go of his guilt and forgive himself, but he doesn't know what that could possibly be referring to?'

He stared at her and she knew he knew it; she could see it in his eyes.

'Lochie, you have to talk, tell me . . . There's a saying that whatever you fight, you strengthen; whatever you resist, persists. Doesn't that resonate in you? You'll never move on if you don't own up to this. Your mind already knows you can't carry on – that's why you said things feel foggy, you're losing sight of the path. You are blocked mentally, emotionally and spiritually by it and it's just going to keep coming back at you; it'll destroy every relationship until you face it.'

She knew her words had hit their mark – she knew he had thrown away his relationships with both Jess and Skye – but he said nothing.

She tried again.

'There's a philosopher called Eckhart Tolle; perhaps you've heard of him. He said something once that really resonates with me: "What could be more futile, more insane, than to create inner resistance to what *already is*?" Do you know it?' she asked.

'I know you like your quotes.'

'I believe in listening to people I think are wiser than me,' she said lightly. 'The point is, you are fighting something that is already present, that has already happened. You are tethered by your past, emotionally and physically. You are taking on *total* responsibility for preventing the company from being taken over and the distillery closed down; you feel that the security of all those people's jobs is on you – but no one person can be expected to do that alone. It's neither fair nor realistic. And it's also not true. It's just a protective measure that your brain has created to keep you here, in this place, in this company, where you've always been. By convincing yourself you can't leave here for the distillery's sake, it takes the problem – the *threat* – of moving on out of your hands.'

He wasn't looking at her now, his gaze stony upon the wall. But she could tell by the rise and fall of his chest that she was pushing on his pressure points. 'What's keeping you here, Lochie . . . ? Your father?'

As she had anticipated, he got up at that, needing to move, to be active, dynamic. He stretched his arms above his head, making himself seem more powerful, masking the fact that he felt vulnerable.

'Tell me about him,' she said, watching as he paced, refusing to stop.

'There's nothing to say.'

'I know he died a few years ago.'

'That's right.'

'Can you tell me what happened?'

'He drank himself to death.' He almost spat the words out. 'That's what happened.'

'I'm sorry,' she said quietly, flinching as she saw his pain suddenly exposed and raw, like a throbbing tumour revealed beneath peeled-back skin. 'I can understand how painful that must have been for you.'

'Can you?' The hint of a sneer was back. 'Really? Or are you just making the right noises?'

She hesitated. '. . . Actually, my father was an alcoholic too. I've seen how it can destroy lives.'

He stopped walking and looked at her. 'Christ, I'm sorry. I didn't know.'

389

'Well, why would you?' she shrugged, forcing a lackadaisical smile. 'It's not something anyone likes talking about, right?'

'No.'

He walked over to the nearest table and leaned against it, his long legs stretched out and crossed at the ankle, his eyes on the ground. He took a deep breath in and held it, before sighing heavily, letting it go.

'The ironic thing is, he never really drank before my mother's death.' He gave a small snort. 'Everyone used to laugh about how he'd never acquired the taste for whisky; a teetotal distillery owner. But when Mum died . . .' He stopped and took another breath. 'When Mum died, it destroyed him. He felt it was his fault.'

'He felt he could have stopped it?' Lochie's head whipped up and she shrugged. 'Daisy told me. I'm so sorry.'

He shrugged but the effort was Herculean, pain twisting the muscles on his face so that the smile was a grimace. 'No, it was a release for her. She'd had a long history of depression. I think that . . . uh . . . part of me always sort of expected it.'

Alex stared at him, glimpsing in this man the boy who had grown up with a mother he knew was going to one day abandon him; it broke her heart to see it and it took everything she had to stay seated in her chair, her hands folded neatly in her lap.

'Almost the bigger shock was that when she did, Dad . . . fell apart.' He didn't speak for a long time nor did Alex fill the silence with platitudes; he had hitched his arms right up now so that they crossed above his heart. 'I can actually remember the very first drink, the one that started it all off – it was the day of the funeral and we came in from the graveyard and he walked straight over to the bar and poured himself a dram – three fingers. And he downed it, there and then. And then he poured himself another.'

His grip on himself tightened, his hands clutching the opposite elbows, his head dropped, making himself small again. Alex felt herself mirror his actions, unable to imagine the pain of watching his only remaining parent slowly kill himself too, waiting for the day he too would manage it. Was it any wonder he didn't trust people when the two who should have put him before everything had put him to the back of the queue, his needs last? Forgotten? He had been abandoned and betrayed – by his parents, by Skye . . .

'He did try to get better. There were several times I thought he was pulling himself back. We would make small targets to aim for – making it to Lord's for the Ashes, pulling off the MacNab . . . but by then, he was too deep in the hole. His body was wrecked and he didn't have the strength of spirit to fight the addiction; it had taken hold of him.' He nodded, biting his bottom lip. 'As he was dying, he apologized for what he'd done, leaving me. And I do believe he was sorry.'

'But you can't forgive him.'

His glance was like the flash of a sword's blade. 'Not yet.'

'Do you feel perhaps you've begun to, with this?'

'How? How does *this* change it?'

'Because now you can see with your own eyes what it's doing to you, the impact it's having on your relationships, your career. You're locked in a cycle you can't break: you're at war with your own family and your board, you don't have a single person here you feel you can trust or rely on, you're working here every day surrounded by the very thing that killed your father. How is that status quo sustainable?' She shrugged. 'It's not. Something has to give.'

'And what would that be? That I quit, is that it? Give them all what they want.'

'That's not what I said. But seeing as you've brought it up, let's explore that: putting aside your sense of responsibility to the workers and the community for a second, is it really such a horrific thought? What's actually keeping you here? Isn't the so-called legacy of this company just chains about your neck?'

He stared at her.

'Is this really how you want to live for the next thirty years? Blocking Sholto with petty moves and counter-moves? What are *your* dreams? Did you ever even consider following them, or did you find yourself down this path before you had a chance to think about it? Are you here simply because you feel you owe it to your parents to continue the so-called legacy? At the end of the day, what's it all for? This is your life.'

She gazed at him, seeing how his breath came fast, high emotion colouring his cheeks. She could see it in him, the need to speak, the blockage at his throat. She felt the same in her own throat, words that could not and would not ever be said, leadening her heart even as she sat here in front of him, smiling like she meant it.

'Lochie, Skye is leaving in a few days. She's got a new job, out of her own father's shadow. Don't you think this could be your chance to step out of your father's shadow too? You could be with her. Start somewhere new.'

'Wha . . . ? No, she's getting married,' he said, a dark expression on his face.

'She's having doubts.'

He frowned, looking away again. 'Why are you saying this to me? You can't honestly think—'

'Skye made you happy once. Yes, she made a mistake – a big one – but I'm guessing you weren't perfect either. Your father was dying and you pushed her away. You've got one chance left to make things right. Be happy, Lochie! Choose happiness! God knows, you deserve it.'

He stood up, making for her. 'Alex, you don't under-stand—'

'No. *You* don't.' She swallowed, wondering whether she would get the words out. 'There's something I need to tell you. Something I found out, only yesterday and . . . I'm sorry, but it's not good news.'

He paled. 'What is it?'

She took a deep breath and made eye contact with him. 'You know your grandfather was adopted?'

He looked puzzled. 'Yes.'

She bit her lip. '. . . The adoption was never made legal.'

'What?' He looked baffled.

'It was after the war, a time of chaos. People were dis-placed, missing . . . It was routine for people to adopt the orphaned children of their friends and relatives. With every-thing else that needed doing, few bothered with going through the legalities of a formal adoption. And it looks like your great-grandmother was one of them.'

He frowned. 'But what . . . what does that have to do with anything? Why does it matter whether or not my grandfather was legally adopted?'

'Because in the company's Articles of Association, it stip-ulates that both the chair and CEO positions must be held by a family member. And according to the legal definition of "family", that means blood relatives, or legal adoptees.'

He was quiet for a long time, a frown puckering his brow, trying to take it all in. It wasn't his Rambo boardroom antics that were going to get him the sack, but *paperwork*? '. . . How do you know all this?'

'By accident. Mrs Peggie and I were looking through some old boxes of photographs. There was one of your great-grandmother Clarissa with your grandfather, and Mrs Peggie said Clarissa had adopted him after the war. It was just a passing comment; I didn't think anything about it at the time until I overheard something the other day that brought it back to mind. I went over to the church and checked the parish records. Sure enough, there's a marriage and death record for your grandfather George, but nothing else. The clerk told me to check online, which I did – I've spent the past couple of days on it while you were in Edinburgh – and although I found a birth record for him in Cumbria, there's no paper trail for the adoption. Nothing at all. Legally it never happened.'

He was staring at her, an inscrutable expression in his eyes. 'No. What I meant was, how exactly did you get hold of the details of our Articles of Association?'

She swallowed at her error; in her nervousness, she had over-explained, a classic sign of anyone telling a lie – or if not telling an outright lie, at least dodging a truth. 'I rang your lawyers in Edinburgh and they sent through a copy.'

'And why would they do that?' he asked, his voice low and slow. 'You're not a shareholder.'

'I know.' Her voice was quiet. 'But Sholto has given me access all areas.'

In a flash, distrust flooded his face, her entrenchment with the enemy suddenly laid bare.

'He said anything that might help me help you—' she said quickly.

'How is this *helping*?' he demanded. 'Do you have any idea of what you've just done? You haven't helped me! You've fucked me over! Thanks to your nosing around in confidential business and family matters, all you've actually managed to do is flag up to the lawyers that I am not legally a Farquhar. And you can rest assured, it's only going to be a matter of time before *that's* brought to Sholto's attention!'

'I know, and I'm so sorry! It wasn't my intention,' she said desperately, trying to keep him calm as he began to pace. 'But that's why I'm still here, saying all this to you. It was why I wanted you to walk through this exercise and see for yourself that you're better off – far better off away from here and the lot of them—'

'This?' He indicated to the constellation on the floor, kicking at the papers. 'You think this can make me feel better?' Scorn ravaged the words.

'Yes! It should! You could be happier than you can possibly imagine being anchored here!' She walked over to him and grabbed his arm. 'Resign, Lochie. There's a golden parachute clause in the articles. Take it. Leave all this and start somewhere new! It's not a loss. You're not losing! You'll be a wealthy man, you'll still have a new venture to pursue with Scotch Vaults. Get Skye back. It can be a win-win for you. Abundant mentality, remember?' She ran out of breath, her hand falling from his arm as she saw the fury burn in his eyes. 'Please, Lochie. You have no choice. There's no way you can win this fight. The facts are the facts – you're finished here.'

Chapter Twenty-Seven

Islay, 13 May 1918

'Next stop, America! I won!' she cried, her arms in the air as she twirled and spun, trampling the buttercups underfoot and feeling the sun on her face.

'That's not fair, you got a head start!' Ed protested, half-laughing, half-panting as he crested the top of the slope and allowed himself to fall headlong into the long grass. 'I'll beat you next time,' he groaned, rolling over onto his back, his arms stretched over his head.

'That's what you always say,' she giggled, flopping onto the ground next to him and seeing how the mild spring was colouring him up, playing its own part as this beautiful, wild, desolate place put him back together again. The cast was off his leg now and he was walking almost all the time without the stick – 'only when you're around,' Sister MacLennan had said, during one of her many tellings-off to Clarissa for exhausting him.

But Clarissa knew she knew what was best for him. They had spent hours walking on the curved golden beach to get him stronger again, exercising the muscles that had withered during his confinement; they had taken rest stops when he'd needed them and eaten from the picnics she'd packed, meaning he'd put on weight too. They had marched and finally raced up these high-slanting *fields to the clifftops, making him fitter and forcing the sea air into his lungs so that his eyes were bright all the time now – 'only when you're around,' Sister MacLennan had tutted.*

He was back to being the man he'd been before he'd hit the rocks, before he'd ever climbed aboard that ship: vital and funny, quietly spoken with his glamorous accent and wistful stories of mountains that made Islay's look like molehills. In a funny way, a shameful way, she was grateful for everything that had happened that night to bring him here: the Germans for the torpedo that had stopped his ship from sailing silently past these shores, the rocks for breaking him and keeping him prisoner when all the other soldiers had left.

She watched him as his breathing returned to normal, his eyelashes throwing shadows on his cheeks, his palms brushing absent-mindedly over the grass as he basked in the gentle warmth, his homeland thousands of miles away behind his head and just over the horizon. So near. So far.

They should never have met. If the world hadn't gone mad, he would be home in Montana and not lying on a clifftop on a Scottish isle with a girl who had pinned her survival to his. But they had met: disease, war, violence – everything that was ugly – had conspired to bring them together, and now growing out of all that, miraculously, was something beautiful. The night stars glistened more brightly now that she knew he was sleeping under them; the flowers nodded more prettily because he ran past them. The world had its song back, life its laughter. Sometimes she didn't know if she could bear it, the beauty too sharp, the sweetness too ripe.

She lay down beside him, rolling her head on the grass and watching the full black moon grow in his eyes as he looked back at her. And it was the strangest feeling, like falling and flying at the same time, the touch of his fingertips against hers, both a burn and a balm. It was the best thing in the world and the worst, because it couldn't last.

Because it wouldn't. She had done too good a job. He was healthy and strong again, fit to fight and his orders had come in. He was leaving in ten days.

Next stop, France.

Islay, Thursday 21 December 2017

The village hall was a short stumpy building, whitewashed with a steepled slate roof and plain windows that looked over the sea with Presbyterian eyes. Its position at the head of the bay – the last building in town before the coast switched back on itself, folding in pleats towards the distillery a mile further on – was isolated and windswept. More snow had been predicted and the sea looked opaque and thick, reflecting back a heavy sky.

Alex pulled up in the old Landy, her chin almost on the steering wheel as she looked for somewhere to turn; the small car park was completely full and cars had been parked at jaunty angles along the approach lane for the past hundred yards. She looked across at the small building – orange curtains obscured her view in but tinsel at the front door glittered in the outdoor lights and even with her windows shut, she could hear the music easily – the sounds of bows dancing upon fiddle strings at a terrific pace, whoops and calls carrying loftily through the night air.

She spotted a muddy bank in the corner; it was too steeply pitched for most of the other cars, small runabout hatchbacks with dented bumpers and rust patches on the wheel arches, but this beast could go anywhere and she rolled up it slowly. She turned off the ignition and the lights and tried to make herself move.

They were in there, the two of them: Skye fishing for clues, throwing out hope and flirtatious smiles; Lochie now only acting the part he had been born and raised for, reduced to a mime artist and merely pretending to be the boss as his employees danced and celebrated around him.

He had left her without a word in the canteen earlier, the roar of the Aston clearly audible even through the thick stone walls. She didn't know where he had gone or what he was doing or what his next move was going to be. She had simply had to cut him loose and trust that she had given him enough upside to act on her advice. But would he? Nothing was ever predictable with him.

She looked over at the golden windows and the raucous party thronging within. She didn't like herself for what she'd done or how she'd made him feel but she couldn't run or look away now; it was almost done. She had to see this through and make sure it happened. Tonight had to be the end of it. All of it.

She pushed on the door and stood, staring in. The sight was joyful and chaotic: kilts were flinging, arms were linking, people were laughing and leaping, others standing by the bar – three deep – holding drinks and chatting. Tinsel had been strung across the roof's timber rafters, a tiny potted Christmas tree sprayed with fake snow and placed on the stage at the far end where the band was playing – fiddlers and an accordionist tapping their feet and bobbing their heads, a giant inflatable snowman and Father Christmas swaying on either side of them, like outriders.

She walked in slowly, her eyes scanning the room for the

only two people she needed to see tonight. In the corner, she saw Hamish and Bruce – both in kilts – talking intently, their heads inclined, drams held between them; Torquil was in trews and chatting to a red-headed girl she had seen a couple of times in the canteen. But where was—?

'Ohmigod, where have you been?'

She felt a hand on her elbow and she turned to find Skye staring at her with dancing eyes. 'I'm so sorry, I got held up.'

'For two hours?' Skye half-laughed, half-wailed.

'I . . . uh . . . had to talk to a client. In New York.' She looked at Skye – her cheeks were flushed, her breath coming fast. 'Have you been dancing?'

'Non-stop,' she said with a 'whew!' 'It's exhausting stuff. You must dance.'

'I can't reel.' Her eyes scanned the room for Lochie. Where was he? Had he skipped this after all?

'Honestly, there's nothing to it. The guys do all the hard work. As long as they know where to put you and when to spin you, you'll be fine.'

'It sounds terrifying.'

Skye laughed. 'You just need a little Dutch courage. Here, have this.' She handed over her dram. 'You've got some catching-up to do, anyway.'

Alex took a sip, anticipating the burn in her throat, enjoying it. 'So how's it going? With you-know-who?'

'We've danced together twice now.'

So he was here then. That was something. She felt herself relax a little. 'Really?'

'Yes. I mean, I say together; it's not like slow-dancing, you know? We're not cheek to cheek but he's been my partner twice, which – given that he's barely been able to look at me all year . . .' She bit her lip.

'Well, that's good.'

'I guess.' She pulled a face.

'What?'

'I just feel so bad. Everyone keeps coming up to me and congratulating me, wishing me luck . . . And I keep thinking about Al.'

'Don't. Don't think about him till you know for sure what you want to do. The decision has to be yours and yours alone. Don't marry him out of guilt.'

'You're right.'

'Just see where tonight takes you. Have the two of you . . . talked yet?'

'Nup. Not yet. But I think maybe he's building up to it, you know? I keep catching him looking at me funny.'

'Sure.' Alex looked around the room. Feeling sick. Wanting to run. 'Where is he?'

'He was just over there, near the bar. Oh yes, there he is, look. In the checked shirt.'

Alex looked over and saw him in profile, the overhead lights cutting angles on his face as he stood with some of the guys from the mash house. But he wasn't talking and his body was too still. He looked lost in thought. Adrift.

'God, he looks so handsome tonight, don't you think?' Skye murmured.

Yes. 'I guess.'

As if sensing that he was being watched, he looked up, falling stiller at the sight of their dual gazes.

She couldn't do this. 'You should go and talk to him,' Alex murmured, nudging Skye with her elbow. *Doing it anyway.*

'Really? You think?'

No. 'Absolutely. It's the perfect opportunity.'

'I guess I do need to get a drink, now that I don't have one,' she giggled.

'Get him to buy one for you. And ask him for the time. Or help with . . . I don't know, your hair or something. Just keep asking him lots of little favours.'

'Why?'

'It tricks the brain, making people believe they like you even more than they already do.'

'Cool!'

Alex watched her go, seeing how Lochie's gaze stayed on her and not Skye.

'Beautiful stranger! Where have you been hiding yourself?'

She looked around to find Callum suddenly standing before her, that cocky smile on his face, genuine pleasure in his eyes. 'Talk about playing hard to get! You've ignored all my texts.'

'I was away for a few days . . . out of range,' she said tightly, feeling a kick of anger in her gut at the sight of him, angry that she had allowed herself to be flattered by a player like him, to have flirted with him. She'd known what he was long before she'd discovered what he'd done to his own cousin, but she had been lonely and worn down, and he was easy on the eye; and for just a moment, it had seemed like an easy option, that maybe she could do as she pleased and be free to act on her impulses. But that was just a fantasy. She lived in the real world, where there were always repercussions, and always – always – obligations to live by.

He took a step closer to her, away from the table. 'I have to see you again. I can't stop thinking about you. What about that dinner we talked about? We could skip out of here now.'

'Not happening,' she said bluntly.

She watched the confusion bloom in his face, that confident smile slipping. 'But . . . we had a good time, didn't we? I thought—'

'You thought wrong.'

She went to move past him but he caught her by the elbow. 'Alex, wait, I don't understand. What's happened? Have I done something?'

'Not to me, Callum, no, you won't be getting that chance.'

'You have completely lost me.'

She took a step closer to him. 'I know about you and Skye,' she said in a low voice.

His expression changed. 'What?'

'After everything you said about how close you used to be, that you were like brothers – and then you did that to him? You disgust me.'

'Now just h—'

'Don't. Don't talk to me, do you understand?' she said, pulling her arm away.

'Alex!'

She pushed through the crowd, away from him, scrummaging towards the bar, ordering another glass. She downed it in one. Skye had been right, she did need some Dutch courage to get through tonight. She'd only been here five minutes and already it was unbearable.

The party was in full swing, everyone having a great time, kicking off their heels. But not her. She was still working. Trying to close the deal.

'What was that about? Lovers' tiff?'

Lochie was beside her; his elbows on the bar like her, a

drink between his hands and his head dipped as he stared at her.

'Nothing.'

'It didn't look like nothing. Not many people can wipe that grin off my cousin's face.'

She swallowed. 'I told him I knew about what he'd done to you.'

Lochie squinted. 'Which was what, exactly?'

She shot him an incredulous look. Did he really want her to spell it out? '. . . Skye?' she whispered.

A look of surprise, then dark amusement dawned on his face. 'Well, I'm grateful for your loyalty, but I'm afraid you've got the wrong cousin.'

'. . . What?' The floor seemed to drop an inch.

'You underestimate the dark horse of the family. Just like I did. He's his father's son, you know,' he said as she looked across at Torquil, now engaged in a deep and intense conversation with the redhead. 'Sholto's heir apparent. The prince regent in the Kentallen crown.'

Torquil had seduced Skye? 'But . . . he's married! He's got a family. Torquil . . . he wouldn't do that,' she blustered. And then when she saw his expression: 'Why would he do that?'

'He'll do whatever it takes to provoke me. Sleeping with my fiancée was an easy way to show everyone I'm what they say I am: unstable, unpredictable, out of control.'

It was true – they were all the things Sholto *had* said to her about him.

'And credit to him, it worked,' he shrugged. 'Punching him at the family assembly wasn't my finest moment, but then I'd only found out the hour before; he took great pleasure in letting it slip over breakfast . . .' He knocked back his drink, finishing it off.

Alex winced. Torquil had told her Lochie had punched him because of the Ferrandor deal. 'High feelings' he'd said, when all along he'd been the antagonist. It wasn't just Lochie who'd been slandered in this. Those things she'd said to Callum . . . She turned, looking for him; he was talking in a small group but his body language was closed, defensive.

'I need to apologize to Callum.'

Lochie placed a hand on her arm. 'Not yet.'

She swallowed as she remembered why her presence was needed here tonight. 'No. Of course.' She put a hand lightly on his forearm. 'How are you doing?'

'Been better.' He looked across at her, locking her gaze to his.

'Where did you go this afternoon? I was worried about you.'

'I went for a run. Needed to think.'

'. . . Lochie, I'm so sorry,' she said quietly.

He gave a hapless shrug. 'It's not your fault.'

Wasn't it? She looked away, feeling wretched. 'Did you think about what I said?'

He snorted. 'Which bit?'

'Grabbing an alternative future to this.'

He turned his head and looked at her again with loaded eyes. 'Yeah.'

'Skye said you've danced together.'

'That's right. She always was a good dancer.' He looked at her. 'Do you reel?'

'God, no.'

'There's nothing to it, so long as you let the man lead.'

She cracked a small smile. 'Not my forte, I'm afraid.'

'Well, you'd better dance with me, then. I'm about the only person in here who can keep you in line.'

'Ha! You wish!' she retorted.

'No?' His eyes suddenly sparkled under the lights and she could see the whisky dancing in them as he grabbed her hand suddenly. 'Well, let's see.'

'Wait! No, Lochie—' But he was pulling her behind him as though she was a kite on a breeze. The fiddles had stopped, she realized, as they moved onto the dance floor, everyone seemingly getting into position for a new dance.

'Alex!' Skye cried excitedly – drunkenly – at the sight of them. 'Lochie! Come dance with us. We need another two for the set.'

'What?' she asked, bewildered, as Skye grabbed her other hand and pulled her into a line opposite Callum. He stared at her with a look of distrust and disappointment and she felt the guilt grab at her then like a hungry child. 'No.' She turned to Skye, panicking. 'I don't . . . I can't reel. I've never done it.'

'Don't worry,' Skye smiled. 'The boys will see you right, isn't that so, Cal?'

But before Cal could react, an accordion belched its first alto notes and everyone stood to attention. She saw that Lochie was standing opposite her.

'This one's Hamilton House,' Skye explained. 'It's basically the girl setting to the man standing beside her husband who is supposedly her lover – but then, when you'd expect man number two, or the lover, to turn her, she turns to the guy next to him and he turns her instead. It's very flirty,' she smiled.

Alex didn't understand a word of it. 'But I don't know

what setting is,' she said in rising horror as the woman to her right began to move and then danced into the space between the middle of the lines.

'Just watch what she's doing,' Skye laughed, as the woman did a sort of step-heel-toe to Lochie, before linking arms with Callum on his right. 'Lochie'll put you where you need to be, isn't that right, Lochie?'

'Aye.'

Alex looked across at him. He was watching her with a smile, enjoying her panic and no doubt relishing seeing her composure slip. It was the night of the gold skirt all over again.

But there was no time to dwell on it for suddenly everyone changed direction by ninety degrees, and Alex found herself at the end of a line, the woman holding her right hand, and she was now facing Skye. What? How had that happened?

Skye winked at her as the two lines moved in towards each other, stamping their feet, before walking back out again and their group changed shape – yet again – into a circle. They went round one way, then another, like nursery-school children and she watched in bafflement as the man and woman then turned in the middle of them.

She couldn't keep up. It happened all over again – lines becoming circles becoming lines again – and she felt the whisky begin to soak into her bloodstream. It may have taken off the edge of her stage fright, but it also blurred her comprehension of the shapes they were making and she let out a yelp in fright when she felt a hand on her back as Skye pushed her into the centre of the two lines.

Lochie was right in front of her and she tried to do the step-heel-toe thing to Callum that she'd seen the woman do, but she was no sooner deciding which foot to start with than she saw the man on Callum's right side lunge for her, turning her fast with both his hands gripping hers. There wasn't even time to gasp as she found herself put between Skye and Callum in a line. They walked, they stamped, they walked back – and then Lochie's hands were upon hers, his grip tight as he spun her round, his eyes never leaving her. She felt her hair lift off her shoulders, the room whizz past at dizzying speed. She laughed – more in fright than exhilaration, although it *was* exhilarating. And then she was in a line again, holding hands between Callum and another man. It repeated – lines, stomping, lines, a circle – and then Lochie again spinning her, making her feel her feet couldn't keep up, that he might lift her from the ground at any moment and send her high in the air, only his eyes – pinned on hers – keeping her rooted, keeping her there.

And then it was over. Just like that, they were back in the line and Skye was dancing with Callum. She tried to get her breath back, following the others as people clapped, laughing as they whooped, aware all the time that his eyes were upon her.

She tried not to return the gaze. It felt loaded somehow. Dangerous. Echoes of the previous weekend were sounding in her ears like warning bells. They couldn't go back there. This wouldn't get him over the line and she had to finish what she had started. She had to.

But the pull was too strong. As the song played on and on – ten minutes, twelve – she let herself be moved like kelp in the sea, allowing people to take her hand and turn her, place her here, set her there; she barely noticed. She saw nothing but him.

She tried deflecting him and when he danced with Skye,

turning her, she joined in with the whooping, clapping harder, throwing her head back in laughter, encouraging him. But when it was their turn again, she felt the spark between their palms as their hands crossed. It was undeniable, inevitable and she saw absolutely no way to stop it . . . not until a warm hand took hers in the line, a hand that had once wanted to feel the touch of her skin too.

The fiddles stopped with an exuberant falsetto, like a car in an emergency stop, and everyone clapped and cheered, some people stomping their feet, others putting their hands to their chests as they tried to get their breath back. But Alex didn't. She kept hold of the hand that had taken hers and without a word, reached up and kissed him – his golden hair in her fingers, that ready smile stretching against her lips.

'Fuck me, I had no idea you and Callum had a thing going,' Skye giggled, from the other side of the loo door.

'We don't.'

'Didn't look like it out there! I told you he was a lady-killer. No one can resist him. Not even you.'

Alex stared at herself in the mirror, the Barbie-pink stippled walls as offensive in the glass as in life. She barely recognized her own reflection. Who was she? When had she become this person? Her eyeliner had smudged à la Debbie Harry and her hair was wild from an evening of being flung about the dance floor. Callum hadn't put her down since she'd kissed him – he hadn't even cared about getting an apology – and they had danced the last six reels in a row. She had no idea what any of them were and she didn't care. She was exhausted, but it was working – as long as she didn't sit down or go anywhere near the bar where Lochie was standing.

'I thought you hadn't either,' Alex said pointedly, perhaps even a little cruelly. But then she was drunk now, as drunk as the rest of them.

'Huh?'

'When I was told you cheated on Lochie, I assumed it was with Callum.'

The toilet flushed and Skye came out, almost hitting the cubicle wall as she staggered over to the basins.

'But Torquil? Really?' Alex asked, pressing her for an answer, an explanation. 'What the hell was that about? He's hardly irresistible . . . Skye?'

Skye looked back at her. 'He was just there, Alex. Whilst Lochie was permanently up some fucking mountain and trying to find different ways to torture himself, Torquil was nice to me: he paid attention to me. Listened to me. He became a friend. I was so lonely.'

'He used you.'

Alex might as well have slapped her. 'What? No!'

'I'm sorry but yes. You were a pawn in his game. He was looking for ways to hurt Lochie, to weaken him. And you allowed him.'

Skye's face fell at her angry, brutally direct words, her lips wobbling as tears threatened.

Alex pulled back, instantly regretful. 'I'm . . . I'm sorry, I didn't mean that to sound so harsh. I'm just . . . it was a shock, that's all. Just another shock. I wish you'd told me.'

'I thought you knew,' Skye implored, the words becoming a wail, and loud, heavy, dramatic, drunken sobs bursting through. 'Y-you said everyone was talking about it.'

She was right, it was a reasonable assumption to make

that his name had come up. Alex grabbed her by the shoulder and squeezed it. Clearly destroying people's lives was her forte tonight. 'I'm being a cow. Ignore me. I've had too much to drink. I'm sorry.'

Skye's head dropped as she wept. 'No, *I've* had too much to drink,' she juddered as Alex began splashing water on her hands and face. 'People have been buying me drinks all night. I feel like such a fraud.'

'You're not. You're not a fraud.'

'But what will they all think when they find out—?'

'It's no one else's business. Who gives a damn what they think? It's not their future happiness on the line, is it?'

Alex wrapped her arms around her and let her cry on her shoulder for a moment. The poor girl was a wreck and it was all Alex's fault. Everything was. The whole sorry mess.

Skye looked up, taking in her reflection too. 'God, I look like shit. I thought flushed cheeks were supposed to be alluring; I look like I'm about to have a stroke.'

'You do not.' She looked at Skye, prettily pink and potentially on the cusp of having everything she never could: *him*. Grabbing a tissue, she gently wiped away Skye's mascara smudges.

'You look so sad,' Skye mumbled, watching her.

'Me? No, I'm fine.' The most common lie in the world.

'Why do you never talk about your problems? We're always talking about mine.'

Alex stalled, her brain suddenly numb. 'My problems are just . . . they're just very boring. And silly.' She forced a smile. 'Are you ready to go back through?'

'I guess I have to. It's now or never with Lochie, right? If we don't say it now, we never will.'

411

Alex nodded, feeling the numbness spread to her heart. 'I guess so.'

They walked back out into the corridor, but as Alex caught sight of the flinging bodies again, she stepped back. She couldn't do this; she couldn't watch it, she couldn't pretend any more with Callum . . .

'Actually, I'm think I'm going to go outside and try to cool down a bit first.'

'Do you want me to come with you?'

'No, you go and do what you need to do. I won't be long. I just need a bit of air. Try to sober up a bit.'

'Okay. That's the back door there,' Skye said, the words a slur as she pointed down the short corridor to a fire exit. 'But you just holler if you need me, okay? I'm here for you, Alex, just like you've been for me. Partners in crime, right?'

Alex tried to smile, to nod, but tears were threatening like a thunderclap and she stumbled her way outside, gasping as the freezing temperatures hit her. She had no coat on; stupid shoes for snow. The music dimmed as the door slammed shut and she turned her face to the night, too miserable even to marvel at the beauty of the diamond-studded sky.

She slumped against the bonnet of a Datsun, her head in her hands. What was she doing?

'You're not fooling anyone, you know.'

Her hands fell away as she looked back to find Lochie leaning against the wall, beside the back door. Had . . . had she just rushed straight past him?

'With the young love scene you've got going on in there, I mean. I assume it's for my benefit but I'm afraid I'm not buying it.' He had a bottle in one hand and appeared to be swigging it neat. His head was tipped back against the wall, looking at her through lowered lids. He was really drunk now, dangerously so, at that point where all bets were off.

She didn't dare deny it, knowing that every word that she used to engage in this conversation was a step off the path she needed him to stay on; she had to remain focused.

He sighed, pulling his gaze away from her, and they were silent for a long time.

'It would appear everything is falling to shit, Hyde.' He took a swig before looking back at her again. 'I take it this wasn't what you had planned as part of my rehabilitation either, getting me to fall for you?'

Her body physically tingled at the words but still she kept quiet.

'Ah, well . . . there it is, anyway. Another problem for you to solve.' He closed his eyes. 'Not that it will matter either way. We could speak all the truths we want tonight but you'll still wake up tomorrow and tell me it's the alcohol. And I guess we'll both pretend to believe that.'

She didn't know what to say. She didn't dare to say anything. Every word that fell from his lips made her want to dance and leap and if she was free to follow her instincts, she'd be in his arms already. But she wasn't. And she couldn't.

He shook his head, looking at her again. 'Did you seriously not know what was happening between us till Saturday?'

'. . . No.'

He closed his eyes and smiled, giving a wry snort. 'I remember exactly when I knew.' He opened his eyes again. 'It was the fire . . . Your voice. It was like you needed me to survive. Like you needed me. There was nothing and then suddenly there was you. You were like an explosion in my mind.'

Tears started flowing down her cheeks, silent in the darkness. Because she wanted to tell him back, to tell him it was the same for her, she felt it too.

From the other side of the building, a door opened and a cone of light spilled onto the ground. The music volume increased tenfold for a moment and she looked over, just in time to see a shining golden head peer round the corner.

'Oh, you're out here!' Callum grinned, lighting up at the sight of her. 'Skye said you were— Ah, Lochie!' He faltered as he caught sight of his cousin in the shadows, leaning against the wall. '. . . Not interrupting anything, I hope?'

'Of course not,' Lochie replied, taking another swig from the bottle. 'We were just having a State of the Nation, weren't we, Hyde?'

'Yes.' She barely recognized the sound of her own voice.

'I was coming out to check everything was okay. It's freezing out here. Aren't you cold?'

'Yes,' she said quietly, looking back at Lochie.

He blinked, the movement slow and heavy, lidding dark eyes that told her everything and nothing all at once.

'You don't mind do you, cuz?' Callum asked.

'Not at all. Take her away,' Lochie murmured, never taking his eyes off her. 'She's all yours.'

Chapter Twenty-Eight

Thompson Falls, Montana, 4 June 1918

The fox had found a mate. For the past few weeks now, she had watched them from her porch, rocking silently on the chair as they frolicked and chased, tumbled and hunted in the small woods at the edge of the clearing. She liked seeing their thick brush tails held aloft in the long grass, watching their pointed ears twitch as raccoons scrabbled up the trees behind them and squirrels dropped cob nuts.

In the distance, the snow was melting off the blue mountaintops and the forests were stirring themselves green. Woodpeckers knocked by day, owls glided on the nights; elks trod their slow path through the trees and the yowl of mountain cats pierced the muffling silence like a knife through silk. The world was coming alive again.

But in another country, across a faraway sea, it was not nature that made the landscape dance but guns – guns that made the earth quake and rivers run red, where the only flowers that grew sprang from trenches and not a bird dared cross the pale sky. And it was in that country that her son's body lay – far from home and left behind by this dawning spring that blossomed without him.

He would never again hear the roar of the meltwater rushing through the rapids, or know the tenderness of daisies against his

415

skin. He wouldn't see the grey fox cubs first stagger into the sunlight, nor grow to be the man he had been born to become. He had been plucked from the face of the world so that no trace remained – no body to bury, no laughter to snatch, as though he had never been at all. Only the newly-hung gold star in the window told otherwise, that a brave soldier had given his life for his country, but there was none but the foxes to see it; they alone were witness to what she had lost.

Islay, Friday 22 December 2017

She had to wipe the snow off the seat with her arm, the sleeve pulled down tight over her reddened hands as she sank onto the bench and looked out to sea. It glistened white like a mirror. Her breathing returned to normal within a minute; her cheeks would take rather longer, but for all her apparent vision of health, her hangover lingered stubbornly in her body. She hadn't been able to look at breakfast and the temptation to climb back into bed and hide under the covers was, for once, overwhelming. It wasn't as though she was going into the distillery today. The boundaries between her and Lochie were too fragile at the moment and she had to keep things clean. Professional. She had to get him over the line.

Would the distillery even be open, anyway? The snow was coming down in thick plumes; the roads could well be closed. Perhaps it wouldn't just be the local kids enjoying a 'snow day' today.

Her phone buzzed with a text and she saw Callum's name on the screen. Again. She bit her lip as she pressed delete without opening it, looking out to the horizon, out towards America. She wasn't proud of herself; she didn't even like herself right now, for she had used him: her weapon of choice for keeping Lochie back – Ha! Like that had worked! – and the ball in the game. She had used him to hurt Lochie and that made her no better than Torquil. Who had she been to stand in judgement of him? A punch on the jaw had been the very least he deserved, but what about her? If he only knew what she had done . . .

She wondered what he was doing right now, now that he was no longer a Farquhar by legal definition. What had happened – if anything – between him and Skye after she had left? Poor Skye. She didn't think he was going to be including her in the calculations for his future.

The phone buzzed again and she looked at it with a sigh. The number was unidentified but as she read the text, it didn't even need to be signed off. She knew perfectly well who it was from.

'Wanted to let you know Lochlan tendered his resignation an hour ago and I happily accepted. Congratulations on a job well done.'

Their breath hung like clouds in the frozen cab. Mr Peggie hadn't said much when Mrs Peggie had explained in brisk tones that if he didn't drive her, Alex would walk across the moors herself; he had 'jobs to do anyway', he'd said, and within the half-hour Mrs Peggie had been packing them both off with a thermos flask and foil-wrapped lardy cake 'just in case'.

The tractor's snow shovel was clearing the single-track road with ruthless efficiency, sprays of snow flying out to the sides and building high banks as the attachment on the back spread salt on the ground behind them. Alex was content to look out of the window, her fingers worrying at the envelope on her lap.

The tractor turned in through the stone-capped gates, Mr Peggie knowing exactly where he was going as they drove through the tree-lined estate. Through the bushes she caught glimpses of the big house, the lights already on in some rooms, the day beginning to die even though it was only just gone two. But that wasn't where they were headed and she gave a murmur of thanks that the old farmer was going along with this, for she would never have found it on her own.

They hooked a right down a narrow track, rolling through an almost alpine landscape, the branches of pine trees laden and drooping under the weight of snow. She knew that if they were to have stopped, utter silence would muffle them. They could as well have been at the very top of the world as on a snowy Scottish isle. There was no sign of any other vehicle tracks – the Aston certainly wasn't an option in these conditions – suggesting he hadn't left the house today.

'Well, there it is,' Mr Peggie said in his usual spare manner as they rounded a bend and the track opened out to a circular drive with a mulberry tree in the middle. The house would have been breathtakingly pretty enough on its own – brown stone in the Regency style, with tall windows and three steps to the front door – but with the snow piled deep on the sills, the roof and the bulbous topiaried-box balls in the flower beds, it was rendered even more enchanting. It might have been only a quarter of the size of the main house but it had three times the charm. 'I'll turn this whilst you knock.'

'Oh, I won't be knocking,' she said hurriedly. 'I'm just

going to put this through the letterbox.' On the far side of the drive, she saw a double garage, the nose of the Aston visible below half-lowered doors.

'You don't need to speak to him?' Mr Peggie frowned.

'Everything he needs to know is in there.'

'Aye, well,' Mr Peggie said after a pause. 'It's up to you. I can wait. Mrs P. has seen to it that I won't starve.'

She jumped down from the cab, landing softly in the snow, and walked towards the front door, unable to resist looking in through the dark windows as she passed. An antique rocking horse stood motionless by one window; a piano was glimpsed through another and she could see lights further on, through the back of the house.

She climbed the steps, looking for the letterbox – but there was none. She looked around. Dammit – had they missed it? Was there a box up by the gates?

She checked again but there was nothing. She was going to have to leave it here. But could she do that? If she left it in the snow, it would get wet and so too would everything inside.

She ran back to the tractor which was now facing up the track. 'Mr P., I'll just be a moment. There's no letterbox. I'll have to find a back door or somewhere out of the snow where I can leave it.'

Mr Peggie toasted her with his flask cap of tea and slice of lardy cake, as though he'd expected as much. 'Aye.'

She shut the door and jogged lightly across the drive again, going past the door this time and in front of the other windows. Inside one she saw weights and a running machine; in the other, a giant TV screen and sofa. It was clear which half of the house he occupied.

She rounded the corner, past a snow-topped hedge, and

stopped. Light pooled on a lawned area and a door was open. She felt her heart catch as she looked around, trying to locate him. Had he heard the tractor? It was hardly a stealth missile, after all.

She heard a sound off to the right and saw a small shed, its door open too. He was in there!

She looked back at the open door to the house and without giving herself a chance to chicken out, ran towards it, tossing the letter onto the safety of a drystone floor. She turned just as she heard another noise coming from the shed and began to run back the way she had come, the snow squeaking beneath her boots.

She was almost there when—

'Alex?'

Oh God. Her stomach dropped at the sound of his voice, flipped at the sight of his face. 'Hi.'

He was holding a stack of logs in his arms, bafflement on his face. 'What are you doing?'

'I . . . I was just leaving.'

'I can see that.'

'I was dropping something off for you.'

He frowned as he looked over to the house and saw the envelope tossed on the floor. 'Is it your bill?'

She snorted, trying to laugh. Failing. 'No.'

'Wait. What's the rush? Come in.'

'I have to get back. Mr Peggie's waiting for me. I didn't mean to disturb you.'

'That's not like you. I thought disturbing me was your favourite thing to do,' he quipped. But she wasn't in the mood for jokes and clearly neither was he. He looked haggard: unshaven with dark circles under his eyes from a bottle of whisky and a night without sleep.

'I was going to put it through your letterbox but . . . well, you don't appear to have one and I couldn't leave it in the snow.'

He stared at her, utterly oblivious to how good he looked standing there with an armful of logs and a deep frown. 'Alex, what exactly is going on?'

'Please, just read it and you'll see.' Her voice wavered. She didn't want to be doing this. Talking to him, engaging . . .

He dropped the logs on the snow and walked over to her. Past her.

'Where are you going?' she asked, watching as he turned the corner out of sight. She waited a moment before following him, finding him talking to Mr Peggie. 'No, wait—!'

But the big wheels were already turning, the old farmer making for home as the snow closed in.

'I've told him I'll drop you back,' Lochie said, walking over and looking down at her, an unspoken conversation coursing between them, and she felt that intensity – aliveness – in her body that she always felt whenever he was near. He took her arm suddenly and led her towards the house.

'Lochie, no—'

'Well, this is a novelty,' he said wryly as he frogmarched her through the door. 'Throwing you in for a change.'

The kitchen was large, with pale blue free-standing units, an enormous preparation unit in the centre with an old oak top and an opened bottle of Merlot on it. He picked up the envelope and dropped it on the unit, walking to a wall cupboard and bringing out another glass. He poured her some wine without asking if she wanted any and handed it to her.

She took a grateful sip as he wandered over to the sink unit and retrieved his own glass. Several plates and a bowl were upended on the drying counter, a jumper strewn across the back of a chair; a copy of *The Times* was open at the sports pages, an iPad charging by the wall. Rona – clearly the world's worst guard dog – pattered through from the hall, checking her bowl for food before becoming aware of Alex's presence and coming over for a pat.

He leaned against the counter, legs crossed at the ankle, watching her. He was saying even less than Mr Peggie which was frankly . . . unnerving.

'You look better than I thought you would,' she said, trying to make small talk. 'How are you feeling?'

'Hungover. Knackered. I haven't slept.'

'No.' She bit her lip. 'What happened last night after I left?'

He paused, tilted his head to the side. 'You mean, did anything happen between me and Skye?'

She looked away. It had been exactly what she'd meant, but the words had no sooner left her than she regretted them.

'Nothing happened and nothing's going to happen. We talked, that was all.'

'About what?'

He shrugged. 'Custody of the dog.'

'Lochie!'

'What?' he demanded. 'What did you think we had to say to each other? That I was going to profess my undying love? That I wanted her back? I don't. She's happy with him and all you're doing is confusing her. They're a good match. I'm not going to get in the way of that.'

'But in the meeting yesterday, you agreed—'

'*I* agreed nothing.'

'You understood, then, that this is your last chance to make it work. Letting her go again doesn't make sense.'

'No. What doesn't make sense is why you are so desperate for me to be with her,' he said in a low, slow voice. 'Why are you pushing for it so hard?'

She blinked at him. 'You know why.'

'Do I? Enlighten me then. Because from where I'm standing, it's pretty bloody obvious what I want.' He held his arms out to the side in a gesture of openness. 'I'm not hiding anything here.'

Her heart was clattering, everything coming too fast. She hadn't come over for this. It was exactly what she'd tried to avoid. 'The Me, the We, the It, remember?'

'Oh, don't give me that bullshit,' he sighed, taking another sip of the wine.

She took a breath, trying to keep calm, feeling the spool beginning to unravel faster and faster through her fingers, burning her skin. 'Your relationship with Skye only failed because—'

'Because she cheated on me.'

'No,' she argued. 'That was just a symptom of the problems that were already there. You were already in trouble. Your father had just died, you were angry, Lochie, you were pushing her away. We walked through the constellation and—'

He was watching her. 'You know, for all your dishing out of advice, I don't get the impression you take any of it yourself. I don't think I'm the only one out of touch with the Me-We-It shit.'

'This isn't about me.'

'On the contrary, I'd say it's all become about you. What was that thing you said yesterday? One of your beloved quotes – something about the madness of resisting something that already is? Well, this thing between us – whatever it is – it's already happening. You're the only one resisting it!'

She looked away. He didn't understand why it could never be and she could never tell him. None of this was supposed to have happened – she hadn't seen it coming – but it was impossible now to loosen the knot that had bound her so tightly in his life. She had wanted to slip away but of course it was never going to be that easy. If she wanted to leave, she would have to cut herself free. 'Look, I didn't come over to fight with you.'

There was a silence. 'Well, it seems to be what we're good at,' he sighed, turning away and topping up his glass. He swigged from it, looking out of the window, the garden still spotlit, the shed door still open, logs scattered in the snow.

'I came to say goodbye. I'm leaving tonight.' Her words bounced off his still back; he didn't reply. 'Everything I wanted to say is in the letter. Please. Just please don't read it till I've gone.'

He turned and looked at her, looked at the envelope on the island. 'Why not?'

'It's better this way,' she said quietly.

It was precisely the wrong thing to have said; 'Lochie, no!' But within two strides he was there, the letter in his hands, scraps of paper fluttering like confetti as he ripped it open and read her goodbye on Mrs Peggie's blue notepaper.

Her heart felt as though it had leapt to her throat and she

turned away in horror, feeling vulnerable, exposed. She should never have come here. Why had she come? It had been a mistake and at some level she must have known it – but she had indulged herself, not quite able to resist the urge to glimpse him one last time.

'Alex.'

The letter was in his hands but as she saw the look on his face, she knew that they were done with words. There would be no more fighting or arguing; he was right – they were resisting something that already was. He crossed the room and picked her up, setting her down on the oak counter as her ankles crossed behind his back, her mouth already on his. Because she knew perfectly well why she had come here: she had come for a proper goodbye.

The firelight made their skin glow, a blanket draped lightly over their hips as they lay intertwined on the sofa, the now-empty bottle of Merlot on the floor beside them along with a half-eaten plate of smoked salmon and lemon wedges, and what had been a bowl of strawberries.

Lochie's fingers grazed her waist, her head on his chest, as they watched the flames flicker and leap. It had been dark outside for hours now, and the snowflakes were still patting at the windowpanes.

'How much has fallen, do you reckon?' she murmured, feeling his chest hair tickle her cheek.

'About a foot, I should think. It's pretty squally out there. The ferries won't be running in this.'

'. . . A Sea King it is then.' It was a joke, but a bad one. Neither of them laughed at the prospect of her leaving; he was silent and she heard the thud of his heart against her ear. She turned her head to look up at him. 'Not that I believe for one minute that you'd be taking me back to the farmhouse tonight, even if they were running.'

'Of course not.' His eyes flashed down at her – confident, assured.

She hid her smile by kissing his chest. 'But the Peggies – they'll be expecting me.'

'I told Mr P. we had business to discuss and that you could stay in one of the spare rooms if necessary.'

'Do you think he bought that?'

Lochie chuckled. 'No.'

She laughed softly too, her amusement fading as the truth pressed in. 'I'm going to miss them.'

His body tensed slightly beneath her. 'They'll miss you.'

'I never expected to become attached.'

'Of course not.' He fell quiet again, his fingers tickling her lightly. 'Alternatively, you could just . . . not leave.'

'I don't belong here.'

'You could.'

'It's beautiful. And you know I love it, but . . . I have my own life. In London. I've got my own company to run, clients, my flat. Commitments.'

'Fine, we'll start small then. At the very least, stay for Christmas.'

She closed her eyes, pushing her face into his armpit, relishing the smell of him. 'I wish I could. But I can't.'

'Why not?'

'I told you. Commitments.'

He looked back at the fire again, his jaw set in that way of his when he was holding back, reining in.

'I don't want you to go.'

She pushed her lips together hard, holding back the tears again. She could hear from his tone that it wasn't the first time he had said these words. Had he said them to his mother? His father?

'I don't want to either,' she whispered, her voice thick, choked with emotion. 'But this isn't real life, for either of us. It could never work.'

'Why not?'

'Because . . .' A single tear slid down her cheek anyway. 'Because this is a disaster for me. Us, together, like this. It's everything that should never have happened. It's unethical, unprofessional. If it was to get out that I fell for my client—'

His hand lifted her chin, making her look at him. 'How many times must I tell you? I'm not your client: I refused to work with you, I didn't hire you. And you failed dismally – far from making me a better boss you found a way to lose me my job. I'm sorry, but you've just been a very beautiful, very annoying woman loitering with intent about my offices for the past three weeks.'

She chuckled, wiping the tear with the back of her hand. 'No one else will see it like that.'

She was right and they both knew it. But his hand found her thigh, lifting it higher on his hip, holding her closer. She felt her pulse quicken, just like that, as he effortlessly pulled her on top of him, framing her face with his hands.

'I thought you were tired,' she said, a slow smile spreading across her lips. 'You said you didn't sleep.'

He smiled back, his eyes both sad and hungry. 'Hyde, you keep telling me you've got a bloody ferry to catch. There's no time to sleep.'

Chapter Twenty-Nine

Islay, Saturday 23 December 2017

The chapel wasn't heated; it was no surprise to anyone, of course, but with the snow lying in deep drifts all around, the tiny electric heater and the candles at the end of each pew could only do so much. Alex pulled her red coat tighter around her; being unlined, it was far too thin but it was the only suitable thing she had up here to wear. They had stopped at the farmhouse on their way past, for her to get changed, the road still gritted and clear from Mr Peggie's foray in the tractor last night, but if Mrs Peggie had wondered at the unusual brightness in her eyes, she didn't comment, making her daily offer of hot kippers before they set out.

Alex was sitting alone in the back row, her knees pressed together as she shivered in the cold, watching the pews fill up. There were no rose windows or stained glass here, no elaborate plasterwork or bountiful flowers, just plain pitched windows high up in each wall, tangles of ivy and rowanberries draping down from the sills.

Alasdair was already at the front, pacing nervously as his best man repeatedly checked for the rings in his jacket pocket. Alex couldn't take her eyes off the groom – soft-faced, young-looking, with ears that stuck out and a shy smile as he kept tugging on his embroidered waistcoat, nodding happily as his friends came up to slap him on the shoulder and wish him luck. The very sight of him made her feel wretched at what she had tried to do – to him, an unwitting stranger who had never even laid eyes on her, who had done her no harm, whose only fault had been to get in her way—

'Hey.' Lochie sat down beside her, his thigh instantly pressed against hers as he undid the buttons on his over-coat. 'Are you warm enough? Do you want this?'

She shook her head, seeing the energy in his movements. 'You're looking very pleased with yourself,' she said, smiling back, wishing she could touch his face again, kiss his mouth. 'Where've you been?'

He inhaled and looked over at her, eyes gleaming. 'Talking to Sholto. I've told him I want to finalize the terms of my exit as soon as possible.'

'You're looking remarkably upbeat about it today.'

'Am I? Well, perhaps I'm beginning to see that there is life beyond this isle,' he murmured, his eyes running over her like mice. 'Christ, you look great in that red. You know, you were wearing that the first time I set eyes on you. Just about floored me.'

'Huh. You did a good job of hiding it,' she scoffed. 'I seem to recall you couldn't get away fast enough.'

'What else could I do? Callum was already trying to make claims on you. It was either punch him or punch the wall.'

'You and walls,' she tutted, holding up his still-bruised knuckles from last weekend.

He blinked at her. 'You're worth it.'

They stared at each other, lost, and she longed to touch him, for things to be different.

'Mind if we sit there?' someone asked, pointing further down the pew.

'No, of course not,' Lochie said, and they stood to allow them past.

Outside, the bagpipes started up and everyone turned in their seats to get a look at the bride.

Alasdair, at the front, looked as though he was going to keel over and the best man shuffled him into position at the front of the aisle as everyone stood to the distinctive strains of 'Highland Cathedral' filling the tiny kirk. Alex stood and turned, just in time to see Skye glide in. Her hair was out of its signature ponytail, instead pinned up in soft ringlets at the side, and she was wearing contacts. The dress was slim-fitting with a furry bolero and she carried a posy of white roses, Bruce holding her arm proudly. She looked nervous, but also very beautiful, and her face relaxed as she saw her groom waiting for her at the end of the aisle.

'She looks so beautiful,' Alex whispered, looking up at Lochie.

'Aye, she does,' he nodded, his eyes on the bride, before looking back down at her and squeezing her hand. 'No regrets,' he mouthed.

The pipes ended as Bruce placed Skye's hand in Alasdair's and everyone took their seats again.

Lochie's hand fell to her thigh and she looked around them nervously, worried that people would see. She had agreed to stay on for the duration of the service; as Lochie had so persuasively argued, Skye would be dismayed if she skipped out just hours before her big moment. And anyway, she was looking for excuses to delay her inevitable departure. He wasn't as easy to leave as she had hoped. 'What are you doing?' she whispered, trying to remove his hand off her leg.

'It doesn't matter now. Let them look.'

'What are you talking about? Of course it matters. This is a small community. People will talk!'

'Let them. I've made a decision.' He pinned her with bright eyes. 'I'm leaving Islay, putting all this behind me. You were right – I need to start afresh. Go somewhere new and begin again.'

He looked at her meaningfully and she felt her own smile begin to play on her lips.

'Oh yes?' she whispered, feeling the butterflies in her stomach take wing. 'Got anywhere particular in mind?'

'Skye! Over here!'

Alex raised her arm and the bride's eyes widened as she caught sight of her standing at the edge of the crowd. Lochie had disappeared again and everyone was talking in huddled groups – the confetti thrown, the photos taken. They were ready to take the celebration back to the reception. She was ready to take her leave.

'You look *so* beautiful,' she gushed, as Skye came over and they hugged.

'Och, I'm going to look a wreck in the photos,' Skye laughed, dabbing at her eyes.

'Rubbish, you've never looked more gorgeous.'

Skye met her gaze. 'I've never felt happier. I had no idea it would feel like this.' She bit her lip. 'I can't believe I nearly—'

Alex grabbed her hands. 'Listen to me, it was my fault. All mine. I was wrong from the start and I dragged you into my mess, confusing you. I'm so sorry. I really am. I made a hash of everything. Can you forgive me?' Urgency tinged her words.

'Of course I can,' Skye said, looking at her with concern. 'There's nothing to forgive. You were only trying to help.'

'No, I was selfish; I nearly ruined everything for you.'

'But you didn't.' Skye squeezed her hand. 'Listen, it's a recognizable condition and there's a name for it: cold feet, right?'

'Well, I can certainly identify with that,' Alex grinned, tucking one leg behind the other, flamingo-style. She had lost feeling in her toes a good twenty minutes earlier, long before they'd taken to standing in the snow, and her suede heels were ruined, but she didn't care. She'd had to do this before she left.

Skye gazed over at her new husband, her eyes soft. 'You know, we have a saying up here: "The little fire that warms is better than the big fire that burns."' She looked back at Alex. 'Besides, Lochie and I did talk finally. After you went the other night, we cleared the air and said all those things we'd been sweeping under the carpet for the past year and a half.' She sighed heavily. 'He was angry, I was panicking and I think we'd both had enough to drink to actually just stop playing games and tell it how it is finally. Things are going to be a lot better between us from now on. I honestly think we can be friends again. I'm so pleased.'

'Who's pleasing my bride?' a voice asked and they turned to see Alasdair standing beside them.

'Oh, Al, this is Alex who I was telling you about.'

'Alex,' he said, shaking her hand with a friendly smile. 'Finally we meet. I've heard more about you than the wedding arrangements for the past three weeks. You must be a force for good.'

'Well, I'm not sure about that,' she laughed as she and Skye exchanged knowing smiles.

He looked at Skye, holding out an arm for her. 'Our carriage awaits. Are you ready, my queen?'

'Lead on, sweet prince,' Skye laughed, having to wipe her cheeks dry again.

'Uh, listen, I'm not going to be able to be there,' Alex said apologetically. 'I'm booked on the two o'clock ferry. I only stayed as late as this in order to see you. I'm sorry.'

Skye looked at her for a moment then burst into a fit of laughter, squeezing more tears from her eyes again. 'Oh, good one, Alex! You almost had me there!'

Alex wouldn't have believed a warehouse could be made to look so fitting for a wedding, but she stood corrected now. The tiers of whisky barrels had each been draped with looping silk ribbons, the struts of the warehouse roof garlanded with ivy, and long refectory tables were set up in the aisles with a mini Christmas tree at the end of each one. At the loading area at the front, a dance floor had been erected, and a harpist was plucking love songs on a small stage to the side, to be replaced by the disco later.

Lochie was caught in conversation with some of the lads who were unwittingly flogging a dead horse in trying to recruit him to their seven-a-side local-league football team, the news of his resignation still confidential until the termination contracts were signed. Alex mingled, working her way through the crowd and chatting easily with the staff and some of Skye's family who had come down – fittingly – from the Isle of Skye. She couldn't believe she was still here. Why *was* she still here? Her mission had been accomplished, it was time to go. And yet . . .

She had warmed up at least; in spite of the deep drifts of snow outside the warehouse walls, the space, although beautifully decorated, was not large and she was even beginning to think about removing her coat. Making her excuses from a group conversation about the marine renewable-energy project in the Sound, she wove through the crowd towards the exit, wanting to touch up her make-up before they sat for the wedding breakfast.

'Oh. Sorry—' Someone bumped into her, standing on her toes in his heavy brogues, and she winced, just as Callum turned around.

There was a momentary pause as he digested the sight of her, back in red, back to the scene of their first meeting. '. . . Excuse me,' he said tersely before moving to head off.

'Callum, wait,' she said, catching him by the arm.

He looked down at her, so handsome, so hurt, his guarded expression almost identical to his cousin's.

'Please. I owe you an apology. I messed you about and—'

'Made false accusations about me.'

'Yes, I made false accusations about you and—'

'You used me.'

'I used you, yes. I'm sorry.'

He let the apology hang like a chandelier – heavy and bright between them – before relinquishing a smile. 'Ach, don't be. It was worth it.'

'Huh?'

'Well, you were never going to kiss me otherwise. As it was, I got an evening of snogging you out of it, whilst you and my cousin played cat and mouse.'

She gasped. 'You . . . you *knew*?'

'Alex, a blind man could have seen what was happening between you two.'

She gawped as he laughed. 'I can't believe you!' she cried, smacking him on the arm.

'Hey, I'm not going to look a gift horse in the mouth. Especially when it's a mouth as pretty as that one,' he grinned.

'You are incorrigible,' she giggled, going to move off, but he caught her by the elbow.

'Hey, Alex . . .?'

She looked back at him.

'Just don't hurt him, okay?'

She blinked, feeling the smile fall from her lips. 'No.'

Callum winked and she slipped out through the barn doors, heading for the nearest toilets in the canteen; a path had been shovelled through the snow and rubber matting laid down. There was a short queue to get in, and a surprised pause stalled the conversation as she walked in. Was it the red, she wondered? Or, as some of the women talked in excited whispers when she went into the cubicle, was it simply that everyone knew about her and the boss?

She fixed her face, aware of the sidelong glances in the mirror at her bespoke make-up, smiling politely at them all as she left. She heard them burst into excited gossip as she stepped back outside, her eyes falling to the lights on in Lochie's office across the courtyard.

She picked her way carefully through the snow which came up to her ankles; if these heels hadn't been ruined before, they certainly were now.

'Hey . . .' she said, peering round the door. 'Oh.'

Two pairs of eyes looked up at her from the desk.

'Ah, Alex,' Sholto said, just as Lochie finished writing

something and handed the sheet of paper over to him. 'What perfect timing.'

'. . . What's going on?' she asked quietly.

'Lochie and I were just signing the termination contracts. He is officially, legally – and soon to be publicly – no longer our CEO,' Sholto smiled. 'Ordinarily, I would offer some platitude that he will be sorely missed, but I think that would offend our mutual intelligence.'

'But he only resigned yesterday,' Alex said, feeling uneasy at the sight of both their smiles. 'How could you have the paperwork—'

'Drawn up so quickly?' Lochie drawled, putting the cap back on his pen. 'Sholto's never one to leave things to chance, are you, cousin? You can be sure he's had this paperwork in his drawer for quite some time, just *itching* for the day when he could get me to sign.' The words tripped off his tongue with wry sprightliness; he looked like a man set free from chains.

Sholto, not bothering to deny it, offered his hand and Lochie shook it, both of them magnanimous – almost cordial – now that the deal was done. 'Well, I must say, you've done well out of me, Lochlan. Golden parachute is an acutely apt term for your exit package. It's a soft landing for you.'

'Actually, thanks to Alex, I've landed on my feet,' Lochie said, talking in code, his eyes settling upon her.

Sholto followed his eyeline and nodded. 'Well, they did tell me she's the best.' He walked over, his small eyes beady upon her. 'Actually, it's fortuitous you've stopped by, Ms Hyde; you were next on my list to come and see, anyway. This is for you.' Reaching into his inner jacket pocket, he held out a slip of paper for her. She didn't need to look at it to know what it was. 'Congratulations on a job well done.'

Alex nodded, watching as Sholto walked out, taking the air in the room with him. She realized she was shivering and she knew that Lochie was staring at her, a question already hanging in the cold night air.

Slowly, she looked back at him. He was ashen-faced as Sholto's words – *'They did tell me she's the best . . . congratulations'* – his victorious manner, began to percolate.

She shivered, hugging her arms around herself in distraction, trying to hold back the boulder Sholto had just pushed on his way out. 'Gosh, it's cold in here,' she said, her voice uncharacteristically faint. 'Shall we go back to the reception? They're getting ready to do the speeches, I think.' She glanced at him, and away again. '. . . Lochie?'

'Congratulations?' His stare was hard. Scrutinizing. 'What's he congratulating you for? You were brought in to save my job; I'm only out on a technicality, so why's he . . . ?' He blinked. 'How is it a job well done if *you* didn't get to do what you were hired to do . . . ?' His expression changed; he got up from his chair and walked over, taking the bank transfer slip from her grasp as though plucking candy from a baby. 'Unless you did?'

He looked down at it, time becoming elastic and stretching out as long as the six zeroes blinking back at him. 'Oh, I see,' he said finally, the words a breath as though they'd been punched up from his stomach. He shook his head, dropping it down, his hands on his hips, and the sight of him like that – like a god, defeated – brought a sob to her throat. Tears sprang to her eyes but she didn't move a hair and he was quiet for a long time, the silence throbbing around them as his breath came in heavy waves. 'So *that* was the game: don't get him better – get him out.' He gave a snort of disbelief. 'Jesus Christ, I did not see that coming.'

'Lochie—'

'Uh-uh.' He stopped her with a silencing finger held inches from her face, shaking his head, his eyes on the floor, still trying to think, to gather his thoughts. She bit her lip as she watched the betrayal bloom on his face like a stain. '"Oh, what a tangled web we weave,"' he murmured. '"When first we practise to deceive."' His voice was quiet, slow, measured; shock slowing his words like a drug, betrayal a slow poison inking his veins. He looked back at her, his sudden gaze like a whip crack. 'You played me from the beginning. It was all a lie, right from the off.'

'No.'

'No?' he mocked, beginning to walk slowly around her, liking how it made her shrink, recoil. Forcing her into the low-power position, his eyes like knives on her body. 'You said to me – and I quote – "I'm not the enemy, Lochlan." Those were your actual words. In our first meeting.'

'I didn't know then. I thought— '

'What?' he snapped. 'What did you think, Alex?'

She looked at him. 'I thought you were what he'd said you were. I thought you were dangerous and reckless and a liability.'

'Oh, I am!' he cried, his eyes shining with an anger that made him look half-crazed. 'I'm all those things.'

'No. You're not.' She shook her head. 'I know you now.'

He stopped walking. 'You know me now?' His eyes were filled with scorn.

'Yes.' She could feel herself trembling under his contempt.

'You know me now?' He began walking again. '. . . You

know me now.' The change in his voice told her the notion had gone from a question to a fact. 'And yet you still went ahead and did it. Even after I told you exactly what he'll do if I go – what'll happen to all those people, those families, their jobs . . . You still did it.' He stared at her with a look of utter disbelief. 'It's all on you now. You know that, right?'

'Lochie, please,' she said, moving now, imploring him to listen, to give her the opportunity to explain. 'You don't understand. It was just supposed to be business. A straight-forward deal to manage you out. It was never personal.'

'*Not personal?*' he whispered, eyes narrowing to danger-ous slits. 'All your fucking talk about my trust issues and being abandoned by my parents, setting myself free, walk-ing my own path . . . that's not personal to you? Because it's personal to me!' he shouted. 'I laid myself open to you, and all the while you were just scanning for pinch spots, trying to find where I was most vulnerable.' He threw his hands up in the air, a hollow laugh escaping him. 'Hey! I can hardly blame you – a cool million would be hard for anyone to walk away from. That I can understand.' He grabbed her chin in his hands, forcing her to look at him. 'But don't try to pretend that you *knowing* me meant anything,' he hissed, his breath hot on her face.

Tears raced down her cheeks, free-flowing over his fin-gers. 'I swear, I never anticipated us.'

'No, you just didn't anticipate getting found out. There was no "us" until I quit – you made sure of that. I could jump or be pushed but you made sure I wouldn't be staying in my job and only once I'd earned you your million was there an "us". You thought you could have your cake and eat it – have me and betray me.' He looked her over as though she was filth. 'I wonder if Sholto really knew what he was getting when he hired you, because up till then, they'd tried every trick in the book: provoking me, baiting me like some kind of tied-up dog, taking Skye from me, ruining that. Until they hit the bull's eye – sending you and making me fall for a lie.'

'It wasn't a lie. I meant all those things I said. I *do* want better for you. I *do* think you needed to go. You were stuck in a stalemate.'

'Stalemate?' He let go of her as though she was tainted, diseased, dirty. 'Well, guess what – we're not there any more. It's checkmate. I'm out. He's won. You've won. *This* is your masterpiece, Alex. Whether it played out the way you imagined, make no mistake, we've all been the puppets in your game. You pull the strings and we dance, baby.'

'No, you're wrong. Everything that happened between us was real. I wanted you. I didn't want to hurt you.'

He quietened. 'And yet you did. The money meant more.' He stared at her for the longest time, desolation in his eyes, and she could see he'd been on this path before; betrayal was nothing new to him. 'I was so wrong about you, you know that? You have got it.'

'G-got what?' she asked.

'The killer instinct, Alex. Sholto was right – congratulations.' He took her hand and brought it up to his forehead, pointing it at him like a gun. 'You took the shot and you got me, sweetheart. Right between the eyes.'

Chapter Thirty

Mayfair, London, Sunday 24 December 2017

'Alex Hyde's office.'

Louise Kennedy's clipped voice pierced the silence of a thickly carpeted room whose still air was only otherwise punctuated by the deep perfume of lilies-of-the-valley.

'No, I'm sorry, she's not available. Who's calling, please?'

Her French-manicured fingertips hovered, poised, above the keyboard, the cursor on the screen flashing as she awaited the name, hardly able to believe her bad luck that the phone had rung in the minute and a half she'd been in here. She'd only swung by to pick up the Fortnum's gift bag she'd accidentally left beneath her desk on Friday afternoon, containing the all-important cranberry sauce for her mother. She should have ignored it, of course, but the habit of picking up on the first ring was a hard one to break.

'I will need a name if she's to—' She was careful to avoid exhaling into the mic of her headset as the caller prevaricated, not believing her, not used to being told no. Her fingers twitched in the air as though twiddling a pen, restless to get on.

'No, that isn't possible, she's not here.' One threaded eyebrow arched as the caller's voice became more strident. 'I'm afraid that's confidential,' she said more briskly, more than used to dealing with self-importance. 'But I can ask her to call you. Does she know what it's in regard to?' Her fingers twitched again.

Outside, the blue lights of a fire engine whirled past the mink-grey slatted windows, the bright sky throwing short shadows on the ground. Shoppers laden with last-minute emergency purchases walked past in profile, heads bent to their phones, shoes clicking on the pavements.

Her lips pursed as the caller talked. She had thought as much. 'I see. So this is a *new* client inquiry.' The woman's presumptive tone had suggested deep personal acquaintance. 'Yes, a lot of people know Miss Hyde . . . I'm sure, but I'm afraid we operate a waiting list and she doesn't have any openings before June. Would you like me to book you in and we'll be in touch nearer the time?'

Her eyebrows buckled as presumptive became didactic; the caller perhaps didn't realize that no one got to Alex without first going past her. 'Well, as I said before, Ms Hyde is away on business with clients but you are very welcome to call back at your convenience if you change your—' Her finger hovered over the disconnect button.

Three, two, o . . .

Her hand dropped to the desk as though shot down, the words still ringing in her ears as though every single one had exploded down the line with a bang. She leaned forward on her elbows, concentrating harder as she stared at her reflection in the blank screen. There was a long pause.

'I'm sorry,' she said finally, an uncharacteristic waver in her cut-glass voice. 'He'll do *what*?'

*

The car had stopped at a set of lights, her face pale behind the glass as she watched the shoppers weave in and out of the city boutiques as though part of an elaborate dance; it was a wonder there weren't more collisions, more standing on toes, she thought blankly, given the sheer numbers involved, but then she knew just how good people were (without even realizing it themselves) at reading micro signs in body language. She didn't look at their faces, just their legs striding, bags swinging, gloved hands interlinked as they moved in couples and pairs and units. Happy, on the final push to Christmas now.

It was sleeting on the east coast and the wet flakes dribbling down the windows made the Christmas lights refract and dazzle hundreds of times over. In the end, she'd come over with a fishing boat, paying a handsome sum to get off the island and away, at last. There hadn't been time to ring Louise – or rather, she hadn't wanted even Louise to hear her in that state – and she'd simply grabbed a local cab in the port; the driver wouldn't need to work for the rest of the week on what she was paying him to get her to Edinburgh airport.

The lights changed and the car began to move again. Her phone rang in her bag and she frowned as she saw the name on the screen.

She took a deep breath. 'Louise, please don't tell me you're working today. You surely don't need me to remind you it's a Sunday *and* it's Christmas Eve?' She stared at the back of the headrest, trying to make her voice sound normal. '. . . Oh, I see. Well, as long as you promise that's all it is. Even I'm not working today.'

She bit her lip, feeling it begin to tremble again. She pressed her index finger against her nose.

'Yes, it's done . . . Yes, thank you.' Her voice wavered. 'Mmhmm, I'm very pleased. I'm on my way to the airport now. We're ten minutes away . . . No, Edinburgh. There was no availability at Glasgow.'

The words came out in a gabble, rising in tone, and she tipped her head back and held the phone away from her head for a moment, closing her eyes and taking another deep breath. '. . . Sorry, yes, I'm here. So what's up?'

She frowned. '. . . Who?'

It was a moment before the name registered. Made sense. 'Yes, I know him,' she said slowly. 'What does he want?'

She snorted as Louise explained. '. . . No, absolutely not. There's no way. It's Christmas Eve. I've been away for three weeks. I need to get home. I'm flying to Switzerland in two days and I need some time to just *stop!*' Her voice had risen again and she dropped her head, squeezing her temples with her free hand. 'Sorry, yes, I'm fine. I'm fine.' She sighed. 'If you could just call him back and explain that I'm now unavailable until the New Year—'

She frowned. 'He's done *what* . . . ? Oh Jesus.'

She gave an exhausted sigh and looked out of the window. The airport was signposted on the upcoming roundabout. This couldn't be happening. But how could she turn away? '. . . *Fuck*,' she hissed savagely, pinching her temples and closing her eyes. 'Is there availability on the evening flights? Something around six?' She swallowed and nodded. 'Seven, then. Yes, fine. Get me on that and text me the exact address . . . Yes, I know I am. Okay, thanks . . . Oh and Louise, if I ever do make it back to London, schedule in a sit-down for the two of us in the New Year. It's time we discussed a raise and getting you on the training programme . . . Of course

I'm serious, I don't know what I'd do without you. Happy Christmas.'

She leaned forward in the seat, the driver already indicating for the third exit to the motorway.

'I'm sorry, there's been a change of plan,' she said wearily. 'Could you take me up to Perth?'

'Thank Christ you're here,' Daisy said, running down the steps to meet her as she paid the taxi an hour later. 'We didn't know who else to call.'

'It's fine. I was in the neighbourhood,' she lied as Daisy threw her arms around her neck. 'How's he doing?'

Daisy shook her head. 'Not good. Ambrose and Max are in with him now.'

'Where are they?' Alex asked, getting her shotgun from the boot and wheeling her suitcase with difficulty over the gravel.

'Oh, leave that there, one of the boys can bring it up the steps later,' Daisy said, waving it away. 'They're in the library. The boys have been trying to keep him calm but he's desperately agitated. It looks like he's lost the whole bloody lot. Everything.'

'Okay,' Alex nodded. 'I'll talk to him.'

'Hey—' Daisy put a hand on her arm, stopping mid-step and looking at her with sudden concern. 'Are you okay? Has something happened?'

'What? With *me*?' Alex asked in surprise, amazed anyone would have even noticed her pale complexion and lacklustre energy. 'God, no, I'm fine,' she said, smiling as she told the most common lie in the world.

'You look pale.'

'Just cold. And tired. I'm looking forward to getting home.'

'I bet,' Daisy agreed, starting up the steps again. 'When are you off?'

'Tonight,' Alex said, generously omitting the fact that she'd been an hour from getting on the plane and escaping from here once and for all.

They walked through the doors against which it had all started with Lochie – the mistletoe was still hanging, of course – and into the panelled hall that she had never expected to see again. Two young boys and three girls – perhaps five, six, sevenish? – thundered down the stairs in full yell, the girls pointing Nerf guns at the boys who were racing ahead and firing neon-green pellets at their backs.

'I said *not* inside!' Emma yelled, leaning over the balcony, her dark hair framing her face. 'Oh, Alex! You're here!'

The others ran out at the sound of their voices – Anna and Elise.

'You came!' Elise cried. 'Thank God!'

'We didn't think there was any chance of getting hold of you, much less getting you *here*,' Anna said as Emma jogged down the stairs and joined them, concern written on all their faces.

'I was pretty much passing anyway,' she mumbled as everyone greeted her with hugs as though she was one of them and not the Judas in their midst, the traitor who had sold out their dear friend. 'Who . . . ?' she asked in bafflement, as the kids tore around the hall before running down the front steps onto the lawns.

'Oh, the muckiest, loudest ones are mine: Bella, Charlie and Miles,' Emma said with a roll of her eyes. 'They've gone feral, I'm afraid – always do when we come to stay here; I haven't been able to get them in the bath since they came on Wednesday.'

'My girls leading them astray,' Daisy tutted. 'They need no excuse.'

'I didn't . . . I didn't know you even had kids,' Alex said in astonishment. 'Where on earth were they hiding last weekend?' Had she somehow overlooked them, Alex wondered? Was she really that self-absorbed?

'They go to stay with my mother when we have our MacNab weekend. Strictly no ankle-biters allowed. It's party-time for the grown-ups.'

'Oh, I see.' She realized they were all looking at her and she tried to draw herself up, move back onto a professional plane. 'And Sam – how is he?'

'Max has looked him over but it's not his area,' Emma continued.

'Well, not unless he gives himself a heart attack,' Max himself said, walking into the hall just at that moment. 'Which is within the realms of possibility, the way he's going. It was good of you to come.' He kissed her lightly on the cheek. 'I've given him a sedative.'

'Do you think you can do anything?' Elise asked, biting her nails.

Alex nodded. 'It's what I do. Crisis callouts are my bread and butter.'

'He's in there,' Daisy said, pointing to the library. 'Ambrose is with him.'

'Okay, thanks.'

'We'll be in the kitchen, okay?' she said. 'I'll make some coffee.'

'Great.' Alex heard their voices – anxious, agitated – recede as she walked over to the library door and knocked lightly.

The door opened almost immediately, making her startle and step back. 'Oh!'

'Sorry,' Ambrose said, slipping out of the room and joining her in the hall. 'I didn't realize you were there. I was just coming to join the others. He's sleeping.'

'Oh,' she said again.

'Max gave him something an hour ago; poor bugger's worn himself out. He didn't sleep at all last night.'

'What's happened, exactly?' she asked, watching him. 'My PA said he backed a bad deal?'

'More than bad, it's catastrophic.' He sighed. 'Look, without sounding crass about it, I'm assuming Lochie must have told you something of Sam's success?'

She nodded.

'The boy had done good. He certainly didn't need to work ever again after he sold the app, but he's not the sort to spend the rest of his life on a yacht on the French Riviera either. He wanted to stay in the game. It didn't matter what the business was, he was up for the challenge. Computer games, whisky trading, you name it – he prided himself on being able to jump between markets. But he backed the wrong horse this time – ploughed ten million sterling into shares of a biotech that was racing to be first to market with an antenatal test based on screening foetal DNA – only for the patent to be denied on a technicality because it's based on natural biological process. Or something.'

'And so the biotech's stock has dived,' she said, predicting the cause of Sam's crisis.

Ambrose nodded.

Ten million was a lot of money. Precious few could take a hit like that and stay on their feet, much less be able to walk away, but Alex still smiled.

'Don't worry. We'll get him through this.'

'Should I wake him up?'

'No, let him sleep. It's the best thing for him if he's been up all night. Even just forty minutes will make him feel better. He should wake up with a clearer perspective.'

'Fancy a coffee then, while we wait?'

'Great.'

Everyone was gathered in the kitchen, sitting around the large farmhouse table when they walked in a moment later, the Christmas carols in the background somewhat para-doxical in mood to the subdued group. They looked up expectantly.

'That was quick!' Daisy said.

'He's sleeping,' Alex replied, shaking her head.

They sighed collectively.

'Well, I guess that's good, right?' Elise said. 'If he didn't sleep last night?'

'Yeah, but not so helpful for Alex,' Emma pointed out.

'It's no problem.'

'But you've come all this way and now he's out for the count? What were you thinking, giving him that sleeping pill?' Emma asked, whacking her husband on the arm.

'I was trying to keep him calm,' Max protested.

'Honestly, it's fine,' Alex said. 'I've changed my flight to the seven ten. As long as I'm away by four thirty, it'll be okay.'

'Well, it's very good of you to do this . . . What are your plans for Christmas anyway?' Max asked, nobly attempting small talk and pulling out a chair for her as Daisy poured a coffee and handed it over.

'I'm just having a quiet one at home. I haven't been home

in almost nine weeks in total, so it'll be good to just get back and . . . flop.'

'Are you spending it with family?' Max asked.

'No. There's only me and my father and he lives in Switzerland so I'm flying out to see him on Boxing Day.'

Max arched an eyebrow, but if he thought it was odd that she wasn't going out in time for Christmas itself, he didn't say. 'That'll be nice.'

'Yes.'

'Will you ski out there?'

Alex hesitated. 'No. Not that.'

'Oh, don't you ski? I sort of assumed you would after the MacNab; you seem very accomplished with all things outdoorsy.'

Alex looked into her coffee. 'Well, I do but Dad doesn't,' she smiled.

'Fair enough. My ortho colleagues are constantly telling their patients there comes an age when it's not worth risking the knocks and bumps. One fall can mean a new hip, right?'

'Yes, right.' She smiled weakly, wanting to get off the topic. 'By the way, where's Jess? Isn't she here?'

'Oh, she had to go into town, get some last-minute bits,' Daisy said, lifting down a bag of potatoes from a shelf in the walk-in larder and bringing it through.

Alex nodded. Wasn't that slightly odd, for a woman to go shopping when her husband was standing in the still-smoking ruins of his financial empire?

'I think she needed to get out,' Anna said as though reading her mind. 'Clear her head a bit.'

'Sure.'

'Right, who's going to help me make a start on these

tatties?' Daisy asked, setting down several large pans in the middle of the table and rifling in the cutlery drawer for vegetable peelers. 'Many hands make light work.'

Everyone groaned.

'What?' Daisy demanded, planting her hands on her hips. 'I'm not cooking for the lot of you on my own.'

'Fine. Give it here,' Anna said, reaching for the peelers and giving one to Elise too.

'And you boys can make yourselves useful too, by filling up the log baskets and coal scuttles. You may as well get the heavy stuff done while we've got a bit of time and it's still light.'

Ambrose and Max got up with dramatic reluctance, but they knew better than to argue and Alex heard them laughing out in the hall a minute later as they pulled on their boots.

'Oh no, I didn't mean you,' Daisy said, reaching to take back the peeler from Alex. 'I'm not putting *you* to work. It's bad enough we've dragged you up here to a sleeping patient when you could have been halfway home by now.'

'But it's no problem. I prefer to keep busy.'

'I think you should take the opportunity to stop for a bit,' Daisy said, reluctantly giving her the peeler anyway as Alex reached for a potato from the bag. 'She looks tired, don't you think?' she asked the others.

'Yeah,' Emma and Anna and Elise agreed.

'It's because you're in black,' Elise said, patting her hand. 'It's a very draining colour.'

'Oh my God, not that again,' Anna chuckled, starting on peeling the potatoes with expert proficiency.

'So, besides Switzerland, what's next for you, Alex?'

Daisy asked interestedly. 'Jess said your PA said you're booked all the way through to June?'

It was Jess who had called? Alex wasn't sure why this should have surprised her; it was her husband who was in crisis, after all. 'Well, yes, but it's not as bad as it sounds – I've got a long trip booked for Sri Lanka at the end of next month.'

'Nice!' Anna said. 'Work or pleasure?'

'Most definitely the latter. It's a yoga retreat, I go there every year.' She rolled her eyes. 'Although they did ask me if I would run a stress-management course within the camp to complement their mindfulness classes.'

'But you're not interested?' Elise asked.

Alex shook her head. 'No, it's where I go to recharge my batteries. I need to keep it reserved for me and *my* headspace. The problem with my job is that by constantly examining other people's problems, it's easy to avoid confronting my own. I have to allocate time in my diary to step away and work on myself or I'd never do it.'

'I expect you have to be disciplined about not blurring the boundaries between work and your private life?' Anna asked.

'That's right. When I'm working with a client, it tends to be to the neglect of my own life; I go to where *they* live and work, I focus entirely on *their* lives, work to *their* schedule, meet *their* colleagues, friends, families.'

'Like us.'

'Oh no, I didn't mean—' Alex said quickly. 'You're different.'

'Are we? Or will you go back to London tonight, step back into your own life and we'll just be the friends of a former client of yours?'

'I feel like we're all friends.' Alex hesitated, detecting an edge. 'Aren't we?'

'Of course we are,' Elise said quickly, patting her hand and shooting Anna a look.

'Of course,' Daisy said, but her eyes were on the vegetables and Alex wasn't convinced.

Everyone fell into an uncomfortable quiet, curls of potato peelings piling up and spilling off the plates onto the refectory table. In the background, Bing Crosby was singing 'Snow' – one of her mother's favourite Christmas songs – as outside the window Ambrose and Max crossed to and fro on the gravel path, lugging coal and logs from the stores, the cold east wind blowing their hair off their faces.

They were moving on to the carrots and parsnips when there was a sudden crash from the other side of the house.

'What was that?' Emma gasped as they all sprang from the table.

'Oh shit,' Daisy hissed as there was the crunch of gravel on the drive. 'That's all we need! Jess is back just as Sam starts bouncing off the walls again.'

'Don't worry, you keep her here, I'll go in to him,' Alex said, grabbing her bag and hurrying from the room, making her way straight over to the library. She took a deep breath and knocked on the door again, noticing that the key had been put on the outside. Were things really that bad? There was no reply but she could hear movement in the room. She walked in.

Sam was in profile, pacing the room, fragments of blue glass peppered across the floor – a vase? An ashtray?

'Sam?' She walked further in and closed the door behind her just as she heard Jess coming into the hall and calling his name.

He looked over, confusion buckling his brow at the sight of her. 'Alex? What are you doing here? Where's Lochie?'

'He's not here. Jess called my office. She thought we could talk, you and I.' He looked back at her blankly and she wasn't even sure he was hearing her. Had he heard Jess's voice in the hall? Perhaps he was wondering where his wife was. 'I'm not sure if you're really aware of what it is I do, but I'm a business coach. I specialize in helping people – leaders – when they're . . . in the kind of trouble you're in.'

He stared at her hard for a moment before gripping his hair and turning away. 'Christ, what good's talking going to do now? It's gone! I fucked up!'

'Yes, I know. I'm sorry.' She watched him closely. 'How are you doing?'

His Adam's apple bobbed in his throat and he planted his hands firmly on his hips, looking down at his feet, trying to hold it together. 'I'm fine,' he said. But the tips of his fingers were blanched and his shoulders were sitting two inches higher than they should.

'Really?'

He looked up at her, his composure fleeing as he saw her concern. '*Fuck no!* What the hell was I thinking? I had every-thing – I'm married to the woman of my dreams, I've got a great house, more money than we could ever need. And I threw it away; I might as well have lit a bloody match under the entire lot of it.'

Alex walked over to the deep partner's desk and leaned against it; she was closer to him now, close enough to be able to lower her voice – which would force him to have to concentrate on her – but not so close that he'd feel trapped or hemmed in. She could see he needed to move and she

wanted him to; as long as he stayed on his feet, his movements would likely remain open and expansive. It was if he
sat down on the sofa that he was at risk of closing down,
physically and mentally.

'Look, I know things seem bleak right at this moment,
but I can assure you, if you made a fortune once, you can
make it twice,' she said, keeping her voice calm and matter-
of-fact; too much sympathy would arouse the panic that
pity was deserved. 'And you will. I work with people like
you all the time Sam – risk-takers, gamblers, entrepreneurs;
losing's just part of the curve of winning. No one who really
makes it big ever got to the top without a knock. You will
get past this.'

'You don't know that.'

'Yes, I do.' Her calmness began to still him.

He narrowed his eyes. 'How?'

'Scotch Vaults for one thing – that's going to be the foundation of your second fortune. It's an excellent idea, plus
you're the first ones in to that particular market.'

'Does Lochie know you think that?'

She shrugged, even though she felt physically jolted at
the sound of his name. 'It doesn't matter what Lochie thinks
about my thoughts. The question is, do you believe in it?'

He looked out of the window, nervously sliding his jaw
from side to side, the gesture a stress tic as his fingers
drummed on his thigh, tension hard-wiring his frame. It
was hard to equate this friable, jittery man with the party
animal leading the drinks last weekend and who had flung
her round the room in a flamboyant salsa. But then how
much had changed for them all since then? Since Lochie
had slept in this room, all their lives had fallen apart.

455

The door behind her opened and she knew it was Jess coming to check on—

'What the fuck?'

She turned and almost dropped on the spot at the sight of Lochie standing there, holding an enormous bunch of yellow tulips, presumably for the now defunct vase on the floor. She looked at him – he was as glassy-eyed as the stressed-out man standing behind her. She couldn't breathe. Couldn't compute. What was he doing here?

There was a sudden scrabbling noise behind her and she turned, startled, again as Sam suddenly appeared in her frame of vision, heading straight for Lochie.

'Sam? What the hell is going on?' Lochie snapped, looking between the two of them in bewilderment. 'Jess told me to put these in the vase and I find *her* in here?'

'Ah, yes, don't worry. I'll put these in water, mate.' Sam patted his shoulder apologetically. 'Just be careful over there, won't you?' He pointed to the glass fragments on the floor. 'I may have slightly had to break some glassware – you know, to get you both in the same room.'

What?

'What the *fuck* is going on?' Lochie thundered, turning on the spot as Sam suddenly darted to the door, hiding behind it for protection, his head and the fingers of one hand all that was visible.

'It's called staging an intervention.' Sam looked across at her and winked. 'You two need to talk this out. Good luck, kids.' And before either of them could even move, he closed the door behind them – and locked it.

'You have got to be kidding me!' Lochie yelled, running over and pulling at the handle. But the key was on the other side and the door was ancient and heavy; it had withstood five hundred years of Ambrose's ancestors; it wasn't going to crumble now. 'This is not fucking funny. Open this door now. Right now! . . . Sam! Ambrose! You fucking fuckers!'

And before Alex could even process what she was seeing, he punched the wall, bending double in the next instant and holding his hand protectively. 'Fuck! Fuck! Fuck!'

Alex watched in mute horror. This had been a set-up? Suddenly the 'off' atmosphere in the kitchen made sense, the other women bringing her back into the fold, just enough to allow this charade to happen, not sure yet whether she was the best thing to have happened to their friend – or the worst.

'Loch—'

'No!' His voice was like venom as he whirled round, one finger pointed at her like a gun. 'You don't get to speak. Your words count for nothing.'

He was right, of course, they didn't – she had lied to him from the start.

'I don't even want to *look* at you. I can't fucking believe—' He began hammering his fist on the ancient oak door again. 'Open this door, you fucking bastards!'

But no one came and she sank down to the sofa, her knees simply refusing to lock any more, her body betraying her mind. After a minute or two of fist-drumming the door, he gave up as well and a silence mushroomed around them, filling the room. Still she didn't dare look at him, but shortly afterwards, she heard his footsteps begin to pace on the parquet.

Alex glanced at the locked door again, wondering how long this would go on for. How could she have escaped from him on a snowed-in island, only to find herself locked in the same room with him a few hours later? Were the others all standing behind the door, listening in? 'How do they even know?' she asked calmly.

'How do you think?' he snapped. 'I rang to tell them that I wasn't coming for Christmas and next thing, it's like the bloody Spanish Inquisition.'

'And yet here you are.'

'Yes. Because they're my *friends*. They wanted to help.'

Alex nodded, indicating their predicament. This was helping?

She sighed and for a second, she caught sight of herself: legs wrapped one around the other, her shoulders hunched, her head dropped – the classic low-power pose she never let her clients sink into. But to her surprise, she found she couldn't pull herself out of it; it was easier to say than to do and her limbs felt leaden, her heart a slow drowsy throb. Because for once, she wasn't 'fine' – she wasn't on top of this, she wasn't in control. She didn't want to be here but she didn't know where she did want to be either. She had no home, simply a base; she had no family, simply obligations; and unlike him, she had no friends, not any more; they had fallen by the wayside of her ambition as her focus steadily closed down to just colleagues and clients, the people who could help. She had scaled the summit of her career-long quest, but at what cost? She was alone, empty and exhausted.

'What did you tell them?'

'Just the truth,' he said coldly. 'That you lied. Set me up.'

The pain in his voice hurt her but she kept her eyes on his and nodded. 'Yes.' She glanced at her hands. 'So why are they doing this then? After hearing all that, surely they think I'm a cold-hearted bitch? A monster?'

He glared at her, wrong-footed by her own harshness at the condemnation upon her. 'Yes, they probably do.'

'So . . . ?'

'I think they think you had a reason.'

Alex went very still, forced a baffled frown. 'Why would they think that?'

'Emma saw something she thinks may explain it.'

'*Emma* did?' Alex scoffed. What on earth could—?

'She saw a business card in your bag. Cereneo, or something?' He watched her closely and she knew she wasn't keeping the alarm off her face. 'She's a neuro nurse; said they've sent patients out to that clinic once or twice. It specializes in pioneering therapies for quadriplegics . . .'

Alex felt the air leave her body, suctioned out by a level of shock that she couldn't comprehend. No. There was no way.

'Apparently you told her you were visiting your father in Switzerland on Boxing Day, but not skiing. It seemed a little odd.' He looked straight at her. 'She also said the treatment he'd require there would be very expensive.' His tone was questioning, uncertain even, but his eyes were steady, assessing her, probing for the truth. '. . . Is it true?' And when she didn't reply – 'You said right at the beginning you needed the money from this job to help someone in your family. I thought it was a joke, but it wasn't, was it?'

Alex tried to breathe in, to make her body work if not her brain. She stood up, moving away from him and hurrying towards the door. She banged on it with her fist. 'Open this door!' she demanded. 'Do you hear me? Someone open this door right now or I'm calling the police!'

She turned around to face him, to make sure he wasn't following her, but the room was a blur; her eyes pooled with hot tears and she could only just make him out on the other side of the ottoman.

'Alex.'

'Stop. Just don't,' she said with as much authority as she could muster.

'Why did you tell me he'd died?'

'I didn't. I never said that.'

'You clearly implied it. It was what you wanted me to infer. You told me he was an alcoholic – past tense. But anyone who's lived with an alcoholic knows there is no past tense. It dies only when you die. My father could have stopped drinking and not touched a drop for forty years and he would still have died *as* an alcoholic. You wanted me to think he was dead.'

Alex willed herself to stay calm. 'So?'

'*So?*' He gave a small snort. 'So, there's a big difference between need and greed, Alex. It changes everything.' He took a step towards her, then stopped again as he saw her recoil. 'If you tell me you did what you did because you needed the money for him, I could understand it. I could forgive it.'

Every word was like a pickaxe to the rock wall around her. 'I don't need your forgiveness. I can live with what I did. I had my reasons.'

There was a hesitation as he tried to see past her front. 'So that million bought you – what? Surgery?' he conjectured. 'A state-of-the-art wheelchair? Care for the rest of his life?'

She didn't reply.

'*Tell* me,' he suddenly demanded, looking angry again. Beginning to walk, to pace. 'Don't you think I deserve to know why you destroyed my life? Was it to save his?'

She shook her head. 'I'm not discussing this.'

'Yes! You are. An explanation is the very least you owe me!'

She shook her head, feeling the adrenaline pitch as he came towards her, black-eyed and red-cheeked.

'Tell me!'

'No.'

He was in front of her now, his hand on her elbow, gripping hard. 'Tell me!'

'It bought me freedom, okay?!' The words burst out of her before she could stop them, panic, fear, frustration, exhaustion bubbling together in a combustible mix. 'He has no one else. Like you said yesterday – it's all on me.'

He watched her, trying to understand, to fill in the blanks. 'What about your mother? Where's she?'

'Gone,' she snapped, the word brittle. 'She left us after the fire.'

'Fire?' His eyes narrowed at the word and she knew he was remembering her desperate shout the night of the distillery blaze and how it had been the only thing to travel through to him as he lay unconscious on the floor. It had been the voice of someone who had lived through those flames before.

She exhaled, all out of fight. He knew most of it now, anyway – pieced together from a single business card and girls' gossip. 'He had been drinking.' Her voice was quiet, her eyes on a spot on the floor past his shoulder. 'And he fell asleep on the sofa and dropped the cigarette on the curtain. And by the time he woke up, the whole room was alight.' She shook her head, feeling the long-repressed memories beginning to surface. 'Somehow he got upstairs and managed to wake me and my mother.' She swallowed, falling back into the terror of that night – the black smoke, his stumbling feet, her mother's high-pitched screams of bewilderment. 'We . . . we couldn't get back down the stairs. The fire was moving so quickly that we had to throw our bed things out of the window and jump. Mum and I went first. Mum was okay but I landed badly and broke my ankle. I couldn't move to get out of the way but Dad was panicking – he was still blind drunk – so he jumped from the other window, thirty feet onto the terrace below. He broke both legs, his pelvis and shattered his spine.'

'Jesus.'

Lochie looked horrified and she stared back at him with pity if he thought broken bones were the worst of it. '. . . It was only when he was being put in the ambulance that he remembered about Amy.'

'Amy?'

The tears began to fall now, hot and heavy globes of anguish, and the words felt suddenly as unstoppable as the tears. 'My sister. I was seventeen, she was nineteen. She was at Bristol Uni but she'd come back unexpectedly because she'd had a fight with her boyfriend. Mum and I were already in bed by the time she got in, so we didn't know she was there. We had no idea. And by the time we did, by the time Dad remembered she'd popped her head in to say "hi" . . .' She scrunched her eyes shut as she remembered her mother's scream and how she'd tried to run back into the house as the flames engulfed the roof. Her head dropped into her hands, the sobs heaving her shoulders as a groan of pain escaped him, and Lochie wrapped his arms around her.

'Oh, Alex,' he breathed into her hair, rubbing her back

gently with his hand as she wept. 'And then our fire too . . . Why didn't you say something?'

She shook her head angrily. How? Where was she supposed to start – with which emotion? Grief for her sister who shouldn't even have been there? Rage at her father whose fault this was? Despair at her mother who had turned and left – left them both – unable to forgive him and unable to look at her?

She pulled back, infuriated by her own tears, and looked past him at the grey day beyond the window. 'Mum finds it very hard, even now, to be with me. Amy and I looked so alike.' She sniffed, pressing the back of her hand to her mouth and trying to steady her breathing again. 'I understand it. She can't help feeling that way. I know she loves me, she just can't . . . be with us at the moment. It's too hard.'

'But—'

'No, there are no buts,' Alex said, stopping him. 'She lost her child. The way she sees it, her husband killed her child and that is a terrible truth to bear. I don't blame her for any of it.'

'What about your father? Do *you* blame him?'

She kept her gaze steady on him, refusing to look away, to face up to the unpalatable, complicated truth. 'Yes. And he pays the price for what he did a million times over every day.' She thought of him, flat on his back and staring at the ceiling. At a stroke, his alcoholism had been cured but only because the urge for a drink was for ever denied by arms which now remained pinned to his sides, the cruel irony of devastating cramps shooting up and down his inert legs leaving him crying in pain. 'He's lost more than any of us – Amy, Mum – his ability to move.' She swallowed, looking at him defiantly. 'What was I supposed to do? Leave him too?'

'No one would blame you.'

'Oh, don't worry – I hate him, just like you hated yours. His weakness destroyed our family; *of course* I wanted to do what my mother did – turn my back on him, just leave him lying there and never go back! But he's my father, the only one I'll ever have. So *this* –' she threw her arms out, indicating the room they were standing in, the two of them here, together – 'working my backside off for the past fourteen years, working with you – it was the solution for me. I told myself that if I could get the money together for his care at that clinic, then that was the most I could be expected to do. I check in with his medical team every bloody day, I visit him every month. There's nothing more that can be done beyond that, short of finding a cure; getting him to the best of the best was what I needed to do and then I'd be free of my duty to him. I could start living my life too.'

He watched her. 'Except – you met me.'

The statement stopped her in her tracks. 'Y-yes.' She lifted her chin higher, trying to pull herself up, become bigger, stronger, more powerful than she felt. 'And so I had to choose and I chose him. And I would do it again,' she said determinedly, but with a tremor in her voice. 'I would.'

'As you should,' he agreed. 'I get it.'

Forgiveness? She had never expected it, never dared to ask for it, but it blew her over like a wind anyway and she felt her shoulders drop down from her ears – she hadn't even noticed they had hunched up. Her body softened.

Understanding bloomed as their eyes met, that familiar zip of electricity charging the air around them. 'Alex . . .' She felt his hand reach for hers, but she pulled away before he could touch her and walked over to the sofa where she had left her bag. It wasn't over yet.

'I have something for you.' He watched as she pulled a large brown A4 envelope from it and held it out for him to take. 'I was intending to send it to you next week. But, well . . . I figure I'll save the postage.'

His eyes flicked up to hers, part amused, part wary. 'What is it?'

'Your insurance policy.' And when she saw his frown, she added, 'Figuratively, I mean. Not literally. It's about your family. You only had half the story.' She swallowed. '*I* only gave you half the story.'

He opened it without a word, confusion clouding his face as he pulled out a wad of photocopies.

'It's proof that you have every right to sit as CEO of Kentallen Distillery Group. You are family in every definition of the word.'

'*What?*' he whispered, frowning deeply as he walked over to the partner's desk, flicking through the sheets – there were photocopies of a handwritten letter, two black-and-white photographs, one colour photograph and a bright landscape painting. He set them all out on the surface and stared at them blankly. 'I don't understand what any of this means.'

Alex walked over and pointed to the colour photograph that Skye had forwarded to her from her phone. 'I take it you heard about this teddy bear they found in the hidden malt barrel on Monday?'

'Vaguely – although with everything going on in Edinburgh, I haven't given it any thought.'

'Well, when Skye showed me this photo, it rang distinct alarm bells with me. Something about the teddy bear seemed familiar but I couldn't think why. It kept bugging me. Then I remembered – I'd seen one in a couple of old photos at the Peggies'.' She pointed to the pictures of the woman and child in the churchyard, and of the nurses and soldiers in the hospital.

'Wait – why are you so intimately acquainted with the Peggies' photo collection?'

She gave a small snort. 'I'm not. But they've got boxes of material that Mr P. inherited from his father who was the local police sergeant – letters, logbooks, photographs; they've been sorting through them with a view to donating it all to the museum. I just happened to come in when Mrs Peggie was going through them.'

'And that was when you first found out my grandfather was adopted,' he clarified, remembering their other conversation in the canteen.

She nodded and pointed to the photograph of the nurse. 'You probably don't need me to tell you that that woman there is Clarissa Farquhar, your great-grandmother. It was she who inherited her brother Percy's forty-per-cent stake in the company when he was killed in the war; which combined with her own thirteen per cent has ultimately given you your majority stake.'

'Yes. I know who she is.'

'But do you know who he is?' She pointed to the photograph again.

'The guy with the broken leg?' he squinted. 'No.'

'He was an American called Edward Cobb – a soldier who was almost killed when the SS *Tuscania* was torpedoed in February 1918.'

Lochie's eyes flashed up to her at the mention of the

troopship. He'd heard of it; it was written into the fabric of the island's history.

'Clarissa saved him. She saw him on the rocks and nursed him back to health. He had a broken leg and various other injuries but he also had Spanish flu. They thought he was going to die from it – most likely he'd had it before they left New York – but she nursed him back to health and he pulled through. He stayed on Islay for another four months whilst his leg healed.'

'What happened to him after then?'

Alex sighed. 'He was sent to France as soon as his leg was mended. He was killed nine days later.'

Lochie winced. 'Christ.'

'Clarissa became a recluse and eventually left the island. Her fiancé had been killed in 1916; her brother just after the *Tuscania* sank; and then Edward too . . . She said she had to get away and she went to live in the Peak District for a short time; her housekeeper went with her.'

He shrugged, clearly baffled as to where she was leading with this. 'Okay.'

She grabbed the photo of the child in the churchyard. 'Who's this, do you think?'

Lochie sighed and stared, easily recognizing the woman with him as Clarissa. 'Well, I would imagine that's my grandfather George. He's the child she adopted – or rather, *didn't* – after the war.'

'Uh-huh. And see what he's holding there?' she said, pointing to the photo and then pulling forward the letter.

'A bear.'

'The same bear Edward Cobb's mother sent over from America when news of the attack broke. See? She says there she was sending it so he wouldn't feel so homesick.'

She watched his eyes move from side to side, reading the letter quickly. 'Okay,' he said again. 'So my grandfather ended up with Edward Cobb's teddy bear. So what?'

'It's the same bear as was found in the hidden malt cask,' she said, pointing again to Skye's photograph of the bear wrapped in the baby blanket at the bottom of the opened cask. 'The obvious question is why was it put there? Skye thought maybe the child had died and the mother had wanted to hide it from sight, but couldn't bear to part with it altogether.'

Lochie frowned. 'It's a stretch.'

'In the absence of any other explanation, it was the most plausible reason anyone could think of.'

He shot her a wry look. 'But you have another explanation, I suppose.'

'Yes. Look at this photograph with the soldiers again,' she said, pointing to the tiny detail she had clocked but not processed on the first viewing. It was barely perceptible in the pale shades of grey, the fact that their hands were touching – only the edges of their little fingers each grazing the other's, but it was enough to make their smiles widen and their eyes shine. Alex knew what love looked like now – it shone like a sunbeam; it was how she felt whenever Lochie looked at her. 'See how they're touching? And there's a bench up on the cliffs by the farmhouse, with an inscription she wrote, about looking over to America. To him, from her. "In memory of EC," it says, and it's signed by "CF". Edward Cobb and Clarissa Farquhar were lovers.' His face roamed hers, the word like a gong, making their bodies vibrate. 'And she had his baby.'

'Wait . . . you're saying my great-grandmother *pretended*

to adopt her own child to cover up the fact that she'd had her American soldier's baby?' he asked in disbelief.

'Yes! That's why there's no paperwork for it. Back then an illegitimate child, born to the best family in the area, would have been an absolute scandal.'

'But how? How did she do it? A pregnancy isn't an easy thing to hide.'

'Precisely. Which is why she disappeared from public view. Her housekeeper, Mrs Dunoon – who had herself only just been widowed – agreed to pretend she was with child and together they left the island, supposedly on account of Clarissa's grief. They travelled to the Peak District where no one knew them; Clarissa gave birth and then she came back to Islay with the baby, pretending she had adopted him after Mrs Dunoon had succumbed to the Spanish flu. But she hadn't.'

He looked baffled. 'And you know that because . . . ?'

'Because Mrs Dunoon was Mrs Peggie's aunt; and that picture –' she pointed to the pastel – 'which she painted and signed, is hanging in my bedroom, dated nine years after she supposedly died. I think Mrs Dunoon stayed out of the way in Cumbria, and Clarissa in return paid her an income for the rest of her life. After all, it's no secret if three know it.'

Lochie looked stunned. She knew it was a lot to take in. It had fried her brain at first too.

'So . . .'

She watched him try to unravel the theory, refusing to believe yet what she was telling him, and what it meant.

'So why put the baby stuff in the cask? What's that about?'

'I'm not certain, but I think she needed to hide anything

that could link the baby with its father. Mrs Peggie told me Edward Cobb's mother came over to the island in 1932 as part of the Gold Star Pilgrimage. Now, if she met Clarissa and her grandson – your grandfather – well, either Clarissa could have told her the truth outright, or she might have seen a likeness in him? George would have been thirteen by then, so who knows? He could have been the spit of his father. But whether or not Dorothy Cobb learnt the truth, Clarissa wouldn't have been able to take any chances with anyone else finding out. Her friendship with Ed was already well known; if she was seen getting close to his mother, people might have begun to wonder and talk . . . She would have wanted to hide the only physical proof that linked him to his father? One of the first things Skye said to me was that the best thing about being a blender is that if you mess up, it's a generation before anyone finds out. Well, guess what? Here we are, only finding out three generations later. She did well.'

He raised an eyebrow. 'Until *you* came along.'

'Sorry,' she smiled.

'No, you're not.'

'No, I'm not.' She watched him as he looked down at the jumbled photos, the letter – the truth. 'Lochie, you may not believe me, but I *was* going to send all this information on to you. I just had to allow for a little distance first.'

He shot her a look. 'Whilst the payment went through, you mean?'

'Yes. The terms of my agreement with Sholto were that I had to get you to resign and think it was your own idea. And I did that. It wasn't anything to do with me if you then came into possession of information clarifying the truth about the so-called adoption.' She arched an eyebrow.

'You're one scary woman, Alex Hyde.'

She smiled. 'Thank you.'

They locked eyes again and she began shuffling the papers back into a neat pile. 'So, what are you going to do? Sholto hasn't announced your resignation yet, has he?'

'No, he said he was going to wait until after Christmas; the distillery's closed for the festive break now anyway.' Lochie sighed, sinking onto the desktop and crossing his ankles. 'But technically I've resigned, he didn't throw me out; regardless of the adoption legalities, it was a voluntary decision to step down. He's not obliged to rehire me.'

Alex felt a chill of panic. She hadn't anticipated that; she'd thought she had all the bases covered. 'But what about the company?' Skye had moved on, of course, but she thought of Bruce and Hamish, the Peggies . . . 'If you don't go back, Sholto can command the proxy shares to facilitate the takeover. They'll close it down.'

Lochie looked at her consideringly for a moment and she could see he was debating whether to share something with her. '. . . Not necessarily,' he said finally. 'I have a feeling Sholto isn't going to want to enforce my termination contract when he sees what I've got in my possession.'

She watched as he walked over to the window and crouched down, picking up the broken shards of glass on the floor. 'Which is?'

He glanced back at her, the shards cupped in his grazed hand. 'The fire report came back just before I left for the party on Thursday night. It wasn't an accident. It was arson.'

Her jaw dropped. 'Oh my God. Do they know who?'

'No. But I do.'

'*Who?*'

'Can't you guess?'

'Sholto?' she gasped, and then when he raised an eyebrow, '*Torquil?*'

'I think it's all part of his and Sholto's plan to destabilize the Islay operations, in preparation for the Ferrandor deal. It's a lot easier to shut down a distillery if part of it's already out of action and razed to the ground.'

Alex couldn't believe what she was hearing. To have seduced Skye to provoke him was one thing, but arson?

'How do you know it was him? Did he confess?'

Lochie smiled at the very thought. 'No, but I've known it was him since the day I got out of hospital, long before that report came in . . . I have the CCTV tapes.'

Alex frowned. 'But – the CCTV isn't working. I was in the meeting. You and Torquil were fighting over the cost of getting it repaired.'

He rose to standing and carefully deposited the broken shards in a neat pile on a high shelf, out of harm's way. 'Exactly. Which meant they went unchecked after the fire. A while back, when the fuse tripped – and that's all it was; no one else bothered to check – I thought it might come in handy one day to have a backup surveillance hidden in plain sight. It's amazing what people will do when they think they're not being watched.'

She laughed in spite of herself, the motion moving her body like a wave. 'Lochie! And you say *I'm* scary!'

'Well, they were playing dirty so . . .' he shrugged.

'Are you going to have him arrested?'

'That depends on Sholto. I could be persuaded to keep the information to myself if he and his son resign with immediate effect. Obviously I'm going to be pretty tied up with Scotch Vaults in London but if I was to come back as non-exec chairman . . .'

London? She watched him as he walked back over to her. 'But that's blackmail.'

'You say blackmail, I say that's how families do business.' He grinned. 'Things need to change from the top – a new board with more external candidates, more women . . .' He arched an eyebrow at her.

'*Me?*'

'Why not? You've just shown me you care about the company's welfare and I already know that even just for the Peggies alone, you'd want to protect its links with the community. Besides, it's only a few days' work a year. I'm thinking Callum can come in as CEO. He's done a good job in the wealth management division.'

'Callum?'

'I know, we've had our differences but he and I were always on the same page about the things that matter.' He took a step closer to her, grabbing her hand suddenly and pressing it to his lips. 'Same taste in women, for one thing.'

The touch of him made her stomach flip, her skin dance, but she pulled back. 'Lochie . . .'

'What?'

She swallowed. 'Too much has happened. Don't you think we've ruined it? Any idea of "us" was jinxed from the start.'

He nodded. 'Before this, I'd have agreed. But things are different now. You know me, but now I know you too. I want you, Alex, and I know you want me.'

'But wanting it isn't enough. There's a million reasons why it won't work.'

He smiled, getting cocky, getting clever, getting closer, his hands on her hips and his head bent. 'Ah, but you see, a wise, scary, very beautiful woman once told me something.'

'What's that?' she whispered, unable not to smile and feeling her resolve weaken as his hands brushed up her waist.

'We only need one reason why it will.'

Chapter Thirty-One

'I've got nothing to wear.'

'Great. Wear that.'

She laughed, falling back on the bed, one arm slung over her face. 'Lochie, I'm serious! Of all the things I didn't think to pack—'

'You mean, apart from for working, shooting, dancing . . . ?'

She threw a lacy cushion at him, which he caught. 'A *toga* was not one of them.'

'Well, I'm afraid Ambrose and Daisy do like their Christmas Eve plays. There's no getting out of it. It's a tradition.'

'But I didn't *know* that,' she said, grinning as he tossed the cushion on the floor and came back to the bed, crawling on hands and knees over her. They had been supposedly 'unpacking' for two hours already, the freezer downstairs now rammed with several magnums of champagne which had to be blast-chilled after tonight's original intended stock had been used up at the celebrations at lunch – although it had been drunk only after she and Lochie had managed to get their own back on the others by escaping through the windows and enacting a dramatic chase scene on the lawns, which had just about given them a collective heart attack.

'No, you didn't know because you thought you could

break my heart and get away with it. Well, we have ways of making you pay. My friends are sick like that.' He kissed her once. Twice. 'Don't worry. It's less *Antony and Cleopatra*, more *Carry On Up the Tiber*.'

'I'm going to have to use a sheet.'

'Good idea. You can use this one,' he said, suddenly ripping away the Egyptian cotton bed linen that was the only thing protecting her modesty and making her shriek. He met her eyes with a wolfish grin. 'It's not like we're going to be needing it.'

Borrodale House, Perthshire, Christmas Day 2017

The table was as dressed up as they were – the men back in their trews and jewel-coloured velvet jackets, the women in their best black (except for Elise, naturally, who was in red). The candles cast a warm, flickering glow that flattered everyone – including the deer heads on the walls – and was complemented by the noisy fire that danced and fussed on the stone hearth.

Rona, who had come over with Lochie on the train that morning, was lying in front of it, groaning in protest whenever any of the numerous crackers were pulled, but not daring to leave her post lest any falling food should require hoovering up; Alex, who had been touched by how pleased even the dog had seemed to see her here, looked down the length of the table with a feeling of peace that she hadn't known the whole of her adult life.

The day had been as perfect as any she could remember. They had all slept late – well, those *without* children – before feasting on cranachan and opening their presents around the tree as the kids played with their stocking fillers. The girls had sweetly put a stocking together for Lochie – her presence here even more unexpected than the previous weekend's – with a miniature bottle of his favourite non-Kentallen malt from Emma, a pair of shooting socks knitted by Daisy, a framed photo of him looking incredibly gorgeous aged twenty-one from Jess, and a copy of *How to Win Friends and Influence People* from Anna and Elise – which he'd promptly given to her. Alex's own last-minute Christmas present to him had been a plane ticket to Geneva for the next day; his to her had been the small-scale model Aston Martin that he'd been gifted when buying his car and which reminded them both of that laughable night in the rain.

Afterwards, they had reinvigorated their appetites with a walk over the moors – Lochie holding her hand whenever he could, Alex unable to wipe the smile from her face – before fighting for the hot water when they got back as they all rushed to run baths.

The kids had long since left the table to go back to playing another game of Poddy 1-2-3 as Alex watched Anna absent-mindedly pull a catkin burr from Elise's hair and Max tried to cheat at pulling a cracker with his wife; as Jess playfully attached a green plastic toy bow tie on top of Sam's silk one and Ambrose squeezed Daisy's waist as he planted a kiss on her cheek for producing such a successful dinner. And Lochie . . . Lochie was sitting beside her, his hand quietly resting on her thigh, their ankles interlinked beneath the table, as Sam talked to him about a biotech company he'd heard was developing an artificial uterine system to support extremely premature births.

Lochie squeezed her thigh and glanced at her, both of

them warmed by the heat between them. She felt changed from the inside out. She felt new.

'A toast,' Ambrose cried, scraping back his chair and holding his whisky glass aloft.

The table fell silent, and Rona looked up expectantly.

'I think we can all agree it's been a pretty tough day to get through. Love's Young Dream here,' he said, nodding his head disparagingly towards the two of them, 'have been absolutely *disgusting* to be around.'

'Disgusting!' everyone cheered as Lochie laughed and shook his head.

'I busted them snogging in the pantry earlier and they're on their final warning. House rules: such happiness in Borrodale will not be tolerated.'

Daisy squawked indignantly, chucking a napkin at him which promptly fluttered onto the candelabra and would have caught fire had Sam not thrown his water over it, soaking Max's lap in the process.

'Hey!' Max protested, jumping up to brush it off as everyone laughed and Rona ran around to him with high hopes.

'. . . But I think I can speak on behalf of everyone here, when I say just what . . . a *bloody relief* it is to see our old pal Lochie here with someone far, far better than he! Alex, you must be a madwoman to be taking him on, but we're certainly grateful you're taking him off our hands and out of my cellars. He's the best of men but life's given him a pretty good kicking up till now and though honey may be sweet, no one licks it off a briar. Am I right?'

Everyone cheered as Lochie groaned. Alex leaned over and kissed him on the cheek.

'But if he's met his match in you, Alex, I have a hunch

you've met yours in him too. As my beloved mother always used to say when she was roundly beating my father in an argument, "Hot water will quench fire." So frankly, you deserve each other.'

Alex laughed.

'So I'm going to say to *all* of you, our wonderful friends, the toast my father always saved for this day – and bear with me, it's a translation from the Gaelic, after all.' He cleared his throat and puffed out his chest.

'*May the best you've ever seen, be the worst you'll ever see.*

May the mouse never leave your pantry, with a tear-drop in his eye.

May you always keep healthy and hearty, until you're old enough to die . . .'

He turned to Alex and Lochie with a face full of emotion.

'*And may you always be just as happy – as we wish you now to be.*'

Welcome to the family, Alex,' he winked, before straightening his arm like Robert the Bruce with a claymore, droplets of whisky flying through the air. 'Happy Christmas, you crazy bastards! Now let's tear up the house!'

Epilogue

Islay, 30 April 1932

The two women sat on the bench, looking out over the great expanse of silver sea that linked their countries like a glass sheet. They were quiet now, their initial frenzy of questions answered and peace settling over them like a cloak. There was comfort to be had in sitting here together, watching the wind dance as it stroked the long grasses and tickled the sea's skin, listening to the puffins hopping just out of sight on the rocky cliffs, their roosting calls like the groans of creaky doors. For this was Scotland, the land that had saved him, and these were the people who had loved him.

'Ed loved to sit here. It was his favourite spot,' Clarissa said, tucking another tendril of hair behind her ear as the sun moved out from behind a cloud and white sunbeams tap-danced on the water. 'When he was getting back on his feet again, we would walk up here together as part of his daily exercise and take our rest here. I think it made him feel closer to you.'

'Bless you.' Dorothy reached for her hand and held it in her own. 'He'd never even seen the sea before he set sail for France; he said it was one of the good things about signing up – he would be getting to see the world.'

But what a world it was, she thought – where men were saved

480

only to be sent to their deaths; where love and loyalty had nothing to do with happy endings. Had it been worth it?

Her eyes fell to the beautiful dark-haired boy, lanky and golden-skinned, sitting cross-legged on the grass before them and whittling a stick. He was thoughtful and composed for one so young, with a kind nature and his father's gentle smile. He had greeted her with a hard-clutched embrace, as though he'd been waiting for her, as though he'd known she would come.

She smiled through her veil of tears and nodded; she was an old woman now, but she still believed what she'd been brought up to believe as a girl: that where God takes away with one hand, he gives back with the other. So perhaps it had been worth it, in the end. Her own child had loved. And he had lost.

But he lived on.

Acknowledgements

Some stories you have to dig for; they're so elusive and hidden away, it's like mining for coal with a spoon. Others simply land in your lap like a ripe peach, and I'm happy to declare that this was the case here – so I'd like to offer my biggest thanks to that dear, shall-remain-nameless friend who told me an anecdote over a customary bottle of champagne last summer and then watched, laughing, as I ran around with it for six months.

In order to write this book, I needed to become a near-expert on whisky and the distilling industry – I kid you not, I actually read cover-to-cover a hazard assessment report and recommended guidelines on fire detection strategies in the brewing and distilling industries! And it was whilst I was researching the history and locale of Islay that I came across the tragic story of the SS *Tuscania* disaster. Although I have fictionalized the characters to coalesce with my plot, the actual details of the events of that night are true and I'd like to make a special mention here of two local farmers, Robert Morrison and Duncan Campbell, who rescued the soldiers from the cliffs and brought them into the safety of their homes. They were subsequently awarded OBEs for their actions and it was Duncan's sister, Anne, who spent the night churning butter in order to feed the survivors.

Also, the local police sergeant, Malcolm MacNeill, who had the grim task of trying to identifying the dead that washed up on the shores – he filled eighty-one pages of his note-book recording the harrowing findings of the disaster and he corresponded with every single one of the American mothers who wrote to him. Although, according to his family, he never spoke of it, all the letters and written material were stored in boxes in the loft of his home and only uncovered after his death; they were donated to the local Museum of Islay Life and can be read there still. If ever you are lucky enough to visit Islay, I would urge you to stop in there for a while, but even if these pages are the closest you come, I hope you'll agree that such bravery and compassion deserves to be acknowledged and remembered, especially as we approach the hundred-year anniversary.

The Islay website www.islayinfo.com was a fantastic source of information about island life, both past and present, and if you'd like to read in further detail about SS *Tuscania*, I highly recommend William Stevens Prince's book *Crusade and Pilgrimage*.

Then, of course, there is my own personal network of clever, fascinating friends who enlighten me with their various wisdoms, in particular, with this book, Isabel Dean on the matter of Socratic questioning, my dinner party mucker WK for introducing me to the frankly brilliant TED lectures where I learnt about non-verbal body language, and TCM for explaining constellations. Thank you, all.

To the entire team at Pan Mac, that thing you're doing? Please keep doing it! You are such an incredibly slick operation and yet all so thoroughly lovely to boot, it is an utter joy to work with you. I know you're like an iceberg and I see only the tip of what you do, but please know that every single effort you make on my behalf is deeply appreciated. It is an honour to be in your gang.

Amanda, my agent and all-round Force of Nature, we've been working together for ten years now (I know, right? Blink of an eye!), and you have been my shadow on this path, never more than a step away in all that time. Thank you so much for your calm steer. I can't sail this boat without you.

As for my family, thanks will never be repayment for what you give me and words will never be able to express it, hence the endless hugs and kisses. I love you all madly. Don't change a thing.

Christmas at CLARIDGE'S
by
Karen Swan

The best presents can't be wrapped . . .

This was where her dreams drifted to if she didn't blot her nights out with drink; this was where her thoughts settled if she didn't fill her days with chat. She remembered this tiny, remote foreign village on a molecular level and the sight of it soaked into her like water into sand, because this was where her old life had ended and her new one had begun.

Portobello – home to the world-famous street market, Notting Hill Carnival and Clem Alderton. She's the queen of the scene, the girl everyone wants to be or be with. But beneath the morning-after make-up, Clem is keeping a secret, and when she goes too far one reckless night she endangers everything – her home, her job and even her adored brother's love.

Portofino – a place of wild beauty and old-school glamour. Clem has been here once before and vowed never to return. But when a handsome stranger asks Clem to restore a neglected villa, it seems like the answer to her problems – if she can just face up to her past.

Claridge's – at Christmas. Clem is back in London working on a special commission for London's grandest hotel. But is this really where her heart lies?

Christmas in
THE SNOW
by
Karen Swan

In London, the snow is falling and Christmas is just around the corner – but Allegra Fisher barely has time to notice. She's pitching for the biggest deal of her career and can't afford to fail. When she meets attractive stranger Sam Kemp on the plane to the meeting, she can't afford to lose her focus. But when Allegra finds herself up against Sam for the bid, their passion quickly turns sour.

In Zermatt in the Swiss Alps, a long-lost mountain hut is discovered in the snow after sixty years. The last person expecting to become involved is Allegra – she hasn't even heard of the woman they found inside. It soon becomes clear the two women are linked and, as she and her best friend Isobel travel out to make sense of the mystery, hearts thaw and dark secrets are uncovered . . .

Christmas on PRIMROSE HILL

by
Karen Swan

On Primrose Hill . . .

Twinkling lights brighten London's Primrose Hill as
Christmas nears – but for Nettie Watson, it's not parties
and presents that she wants.

Promises are made

For Nettie, Christmas only serves as a stark reminder
of the life she used to have . . . One day she made
a promise to never leave home, and so far she's
stayed true to her word.

Promises are broken

Under the glaring spotlight of the world's media, Nettie
is unexpectedly caught up in a twenty-first-century
storm . . . Her exploits have made her a global name and
attracted the attention of one of the world's most eligible
men – famous front man, Jamie Westlake. But now she
has his attention, does she want to keep it?

Christmas
UNDER
THE STARS
by
Karen Swan

Worlds apart. A love without limit.

In the snow-topped mountains of the Canadian Rockies, Meg and Mitch are living their dream. Just weeks away from their wedding, they work and play with Tuck and Lucy, their closest and oldest friends. Meg and Lucy are as close as sisters – much to Meg's real sister's dismay – and Tuck and Mitch have successfully turned their passion for snowboarding into a booming business.

But when a polar storm hits, tragedy strikes. Alone in the tiny mountain log cabin she shares with Mitch, Meg desperately tries to radio for help – and it comes from the most unexpected quarter, a lone voice across the airwaves that sees what she cannot.

As the snow melts and the friends try to live with their loss, the relationships Meg thought were forever are buckled by tensions, rivalries and devastating secrets. Nothing is as she thought and only her radio contact understands what it is to be truly alone. As they share confidences in the dark, witnessed only by the stars, Meg feels her future begin to pull away from her past and is forced to consider a strange truth – is it her friends who are the strangers? And a stranger who really knows her best?

The Rome Affair

by
Karen Swan

A love that can't be stopped. A secret that can't be kept.

1974 and Elena Damiani lives a gilded life. Born with extreme wealth and beauty, no door is closed to her, no man can resist her. At twenty-six, she is already onto her third husband when she meets her love match. But he is the one man she can never have, and all the riches in the world can't change it.

2017 and Francesca Hackett is living *la dolce vita* in Rome, leading tourist groups around the Eternal City and forgetting the ghosts she left behind in London. When she finds a stolen designer handbag in her dustbin and returns it, she is introduced to the grand neighbour who lives across the piazza – famed socialite and Viscontessa, Elena. Elena is overjoyed: the bag contains an unopened letter written by her husband on his deathbed, twelve years earlier.

The two women begin to work together on the Viscontessa's memoirs. As summer unfurls, Elena tells her sensational stories, leaving Cesca in her thrall. But when a priceless diamond ring is found in an ancient tunnel and ascribed to Elena, Cesca begins to suspect a shocking secret at the heart of her new friend's life . . .

It's time to relax with your next good book

THE WINDOWSEAT.CO.UK

If you've enjoyed this book, but don't know what to read next, then we can help. The Window Seat is a site that's all about making it easier to discover your next good book. We feature recommendations, behind-the-scenes tales from the world of publishing, creative writing tips, competitions, and, if we're honest, quite a lot of lists based on our favourite reads.

You'll find stories and features by authors including Lucinda Riley, Karen Swan, Diane Chamberlain, Jane Green, Lucy Diamond and many more. We showcase brand-new talent as well as classic favourites, so you'll never be stuck for what to read again.

We'd love to know what you think of the site, our books, and what you'd like us to feature, so do let us know.

 @panmacmillan.com

 facebook.com/panmacmillan

WWW.THEWINDOWSEAT.CO.UK